EISENHORN

HERETICUS

A WARHAMMER 40,000 NOVEL

EISENHORN

HERETICUS

DAN ABNETT

BLACK LIBRARY

For Mark Bedford.

A BLACK LIBRARY PUBLICATION

Backcloth for a Crown Additional first published in *Inferno!* magazine
in 2002
Hereticus first published in Great Britain in 2002
This edition published in 2015 by
Black Library
Games Workshop Ltd
Willow Road
Nottingham NG7 2WS UK

10 9 8 7 6 5 4 3 2 1

Cover illustration by Alexander Ovchinnikov

A CIP record for this book is available from the British Library.

UK ISBN 13: 978 1 84970 965 1
US ISBN 13: 978 1 84970 966 8

See Black Library on the internet at

blacklibrary.com

Find out more about Games Workshop
and the world of Warhammer 40,000 at

games-workshop.com

Printed and bound by CPI Group (UK) Ltd, Croydon, CR0 4YY

It is the 41st millennium. For more than a hundred centuries the Emperor has sat immobile on the Golden Throne of Earth. He is the master of mankind by the will of the gods, and master of a million worlds by the might of his inexhaustible armies. He is a rotting carcass writhing invisibly with power from the Dark Age of Technology. He is the Carrion Lord of the Imperium for whom a thousand souls are sacrificed every day, so that he may never truly die.

Yet even in his deathless state, the Emperor continues his eternal vigilance. Mighty battlefleets cross the daemon-infested miasma of the warp, the only route between distant stars, their way lit by the Astronomican, the psychic manifestation of the Emperor's will. Vast armies give battle in His name on uncounted worlds. Greatest amongst his soldiers are the Adeptus Astartes, the Space Marines, bioengineered super-warriors. Their comrades in arms are legion: the Astra Militarum and countless planetary defence forces, the ever-vigilant Inquisition and the tech-priests of the Adeptus Mechanicus to name only a few. But for all their multitudes, they are barely enough to hold off the ever-present threat from aliens, heretics, mutants — and worse.

To be a man in such times is to be one amongst untold billions. It is to live in the cruellest and most bloody regime imaginable. These are the tales of those times. Forget the power of technology and science, for so much has been forgotten, never to be re-learned. Forget the promise of progress and understanding, for in the grim dark future there is only war. There is no peace amongst the stars, only an eternity of carnage and slaughter, and the laughter of thirsting gods.

CONTENTS

BACKCLOTH FOR
A CROWN ADDITIONAL

Lord Froigre, much to everyone's dismay including, I'm sure, his own, was dead.

It was a dry, summer morning in 355.M41 and I was taking breakfast with Alizebeth Bequin on the terrace of Spaeton House when I received the news. The sky was a blurry blue, the colour of Sameterware porcelain, and down in the bay the water was a pale lilac, shot through with glittering frills of silver. Sand doves warbled from the drowsy shade of the estate orchards.

Jubal Kircher, my craggy, dependable chief of household security, came out into the day's heat from the garden room, apologised courteously for interrupting our private meal, and handed me a folded square of thin transmission paper.

'Trouble?' asked Bequin, pushing aside her dish of ploin crepes.

'Froigre's dead,' I replied, studying the missive.

'Froigre who?'

'Lord Froigre of House Froigre.'

'You knew him?'

'Very well. I would count him as a friend. Well, how very miserable. Dead at eighty-two. That's no age.'

'Was he ill?' Bequin asked.

'No. Aen Froigre was, if anything, maddeningly robust and healthy. Not a scrap of augmetics about him. You know the sort.' I made this remark pointedly. My career had not been kind to my body. I had been repaired, rebuilt, augmented and generally sewn back together more times than I cared to remember. I was a walking testimonial to Imperial Med-icae reconstruction sur-gery. Alizebeth, on the other hand, still looked like a woman in her prime, a beautiful woman at that, and only the barest minimum of juvenat work had pre-served her so.

'According to this, he died following a seizure at his home last night. His family are conducting thorough investigations, of course, but...' I drummed my fingers on the table-top.

'Foul play?'

'He was an influential man.'

'Such men have enemies.'

'And friends,' I said. I handed her the communique. 'That's why his widow has requested my assistance.'

But for my friendship with Aen, I'd have turned the mat-ter down. Alizebeth had only just arrived on Gudrun after an absence of almost eighteen months, and would be gone again in a week, so I had resolved to spend as much time with her as possible. The operational demands of the Dis-taff, based on Messina, kept her away from my side far more than I would have liked.

But this was important, and Lady Froigre's plea too dis-traught to ignore.

'I'll come with you,' Alizebeth suggested. 'I feel like a jaunt in the country.' She called for a staff car to be brought round from the stable block and we were on our way in under an hour.

Felippe Gabon, one of Kircher's security detail, acted as our driver. He guided the car up from Spaeton on a whisper of thrust and laid in a course for Menizerre. Soon we were cruising south-west over the forest tracts and the verdant cultivated belt outside Dorsay and leaving the Insume headland behind.

In the comfortable, climate-controlled rear cabin of the staff car, I told Alizebeth about Froigre.

'There have been Froigres on Gudrun since the days of the first colonies. Their house is one of the Twenty-Six Venerables, that is to say one of the twenty-six original noble fiefs, and as such has an hereditary seat in the Upper Legislature of the planetary government. Other, newer houses have considerably more power and land these days, but nothing can quite eclipse the prestige of the Venerables. Houses like Froigre, Sangral, Meissian. And Glaw.'

She smiled impishly at my inclusion of that last name.

'So... power, land, prestige... a honeytrap for rivals and enemies. Did your friend have any?'

I shrugged. I'd brought with me several data-slates Psullus had looked out for me from the library. They contained heraldic ledgers, family histories, biographies and memoirs. And very little that seemed pertinent.

'House Froigre vied with House Athensae and House Brudish in the early years of Gudrun, but that's literally ancient history. Besides, House Brudish became extinct after another feud with House Pariti eight hundred years ago. Aen's grandfather famously clashed with Lord Sangral and the then Governor Lord Dougray over the introduction of Founding

Levy in the one-nineties, but that was just political, though Dougray never forgave him and later snubbed him by making Richtien chancellor. In recent times, House Froigre has been very much a quiet, solid, traditional seat in the Legislature. No feuds, that I know of. In fact, there hasn't been an inter-house war on Gudrun for seven generations.

'They all play nicely together, these days, do they?' she asked.

'Pretty much. One of the things I like about Gudrun is that it is so damned civilised.'

'Too damned civilised,' she admonished. 'One day, Gregor, one day this place will lull you into such a deep sense of tranquil seclusion that you'll be caught with your pants down.'

'I hardly think so. It's not complacency, before you jump down my throat. Gudrun – Spaeton House itself – is just a safe place. A sanctuary, given my line of work.'

'Your friend's still dead,' she reminded me.

I sat back. 'He liked to live well. Good food, fine wines. He could drink Nayl under the table.'

'No!'

'I'm not joking. Five years ago, at the wedding of Aen's daughter. I was invited and I took Harlon along as... as I don't know what, actually. You weren't around and I didn't want to go alone. Harlon started bending his lordship's ear with tales of bounty hunting and the last I saw of them they were sprinting their way down their fourth bottle of anise at five in the morning. Aen was up at nine the next day to see his daughter off. Nayl was still asleep at nine the following day.'

She grinned. 'So a life of great appetites may have just caught up with him?'

'Perhaps. Though you'd think that would have shown up on the medicae mortus's report.'

'So you do suspect foul play?'

'I can't shake that idea.'

I was silent for a few minutes, and Alizebeth scrolled her way through several of the slates.

'House Froigre's main income was from mercantile dealings. They hold a twelve point stock in Brade ent Cie and a fifteen per cent share in Helican SubSid Shipping. What about trade rivals?'

'We'd have to expand our scope off-planet. I suppose assassination is possible, but that's a strange way to hit back at a trade rival. I'll have to examine their records. If we can turn up signs of a clandestine trade fight, then maybe assassination is the answer.'

'Your friend spoke out against the Ophidian Campaign.'

'So did his father. Neither believed it was appropriate to divert funds and manpower into a war of reconquest in the sub-sector next door when there was so much to put in order on the home front.'

'I was just wondering...' she said.

'Wonder away, but I think that's a dead end. The Ophidian War's long since over and done with and I don't think anyone cares what Aen thought about it.'

'So have you got a theory?'

'Only the obvious ones. None of them with any substantiating data. An internecine feud, targeting Aen from inside the family. A murder driven by some secret affair of the heart. A darker conspiracy that remains quite invisible for now. Or...'

'Or?'

'Too much good living, in which case we'll be home before nightfall.'

Froigre Hall, the ancestral pile of the noble House Froigre, was a splendid stack of ivy-swathed ouslite and copper tiles overlooking the Vale of Fiegg, ten kilometres south of Menizerre. Water meadows sloped back from the river, becoming wildflower pastures that climbed through spinneys of larch and fintle to hem the magnificent planned gardens of the house; geometric designs of box-hedge, trim lawn, flowering beds and symmetrical ponds. Beyond the sandy drive, darkened woods came right down to skirt the back of the great hall, except for where a near-perfect sulleq lawn had been laid. Aen and I had spent several diverting afternoons there, playing against each other. A kilometre north of the house, the gnarled stone finger of the Folly rose from the ascending woods.

'Where to put down, sir?' Gabon asked over the intercom.

'On the drive in front of the portico, if you'd be so kind.'

'What's been going on here?' Alizebeth asked as we came in lower. She pointed. The lawn areas nearest to the hall were littered with scraps of rubbish – paper waste and glittery bits of foil. Some sections of grass were flat and yellow as if compressed and starved of light.

Tiny stones, whipped up by our downwash, ticked off the car's bodywork as we settled in to land.

'Oh, my dear Gregor!' Lady Freyl Froigre almost fell into my arms. I held her in a comforting embrace for a few patient moments as she sobbed against my chest.

'Forgive me!' she said suddenly, pulling away and dabbing her eyes with a black lace handkerchief. 'This is all so very terrible. So very, very terrible.'

'My deepest sympathies for your loss, lady,' I said, feeling awkward.

A houseman, his arm banded in black, had led us into a stateroom off the main hall where Lady Froigre was waiting.

The blinds were drawn, and mourning tapers had been lit, filling the air with a feeble light and a sickly perfume. Freyl Froigre was a stunning woman in her late sixties, her lush red hair, almost flame-pink it was so bright, pulled back and pinned down under a veil coiff of jet scamiscoire. Her grief-gown was slate epinchire, the sleeves ending in delicate interwoven gloves so that not one speck of her flesh was uncovered.

I introduced Alizebeth, who murmured her condolences, and Lady Froigre nodded. Then she suddenly looked flustered.

'Oh, my. Where are my manners? I should have the staff bring refreshments for you and–'

'Hush, lady,' I said, taking her arm and walking her down the long room into the soft shade of the shutters. 'You have enough on your mind. Grief is enough. Tell me what you know and I will do the rest.'

'You're a good man, sir. I knew I could trust you.' She paused and waited while her current wracks subsided.

'Aen died just before midnight last night. A seizure. It was quick, the physician said.'

'What else did he say, lady?'

She drew a data-wand from her sleeve and handed it to me. 'It's all here.' I plucked out my slate and plugged it in. The display lit up with the stored files.

Death by tremorous palpitations of the heart and mind. A dysfunction of the spirit. According the the medicae's report, Aen Froigre had died because of a spasm in his anima.

'This means...' I paused, '...nothing. Who is your physician?'

'Genorus Notil of Menizerre. He has been the family medicae since the time of Aen's grandfather.'

'His report is rather... non-specific, lady. Could I present the body for a further examination?'

'I've already done that,' she said softly. 'The surgeon at Menizerre General who attended said the same. My husband died of terror.'

'Terror?'

'Yes, inquisitor. Now tell me that isn't the work of the infernal powers?'

There had, she told me, been a celebration. A Grand Fete. Aen's eldest son, Rinton, had returned home two weeks before, having mustered out of his service in the Imperial Guard. Rinton Froigre had been a captain in the Fiftieth Gudrunite and seen six years' service in the Ophidean sub-sector. Such was his father's delight on his return, a fete was called. A carnival feast. Travelling players from all around the canton had attended, along with troupes of musicians, acrobats, armies of stall holders, entertainers, and hundreds of folk from the town. That explained the litter and faded patches on the lawn. Tent pitches. The scars of marques.

'Had he any enemies?' I asked, pacing the shuttered room.

'None that I know of.'

'I would like to review his correspondence. Diaries too, if he kept them.'

'I'll see. I don't believe he kept a diary, but our rubricator will have a list of correspondence.'

On the top of the harpsichord was a framed portrait, a hololith of Aen Froigre, smiling.

I picked it up and studied it.

'The last portrait of him,' she said. 'Taken at the fete. My last connection with him.'

'Where did he die?'

'The Folly,' said Lady Froigre. 'He died in the Folly.'

The woods were damp and dark. Boughs creaked in the late afternoon wind and odd birdsong thrilled from the shadows.

The Folly was a stone drum capped by a slate needle. Inside, it was bare and terribly musty. Sand doves fluttered up in the roof spaces. Cobwebs glazed the bare windows.

'This is where I found him,' said a voice from behind me.

I turned. Rinton Froigre stooped in under the doorframe. He was a well-made boy of twenty-five, with his mother's lush red hair. His eyes had a curious, hooded aspect.

'Rinton.'

'Sir,' he bowed slightly.

'Was he dead when you found him?'

'No, inquisitor. He was laughing and talking. He liked to come up here. He loved the Folly. I came up to thank him for the fete that he had thrown in my honour. We were talking together when suddenly he went into convulsions. Just minutes later, before I could summon help, he was dead.'

I didn't know Rinton Froigre well, though his service record was very respectable, and I knew his father had been proud of him. Aen had never mentioned any animosity from his son, but in any noble house there is always the spectre of succession to consider. Rinton had been alone with his father at the time of death. He was a seasoned soldier, undoubtedly no stranger to the act of killing.

I kept an open mind – literally. Even without any invasive mental probing, it is possible for a psionic of my ability to sense surface thoughts. There was no flavour of deceit about Rinton's person, though I could feel carefully contained loss, and the tingle of trepidation. Small wonder, I considered. Uncommon are the citizens of the Imperium who do not register anxiety at being quizzed by an inquisitor of the Holy Ordos.

There was no point pressing him now. Rinton's story might easily be put to the test with an auto-seance, during which psychometric techniques would simply reveal the truth of his father's last moments to me.

Rinton walked me back to the Hall, and left me to my pon-
derings in Aen's study. It was as he had left it, I was told.

The room was half–panelled and lined for the most part
with glazed shelves of neatly bound books and data-slates.
Discreet glow-globes hovered around the edges of the
room at head-height, set to a low luminosity, and a selec-
tion of scroll-backed couches and over-stuffed chairs were
arranged in front of the high-throated ceramic fireplace with
its wood-burning fusion stove.

The desk, under the diamond-paned west windows, was a
wide crescent of polished duralloy floated a metre off the carpet by passive suspensor pods. The desk was clean and bare.

I sat at it, depressing slightly the hydraulics of the writing
chair – I was half a head taller than Aen Froigre. I studied the
mirror-smooth, slightly raked surface of the desk. There was
no sign of any control panel, but a gentle wave of my hand
across it woke up heat-sensitive touch-plates engraved into
the duralloy's finish. I touched a few, but they needed Aen's
touch – probably a combination of palmprint and genekey –
to unlock them.

That, or Inquisition-grade software. I unpinned my Inquisitorial rosette, which I had been wearing on the sternum of a
my black leather coat, and slid open the signal port. Holding
it low over the desk, I force fed the touch-plates with several
magenta-level security override programs. It gave up the fight
almost at once, opening systems without even the need for
passwords.

Built into the stylish desk – an item of furniture that had
clearly cost Aen a lot of money – was a fairly powerful cogitator, a vox-pict uplink, a message archive, two filing archives,
and a master control for the simple, limited electronic systems
built into the Hall. Separate pages of each file and message

could be displayed as a facsimile on the blotter plate and a touch of a finger turned them or put them away. Aen had destroyed all paper records.

I played with it for some time, but the most interesting thing I found was a log of invoices for services provided at the fete, and a list of the invitations. I copied both into my own data-slate.

Alizebeth and Gabon arrived while I was busy with that. Alizebeth had been interviewing the household staff, and Gabon had been out, walking the grounds.

'There were over nine hundred guests here, sir,' he said, 'and maybe another five hundred players, musicians, entertainers and carnival folk.'

'Where from?'

'Menizerre, mostly,' he replied. 'Local entertainers, a few troubadours and some street tumblers from the biweekly textile market. The biggest individual groups were Kalikin's Company, an acclaimed troupe of travelling actors, and Sunsable's Touring Fair, who provided the games and rides and diversions.'

I nodded. Gabon was as thorough as usual. A short, spare man in his one fifties with cropped black hair and a bushy moustache, he had been with the Dorsay Arbites for about seventy years before retiring into private service. He wore a simple, refined dark blue suit that had been ingeniously tailored to hide the fact that he was wearing a handgun in a shoulder rig.

'What about you?' I asked Alizebeth. She sat down on one of the couches.

'Nothing scintillating. The staff seem genuinely shocked and upset at the death. They all react with outrage at the idea your friend might have had any enemies.'

'It seems quite clear to me that he did have some,' I said.

Alizebeth reached into the folds of her gown and fished out a small, hard object. She tossed it across onto the desk top and it landed with a tap. There it extended four, multi-jointed limbs and scurried across onto my palm.

I turned the wriggling poison-snooper over and pressed the recessed stud on its belly. A little ball of hololithic energy coalesced above its head-mounted projector and I read it as slowly scrolled around on its own axis.

'Traces of lho, obscura and several other class II and III narcotics in the garden area and the staff quarters. Penshel seed traces found in the stable block. More lho, as well as listeria and e. coli in small amounts in the kitchen section... hmmm...'

Alizebeth shrugged. 'The usual mix of recreational drugs one might expect, none in large quantities, and the kitchens's as hygienic as anywhere. You'd probably get the same sort of readings from Spaeton House.'

'Probably. Penshel seeds, they're quite unusual.'

'A very mild stimulant,' said Gabon. 'I didn't know anyone still used that stuff. Time was, it was the drug of choice in the artists' quarter of Dorsay, back when I was on the force. The seeds are dried, rolled and smoked in pipes. A little bohemian, an old man's smoke.'

'Most of the outdoor traces can be put down to the visiting entertainers,' I mused, 'plus a little off-duty pleasure from the staff or loose-living guests. What about the stable block? Are any of Froigre's ostlers penshel smokers?'

Alizebeth shook her head. 'They'd cleared large parts of the stable area to provide spaces for the fair stall-holders.'

I put the snooper down on the desk and it wriggled back and forth for a few moments until it got enough purchase to right itself. 'So nothing untoward, in fact. And certainly no significant toxins.'

'None at all,' said Alizebeth.

Damn. Given the description of Aen's death, I had been quite sure poison was the key, perhaps some assassin's sophisticated toxin that had not shown up on the initial medicae report. But Alizebeth's snooper was high-grade and thorough.

'What do we do now?' she asked.

I passed her my data-slate. 'Send the contents of this to Aemos by direct vox-link. See what he can come up with.'

Uber Aemos was my ancient and trusted savant. If anyone could see a pattern or make a connection, it was him.

Evening fell. I went outside, alone. I felt annoyed and frustrated. In fact, I felt thwarted. I'd come there as a favour to my old friend's widow, offering my services, and in most respects I was overqualified. I was an Imperial inquisitor, and this was most likely just a job for the local Arbites. I had expected to have the entire matter sewn up in a few hours, to settle things swiftly in a quick, unofficial investigation, and leave with the thanks of the family for sparing them a long, drawn-out inquest.

But the clues just weren't there. There was no motive, no obvious antagonist, no aggressor, but still it seemed likely that Aen Froigre had been killed. I looked at the medicae report again, hoping to find something that would establish natural causes.

Nothing. Something, someone, had taken my friend's life, but I couldn't tell what or who or why.

The evening skies were dark, stained a deep violet and smeared with chasing milky clouds. An early moon shone, passing behind the running trails of cloud every minute or so. A wind was gathering, and the stands of trees beside the lawn were beginning to sway and swish. The leaves made a cold sound, like rain.

I walked over to my flyer, popped the cargo trunk and took out Barbarisater. I slowly freed it from its silk bindings and drew the long, gleaming blade from its machined scabbard. Barbarisater had been an heirloom sword, a psychically-attuned weapon from the forges of distant Carthae and slaved to the minds of the generations of warrior women who had wielded it. Enhancing its strength with pentagrammic wards, I had used the long sabre in my battle against the heretic Quixos, during which struggle it had been broken below the tip. Master swordsmiths had remade the blade from the broken main portion, creating a shorter, straighter blade by rounding off and edging the break and reducing the hilt. A good deal smaller than its old self, now more a single-handed rapier than a hand-and-a-half sabre, it was still a potent weapon.

Naked, in my hand, it hummed and whined as my mind ran through it and made it resonate. The incised wards glowed and sobbed out faint wisps of smoke. I walked out over the grass under the seething trees, holding the blade out before me like a dowsing rod, sweeping the scene, letting the blade-tip slide along the invisible angles of space. Twice, on my circuit of the lawns, it twitched as if tugged by sprite hands, but I could discern nothing from the locations.

But there was something there. My first hint of a malign focus. My first hint that not only was foul play involved, but that Lady Froigre might be right.

Though they had left only the slightest traces behind them, infernal powers had been at work here.

Alizebeth came into my room at eight the next morning. She woke me by sitting down on the side of my bed and handed me a cup of hot, black caffeine as I roused.

She was already dressed and ready for work. The day was bright. I could hear the household coming to life: pans clattering the kitchen block and the butler calling to his pages in the nearby gallery.

'Bad storm in the night,' she said. 'Brought trees down.'

'Really?' I grumbled, sitting up and sipping the sweet, dark caffeine.

I looked at her. It wasn't like Bequin to be so perky this early.

'Out with it,' I said.

She handed me a data-slate. 'Aemos has been busy. Must've worked all night.'

'Through the storm.'

'There was no storm up his way. It was local.' I didn't really hear that reply. I was caught up in a close reading of the slate.

Failing to cross-match just about every detail I had sent him, Aemos had clearly become bored. The list of guests I had sent him had led to nothing, despite his best efforts to make connections. The caterers and performers had revealed nothing either. No links to the underworld or cult activity, no misdeeds or priors, except for the usual clutch of innocent and minor violations one might expect. One of the travelling actors had been charged with affray twenty years before, and another had done time for grievous wounding, that sort of thing.

The only item that had flagged any sort of connection was the description of Aen Froigre's death. Aemos had only turned to that rather vague clue once he'd exhausted all others.

In the past twenty months, eleven people in the Drunner Region of Gudrun, which is to say the coastal area encompassing Menizerre, Dorsay and Insume all the way to Madua chapeltown, had died of a similar, mystery ailment. Only a tight, deliberate search like the one Aemos had conducted would have shown up such a connection, given the scale of area involved and the size of population. Listed together, the deaths stood out like a sore thumb.

Here, Aemos had come into his own. Another clerk might have sent those findings to me and waited for direction, but Aemos, hungry to answer the questions himself, had pressed on, trying to make a pattern out of them. No simple task. There was nothing to demo-graphically or geographically link the victims. A housewife here, a millkeeper there, a landowner in one small village, a community doctor in another, seventy kilometres away.

The only thing they had in common was the sudden, violent and inexplicable nature of their demises: seizures, abrupt, fatal.

I set down my cup and scrolled on, aware that Alizebeth was grinning at me.

'Get to the last bit,' she advised. 'Aemos strikes again.'

Right at the last, Aemos revealed another connection.

A day or two before each death, the victim's locality had been paid a visit by Sunsable's Touring Fair.

Lady Froigre was most perturbed to see us about to leave. 'There are questions here still...' she began.

'And I'm going to seek the answers,' I said. 'Trust me. I believe my savant has hit upon something.'

She nodded, unhappy. Rinton stepped forward and put his arm around his mother's shoulders.

'Trust me,' I repeated and walked out across the drive to my waiting flyer.

I could hear the sound of chain blades, and turned from the car to walk around the side of the hall. One of the trees brought down in the night's freak storm had crushed part of the stable block and the housemen were working to saw up the huge trunk and clear it.

'Is that where you detected Penshel seed?' I asked Alizebeth when she came to find out what was keeping me.

'Yes,' she said.

'Fetch my blade.'

I called the housemen away from their work, and walked into the collapsed ruin of the stable, crunching over heaps of coarse sawdust. The ivy–clad tree still sprawled through the burst roof.

Alizebeth brought me Barbarisater and I drew it quickly. By then Lady Froigre and Rinton Froigre had emerged to see what I was doing.

Barbarisater hummed in my hand, louder and more throatily than it had done the previous night. As soon as I entered that part of the stable block, the particular stall the tree had smashed, it jumped. The taste of Chaos was here.

'What was this used for?' I asked. 'During the fete, what was this area used for?'

'Storage,' said Lady Froigre. 'The people from the fair wanted to keep equipment and belongings out of sight. Food too, I think. One man had trays of fresh figs he wanted to keep out of the light.'

'And the hololithographer,' said Rinton. 'He used one of those stalls as a darkroom.'

So how do you find a travelling fair in an area the size of the Drunner Region? If you have a copy of their most recent invoice, it's easy. The fair-master, eager to be paid for his services at Froigre Hall, had left as a payment address an inn eighty kilometres away in Seabrud. From the invoice, I saw that Aen had been asked to mail the payment within five days. The fair moved around a great deal, and the travelling folk didn't believe much in the concept of credit accounts.

From Seabrud, we got a fix on the location of Sunsable's Fair.

They had pitched on a meadow outside the village of Brudmarten, a little, rustic community of ket-herds and weavers that was flanked by a lush, deciduous woodland hillside to the east and marshy, cattle-trampled fields below at the river spill to the west.

It was late afternoon on a hot, close day, the air edged with the heavy, fulminous threat of storms. The sky was dark overhead, but the corn was bright and golden down in the meadows, and pollen balls blew in the breeze like thistle-fibres. Grain-crakes whooped in the corn stands, and small warblers of the most intense blue darted across the hedges.

Gabon lowered the limo to rest in a lane behind the village kirk, a pale, Low Gothic temple in need of up-keep. A noble statue of the Emperor Immaculate stood in the overgrown graveyard, a roost for wood doves. I buckled on my sword and covered it with a long leather cloak. Gabon locked the car.

'Stay with me,' I told Alizebeth, and then turned to Gabon. 'Shadow us.'

'Yes, sir.'

We walked down the lane towards the fair.

Even from a distance, we could hear the noise and feel the energy. The arrival of the fair had brought the folk of Brudmarten and the neighbouring hamlets out in force. Pipe organs were trilling and wheezing in the lank air, and there was the pop and whizz of firecrackers. I could hear laughter, the clatter of rides, the ringing of score bells, children screaming, rowdy men carousing, pistons hissing. The smell of warm ale wafted from the tavern tent.

The gate in the meadow's hedge had been turned into

an entranceway, arched with a gaudy, handpainted sign that declared Sunsable's Miraculous Fair of Fairs open. A white-eyed twist at the gateway took our coins for admission.

Inside, on the meadow, all manner of bright, vulgar sights greeted us. The carousel, lit up with gas-lamps. The ring-toss. The neat, pink box-tent of the clairvoyant. The churning hoop of the whirligig, spilling out the squeals of children. The colourful shouts of the freak show barker. The burnt-sugar smell of floss makers. The clang of test-your- strength machines.

For a penny, you could ride the shoulders of a Battle Titan – actually an agricultural servitor armoured with painted sections of rusty silage hopper. For another penny, you could shoot greenskins in the las-gallery, or touch the Real and Completely Genuine shin bone of Macharius, or dunk for ploins. For tuppence, you could gaze into the Eye of Terror and have your heroism judged by a hooded man with a stutter who claimed to be an ex-Space Marine. The Eye of Terror in this case was a pit dug in the ground and filled with chemical lamps and coloured glass filters.

Nearby, a small donation allowed you to watch an oiled man struggle free from chains, or a burning sack, or a tin bathtub full of broken glass, or a set of stocks.

'Just a penny, sir, just a penny!' howled a man on stilts with a harlequined face as he capered past me. 'For the young lady!'

I decided not to ask what my penny might buy.

'I want to go look at the freak show,' Alizebeth told me.

'Save your money... it's all around us,' I growled.

We pushed on. Coloured balloons drifted away over the field into the encroaching darkness of the thunderhead. Corn crickets rasped furiously in the trampled stalks all about us. Drunken, painted faces swam at us, some lacking teeth, some with glittering augmetic eyes.

'Over there,' I whispered to Alizebeth.

Past the brazier stand of a woman selling paper cones of sugared nuts, and a large handcart stacked with wire cages full of songbirds, was a small booth tent of heavy red material erected at the side of a brightly painted trailer. A wooden panel raised on bunting–wrapped posts announced 'Hololiths! Most Lifelike! Most Agreeable!' below which a smaller notice said 'A most delightful gift, or a souvenir of the day, captured by the magic art of a master hololithographer.' A frail old man with tufted white hair and small spectacles was seated outside the booth on a folding canvas chair, eating a meat pie that was so hot he had to keep blowing on it.

'Why don't you go and engage his interest?' I suggested.

Alizebeth left my side, pushed through the noisy crowd and stopped by his booth. A sheet of flakboard had been erected beside the booth's entrance, and on it were numerous hololithic pictures mounted for display: some miniatures, some landscapes, some family groups. Alizebeth studied them with feigned interest. The old man immediately leapt up off his chair, stowed the half-eaten pie behind the board and brushed the crumbs off his robes. I moved round to the side, staying in the crowd, watching. I paused to examine the caged birds, though in fact I was looking through their cages at the booth tent.

The old man approached Bequin courteously.

'Madam, good afternoon! I see your attention has been arrested by my display of work. Are they not fairly framed and well-composed?'

'Indeed,' she said.

'You have a good eye, madam,' he said, 'for so often in these country fairs the work of the hololithgrapher is substandard. The composition is frequently poor and the plate quality fades with time. Not so with your humble servant. I have plied this trade of portraiture for thirty years and I fancy I have skill for it. You see this print here? The lakeshore at Entreve?'

'It is a pleasing scene.'

'You are very kind, madam. It is handcoloured, like many of my frames. But this very print was made in the summer of... 329, if my memory serves. And you'll appreciate, there is no fading, no loss of clarity, no discolouration.'

'It has preserved itself well.'

'It has,' he agreed, merrily. 'I have patented my own techniques, and I prepare the chemical compounds for the plates by hand, in my modest studio adjoining.' He gestured to his trailer. 'That is how I can maintain the quality and the perfect grade of the hololiths, and reproduce and print them to order with no marked loss of standard from original to duplicate. My reputation rests upon it. Up and down the byeways of the land, the name Bakunin is a watchword for quality portraiture.'

Alizebeth smiled. 'It's most impressive, Master Bakunin. And how much...?'

'Aha!' he grinned. 'I thought you might be tempted, madam, and may I say it would be a crime for your beauty to remain unrecorded! My services are most affordable.'

I moved round further, edging my way to the side of his booth until he and Alizebeth were out of sight behind the awning. I could hear him still making his pitch to her.

On the side of the trailer, further bold statements and enticements were painted in a flourishing script. A large sign read 'Portraits two crowns, group scenes three crowns, gilded miniatures a half-crown only, offering many a striking and famous backcloth for a crown additional.'

I wandered behind the trailer. It was parked at the edge of

the fairground, near to a copse of fintle and yew that screened
the meadow from pastures beyond the ditch. It was damp and
shaded here, small animals rustling in the thickets. I tried to
look in at one small window, but it was shuttered. I touched
the side of the trailer and felt Barbarisater twitch against my
hip. There was a door near the far end of the trailer. I tried it,
but it was locked.

'What's your business?' growled a voice.

Three burly fairground wranglers had approached along the
copse-side of the booths. They had been smoking lho-sticks
behind their trailer on a break.

'Not yours,' I assured them.

'You had best be leaving Master Bakunin's trailer alone,'
one said. All three were built like wrestlers, their bared arms
stained with crude tattoos. I had no time for this.

'Go away now,' I said, pitching my will through my voice.
They all blinked, not quite sure what had happened to their
minds, and then simply walked away as if I wasn't there.

I returned my attention to the door, and quickly forced the
lock with my multi-key. To my surprise, the thin wooden door
still refused to open. I wondered if it was bolted from inside,
but as I put more weight into it, it did shift a little, enough
to prove there there was nothing physical holding it. Then it
banged back shut as if drawn by immense suction.

My pulse began to race. I could feel the sour tang of warpcraft in the air and Barbarisater was now vibrating in its
scabbard. It was time to dispense with subtleties.

I paced around to the front of the booth, but there was no
longer any sign of Bequin or the old man. Stooping, I went in
under the entrance flap. An inner drop curtain of black cloth
stopped exterior light from entering the tent.

I pushed that aside.

'I will be with you shortly, sir,' Bakunin called, 'if you would give me a moment.'

'I'm not a customer,' I said. I looked around. The tent was quite small, and lit by the greenish glow of gas mantles that ran, I supposed, off the trailer supply. Alizebeth was sat at the far side on a ladderback chair with a dropcloth of cream felt behind her. Bakunin was facing her, carefully adjusting his hololithic camera, a brass and teak machine mounted on a wooden tripod. He looked round at me curiously, his hands still polishing a brass-rimmed lens. Alizebeth rose out of her seat.

'Gregor?' she asked.

'The good lady is just sitting for a portrait, sir. It's all very civilised.' Bakunin peered at me, unsure what to make of me. He smiled and offered his hand. 'I am Bakunin, artist and hololithographer.'

'I am Eisenhorn, Imperial inquisitor.'

'Oh,' he said and took a step backwards. 'I... I...'

'You're wondering why a servant of the Ordos has just walked into your booth,' I finished for him. Bakunin's mind was like an open book. There was, I saw at once, no guile there, except for the natural money-making trickery of a fairground rogue. Whatever else he was, Bakunin was no heretic.

'You took a portrait of Lord Froigre at the fete held on his lands just the other day?' I said, thinking of the picture on the harpsichord back at the hall.

'I did,' he said. 'His lordship was pleased. I made no charge for the work, sir. It was a gift to thank his lordship for his hospitality. I thought perhaps some of his worthy friends might see the work and want the like for themselves, I...'

He doesn't know, I thought. He has no clue what this is about. He's trying to work out how he might have drawn this investigation to himself.

'Lord Froigre is dead,' I told him.

He went pale. 'No, that's... that's...'

'Master Bakunin... do you know if any other of your previous subjects have died? Died soon after your work was complete?'

'I don't, I'm sure. Sir, what are you implying?'

'I have a list of names,' I said, unclipping my data-slate. 'Do you keep records of your work?'

'I keep them all, all the exposed plates, in case that copies or replacements are needed. I have full catalogues of all pictures.'

I showed him the slate. 'Do you recognise any of these names?'

His hands were shaking. He said, 'I'll have to check them against my catalogue,' but I knew for a fact he'd recognised some of them at once.

'Let's do that together,' I said. Alizebeth followed us as we went through the back of the tent into the trailer. It was a dark, confined space, and Bakunin kept apologising. Every scrap of surface, even the untidy flat of his little cot bed, was piled with spares and partly disassembled cameras. There was a musty, chemical stink, mixed with the scent of Penshel seeds. Bakunin's pipe lay in a small bowl. He reached into a crate under the cot and pulled out several dog-eared record books.

'Let me see now,' he began.

There was a door at the end of the little room. 'What's through there?'

'My darkroom, along with the file racks for the exposed plates.'

'It has a door to the outside?'

'Yes,' he said.

'Locked?'

'No...'

'You have an assistant then, someone you ordered to hold the door shut?'

'I have no assistant...' he said, puzzled.

'Open this door,' I told him. He put down the books and went to the communicating door. Just from his body language, I could tell he had been expecting it to open easily.

'I don't understand,' he said. 'It's never jammed before.'

'Stand back,' I said, and drew Barbarisater. The exposed blade filled the little trailer with ozone and Bakunin yelped.

I put the blade through the door with one good swing and ripped it open. There was a loud bang of atmospheric decompression, and fetid air swept over us. A dark, smoky haze drifted out.

'Emperor of Mankind, what is that?'

'Warpcraft,' I said. 'You say you mix your own oxides and solutions?'

'Yes.'

'Where do you get your supplies from?'

'Everywhere, here and there, sometimes from apothecaries, or market traders or...'

Anywhere. Bakunin had experimented with all manner of compounds over the years to create the best, most effective plates for his camera. He'd never been fussy about where the active ingredients came from. Something in his workshop, something in his rack of flasks and bottles, was tainted.

I took a step towards the darkroom. In the half-light, things were flickering, half-formed and pale. The baleful energies lurking in Bakunin's workshop could sense I was a threat, and were trying to protect themselves by sealing the doors tight to keep me out.

I crossed the threshold into the darkroom. Alizebeth's cry of warning was lost in the shrieking of tormented air that suddenly swirled around me. Glass bottles and flasks of mineral tincture vibrated wildly in metal racks above Bakunin's work bench. Jars of liquid chemicals and unguent oils shattered and sprayed their contents into the air. The little gas-jet burner flared and ignited, its rubber tube thrashing like a snake. Glass plates, each a square the size of a data-slate, and each sleeved in a folder of tan card, were jiggling and working themselves out of the wooden racks on the far side of the blacked out room. There were thousands of them, each one the master exposure of one of Bakunin's hololiths. The first yanked clear of the shelf as if tugged by a sucking force, and I expected it to shatter on the floor, but it floated in the air. Quickly others followed suit. Light from sources I couldn't locate played in the air, casting specks and flashes of colour all around. The air itself became dark brown, like tobacco.

I raised my sword. A negative plate came flying at my head and I struck at it. Shards of glass flew in all directions. Another came at me and I smashed that too. More flew from the shelves like a spray of playing cards, whipping through the air towards me. I made a series of quick *uwe sar* and *ulsar* parries, bursting the glass squares as they struck in. I missed one, and it sliced my cheek with its edge before hitting the wall behind me like a throwing knife.

'Get him out of here!' I yelled to Alizebeth. The trailer was shaking. Outside there was a crash of thunder and rain started to hammer on the low roof. The hurtling plates were driving me back, and Barbarisater had become a blur in my hands as it struck out to intercept them all.

Then the ghosts came. Serious men in formal robes. Gentlewomen in long gowns. Solemn children with pale faces. A laughing innkeeper with blotchy cheeks. Two farmhands, with their arms around each other's shoulders. More, still more, shimmering in the dirty air, made of smoke, their skins white, their clothes sepia, their expressions frozen at the moment they had been caught by the camera. They clawed and tugged at me with fingers of ice, pummelled me with psychokinetic fists. Some passed through me like wraiths, chilling my marrow. The malevolence hiding in that little trailer was conjuring up all the images Bakunin had immortalised in his career, ripping them off the negative plates and giving them form.

I staggered back, tears appearing in my cloak. Their touch was as sharp as the edge of the glass plates. Their hollow screaming filled my ears. Then, with a sickening lurch, the world itself distorted and changed. The trailer was gone. For a moment I was standing on a sepia shoreline, then I was an uninvited guest at a country wedding. My sword hacking and flashing, I stumbled on into a baptism, then a colourised view of the Atenate Mountains, then a feast in a guild hall. The ghosts surged at me, frozen hands clawing. The innkeeper with the blotchy cheeks got his icy fists around my throat though his face was still open in laughter. I chopped Barbarisater through him and he billowed like smoke. A sad-faced housemaid pulled at my arm and a fisherman struck at me with his boat hook.

I began to recite the Litany of Salvation, yelling it into the leering faces that beset me. A few crumpled and melted like cellulose exposed to flame.

I heard gunshots. Gabon was to my right, firing his weapon. He was standing on the pier at Dorsay at sunset, in the middle of a inter-village game of knockball, and a harvest festival, all at the same time. The conflicting scenes blurred and merged around him. A bride and her groom, along with five mourners from a funeral and a retiring Arbites constable in full medals, were attacking him.

'Get back!' I yelled. Barbarisater was glowing white-hot. Thunder crashed again, shaking the earth. Gabon shrieked as the bride's fingers ripped through his face, and as he stumbled backwards, whizzing glass plates chopped into him like axe heads.

His blood was in the air, like rain. It flooded into the ghosts and stained their sepia tones crimson and their pale flesh pink. I felt fingers like knives draw across the flesh of my arms and back. There were too many of them.

I couldn't trust my eyes. According to them, I was standing on a riverbank, and also the front steps of an Administratum building. The locations overlaid each other impossibly, and neither was real.

I leapt, and lashed out with my blade. I hit something, tore through and immediately found myself rolling on the rain-sodden turf behind the trailer.

Lightning split the darkness overhead and the rain was torrential. The storm and the bizarre activity around Bakunin's booth had sent the commonfolk fleeing from the meadow. The trailer was still vibrating and shaking, and oily brown smoke was gushing from the hole in the side wall I'd cut to break my way out. Inside, lights crackled and flashed and the phantom screaming continued. The warpaint was berserk.

Bakunin appeared, looking desperate, with Alizebeth close behind him. He put his hands to his mouth in shock at the sight of me torn and bloodied.

'Where is it?' I snarled.

'Third shelf up, above the workbench,' he stammered. 'The green bottle. I needed tincture of mercury, years ago, years ago, and an old woman in one of the villages gave it to me and said it would do as well. I use it all the time now. The emulsions it mixes are perfect. My work has never been better.'

He looked down at the grass, shaking and horrified. 'I should have realised,' he muttered. 'I should have realised. No matter how much I used, the bottle never emptied.'

'Third shelf up?' I confirmed.

'I'll show you,' he said, and sprang to the trailer, clambering in through the hole I had smashed.

'Bakunin! No!'

I followed him inside, tumbling back into the jumble of landscapes and the maelstrom of screaming ghosts. Just for a moment, a brief moment, I saw Aen Froigre amongst them.

Then I was falling through another wedding, a hunting scene, a stockman's meeting, a farrier's smithy, the castle of Elempite by moonlight, a cattle market, a–

I heard Bakunin scream.

I deflected three more deadly hololith plates, and slashed through the thicket of howling ghosts. Spectral, as if it wasn't there, I saw the workbench and the shelves. The green bottle, glowing internally with jade fire.

I raised Barbarisater and smashed the bottle with the edge of the shivering blade.

The explosion shredded the inner partition wall and lurched the trailer onto its side. Dazed, I lay on the splintered wall, sprawled amongst the debris of glass and wood.

The screaming stopped.

Someone had called the local Arbites. They moved in through the crowds of onlookers as the last of the rain fell and the skies began to clear.

I showed them my credentials and told them to keep the crowd back while I finished my work. The trailer was already burning, and Alizebeth and I threw the last few hololith prints into the flames.

The pictures were fading now. Superimposed on each one, every portrait, every landscape, every miniature, was a ghost exposure. An after-image.

Bakunin, screaming his last scream forever.

HERETICUS

For Mark Bedford

BY ORDER OF HIS MOST HOLY MAJESTY
THE GOD-EMPEROR OF TERRA

SEQUESTERED INQUISITORIAL DOSSIERS
AUTHORISED PERSONS ONLY

CASE FILE 442:41F:JL3:Kbu

Please enter your authority code > `••••••••••••••`

Validating...

Thank you, inquisitor.

You may proceed.

To Gregor Eisenhorn, a communiqué
  Carried by Guild Astropathica (Scarus) via meme-wave
  45~a.639 triple intra
Path detail:
  Origin: Thracian Primaris, Helican Sub 81281 origin date:
  142.386.M41
  (relayed: divergent M-12/Ostall VII)
  Received: Durer, Ophidian Sub 52981 reception date:
  144.386.M41
  Transcript carried and logged as per header
  (redundant copy filed buffer 4362 key 11)

Author: Lord Inquisitor Phlebas Alessandro Rorken
  Master of the Ordo Xenos Helican,
  Inquisition High Council Officio, Scarus Sector

My dear Gregor,

In the name of the God-Emperor, and of the Holy Inquisition, greetings.

I trust the elders of Durer have welcomed you in a manner befitting your status. Hierarch Onnopel has been charged by my officio to ensure that you are provided with all requirements for the long task ahead. May I take this opportunity to express my gratitude to you again for agreeing to conduct this Examination in my stead. My health, so it would appear to everyone but me, is still a matter for concern. My physician clucks over me night and day. They have changed my blood a number of times and talk of further surgery, but it is all for naught. I am healthy and sound and would be on the road to recovery but for their coddling. Indeed, I would be on the road to Durer too but for that.

Yet it seems a quack from the Officio Medicae has authority over even one such as I. The work I have done to bring the heretics of Durer to trial must be finished in my absence, and I can think of no surer hand than yours to steer the business.

I write to you for two reasons – apart, that is, for expressing my thanks. Despite my efforts, Sakarof Lord Hereticus has insisted on sending two of his own delegates to the Examination: Koth and Menderef, you know them both. I'm sorry, Gregor, but you must tolerate them. They are a burden I would have spared you from.

Secondly, I am forced to saddle you with Inquisitor Bastian Verveuk. He was an interrogator under Lord Osma, and had come to my staff to finish his preparation. I had promised him a hand in the Examination, primarily because of his good offices in securing the central prosecutions. Please accommodate him in your counsel, for my sake. He is a good man, young and untried, but capable, though he reeks of the puritan. Didn't we all at that age? He will arrive with you on the 151st. Make him as welcome as you can. I know you hate to incorporate unknowns into your camp, but I ask this as a personal favour. Osma will make things very difficult for me if I retard his pupil's progress at this late stage.

I wish you speed, wisdom and success in the closure of this inspection.

Sealed and notarised by astropathicae clerk, this 142nd day of 386.M41.

The Emperor protects!

Rorken

[message ends]

To Gregor Eisenhorn, a communiqué
　　Carried by Guild Astropathica (Scarus) via meme-loop
　　repeat 45~3.5611 secure
Path detail:
　　Origin: Thracian Primaris, Helican Sub 81281 origin date:
　　142.386.M41
　　(relayed: loop navigatus 351/echo Gernale beacon)
　　Received: Durer, Ophidian Sub 52981 reception date:
　　144.386.M41
　　Transcript carried and logged as per header
　　(redundant copy filed buffer 7002 key 34)

Author: Inquisitor Bastian Verveuk, Ordo Xenos
　　Inquisition High Council Officio, Scarus Sector,
　　Scarus Major

Salutations, sir!

In the name of the God-Emperor, hallowed be his eternal vigil, and by the High Lords of Terra, I commend myself your eminence and trust that this communiqué finds your eminence in good health.

　　Great was my excitement when my Lord Rorken informed me that I was to take a part, at his side, in the formal Examination of the vile and abominated heretics of Durer. At once, I threw myself into the cataloguing of advance discovery, and assisted in the compilation of the evidentiary archive that would support the particulars of the Examination.

　　You may then imagine my terrible disappointment when my lord's sudden and lamentable illness seemed to cast the very occurrence of that divine work into doubt. Now, this very hour, my lord has informed me that you are to oversee the matter as his proxy and that you have agreed to find a place for me at your side.

I cannot contain my exhilaration! The chance to work at close hand with one such as you! I have studied your holy work with awe since my earliest days in the preparatory scholams. You are an object lesson in devotion and puritanical duty, an example to us all. I look forward with great eagerness to discussing matters of contra-heretical law with you, and perhaps hearing first hand a few scraps of your dazzling insight. It is my most fervent ambition to pursue the rank of inquisitor in the Ordo Hereticus, and I am sure I would be better armed for such duty if I had the benefit of learning from your own first-hand accounts of such infamous beings as the dread Quixos.

You will find me a devoted and hard-working colleague. I count the days until we can begin this sacred work together.

Hallowed be the Golden Throne!

Your servant,

Bastian Verveuk

[message ends]

To Lord Rorken, a communiqué
  Carried by Guild Astropathica (Ophidia) via meme-wave
  3Q1~c.122 double intra
Path detail:
  Origin: Durer, Ophidian Sub 52981 origin date: 144.386.M41
  (relayed: divergent B-3/loop Gernale beacon)
  Received: Thracian Primaris, Helican Sub 81281 reception
  date: 149.386.M41
  Transcript carried and logged as per header
  (redundant copy deleted from buffer)

Author: Gregor Eisenhorn, Inquisitor

re: Bastian Verveuk

My lord, what foetid corner of the Imperium breeds these fawning idiots?
  Now you really owe me.

G. E.

[message ends]

ONE

The case of Udwin Pridde
Small talk with Verveuk
Something like vengeance

When the time came, Fayde Thuring was damn near impossible to stop.

I blame myself for that. I had let him run on for too long. For the best part of eight decades he had escaped my attentions, and in that time he had grown immeasurably from the minor warp-dabbler I had once let slip away.

My mistake. But I wasn't the one to pay.

On the 160th day of 386.M41 a nobleman in his late one sixties appeared at the Examination hearings held in the Imperial Minster of Eriale, the legislative capital of the Uvege in the south-west of Durer's third largest landmass.

He was a landowner, widowed young, and he had built his fortune in post-liberation Durer society on a successful agri-combine venture and the inherited wealth of his late wife. In 376, as a mature, successful and highly eligible newcomer

amongst the gentry of the Uvege, a prosperous region of verdant farmland, he had made a socially-advancing second
marriage. His new bride was Betrice, thirty years his junior, the
eldest daughter of the venerable House Samargue. The Samargue family's ancient wealth was at that time seeping away
as the efficient land-use policies of Administratum-sponsored
combines slowly took control of the Uvege's pastoral economy.

The nobleman's name was Udwin Pridde, and he had been
summoned by the hierarch of the See of Eriale to answer
charges of recidivism, warpcraft and, above all, heresy.

Facing him across the marble floor of the Minster was a dignified Inquisitorial body of the most august quality. Inquisitor
Eskane Koth, an Amalathian, born and bred on Thracian Primaris, one day to be known as the Dove of Avignon. Inquisitor
Laslo Menderef, a native of lowland Sancour, Menderef the
Grievous as he would become, an Istvaanian with a cold
appreciation of warp-crime and poor body hygiene. Inquisitor Poul Rassi, son of the Kilwaddi Steppes, a sound, elderly,
even-handed servant of order. The novice Inquisitor Bastian
Verveuk.

And myself. Gregor Eisenhorn. Inquisitor and presiding
examiner.

Pridde was the first of two hundred and sixty individuals
identified by Lord Rorken's work as possible heretics to be
weighed by this Formal Court of Examination. He looked
nervous but dignified as he faced us, toying with his lace collar. He had hired a pardoner called Fen of Clincy to speak on
his behalf.

It was the third day of the hearings. As the pardoner droned
on, describing Pridde in terms that would have made a saint
blush for want of virtue, I thumbed half-heartedly through

the catalogue of pending cases and sighed at the scale of the
work to come. The catalogue – we all had a copy – was thicker
than my wrist. This was the third day already and still we had
not progressed further than the preamble of the first case. The
opening rites had taken a full day and the legal recognition
of the authority of the Ordos Helican here on Durer, together
with other petty matters of law, yet another. I wondered, may
the God-Emperor forgive my lack of charity, if Lord Rorken's
illness was genuine or just a handy excuse to avoid this tedium.

Outside, it was a balmy summer day. Wealthy citizens of
Eriale were boating on the ornamental lakes, lunching in the
hillside trattorias of the Uvege, conducting lucrative business
in the caffeine houses of the city's Commercia.

In the echoing, cool vault of the Minster, there was nothing but the whining voice of Fen of Clincy.

Golden sunlight shafted in through the celestory windows
and bathed the stalls of the audience gallery. That area was
half empty. A few dignitaries, clerks, local hierarchs and archivists of the Planetary Chronicle. They looked drowsy to me
and I knew their account of these proceedings would be at
odds with the official log recorded by the pict-servitors. Hierarch Onnopel himself was already dozing. The fat idiot. If his
grip on the spiritual fibre of his flock had been tighter, these
hearings might not have been necessary.

I saw my ancient savant, Uber Aemos, apparently listening
intently, though I knew his mind was far away. I saw Alizebeth Bequin, my dear friend and colleague, reading a copy
of the court briefing. She looked stately and prim in her long
dark gown and half-veil. As she pretended to turn the pages,
I glimpsed the data-slate concealed inside its cover. Another
volume of poetry, no doubt. The glimpse made me chuckle,
and I hastened to stifle the sound.

'My lord? Is there a problem?' the pardoner asked, breaking off in mid-flow.

I waved a hand. 'None. Please continue, sir. And hasten to your summary, perhaps?'

The Minster at Eriale was only a few decades old, rebuilt from war rubble in a triumphant High Gothic style. As little as half a century before, this entire sub-sector – the Ophidian sub-sector – had been in the embrace of the arch-enemy. In fact, it had been my honour to witness the embarkation of the great Imperial taskforce that had liberated it. That had been on Gudrun, the former capital world of the Helican sub-sector, one hundred and fifty years previously. Sometimes I felt very old.

I had lived, by that time, for one hundred and eighty-eight years, so I was in early middle age by the standards of privileged Imperial society. Careful augmetic work and juvenat conditioning had retarded the natural deteriorations of my body and mind, and more significant artifice had repaired wounds and damage my career had cost me. I was robust, healthy and vigorous, but sometimes the sheer profusion of my memories reminded me how long I had been alive. Of course, I was but a youth compared to Aemos.

Sitting there, in a gilt lifter throne at the centre of the high table, dressed in the robes and regalia of a lord chief examiner, I reflected that I had perhaps been too hard on that duffer Onnopel. Any reconquered territory, taken back from the taint of the warp, would perforce be plagued by heresy for some time as Imperial law reinstated itself. Indeed, ordos dedicated to the Ophidian sub-sector had yet to be founded, so jurisdiction lay with the neighbouring Officio Helican. An Examination such as this was timely. Fifty years of freedom and it was right for the Inquisition to move in and inspect the fabric of the new society. This was necessary tedium, I tried to remind myself, and Rorken had been correct in calling for it. The Ophidian sub-sector, thriving in its recovery, needed the Inquisition to check on its spiritual health just as this rebuilt Minster needed stonemasons to keep an eye on its integrity as it settled.

'My lord inquisitor?' Verveuk whispered to me. I looked up and realised Fen the pardoner had finished at last.

'Your duty is noted, pardoner. You may retire,' I said, scribing a mark on my slate. He bowed.

'I trust the accused has paid you in advance for your time,' said Inquisitor Koth archly. 'His assets may be sequestered, 'ere long.'

'I have been paid for my statement, sir,' confirmed Fen.

'Generously, it seems,' I observed. 'Was it by the word?'

My fellow inquisitors chuckled. Except Verveuk, who barked out a over-loud whinny as if I had just made the finest jest this side of the Golden Throne. By the Throne, he was a sycophantic weasel! If ever a windpipe cried out for a brisk half-hitch, his was it.

At least his snorting had woken Onnopel up. The hierarch roused with a start and growled 'hear, hear!' with a faux-knowing nod of his many chinned head as if he had been listening intently all along. Then he went bright red and pretended to look for something under his pew.

'If there are no further comments from the Ministorum,' I said dryly, 'perhaps we can move on. Inquisitor Menderef?'

'Thank you, lord chief examiner,' said Menderef politely, rising to his feet.

The pardoner had scurried away, leaving Pridde alone in the open expanse of the wide floor. Pridde was in chains, but his fine garb with its lace trim seemed to discomfort him more than the shackles. Menderef walked around the high table to face him, turning the pages of a manuscript slowly.

He began his cross-examination.

Laslo Menderef was a slender man a century old. His thin brown hair was laquered up over his skull in a hard widow's peak and his face was sallow and taut-skinned. He wore a long, plain velvet robe of selpic blue with his rosette of office and the symbol of the Ordo Hereticus pinned at his breast. He had a chilling manner that I admired, though I cared not at all for the man's radical philosophy. He was also the most articulate interrogator in Sakarof's officio. His long-fingered, agile hands found a place in the manuscript and stopped there.

'Udwin Pridde?' he said.

'Sir,' Pridde answered.

'On the 42nd day of 380.M41, you called upon the house of an unlicensed practitioner of apothecary in Clude and purchased two phials of umbilical blood, a hank of hair from the head of an executed murderer and a fertility doll carved from a human finger bone.'

'I did not, sir.'

'Oh,' said Menderef amiably, 'then I am mistaken.' He turned back and nodded to me. 'It appears we are done here, lord examiner,' he said. He paused just long enough for Pridde to sag with relief and then wheeled round again. Glory, but his technique was superb.

'You're a liar,' he said. Pridde recoiled, suddenly alert once more.

'S-sir–'

'The apothecary was executed for her practices by the Eriale Arbites in the winter of 382. She kept annotated records of her dealings which, I presume, she foolishly thought might serve as some kind of bargaining tool in the event of her apprehension. Your name is there. The matter of your purchases is there. Would you like to see it?'

'It is a fabrication, sir.'

'A fabrication... uhm...' Menderef paced slowly around the defendant. Pridde tried to keep his eyes on him but didn't dare turn from his spot. Once Menderef was behind him, Pridde started to shake.

'You've never been to Clude?'

'I go there sometimes, sir.'

'Sometimes?'

'Once, maybe twice every year.'

'For what purpose?'

'There is a feed merchant in Clude who—'

'Yes, there is. Aarn Wisse. We have spoken with him. Though he admits to knowing you and doing business with you, he says he never saw you at all in 380 or the year after. He has no receipt of purchase for you in his ledger.'

'He is mistaken, sir.'

'Is he? Or are you?'

'Sir?'

'Pridde... your pardoner has already taken up too much of the day extolling – and magnifying – your multiple virtues. Do not waste any more of our time. We know you visited the apothecary. We know what you purchased. Make us like you more by collaborating with this line of questioning.'

Pridde shuddered. In a small voice, he said, 'I did make those purchases, sir. Yes.'

'Louder, for the court, please. I see amber lights winking on the vox-recorders. They're not picking up your voice. The lights have to glow green, you see. Like they are now, hearing me. Green means they hear you.'

'Sir, I did make those purchases!'

Menderef nodded and looked back at his manuscript. 'Two phials of umbilical blood, a hank of hair from the head of an executed murderer and fertility doll carved from a human finger bone. Are those the purchases you mean?'

'Yes, sir...'

'Green lights, Pridde, green lights!'

'Yes, sir!'

Menderef closed the manuscript and stalked round in front of Pridde again. 'Would you like to explain why?'

Pridde looked at him and swallowed hard. 'For the stock.'

'The stock?'

'My breeding stock of cattle, sir.'

'Your cattle asked you to make these purchases?'

Koth and Verveuk laughed.

'No, no, sir... I had purchased fifty head of breeding stock from a farm in the South Uvege two years before. Cosican Red-flank. Do you know the breed, sir?'

Menderef looked back at us, playing to the gallery with raised eyebrows. Verveuk laughed again. 'I am not on first name terms with cattle, Pridde.'

'They're good stock, the best. Certificated by the Administratum Officio Agricultae. I was hoping to breed from them and establish a commercial herd for my combine.'

'I see. And?'

'They sickened, over winter. None would carry to term. The things they whelped were still-born... such things... I had to burn them. I asked the Ministorum for a blessing, but they refused. Said it was a failing in my stockmanship. I was desperate. I had sunk a lot of capital into the herd, sir. Then this apothecary told me...'

'Told you what?'

'That it was the warp. Said the warp was in the feed and the land, the very meadows. She said I could cure the trouble if I followed her guidance.'

'She suggested you used rural warpcraft to mend your ailing cattle?'

'She did.'

'And you thought that was a good idea?'

'As I said, I was desperate, sir.'

'I know you were. But it wasn't for the cattle, was it? Your wife had asked you to make the purchases, hadn't she?'

'No, sir!'

'Yes, sir! Your wife, of the Samargue bloodline, desperate to restore power and vigour to its ailing fortunes!'

'Y-yes...'

'Green light, Pridde!'

'Yes!'

From the documentation and my preparation, I already knew that House Samargue was the biggest game we were after on Durer. To his credit, Verveuk had suggested we begin with Pridde, a minor player, no more than an accomplice really, and use him as a lever to open up the noble family. On the basis of his testimony, the corruption of the ancient House would be easy to force out into the open.

Menderef continued his questioning for over an hour and, to tell the truth, it made for captivating theatre. When the Minster bell sounded nones, he cast a subtle glance at me to indicate there was no point pressing Pridde further for the time being. A break, with opportunity for the defendant to pace and worry, would serve us well for the day's second session.

'We will suspend the hearing for a brief term,' I declared. 'Bailiffs, conduct the accused to the cells. We will resume at the chime, an hour from now.'

I was hungry and stiff. Lunch offered a decent respite, even if I would have to tolerate Verveuk.

Bastian Verveuk was thirty-two standard years old and had been an inquisitor for seven months. He was a fresh-faced boy, he seemed to me, of medium height with a centre-parted bowl of heavy blond hair and slightly hooded, earnest eyes. He looked like he was yearning all the time. Yearning and swept up in some spiritual rapture.

He had a brilliantly ordered mind and had doubtlessly served Osma well as an interrogator. But now his hour had come and he was pushing up the ranks with immodest ambition. His transfer to Rorken's staff – for 'supplementary schooling' – had probably been the result of Osma losing patience with him. Osma was like that. Osma was still the same Osma who had plagued me fifty years before. Except that now he was set to inherit Orsini's role as Grand Master of the Inquisition, Helican sub-sector. Grand Master Orsini was dying and Osma was his chosen heir. It was just a matter of time.

Rorken was dying too, if the rumours were true. Soon, I would be friendless in the high ranks of the Ordos Helican.

Thanks to Rorken's infirmity, I had acquired Verveuk. He was simply a burden I had to carry. His manner, his yearning, his bright eagerness; his damned questions.

I stood in the Minster's warm sacristy, sipping wine and eating thick seed-bread, smoked fish and a strong, waxy cheese locally produced in the Uvege. I was chatting with Rassi, a pale, quiet senior inquisitor from the Ordo Malleus who had become a firm friend in recent years despite his association with the caustic Osma.

'A month, you think, Gregor?'

'For this, Poul? Two, maybe three.'

He sighed, toying his fork around his plate, his silver-headed cane tucked under his arm to free his hands. 'Maybe six if they each bring a bloody pardoner, eh?'

We laughed. Koth slid past us to refill his glass and cast us a nod.

'Don't look now,' Rassi murmured, 'but your fan club is here.'

'Oh, crap. Don't leave me with him!' I hissed, but Rassi had already moved away. Verveuk slid up beside me. He was balancing a dish of game terrine, pickles and salted spry that he clearly had no intention of eating.

'It goes well, I think!' he started.

'Oh, very well.'

'Of course, you must have great experience of these sessions, so you know better than I. But a good start, would you not say?'

'Yes, a good start.'

'Pridde is the key, he'll turn the lock of House Samargue.'

'I'm quite sure of it.'

'Menderef's work was something, wasn't it? The cross-exam? So deft, so well-judged. The way he broke Pridde.'

'I – uh – expected no less.'

'Quite something, yes indeed.'

I felt I had to say something. 'Your choice of Pridde. As the first accused. Well judged, well... well, a good decision, anyway.'

He looked at me as if I was his one true love and I'd just promised to do something significant.

'Lord, I am truly honoured that you say so. I only did what I thought best. Really lord, to hear that from you, fills my heart with–'

'Stewed fish?' I asked, offering him the bowl.

'No, thank you, lord.'

'It's very good,' I said, slathering my bread with it. 'Though like so many fine things in life, you can quite quickly have too much of it.'

He didn't take the hint. The hint would most likely have to be embossed on the tip of a hi-ex bolter round and fired up his nose before he'd notice it.

'I feel, lord,' he said, setting his untouched dish aside, 'that I can learn so much from you. This is an opportunity that few of my status get.'

'I can't fathom why,' I said.

He smiled. 'I almost feel I should thank the miserable tumors eating at my Lord Rorken for this chance.'

'I feel I owe some sort of payback to them too,' I muttered.

'It's so rare that a – if I may say – veteran inquisitor such as yourself... a field inquisitor, I mean, not a desk-bound lord... participates in a process like this and mingles with lesser officers such as me. Lord Rorken has always spoken so highly of you. There is much I want to ask you, so many things. I have read up on all your works. The P'Glao Conspiracy, for example. I have reviewed that from end to end, and I have so many queries. And other matters–'

Here it comes, I thought.

And there it came.

'The daemonhosts. And Quixos. There is, oh, so much in that that demands the attention of a scholar such as myself. Can you give me personal insight? Perhaps not now... later... we could dine together and talk...'

'Well, perhaps.'

'The records are so incomplete – or rather, restricted. I yearn to know how you dealt with Prophaniti. And Cherubael.'

I was waiting for the name. Still, hearing it, I winced.

Cherubael. That's what they all asked. Every last neophyte inquisitor I met. That's what they all wanted to know. Damn their interest. It was over and done with.

Cherubael.

For one hundred and fifty years, the daemon had plagued my dreams and made each one a nightmare. For a century and a half, it had been in my head, a shadow at the horizon of sanity, a softly breathing shape in the dark recesses of my consciousness.

I had done with Cherubael. I had vanquished it.

But still the neophytes asked, and swirled up the memories again for me.

I would never tell them the truth. How could I?

'Lord?'

'I'm sorry, Verveuk, my mind wandered. What did you say?'

'I said, isn't that one of your men?'

Godwin Fischig, dressed in a long black coat, still powerful and imposing after all these years, had entered the sacristy by the rear door and was looking around for me.

I handed my plate and glass to the startled Verveuk and went directly across to him.

'I didn't expect to see you here,' I whispered, drawing him aside.

'Not really my thing, but you'll thank me for busting in.'

'What is it?'

'Paydirt, Gregor. You'll never guess in a hundred centuries who we've turned up.'

'Presuming we don't have a million years, Fischig, tell me.'

'Thuring,' he said. 'We've found Thuring.'

* * *

Vengeance, in my opinion, is never an adequate motive for an inquisitor's work. I had sworn to make Thuring pay for the death of my old friend Midas Betancore, of course, but the eighty years since Midas's murder had been filled to distraction with more weighty and more pressing cases. There had not been time or opportunity to spare the months – perhaps years – required to hunt Thuring down. He was... not worth the effort.

At least, that is what Lord Rorken always counselled me when I brought the matter up. Fayde Thuring. An inconsequential player in the shadow-world of heresy that lurks within Imperial society. A nothing who would run foul of justice soon enough all by himself. Undeserving of my attention. Not worth the effort.

Indeed, for a long time, I had believed him dead. My agents and informants had kept me appraised of his activities, and early in 352.M41 I had learned he had fallen in with an out-world fraternity of Chaos called the Hearthood, or sometimes the Chimes of the World Clock. They practised a stylised worship of the Blood God, in the form of a local tribe's minor swine-deity called Eolkit or Yulquet or Uulcet (the name differed in every source consulted) and for some months had plagued the crop-world Hasarna. Their cult-priest took the ceremonial guise of the swine-butcher or culler who, in older times, had travelled between the communities of Hasarna at the end of each autumn, slaughtering the livestock ready for the cold months. It was an old tradition, one that mixed ritual blood-letting with the dying of the calendar year, and is common throughout the Imperium. Pre-Imperial Terra had just such a myth once, called the Hallows, or the Eve of Hallowing.

The cult leader was Amel Sanx, the Corruptor of Lyx,

reappearing for the first time after a century of hiding to spread his poisons. Sanx was so notorious a heretic that once it became known he was involved, the initial Inquisitorial efforts to prosecute the Hearthood multiplied a hundredfold and a kill-team of the Adepta Sororitas led by Inquisitor Aedelorn obliterated them in a raid on Hasarna's northern capital.

In the aftermath, it was discovered that Sanx had already sacrificed most of his minor followers as part of a ritual that Aedelorn's raid had interrupted. Thuring was one of his second tier of trusted acolytes in the Hearthood. His body was listed as amongst the ritual victims.

Midas's killer was dead. Or so I had thought until that moment in the sacristy of Eriale's Minster.

'Are you sure of this?'

Fischig looked at me with a shrug as if I should have trouble doubting his words.

'Where is he?'

'That's the part you've going to love. He's here.'

They had taken their places already in the main vault of the Minster by the time I joined them. House Samargue had brought out a militant advocate to answer for them and already he was strenuously trying to establish the fragility of Udwin Pridde's testimony.

I slammed my fist on the table to shut him up.

'Enough! This Examination is suspended!'

My fellow inquisitors swung round to look at me.

'It's what?' asked Menderef.

'Until further notice!' I added.

'But–' Koth began.

'Gregor–?' asked Rassi. 'What are you doing?'

'This is highly irregular–' Verveuk said.

'I know!' I told him, right into his face. He flinched.

'My lord chief examiner,' asked the Samargue's advocate, stepping towards the bench nervously, 'may I presume to ask when this hearing might recommence?'

'When I'm ready,' I snarled. 'When I'm good and ready.'

TWO

Betancore, blood up
Fischig's briefing
Arming for battle

It caused quite a stir. What am I saying? Of course it caused
quite a stir. Crowds quickly gathered outside the Minster in
the bright afternoon sunshine. The archivists and pamphlet-
eers who had been dozing in the public gallery scampered off
to promulgate the news. Even the confessors and preachers
who had been wandering the streets, lambasting the commonfolk with bilious sermons against heresy, followed the
crowds to the Minster square.

'You can't just suspend a Court of Examination!' Menderef
raged at me. I shoved him aside and strode on down the
long aisle towards the main doors of the Minster. Bequin
and Fischig were in step with me, and Aemos scurried to
catch up.

'You say "here", what do you mean?' I asked Fischig, dragging off my fur-trimmed cloak and my chain of office and
tossing them onto a pew.

'Miquol,' he said. 'It's an island in the northern polar circle. About two hours' transit time.'

'Eisenhorn! Eisenhorn!' Menderef yelled behind me, a twitter of agitated voices around him.

'You sure it's him?'

'I've reviewed Godwin's findings,' snapped Bequin. 'It's Thuring, all right. I'd put money on it.'

We reached the end of the Minster's nave and were crossing towards the entrance arch and daylight. A hand caught my sleeve.

I turned. It was Rassi.

'What are you doing, Gregor? This is holy work you're abandoning.'

'I'm not abandoning anything, Poul. Didn't you hear me? I'm suspending it. This Examination is all about feeble little recidivists and their ungodly habits. I'm set on a true heretic.'

'Really?'

'Come along if you don't believe me.'

'Very well.'

As I pressed on through the great doorway, Rassi turned and intercepted Koth and Menderef. He shouted down their objections. 'I'm going with him,' I heard him say to them. 'I trust Eisenhorn's judgment. If he was wrong to break the court here, I'll testify to that when I return.'

We were out in the daylight. Mobs of civilians gazed at us, some shielding their eyes from the sun's glare where the blossom-heavy trees of the square failed to shade them.

'Medea?' I asked Fischig.

'Already called in. I presumed; I hope that's all right.'

'Does she know?'

Fischig glanced at Bequin and Aemos. 'Yes. I couldn't hide it from her.'

Almost on cue, Medea's voice crackled over my vox-link.

'Aegis descending, the Armour of God, by two,' she reported in Glossia code, her voice hard-edged and bitter.

'Damn it!' I said. 'Clear the square!'

Fischig and Bequin ran forward into the crowd. 'Clear the area!' Bequin yelled.

'Come on, move! Move now!' Fischig bellowed.

No one obeyed.

Fischig pulled out his handgun and fired into the air. Shrieking, the crowd surged back and streamed away down the approach streets.

Just in time.

My gun-cutter, all four hundred and fifty tonnes of it, swung in over the roof of the Eriale Municipal Library and descended on wailing thrusters into the Minster square. The downwash blew the blossom off the trees and filled with air with petals like confetti.

I felt the ground shake as the vessel set down hard. Flagstones cracked under the steel pads of the extended landing struts. Casements around the square shattered. The trees in the square billowed furiously in the outrush of the jets. The nose ramp whined open.

I hurried up the ramp with Aemos and Bequin, pausing to beckon Rassi aboard. Leaning on his cane, he walked more slowly than us. Fischig waited at the foot of the ramp, sternly ushering in the other members of my retinue who had been stationed in the vicinity of the Minster. Kara Swole, who had been monitoring the crowd from a caffeine house opposite the library. Duclane Haar, whose sniper-variant long-las had been tracking the traffic around the Minster's main door from the roof of the Administratum's tithe barn. Bex Begundi, who had been posing as a homeless mutant begging for alms in the porch of Saint Becwal's Chapel, his pistols concealed under his pauper's bowl.

Fischig pulled them all in and then ran up the ramp, hauling on the lever that slammed the ramp shut.

Almost immediately, the gun-cutter rose again, puffing out a cloud of blossom.

In the entry bay, I took a quick head count.

'Verveuk! What are you doing here?'

'As my Lord Rorken instructed,' he said, 'I go where you go, lord.'

We gained altitude, climbing into the stratosphere for the transit north. My own people knew their places and tasks, but I pulled Kara Swole aside and told her to make sure Rassi and Verveuk were comfortable. 'Inquisitor Rassi deserves every courtesy, but don't give Verveuk a millimetre. Don't let him get in the way.'

Kara Swole was a well-muscled acrobat-dancer from Bonaventure who had assisted one of my investigations three years before and had enjoyed the experience so much she'd asked to join my retinue permanently. She was small and lithe, with very short red hair, and her muscular frame made her look almost stocky, but she was nimbler and more agile than just about anyone I had ever met and had a genuine flair for surveillance. She'd become a valued member of my team and she'd told me more than once that the employment I offered her was infinitely preferable to her previous life in the circus arenas of her homeworld.

Kara glanced in Verveuk's direction. 'He looks like a ninker to me,' she murmured. 'Ninker' was her insult of choice, a slang term from the circus creole. I'd never had the heart to ask her what it meant.

'I believe you're right about that,' I whispered back. 'Keep an eye on him... and make sure Rassi's happy. When we get to the destination, I want you and Haar guarding them with your lives.'

'Understood.'

I gathered Fischig, Bequin, Aemos, Haar and Begundi around the chart table for a briefing, and also summoned Dahault, my astropath.

'All right... how did you find him?'

Fischig smiled. He was obviously pleased with himself. 'The audit turned him up. At least, it turned up some appetising clues that made me look harder and find him. He'd been operating in three of the northern seaports, and also in the capital. I couldn't believe it at first. I mean, we thought he was dead. But it's him.'

An audit was part of my standard operating practice, and I'd set one going the moment Lord Rorken prevailed on me to conduct the Examination, four months earlier. Under Fischig's leadership, a large part of my support staff – over thirty specialists – had gone ahead to Durer to carry it out. The purpose of an audit was twofold. First, to review and recheck the cases to be presented for Examination to make sure we weren't wasting our time and that we were in possession of all the relevant data. It wasn't that I didn't trust Lord Rorken's preparation, I just like to be certain about what I'm prosecuting. Secondly, it was to investigate the possible existence of heretical cases that might have been overlooked by the Examination. I was going to be devoting a lot of my time and resources to this clean up of Durer, and I wanted to make sure I was being thorough. If there was other recidivism here, I wanted to root it out at the same time.

Fischig and the audit team had made a virtual fingertip search of the planetary records, cross-checking even minor anomalies against my database. It proved that Rorken's preparatory work had been excellent, for very little turned up.

Except Fayde Thuring. Fischig had first discovered some off-world financial transactions that flagged because they linked to merchant accounts on Thracian Primaris that Thuring had been associated with twenty years earlier. Fischig had backtracked painstakingly through shipping registers and accommodation listings and had lucked upon some footage recorded by a mercantile company's security pict. The man captured digitally by the pict-recorder bore a striking similarity to Fayde Thuring.

'As far as we can make out,' said Fischig, 'Thuring's been on Durer for about a year. Arrived aboard a free trader last summer and took up residence in Haynstown on an eighteen month merchant's visa. Uses the name Illiam Vowis and claims to be a dealer in aeronautical engineering. Not short of cash or connections. Most of the business seems legit, though he's been buying up a lot of machine parts and tooling units and hiring on a fair number of local tech-adepts. From the outside, it looks like he's setting up a repair and servicing outfit. What he's actually doing is not yet clear.'

'Has he purchased or rented any workspace property?' asked Begundi.

'No. That's one of the discrepancies.' Fischig looked up at me. 'He keeps moving around. Difficult to track. But four days ago, I got a good lead that he was in the northern seaport, Finyard. So I sent Nayl to get a proper look.'

Harlon Nayl, a long serving member of my cadre and an ex-bounty hunter, was one of my finest. 'What did he find?'

'He was too late to catch Thuring. He'd already gone, but Nayl got into the hotel suite he had been using before their housekeeping could clean it up, and got enough hair and tissue fibres to run a gene-scan against the samples we hold on file. Perfect match. Illiam Vowis is Fayde Thuring.'

'And you say he's now on a polar island?'

Fischig nodded. 'Nayl took off after Thuring, found out he had arranged passage to this place Miquol. Used to be a PDF listening station there, years ago, but it's uninhabited now. We don't know what he's doing there, or even if he's been there before. Nayl should have reached the island himself by now. He hasn't checked in, but the magnetosphere is wild as hell up near the pole, so comms are out. Long-range, anyway.'

'This is excellent work, old friend,' I told Fischig, and he smiled appreciatively. Godwin Fischig, once a chastener in the Arbites of Hubris and a law enforcer of considerable ability, was one of my real veterans. He'd served at my side for fifteen decades now, for as long as Alizebeth Bequin. Only Aemos had been with me longer. The three of them were my rock, my foundation, the cornerstones of my entire operation. And they were my friends. Aemos provided wisdom and an unimaginably vast resource of knowledge. Bequin was an untouchable, and ran an academy of similarly gifted individuals called the Distaff. They were my greatest weapon, a corps of psychically blank individuals who could be used to block even the most powerful psykers. Bequin was also my emotional rudder. I confided in her more than the others and looked to her for support when I was troubled.

Fischig was my conscience. He was an imposing man with an age-grizzled face that was now quite jowly. A thin down of grey hair covered his scalp where once he had been blond. The scar under his milky eye had gone pink and glossy over time. Fischig was a formidable warrior and had gone through some of the worst times at my side. But there was none more single-minded than he, none so pure... puritanical, if you will.

Good and evil, Law and Chaos, humanity and the warp... they were simple, black and white distinctions for him. I admired that so. Time, experience and incident had greyed my attitudes somewhat. I depended on Fischig to be my moral compass.

It was a role he seemed happy to perform. I think that's why he had stayed with me so long, when by now he could have become a commissioner of Arbites, a divisional prefect, maybe even a planetary governor. Being the conscience of one of the sub-sector's most senior inquisitors was a calling that gave him satisfaction.

I wondered sometimes if Fischig regretted the fact that I had never sought higher office in the Inquisition. I suppose, given my track record and reputation, I could have become the lord of an ordo by now, or at least been well on my way. Lord Rorken, who had become something of a mentor to me, had often expressed his disappointment that I had not taken up the opportunities he had offered to become his heir. He had been grooming me for a while as successor to the control of the Ordo Xenos, Helican sub. But I had never fancied that kind of life. I was happiest in the field, not behind a desk.

Of all of them, Fischig would have benefitted most if I had followed that kind of course. I could well imagine him as the commander-in-chief of the Inquisitorial Guard Helican. But he had never expressed any hint of unhappiness in that regard. Like me, he liked the challenge of field work.

We made a good team, for a long time. I'll never forget that, and despite what fate was to bring, I'll always thank the God-Emperor of mankind for the honour of working alongside him for as long as I did.

* * *

'Aemos,' I said, 'perhaps you'd like to review Fischig's data and see if you can make any further deductions. I'm interested in this island. Punch up the data, maps, archives. Tell me what you find.'

'Of course, Gregor,' Aemos said. His voice was very thin and reedy, and he was more hunched and wizened than ever. But knowledge still absorbed him, and I think it nourished him in the way that food or wealth or duty or even love kept other men going way past their prime.

'Fischig will assist you,' I said. 'And perhaps Inquisitor Rassi too. I want a workable plan of operations in-' I checked my chronometer '-sixty minutes. I need to know everything it is possible or pertinent to know before we hit the ground. And I want a positive, uncomplicated plan of what we do when we get there. Alizebeth?'

'Gregor?'

'Get in contact with as many of our specialists here on Durer as you can find and get them moving in to support us. Distaff especially. I don't care how long it takes or what it costs. I want to know we have solid backup following us.'

She nodded graciously. She was a brilliant man-manager. Bequin was still as demure and beautiful as the day I had met her, a century and a half before, a spectacular testament of the way Imperial science can counter the effects of aging. Only the faintest creases in the corners of her eyes and lips betrayed the fact that she was not a stunning woman in her late thirties. Lately, she had taken to walking rather regally with a shoulder-high ebony cane for support, claiming that her bones were old, but I believed that to be an affectation designed to reinforce her very senior and matriarchal role.

Only when I looked into her eyes could I see the distances of age. Her life had been hard and she had witnessed many terrible things. There was a sort of wistful pain in the depths of her gaze, a profound sadness. I knew she loved me, and I loved her as much as any being I had ever known. But long ago, mutually, we had set that aside. I was a psyker and she was an untouchable. Whatever the sadness we both felt because of our denied love, being together would have been so much more agonising.

'Dahault...'

'Sir?' the astropath answered smartly. He had been with me for twenty years, by far the longest stretch any astropath had managed in my employ. They wear out so quickly, in my experience. Dahault was a vital, burly man with a spectacular waxed moustache that I believe he grew to compensate for his shaved head. He was certainly powerful and able, and had taken to my regime of work well. Only in the past few years had he started to show the signs of psychic exhaustion – the shallow, drawn skin, the hunted look, the aphasia. I dearly hoped I would be able to retire him on a pension before his calling burned out his mind.

'Check ahead,' I told him. 'Fischig says the magnetosphere is blocking vox traffic, but Thuring may be using astropaths. See what you hear.'

He nodded and shuffled away to his compact, screened cabin under the bridge to connect his skull-plugs to the astro-communication network.

I turned last to Bex Begundi and Duclane Haar. Haar was an ex-Imperial Guard marksman from the 50th Gudrunite Rifles, a regiment I had an old association with. Of medium build, he wore a matt anti-flect bodyglove, the cap-pin of his old outfit dangling round his neck on a cord. He had lost a leg in action on Wichard, and been invalided out of service. But he was as good a shot with the sniper-variant long-las as Duj Husmaan, now long gone and in a manner I sorely regretted.

Haar was clean shaven and his brown hair was as neatly trimmed as it had been in the days of parade ground drill. He wore an optic target enhancer that clamped around the side of his skull, looping over his ear, and could drop the articulate arm of the foresight down over his right eye for aiming. He preferred the enhancer to a conventional rifle-mounted scope, and with his tally of clean hits, I wasn't about to argue.

Bex Begundi was a rogue, in the strictest sense of the term. A desperado, old Commodus Voke would have called him. An outlaw, scammer, con-artist and low-life, born in the slums of Sameter, a world I had no love for as I'd once left a hand there. He was one of Harlon Nayl's recruits – possibly one of his intended bounties who had been offered a life or death choice – and had joined my team six years before. Begundi was unspeakably cocky and prodigiously skilled with handguns.

Tall, no more than thirty-five years old, he was not exactly handsome but oozed a devastating charisma. He was dark haired, a jet-black goatee perfectly trimmed around his petulant smile, with hard cheekbones, and corpse-white skin dye contrasting with the wipes of black kohl under his dangerously twinkling eyes, as was the gang-custom of the slums. He was dressed in a leather armour body jacket embroidered with rich silk thread and preposterous panels of sequins. But there was nothing remotely comical about the paired Hecuter autopistols holstered under his arms in a custom-made, easy-draw rig.

'We're in for a fight when we get down, make no mistake,' I told them.

'Rockin' good news,' said Begundi with a hungry smile.

'Just point me at the target, sir,' said Haar.

I nodded, pleased. 'No showboating, you hear me? No grandstanding.'

Begundi looked hurt. 'As if!' he complained.

'Actually, I was thinking of you, Haar,' I replied. Haar blushed. He had proved to be extremely... eager. A killer's instinct.

'You can trust me, sir,' he said.

'This is important. I know it's always important, but this is... personal. No screw ups.'

'We're after the guy who popped Dee's dad, right?' asked Begundi.

Dee. That's what they called Medea Betancore, my pilot.

'Yes, we are. For her sake, stay alert.'

I went up into the cockpit. The high-altitude cloudscape was sliding past outside. Medea was flying like a daemon.

She was just over seventy-five years old, just a youngster still. Stunning, volatile, brilliant, sexy, she had inherited her late father's pilot skills as surely as she had inherited his dark Glavian skin and fine looks.

She was wearing Midas's cerise flying jacket.

'You need to stay focused, Medea,' I said.

'I will,' she replied, not looking up from the controls.

'I mean it. This is just a job.'

'I know. I'm fine.'

'If you need to stand down, it can be arranged.'

'Stand down?' She snapped the words and looked round at me sharply, her large, brown eyes wet with angry tears. 'This is my father's killer we're going for! All my life I've waited for this! Literally! I'm not going to stand down, boss!'

She had never known her father. Fayde Thuring had murdered Midas Betancore a month before her birth.

'Fine. I want you with me. I'd like you with me. But I will not allow emotion to cloud this.'

'It won't.'

'I'm glad to hear it.'

There was a long silence. I turned to go.

'Gregor?' she said softly.

'Yes, Medea?'

'Kill the bastard. Please.'

In my cabin, I made my preparations. The soft robes I had been wearing as lord chief examiner went in favour of an armoured bodyglove, steel-reinforced knee boots, a leather jacket and a heavy storm coat with armoured shoulder panels. I pinned my badges of office on my chest, my Inquisitorial rosette at my throat.

I selected my three primary weapons from the safe: a large calibre bolt pistol, the runestaff handmade for me by Magos Bure of the Adeptus Mechanicus, and the curved, pentagram-engraved force sword that I had commissioned to be forged from the broken half of the Carthaen warblade, Barbarisater.

I blessed each one.

I thought of Midas Betancore, dead nearly a century now. Barbarisater purred in my hands.

THREE

Miquol
Durer PDF listening station 272
The turnabout

Miquol was a vast volcanic slab jutting from the black waters of the polar ocean, sixteen kilometres long and nine wide. From the air, it looked bleak and lifeless. Sheer cliffs a hundred metres high edged its shape but its interior was a ragged desert of crags and rock litter.

'Life signs?' I asked.

Medea shrugged. We weren't picking anything up, but it was obvious from the jumping, hiccuping displays that the magnetics were playing hell with our instruments.

'Shall I set down topside?' she asked.

'Maybe,' I said. 'Bring us around for another pass to the south first.'

We banked. Cloud cover was low, and banks of chill fog swathed the island's gloomy sprawl.

Fischig joined us in the cockpit.

'You said there was an old facility here?' I said.

He nodded. 'A listening station, used by the Planetary Defence Force in the early years after the liberation. Been out of use for a couple of decades now. It's high up in the interior. I've got a chart-ref.'

'What's that?' Medea asked, pointing down at the southern cliffs. Down below, we could make out some derelict jetties, landing docks and prehab sheds clustered on a sea-level crag at the foot of the cliff. Some kind of vertical trackway, a row of rusting pylons, ran from the back of some of the larger sheds up the face of the cliff.

'That's the landing facility,' said Fischig. 'Used to serve the island when there were still PDF staffers stationed here.'

'There's a sea-craft down there,' I said. 'Fairly large.'

I looked across at Medea. 'Put down there. The crag there beside the sheds. The cliffs will keep the cutter out of sight too.'

It was bitingly cold, and the air was dank with fog and sea-spray. Aemos and Dahault stayed with Medea aboard the cutter and the rest of us ventured out. On the ramp, I turned to Verveuk. 'You stay aboard too, Bastian.'

He looked dismayed. That damned yearning look again.

'I'd like to feel I have someone I can count on watching the cutter,' I lied smoothly.

His expression changed immediately: pride, self-importance. 'But of course, lord!'

We crossed the crag in the lee of the high cliffs towards the prefabs. They were old-pattern Imperial modulars, shipped in and bolted together. Time and weather had much decayed them. Windows were boarded and the fibre-ply walls were rotten and patched. Rain and spray had scrubbed away most of the surface paint and varnish, but in places you could just make out the faded crest of the Durer PDF.

Haar and Fischig led the way. Haar had his long-las raised to his shoulder, his fore-sight dropped into place, hunting for targets as he paced forward. Fischig carried a las-rifle in one hand. A motion tracker unit was buckled over his left shoulder, whirring and ticking as it subjected Fischig's immediate vicinity to invisible waves of vigilance. Rassi and I were close behind them, with Alizebeth, Kara and Begundi at the rear.

Fischig pointed to the vertical trackway we had seen from the air. 'Looks like a cable-carriage or a funicular railway. Runs up to the cliff top.'

'Functional?' Rassi inquired.

'I doubt it, sir,' said Fischig. 'It's old and hasn't been maintained. I don't like the look of those cables.' The main lifting lines were heavy-gauge hawsers, but they swung slackly in the wind between the pylons and showed signs of fraying. 'There are stairs, though,' Fischig added. 'Right up the cliff alongside the track.'

We crossed to the jetties. They too were badly decayed. Rusting chains slapped and clanked with the sea-swell. The craft moored there was a modern, ocean-going ekranoplane, twenty metres long and sleekly grey. Stencils on the hull told us it was a licensed charter vessel from Finyard, presumably the vessel Thuring had hired to bring him here.

There was no sign of crew, and the hatches were locked down. There wasn't even a hint of standby automation.

'Want me to force entry?' asked Kara.

'Maybe–' I was interrupted by a shout from Haar. He was standing in the entrance of the nearest prefab, a docking shed that stood over the water on stilt legs. Haar gestured inside as I joined him. In the half-light, I could see four bodies slumped on the duckboards of the dry well. Fischig was kneeling beside them.

'Local mariners. Their papers are still in their pockets. Registered operators from Finyard.'

'Dead how long?'

Fischig shrugged. 'Maybe a day? Single shot to the back of the head in each case.'

'The crew from the sea-craft.'

He rose. 'Makes sense to me.'

'Why didn't they dump the bodies at sea?' Haar wondered.

'Because an ekranoplane is a specialist vehicle and they needed the crew alive to get them here,' I suggested.

'But if they killed them once they were here–' Haar began.

I was way ahead of him. 'Then they're not planning on leaving the island. Not the way they arrived, at any rate.'

I had Kara Swole break into the ekranoplane. There was nothing useful inside, just a few items of equipment and personal clutter belonging to the murdered crew. The passengers had taken everything else with them.

The only thing we learned was that Thuring might have as many as twenty men with him on Miquol, given the ekranoplane's load capacity and the number of emergency life jackets.

'They've gone inland,' I decided. 'And that's where we're going too.'

'Shall I get Dee to fire up the cutter?' Begundi asked.

'No,' I said. 'We'll go in on foot. I want to get as close to Thuring as possible before he makes us. We can call in the cutter if we need it.'

'Medea won't like that, Gregor,' said Bequin.

I knew that damn well.

* * *

I believed Medea deserved every chance to avenge her father. Vengeance might not be an appropriate motive for an inquisitor, but as far as I was concerned it was perfectly fine for a headstrong, passionate combat-pilot.

However, her passion could become a liability. I wanted Thuring taken cleanly and I didn't relish the prospect of Medea going off in a blind fury.

Bequin was right, though. Medea really didn't like it.

'I'm coming!'

'No.'

'I'm coming with you!'

'No!' I caught her by the arms and stared into her face. 'You are not. Not yet.'

'Gregor!' she wailed.

'Listen! Think about this logic–'

'Logically? That bastard killed my father an–'

'Listen! I don't want the cutter giving us away too early. That means leaving it here. But I do want the cutter ready to respond at a moment's notice, and that means you have to stay here on standby! Medea, you're the only one who can fly it!'

She shook off my grip and turned away, gazing at the rolling surge of the ocean.

'Medea?'

'Okay. But I want to be there when–'

'You will. I promise.'

'You swear it?'

'I swear it.'

Slowly, she turned look at me. Her eyes were still bright with hurt. 'Swear it on your secrets,' she said.

'What?'

'Do it the Glavian way. Swear it on your secrets.'

I remembered this now. The Glavian custom. They considered an oath most binding if it was sworn against private, personal secrets. In the old days, I suppose, that meant one Glavian pilot swearing to exchange valuable technical or navigational secrets with another as an act of faith and honour. Midas had made me do it once, years before. He'd made me swear to a three-month sabbatical at a time when I was working too hard. It hadn't been possible, because of one case or another, and I'd ended up having to tell him that I adored Alizebeth and wished with every scrap of my being that we could be together.

That was the deepest, darkest secret I had been carrying at the time. How things change.

'I swear it on my secrets,' I told her.

'On your gravest secret.'

'On my gravest secret.'

She spat on the ground and then quickly licked her palm and held out her hand. I mirrored her gestures and clasped her hand.

We left her with Aemos, Dahault and Verveuk at the gun-cutter and made our way up the cliff stairs.

It was raining by the time we reached the top, and the last few flights were treacherously wet. Salty wind flapped in from the sea, gusting into our coats and clothes.

I was worried about Poul Rassi. Though he didn't look it, he was over a century older than me, and the climb left him pale and breathless. He was relying on his cane more than before.

'I'm all right,' he said. 'Don't fuss.'

'Are you sure, Poul?'

He smiled. 'I've been in the courts and privy chambers for too many of the last few years, Gregor. This is almost an adventure. I'd forgotten how much I liked this.' Rassi raised his cane and flourished it ahead of us like a sabre. 'Shall we?'

We advanced into the hinterland of Miquol. Fischig had an auspex locked off on the old PDF base, so we headed for that as a place to start.

The sky was the luminous, hazy white of a blown valve-screen. Stripes of fog clung to the ground like walls of smoke. The rain was constant. The landscape was a mix of jagged upthrust outcrops and steep, shadowy valleys littered with scree. Boulders were scattered all around, some the size of skulls, some the size of battle tanks. The rock was dark, almost the colour of anthracite, and occasionally it was splintered out in cascades of volcanic glass. A forbidding, grey place. A monochrome world.

After two hours, we passed a rust-eaten tower of girders capped by sagging, corroded alloy petals that had once been a communications dish. One of the peripheral receivers of the listening station.

'We're close,' said Fischig, consulting his auspex. 'The PDF base is over the next headland.'

Durer PDF listening station 272 had been established shortly after the planet's liberation by the newly formed Planetary Defence Force as part of a global overwatch program. Through it, and around three hundred facilities like it, the Durer PDF had been able to maintain a round-the-clock watch of orbital traffic, local shipping lane activity and even general warp space movements, providing the planet with an early warning network and gathering vital tactical intelligence for this part of the sub-sector in general. Over a period of twenty years following the annexation of the territory, the network had gradually been run down, eventually supplanted by a string of scanner beacons in high orbit and a slaved sub-net of sensor buoys seeded throughout the Durer system.

The PDF had finally vacated the obsolete station some three decades before, undoubtedly grateful that they would never have to tolerate a tour of duty on this harsh rock again.

The station lay on the shore of a long polar lake, framed by ragged infant mountains to the north. It was an exposed place, bitten by the sub-zero winds. The lake, smudged with mist, was a flat, gleaming mirror of oil-dark water, its glassy surface occasionally disturbed by a flurry of wind ripples.

On the grey shore there were eighteen longhouses arranged in a grid around a drum-like generator building, a hangar large enough to shelter several troop carriers or orbital interceptors, a cluster of store barns, a number of machine shops, a small Ecclesiarchy chapel, a central command post with adjoining modules arranged in a radial hub and the main dish array.

All of it had succumbed to the feral ministry of the environment. The modules and prefabs were aged and dilapidated, windows covered with boards. The roadways between the prefabs were littered with rusting trash: old fuel drums, the carcasses of trucks, piles of flaking storm shutters. The vast main dish, angled towards the west, was a skeleton of its former self, just a hemisphere described by bare girders and dangling struts. In the black mirror of the lake, its reflection seemed like that of a giant, bleached ribcage. But it looked to me more like the ruins of an orrery, just the shattered remains of the central solar ball, permanently peering in the direction it had last been turned.

Hugging cover, we made our way onto the cold shore and crossed the short distance to the nearest longhouse. We all had weapons drawn by now, except Begundi. Fischig's auspex and motion tracker both indicated life-signs close by, but how close they weren't telling. Thanks to the damn magnetic interference we were forewarned but as good as blind.

We were non-verbal by now. I gestured and sent Haar ahead down the left side of the street, Fischig down the right. I'd have liked to deploy Kara too, but she was keeping to my orders and sticking close to Rassi, her assault weapon tight in her gloved hands. Rassi, his sombre, fur-trimmed robes flapping in the wind, had produced a multi-barrel pepperpot handgun of exotic manufacture.

Bequin hung back from me so that her psychic deadness wouldn't conflict with my mind. For the trek across Miquol she had changed her formal gown for a quilted body suit and stout boots, with a hooded cloak of dark green, embroidered velvet wrapped around her. I noticed she had also left her long walking cane aboard the cutter. She had drawn a slim, long-nosed micro-las that I had given her on her hundred and fiftieth birthday. It had pearl-inlaid grips and was a custom masterpiece, an antique made by Magos Nwel of Gehenna.

The pistol suited her. It was slender and elegant and devastatingly potent.

Up ahead, I saw Fischig signal to Haar. Haar knelt down and gave the big man some cover as he crossed to the back door of the next longhouse. I sent Begundi forward in support. Begundi still hadn't drawn his hand cannons from their shoulder rig, and ran with an easy, loping gait.

Once Begundi had reached him, Fischig slipped inside the longhouse. There was a pause, and then Begundi went in too.

We waited.

Begundi appeared in the doorway and beckoned to us.

* * *

It was good to be out of the damp, though the dark, rot-stinking interior of the old prefab barrack wasn't much better. We got inside, and Haar and Kara stood guard at the doorway, with Begundi covering the front.

Fischig had found something.

Fischig had found someone.

It was an old man. Filthy, wizened, lice-ridden and diseased. He cowered in the corner, whining each time the beam of Fischig's hand-lamp probed at him. If I'd passed him on the streets of Eriale, I'd have taken him for a beggar and not given him a second look. Out here, though, it was different.

'Give me the lamp,' I said. The old man, who seemed more animal than human, shrank back as I turned the hard white light on him. He was caked in filth, starving and gripped by fear.

But despite the dirt, I could recognise his robes.

'Father? Father hierarch?'

He moaned.

'Father, we're friends.' I unclasped my rosette and held it out to show him.

'I am Inquisitor Gregor Eisenhorn, Ordo Xenos Helican. We are here in an official capacity. Don't be afraid.'

He looked at me, blinking and slowly reached out a dirt-blackened hand towards the rosette. I let him take it. He looked at it for a long time, his hands trembling. Then he started to weep.

I waved Fischig and the others back and knelt down beside him.

'What's your name?'

'D-Dronicus.'

'Dronicus?'

'Pater Hershel Dronicus, hierarch of the parish of Miquol, blessed be the God-Emperor of Mankind.'

'The God-Emperor protects us all,' I answered. 'Can you tell me how you come to be here, father?'

'I've always been here,' he replied. 'The soldiers may have gone, but while there is a chapel here, there is a parish, and so long as there is a parish then there is a priest.'

By the Golden Throne, this old fellow had lived here alone for thirty years, maintaining the chapel.

'They never deconsecrated the ground?'

'No, sir. And I am thankful. My duty to the parish has given me time to think.'

'Go mad, more like,' Haar muttered.

'Enough!' I snapped over my shoulder.

'Let me see if I understand this right,' I said to Dronicus. 'You served here as a priest and when the PDF abandoned the site, you stayed on and looked after the chapel?'

'Yes, sir, that is the sum of it.'

'What did you live on?' asked Fischig. That detective brain, looking for holes in the story.

'Fish,' he said. From his astonishingly foul breath, I believed that.

'Fish... I went down to the landing point once a week and fished, smoking and storing the catch in the hangar. Besides, the soldiers left a lot of canned produce. Why? Are you hungry?'

'No,' said Fischig, unprepared for the generosity of the question.

'Why are you hiding in here?' Bequin asked softly.

Dronicus looked at me as if needing my permission to answer.

'Go ahead,' I nodded.

'They drove me out,' he said. 'Out of my hangar. They were mean. They tried to kill me, but I can run, you know!'

'I have no doubt.'

'Why did they drive you out?' Fischig asked.

'They wanted the hangar. I think they wanted my fish.'

'I'm sure they did. Smoked fish, that's worth something out here. But they wanted something else, didn't they?'

He nodded, a bleak look on his face. 'They wanted the space.'

'What for?'

'For their work.'

'What work?'

'They are mending their god.'

I glanced sidelong at Fischig.

'Their god? What god is that?'

'Not mine, that's for sure!' Dronicus exclaimed. Then he suddenly looked reflective. 'But it's a god, nevertheless.'

'Why do you say that?' I asked.

'It's big. Gods are big. Aren't they?'

'Usually.'

'You said "they",' said Rassi, crouching down next to me. 'Who do you mean? How many of them are there?'

Rassi's tone was admirably calm and reassuring, and I could feel the gentle bow-wake of the psychic influence he was cautiously bringing to bear. No wonder he had such a great reputation. I almost felt stupid for not asking such obvious questions.

'The god-smiths,' the old priest replied. 'I do not know their names. There are nine of them. And also the other nine. And the fourteen others. And the other five.'

'Thirty-seven?' breathed Fischig.

Dronicus screwed up his face. 'Oh, there's a lot more than that. Nine and nine and fourteen and five and ten and three and sixteen...'

Rassi looked at me. 'Dementia,' he whispered. 'He's able

to account for them only in the groups he's seen them. He's not capable of identifying a whole. They are just numbers of people that he's seen at various times.'

'I'm not stupid,' cut in Dronicus simply.

'I never said you were, father,' Rassi replied.

'I'm not mad either.'

'Of course.'

The old man smiled and nodded and then, very directly, asked, 'Do you have any fish?'

'Boss!' Haar hissed suddenly. I rose quickly.

'What is it?'

'Movement... thirty metres...' His fore-sight was twitching as it downloaded the data. He knelt in the doorway and eased his rifle up to a firing position.

'What do you see?'

'Trouble. Eight men, armed, moving like an infantry formation. Coming this way.'

'We must have tripped something on the way in,' said Begundi.

'I don't want a fight. Not yet.' I looked at the others. 'Let's exit that way and regroup.'

'We have to take him,' said Rassi, indicating the old priest.

'Agreed. Let's go.'

Begundi opened the far door of the hut and led the way out. Bequin followed him, then Fischig. Rassi reached out to help the old priest up.

'Come on, father,' he said.

Seeing the hand coming for him, Dronicus yelped.

'Shit! We're rumbled!' said Haar. 'They're coming!'

Las-fire, bright and furious, suddenly hammered at the doorway and blew holes through the rotten fibre-ply.

Kara dived down for cover. Haar kept his place and I heard his long-las crack.

'One down,' he said.

Rassi and I hauled the old priest to his feet and bundled him towards the back exit. Behind us, the long-las cracked again, and was joined by the chatter of Kara Swole's assault weapon. Return fire hammered into the side of the longhouse, perforating the wall.

'Get him out,' I told Rassi and ran to the door.

Standing over Kara as she fired, I shot several bolt rounds through the gaping window. Las-shots seared down the street and burst against the side of the hut. I got a glimpse of figures in bulky grey combat fatigues scurrying closer and pausing to unload their lasrifles in our direction.

A sudden thought, true and clear, lanced into my brain. I grabbed Kara and Haar. 'Move!' I howled.

We had made it to the rear door when the grenade took the front off the hut. The entire doorway area where Haar had been crouching erupted in a flash of flame and shredded fibre-ply.

The blast-rush blew us out into the street.

Fischig hauled me up.

'Go! Go!'

Kara was bleeding from a shrapnel wound on her temple and Haar was dazed. But we ran, dragging them with us, up the muddy roadway towards the main dish.

Three men in insulated combat armour raced into the street ahead of us, raising lasrifles.

Begundi's Hecuter pistols were in his hands faster than any of us could raise the weapons we already held. He blazed out twin streams of shots, the shell cases spraying out from the slide-slots of his weapons. All three men ahead of us lurched back and sprawled.

Begundi ran ahead, chopping down another two as they emerged, his handguns roaring. Then he dropped suddenly onto his back, rolled round and blasted another assailant off the roof where he had suddenly appeared.

Five more loomed behind us, breaking out of the rear door we had escaped through.

Fischig and Kara turned, firing. They dropped three of them. Bequin brought down the fourth with a single well-placed head-shot. A round from my bolt pistol knocked the fifth five metres back down the road.

'Thorn? Desiring Aegis? Pattern oath?' my vox suddenly squawked. Medea was monitoring the activity over the vox-link.

'Negative! Thorn wishes Aegis repose under wing!' I replied, using Glossia, the informal private code I shared with my staff.

'Aegis stirred. The flower of blood.'

'Aegis repose, by the thrice ignited. As a statue, to the end of Earth.'

'Gregor! Let me come!'

'No, Medea! No!'

We were in a serious firefight now. Las-shots and hard rounds whipped in all directions. Fischig and Haar laid down heavy cover fire. Kara and Bequin selected targets more particularly and hit most of them. Begundi blazed away with his matched handguns. I fired carefully, cautiously, keeping the old priest behind me. Rassi's fission-lock pepperpot banged and sparked and hailed lead balls at the enemy. Every few seconds, he raised his cane and sent forth a drizzle of psycho-thermic flame from the silver tip.

'Brace yourselves,' I yelled. 'You especially, Poul.'

He nodded.

Reveal yourselves! I urged, using the will at full force.

Such a raw outburst would usually have floored all those around me, but Haar, Begundi and Kara had all been mentally conditioned during rigorous training to black out my psy-streams. Bequin was untouchable and Fischig wore a torc that protected him.

Rassi, forewarned, put up a mental wall. The old priest screamed, stood up and wet himself.

He wasn't the only one to stand up. Our attackers rose into view, each one clutching a smoking weapon, each one blinking in dumb confusion.

Begundi, Fischig and I cut them all down in a few, lethal seconds.

Victory.

For a moment.

Suddenly, Dronicus was running away down the street and Rassi was doubled up by convulsions. I felt it too. A sudden jolt in the background psionic resonance. Like a painfully bright flash of light.

I staggered back and slammed into the side of the nearest hut. Blood spurted out of my nose. Begundi and Kara fell to their knees. Haar sat down hard, sobbing. Even Fischig, protected by his torc, felt it and staggered.

Alizebeth, the only one unmoved, glanced around at us and yelled, 'What? What is it?'

I knew where it had come from. The hangar. I struggled upright in time to see the hangar roof quiver and buckle as something broke through it from inside.

Something huge that smashed entire roof panels out of the way as it got to its feet.

It must have been lying down in the hangar, I realised. Now it was rising and activated. What we had felt had simply been the backwash of its mind-link going live.

With dreadful certainty, I realised that Fayde Thuring was going to be damn near impossible to stop.

I had made an unbelievable, unforgivable mistake. I had underestimated him and his resources. He was nothing like the minor warp-dabbler I had once let slip away.

He had a Titan, Emperor damn him.

He had a Battle Titan.

FOUR

Cruor Vult
Fleeing the giant
A terrible long shot

Its name was *Cruor Vult*. It weighed two and half thousand tonnes and stood sixty metres tall. Like all the great Warlord-class Battle Titans, it was a biped, almost humanoid in its proportions. Hooved with immense three-toed feet of articulated metal, its massive legs supported a colossal pelvic mount and the great, riveted torso that housed its throbbing atomic furnaces. Broad shoulders provided ample space for turbo-laser batteries. Beneath the shoulder armour, the Titan's arms elevated the machine's primary weapons: a gatling blaster as the right fist, a plasma cannon as the left. The head was comparatively small, though I knew it was large enough to contain the entire command deck. It was set low down between the shoulders, making the monster ogrish and hunched.

I have seen Titans before. They are always a terrifying sight. Even the Imperial Battle Titans are awful to behold.

The Adeptus Mechanicus, who forge and maintain the war machines for the benefit of mankind, regard them as gods. They are perhaps the greatest mechanical artefacts the human race has ever manufactured. We have made more powerful things – the starships that can cross the void, negotiate warp space and reduce continents to ashes with their ordnance – and we have made more technically sophisticated things – the latest generations of fluid-core autonomous cogitators. But we have made nothing as sublime as the Titan.

They are built for war and war alone. They are created only to destroy. They carry the most potent armaments of any land-based fighting vehicle anywhere. Only fleet warships can bring greater firepower to bear. Their image, bulk, their sheer size, is intended to do nothing except terrify and demoralise a foe.

And they are alive. Not as you or I would understand it, perhaps, but there is an intellect burning inside the mind-impulse link that connects the drivers and crew to the Titan's function. Some say they have a soul. Only the Priests of Mars, the adepts and tech-mages of the Cult Mechanicus, truly understand their secrets and they guard that lore ruthlessly.

Perhaps the only thing more terrifying than a Battle Titan is a Chaos Battle Titan, the infamous metal leviathans of the arch-enemy. Some are manufactured in the smithies and forges of the warp, their designs copied and parodied from the Imperial originals, sacrilegious perversions of the Martian god-machines. Others are ancient Imperial Titans corrupted during the Great Heresy, traitor legions that have lurked in the Eye of Terror for ten thousand years in defiance of the Emperor's will.

Which this was, frankly I cared little. It looked deformed, blistered with rust, draped with razorwire and covered with blade-studs that sprouted like thorns. What I first took to be strings of yellow beads hanging from its shoulders and blade-studs were actually chains of human skulls, thousands of them. Its metal was a dull, dirty black and inscribed with the unutterable runes of Chaos. Its head was a leering skull plated in glinting chrome. Its name was wrought in brass on a placard across its gigantic chest.

It stepped forward. The ground shook. The ruptured roof panels of the hangar squealed as they tore and caved in around its swinging thighs. It strode through the fabric of the hangar like a man wading through a stream. The building's front burst out and fell away with a tremendous crash as the Titan broke its way through.

And then it howled.

Great vox-horns fixed to the sides of its skull blared out the berserk war-cry of the monster. It was so painfully loud, so deep in the infrasonic register, that it reflexively triggered primal fear and panic in us. The earth shook even more than it had done under the weight of its footsteps.

It was coming our way. Now it was clear of the hangar, I could see the long segmented tail it dragged and whipped behind it.

Move! I said, directing my will at my colleagues in the hope of snapping them into some sort of rational response. Every few seconds, the rock under our feet vibrated as it took another step.

We started to run through the streets of the deserted station, trying to keep as much of the buildings as possible between us and it. Our one advantage was our size. We could evade it by staying hidden.

With a metallic screech of badly lubricated joints, it slowly turned its head and waist to look in our direction and then stomped heavily round to follow us. It walked straight through a longhouse, shattering it like matchwood.

'It knows where we are!' Rassi cried, desperately.

'How can it?' Haar whined.

Military grade sensors. Heavy-duty auspex. Devices so powerful that they could overcome the island's magnetic distortions. This beast had been made to fight in horrifically inhospitable theatres, resisting toxins, radiations, vacuums, bombardments. It needed to be able to see and hear and smell and target in the middle of hell. The local magnetics that had bested our civilian instruments were nothing to it.

'It's so... big...' Bequin stammered.

Another crash. Another longhouse kicked over and splintered. A squeak of protesting metal as a derelict troop truck was pulverised underfoot.

We turned back, running back almost the other way now, passing south of the chapel and the command centre. Again, with an echoing grind of engaging joints, it came about and renewed its inexorable pursuit.

I felt a spasm, a pulse on a psychic level. I was feeling the surge and flicker of its mind-impulse link.

'Get down!' I yelled.

The gatling blaster opened fire. The sound was a single blur of noise. A huge cone of flaming gases flickered and twitched around the blaster muzzles.

A storm of destruction rained around us. Hundreds of high-explosive shells hosed the street, blitzing the fronts of the buildings, pulping them. Firestorms sucked and rushed down the street. Billions of cinders and debris scarps sprayed all around. The stench of fyceline was chokingly strong.

I got up in a blizzard of ash and settling sparks. We were all still alive, if chronically dazed by the concussive force. Either the Titan's targeting systems were off-set, or the crew were still getting used to its operation. The sensors might be capable of tracking our movement, but the Titan still had to get its eye in. Perhaps it could only sense us in a general way.

'We can't fight that!' said Fischig.

He was right. We couldn't. We had nothing. This was so one-sided it wasn't even tragic. But we couldn't run, either. Once we left the cover of the station's buildings, we would be in the open and easy targets.

'What about the gun-cutter?' blurted Alizebeth.

'No... no,' I said. 'Even the cutter hasn't got enough kill-power. It might make a dent, but it wouldn't stand a chance. That thing would shoot it out of the sky before it even got close.'

'But–'

'No! It's not an option!'

'What is then?' she wanted to know. 'Dying? Is that an option?'

We were running again, away from the burning zone of devastation. With another overwhelming blurt of decibels, the blaster cut loose again. A longhouse and part of the command centre to our right disintegrated in a volcanic flurry of spinning wreckage and fire. There were walls of flame everywhere, gusting yellow and bright into the grey gloom.

Begundi led us down a side street between the ends of longhouses, Fischig and Kara Swole almost carrying the exhausted Rassi. We ducked down in the shadows against the rotting side wall.

Hiding, we could no longer see the Titan. There was silence, interrupted only by the crackle of blazing fibre-ply and the creak of prefab frames slowly slumping.

But I could feel it. I could feel its abhuman mind seething malevolently through the deepest harmonics of the psyk-range. It was north of us, on the other side of the chapel and the store barns, waiting, listening.

A vibrating thump. It was moving again. The rate of the footsteps increased as it picked up speed until the ground no longer had time to stop shaking between thumps. Pebbles skittered on the ground and loose glass dislodged from the broken windows of the nearby longhouses.

'Go!' growled Fischig. He broke and started to run east across the main street. The others began to follow his lead.

'Fischig! Not that way!' I leapt after him, grabbing him in the middle of the roadway. There was a groan of tortured metal and the Titan itself appeared at the end of the street, traversing its mighty upper body to face us.

Fischig froze in terror. I threw us both forward behind the rusted hulk of an old PDF troop carrier.

Blaster fire ripped down the street, kicking up a wild row of individual impacts that pitted the rocky ground, demolished the edge of a barn and filled the air with greasy flame, smoke and powdered rock.

A flurry of shots sliced through the shell of the troop carrier, splitting its fatigued armour wide open and hurling rusty shrapnel in all directions. The force of the hits actually lifted the carrier's mouldering bulk and spun it around, end to end. I dragged Fischig behind a longhouse and just prevented us from being crushed under the lurching metal shape. The carrier came to rest against the side wall of the prefab, stoving in the wall panels.

The earthshaking footsteps resumed. The Titan was advancing down the street. I looked at Fischig. He was dazed and pale. A ragged chunk of shrapnel had embedded itself in his left shoulder. It would have decapitated him if it hadn't been for the motion tracker unit strapped there. As it was, the tracker was a smouldering wreck and blood poured from the hunk of metal projecting from his trapezius.

'Holy Throne,' he murmured.

I hoisted him up and glanced back across the street. Begundi and Swole had managed to get everyone else back into cover before the barrage. I could see them through the smoke, huddled in the shadows.

I raised my free hand and made gestures that were as clear as possible. I wanted them to back off and regroup. We would have to split up. There was nowhere we dared cross the open street in either direction.

Fischig and I blundered off in the opposite direction, coming out in a drain gully behind the row of longhouses where a stream emptied down through the station to the lake. We crossed it using a small wire-caged footbridge and then fell into cover on the far side of a machine shop.

'Where is it?' Fischig wheezed in pain.

I checked. I could see the huge machine towering above the prefabs two hundred metres back, shrouded in the black smoke that was roiling up from its last onslaught. It had reached the old troop carrier and was standing there. It looked for all the worlds as if the giant war-engine was sniffing the air.

It turned again suddenly, filling the air with the sound of whirring gears and clanking joints, and smashed through the longhouse as it moved off after us.

'It's coming this way,' I told Fischig. We started to run again, across the levelled rockcrete apron of the machine shop and then down the gently sloped street towards the command centre.

Fischig had slowed right down. It was gaining on us.

There was a distant, booming roar that echoed around the entire lake basin. A ball of flame rose into the air from the very western end of the station area.

'What the hell was that?' Fischig growled.

The Titan clearly wanted to know too. It adjusted its path and moved away from us, striding towards the site of the unexplained blast, oblivious to the collateral damage it was leaving in its wake.

'That,' said a voice behind us, 'was the best diversion I could come up with.'

We looked around and there was Harlon Nayl.

Nayl was a good friend and a respected member of my team. I hadn't seen the old bounty hunter since he had set off for Durer with Fischig's party to conduct the audit. He was a big man, dressed as always in a black combat-armoured body-glove. With his heavy skull shaved and polished and his grizzled face, he looked a fierce brute, but there was a grace to his movements and a nobility to his stature that always set me in mind of Vownus, the rogue hero of Catuldynus's epic verse allegory *The Once-Pure Hive*.

He held a vox-trigger detonator in his hand.

We followed Nayl into the shelter of a storebarn and the bounty hunter immediately began to field dress Fischig's wound. The Battle Titan was still prowling around west of us, investigating the mysterious blast.

'I tried to raise you on the vox, but the channels were screwed,' Nayl said.

'Magnetics,' I said. 'How long have you been here?'

'Since first light. I rented a speeder to follow Thuring. It's hidden up in the hills on the far side of the lake.'

'What have you found?' Fischig asked, wincing as Nayl sprayed his wound with antisept.

'Apart from the obvious, you mean?'

'Yes,' I said.

'Thuring's got backing. Serious capital support. Maybe a powerful local cult we don't know about, more likely an off-world cabal. He's got manpower, resources, equipment. When I first arrived, I poked around, got a glimpse of what was in the hangar... that took my breath away, I can tell you. Then I "borrowed" one of his men and asked some questions.'

'Did you get any answers?'

'A few. He was... trained to resist.'

I knew Nayl's interrogation techniques were fairly basic.

'How long did he last?'

'About ten minutes.'

'And he told you–'

'Thuring has known for some time that the Titan was here. Probably information received from his backers. It seems no one knew that Miquol was used by the arch-enemy as a Titan pen during the occupation. The bloody PDF were stationed here for years and never realised what was hidden just up there in the mountains.'

I peered out of the barn door. The Titan had come about and was plodding back in our direction. I could taste its bitter psychic anger and feel the earth quivering under my feet.

'Harlon!'

He leapt up and came to join me. 'Damn,' he hissed, viewing the Titan. He took out his detonator again, selected a fresh channel and thumbed the trigger.

There was a flash, a rolling report, and another mass of fire blossomed from the western shore of the lake. The Titan turned immediately and stomped towards the fresh blast.

'It's not going to fall for that many more times,' said Nayl.

'So there was a Titan... that damn thing... abandoned and dormant in the mountains?'

'That's about the size of it. Left behind in the mass retreat, never found by Imperial liberators. Sealed in a shielded cavern... along with two more like it.'

'Three Titans?' snarled Fischig.

'They've taken this long to get just that one working,' said Nayl. 'Thuring's aboard that thing, commanding it personally. He's delighted with his new toy, even though it's not up to optimum. You'll notice it's only used its solid munition weapon. I don't think its reactors are generating enough juice yet to power up its energy batteries.'

'Lucky us,' I said.

'What I can't tell you is why Thuring is restoring a monster like that.'

There could be many reasons, I thought. He could be doing it on the behest of his rich sponsors, which seemed likely. He could be intending to sell it to the highest bidder. There were cult groups in the Ophidian sub-sector that would love to own that sort of power. He could even be working for some higher power, perhaps enlisted by the actual legions of the arch-enemy.

Or he could be doing this for himself. That idea chilled me. Thuring was evidently a more significant player than I had estimated. He could have designs of his own, and with a Battle Titan at his command those designs could be very bloody. He could hold cities to ransom, here on Durer or elsewhere. He could raze population centres, slaughter millions, particularly once the turbines of *Cruor Vult* were operating at full power.

Whatever the truth, the dismal fate of the ekranoplane's crew told me he wasn't intending to leave the island the way he had come in. A bulk lifter could easily land here, pick up the Titan and be away before the frankly paltry watch forces of Durer could react. Thuring was planning to leave here with the Titan. I knew that as a certainty. It didn't matter where he was going after that. Imperial blood would be spilled as a result. We had to stop him.

Which brought me back to my original problem.

How the hell were we going to fight that?

Frantically, with the Titan now turning back from the second diversion, I considered the tools at our disposal. It was hard to concentrate, because the angry flutter of the Titan's mind link was interfering with my mind. I suppose that's what gave me the idea. The desperate idea.

I reached to key my vox link and then paused. The behemoth would detect vox transmissions effortlessly. Instead, I stretched out with my mind, trying to find Rassi.

'Nayl?' I asked. 'What's the most secure structure here?'

'The chapel,' he said. 'It's reinforced stone.'

I opened my mind fully. *Thorn enfolds kin, within a seal, the worshipful place.* If Rassi could hear me, he wouldn't understand Glossia, but I figured he'd have the sense to consult the others.

After a long pause, the answer came.

Kin come to Thorn, in sealed worship, abrupt.

'Let's move!' I told Nayl and Fischig.

We reached the chapel first. The dread Titan had begun to stride our way again by then, but Nayl fired the last of his diversions and distracted it east.

We tumbled into the ancient church. It was generally stripped bare and full of slimy black mold. A few remaining wooden pews were sagging with damp corruption. The double-headed eagle from the altar lay trampled on the floor.

I noticed that its dented wings were polished brightly. Dronicus had tended this place fervently until Thuring's men had arrived and smashed up his diligently maintained shrine. It was a heartbreaking sight.

I bowed to the altar and made the sign of the eagle across my chest with both hands.

The others arrived in a hurry, weapons drawn, slamming the door shut behind them: Bequin, Haar, Begundi, Swole and Rassi.

Rassi was panting hard. Bequin was pale. Both Haar and Swole had cuts and contusions from near misses.

'You have a plan?' asked Rassi, almost immediately.

I nodded. 'It's a terrible long shot, but I don't know what else to do.'

'Let's hear it,' said Fischig.

I do not pretend, as I have already reflected, to have any specific understanding of the workings of a Battle Titan. No man does, unless he be a priest of Mars or, like Thuring, the owner of illicitly transmitted lore. Aemos probably knew a thing or two. I knew for certain he had seen Adeptus Mechanicus mind-impulse units firsthand, for he'd told me as much, long before, in the cryogenerator chamber of the tomb-vault Processional Two Twelve on Hubris.

But he was not with me in that chilly, ransacked chapel, nor was a decent conversation with him viable.

However, I knew enough to understand that the function of a Titan depended on the connection between man and machine, between the human brain and the mechanical sentience. That was achieved – miraculously – through the psychic interface of the mind-impulse unit.

Which meant, in very simple terms, that the root of our

problem was essentially a psychic one. If we could disrupt or, better still, destroy, the mind link...

'This runestaff was made for me by Magos Geard Bure of the Adeptus Mechanicus,' I told Rassi, letting him feel the weight of the weapon. It was a long, runic steel pole with a cap-piece in the form of a sun's corona, fashioned in electrum. The lode-stone at the cap's centre was a skull, a perfect copy of my own, marked with the thirteenth sign of castigation, that had been worked from a hyper-dense geode of tele-empathic mineral called the Lith that Bure had found on Cinchare. It was a psionic amplifier of quite devastating power.

'We use it to boost our collaborating minds. Force a way into the machine's consciousness.'

'Indeed. And then?'

I glanced over at Alizebeth. 'Then Madam Bequin takes hold of the runestaff and delivers her untouchable blank-ness into the heart of it.'

'Will that work?' Kara Swole asked.

There was a long pause.

Bequin looked at me and then at Rassi. 'I don't know. Will it?'

'I don't know either,' I said. 'But I think it's the best chance we have.'

Rassi breathed deeply. 'So be it. I don't see another hope, not even a remote one. Let's get on with it.'

Poul Rassi and I took the runestaff between us, our hands clamped around the long haft.

He closed his eyes.

I tried to relax, but the instinctual barriers of self protection that exist in every mind kept mine from letting go. I didn't want to get inside that thing. Even from a distance, it stank of putrid power. It reeked of the warp.

'Come on, Gregor,' Rassi whispered.

I concentrated. I closed my eyes. I knew the Titan was treading nearer, because I could feel the chapel floor shaking.

I tried to let myself go.

It was like clinging to a precious handhold when you are dangling over a pit of corrosive sludge. I couldn't bear to submit and slide away. What waited for me down there was cosmic horror, a broiling mass of filth and poison that would dissolve my mind, my sanity, my soul.

Chaos beckoned, and I was trying to find the courage to jump into its arms.

I could feel the sweat dribbling down my brow. I could smell the rotten odour of the derelict chapel. I could feel the cold steel in my hands.

I let go.

It was worse than anything I could have imagined.

Drowning. I was drowning, face down, in black ooze. The sticky, foetid stuff was filling my nostrils and my ears, trying to pour like treacle down into my mouth and choke me. There was no up, no down, no world.

There was just viscous blackness and the unforgettable smell of the warp.

A hand grasped me by the back of the jacket and yanked me up. Air. I spluttered, puking out filmy strings of phlegm stained black by the ooze.

'Gregor! Gregor!'

It was Rassi. He stood beside me, knee deep in the warp mud. God-Emperor, but his mind was strong. I'd have been dead already but for him.

He looked drawn and weak. Warp-induced pustules were spotting his face and crusting his neck. Blowflies billowed around us, their buzzing incessant in our ears.

'Come on,' he said. 'We've come this far.' His words came broken up as he was repeatedly forced to spit out flies that mobbed around his dry lips.

I looked around. The sea of black ooze went on forever. The sky over our heads was thickly dark, but I realised that the billowing clouds were impossibly vast swarms of flies, blocking out the light.

Firelights, distant, flashing, reflected across the slime.

We were in the outer reaches of the Chaos Titan's mind-link.

Swathed in films of ectoplasmic ooze, we struggled forward, holding each other for support. Rassi was moaning. His psychic self had brought no cane to support him.

Flames underlit the horizon and the sea of sludge rolled nauseatingly. I had not encountered a mental landscape this abominable since my first dreams of Cherubael, years before.

Cherubael.

Just the thought of him in my mind brought the flies rushing around me. The slime reacted too, popping and bubbling about my knees. I felt a keening, a sharp need, that filled the polluted air around me.

Cherubael. Cherubael.

'Stop it!' wailed Rassi.

'Stop what?'

'Whatever you're thinking about, stop it. The whole world is reacting.'

'I'm sorry...' I suppressed the notion of Cherubael in my mind with every ounce of my will. The tremors subsided.

'Throne, Gregor. I don't know what you've got in your head, I don't want to know...' said Rassi. 'But... I pity you.'

We trudged forward, first one of us slipping over, then the other, then one bringing the other down. The deep slime licked at us, hungry.

Thousands of kilometres ahead of us, a source of power throbbed. I could dimly make out the silhouette of a man. But it wasn't a man. It was *Cruor Vult*. 'Blood wills it', that would be the simplest Low Gothic translation. The Titan stood there, distant, the master of this psychic realm.

Daemonic forms ghosted around us. Their spectral, screaming faces were madness to behold. They were like smoke, like shadowplay. They snarled at us.

Another few hundred metres and images began to flash into my mind. We were breaking into the edges of the Titan's memory sphere.

I saw such things.

May the God-Emperor spare me, I saw such things then.

I stood on the brink and peered into the abyss of the Titan's memories. I saw cities die in flames. I saw legions of the Imperial Guard incinerated. I saw Space Marines die in their hundreds, scurrying around my feet like ants.

I saw planets catch fire and burn to ashes. I saw Imperial Titans, proud warlords, burst apart and die under the onslaught of my hands.

I saw the gates of the Imperial Palace on Terra through a blizzard of fire. I saw down through many thousands of years.

I saw Horus, vile and screaming out his wrath.

I saw the whole Heresy played out in front of my eyes.

I saw the Age of Strife, and witnessed first hand the Dark Age of Technology that preceded it.

I fell, plummeting through history, through the stored memory of *Cruor Vult*.

I saw too much. I started to scream.

Rassi slapped me hard around the face.

'Gregor! Come on now, we are almost there!'

We were at the heart of it all now, frail as whispers. We were in the bridge of the Titan, seeing the multiple, overlapping spectres of the men who had commanded it, all sat in the princeps's throne, all dead.

Daemons crouched on my back, writhed on my shoulders, gnawed at my ears and cheeks.

I saw horror. Absolute horror.

Beside me, Rassi reached out and touched the mind-impulse unit built into the floor of the bridge.

'Now, I think...' he said.

'Alizebeth!' I yelled.

In the rank confines of the chapel, Bequin leapt forward and grabbed the runestaff from the hands of two inquisitors who were quivering with power, stress and terror, our eyes rolled up blankly so that only the whites showed.

She gripped the runestaff, focused her untouchable force and–

FIVE

My plan fails
Damn Verveuk all to hell
The unthinkable

She was killed.

Not at once, of course. The backrip of the Titan's terrible sentience tore into her, overwhelmed her untouchable quality by dint of its sheer force, and broke her mind.

Electrical discharge crackled down the haft of my runestaff, throwing Rassi and myself away and blasting Alizebeth back across the chapel. The scorch marks are still visible on the uncorruptible steel: the perfectly etched fingerprints of Poul Rassi, Gregor Eisenhorn and Alizebeth Bequin.

Nayl told me afterwards that the psychic recoil had tossed Rassi and myself to either side like dolls, but the main force had been directed at Bequin. She had flown through the air a dozen metres, her cloak fluttering out and cracked off the back wall of the chapel with a sound that Nayl knew meant snapping bones.

He ran to her, calling her name. Fischig lurched forward too. Rassi and I lay on the ground, weeping and gasping. The runestaff, steaming, had landed on the stone floor between us with a clang.

My plan had failed dismally and completely.

Blood trickling from my nose, I got up, Swole and Haar helping me. I had little idea where I was. Images of the Age of Strife still permeated my mind.\

'Rassi?' I gasped.

'Alive!' said Begundi, crouching next to the sprawled inquisitor. 'But he's weak...'

'Alizebeth?' I asked softly, looking to where she lay. Fischig and Nayl were huddled over her. Nayl looked back at me, and shook his head.

'No...' I said, pushing Kara Swole away as I stepped forward. Not Alizebeth. Not her, after all this time.

'She's hurt bad, boss,' Nayl said. 'I'll try to make her comfortable, but...'

The tread of *Cruor Vult* echoed outside.

I staggered towards Bequin. She looked so still. So broken.

'Oh sweet Emperor, please, no–'

'Inquisitor...' said Haar. 'We're dead now, aren't we, for sure?'

I realised slowly that the Titan was right outside.

'What are you doing?' Begundi yelled at me.

I had no idea. I was only partially conscious. I had Barbarisater in my fist and was running for the door. I think I meant to go out and face the Titan with my sword. That's how far gone I was.

One man with a sword, intent on facing down a Battle Titan.

Before I could reach the door, I heard the scream of down-jets and the chatter of cannon-fire.

I didn't have to look out to know it was my gun-cutter. Damn Medea.

'Thorn to Aegis, the spite of justice! Belay! Belay!'

'Thorn requires Aegis, the shades of Eternity, Razor Delphus Pathway! Pattern Ivory!'

'Thorn denies! The cover of stillness! Belay!

'Aegis responds to Verveuk. The matter, quite done.'

'No!' I bellowed. 'Nooo!' Medea's response had told me that she was following Bastian Verveuk's orders now. He had commanded her to take the gun-cutter up. He had ordered her to attack the Titan.

I honestly believe that he thought he was helping me. That he could do some good.

Damn Verveuk. Damn Verveuk all to hell.

I ran outside in time to see the majestic raptor-shape of my gun-cutter burning in low across the PDF station, blazing its guns at the slowly turning Titan. The streams of hi-calibre shells were just pinging off the giant's thick, armoured skin.

Cruor Vult turned with a scrape of metal against metal, raised its right fist and fired. The conical flame-flash of its muzzle gases, white-hot to the point of incandescence, twitched and flickered around the gatling blaster

The cutter bucked and lurched as the first rounds struck it. It tried to evade, but the air was air was too thick with pelting bolts.

The ferocious salvo ripped the belly out of my beloved gun-cutter and tore off a tail-wing. Spewing flames and smoke, the cutter veered off, debris cascading away from its shredded hull. It tried to climb.

Its main engines stalled out.

Leaving a wide streak of smoke behind it in the air, the cutter banked violently to the left, ripped a wing strut through the edge of the ancient, rusted dish, and dropped. It hit the shore of the lake, burying itself in the beach mud and shingle, leaving a smouldering groove thirty metres long behind it.

I stumbled forward, trying to see, but the main bulk of the downed cutter was obscured by buildings. It was ablaze, I could tell that much. *Cruor Vult* began to pace slowly towards the beach.

I had a sudden mental image of a hunter walking to his wounded quarry, preparing to fire a final, point-blank kill-shot.

Around the corner of the next longhouse, I could see down the glinting shingle of the icy lakeshore. The Titan was crunching away from me, its vast treads leaving perfect indentations of pulverised pebbles behind it. The cutter was half on its side, a mangled, truncated wreck, driven down into the scree and hard, cold mud of the shoreline. Wretched black fumes were boiling out of its innards, and curls of steam were rising where the lake water was in contact with flaming debris.

There was a little, tinny bang, and an exit hatch blew out of the cutter's flank, fired off by explosive bolts. A figure, clearly injured, fell out of the hatch, and began to struggle up the beach.

It looked like Verveuk.

The Titan was only about fifty metres from the crashed vessel now, its feet lifting sprays of water as it strode through the beachline shallows.

I became aware of movement beside me. It was Haar, his long-las raised and aimed at the Titan, a defiant gesture so full of courage it quite eclipsed its own basic stupidity. Kara Swole was close behind him, anxiously accompanying Rassi, who had dragged himself out to join me. He looked half-dead from his trials in the mind-link, his eyes sunken and dark, his lips tight and bloodless.

I wonder how the hell I looked.

Begundi followed after them. He'd holstered his pistols again. He knew firepower like that was pointless. Fischig and Nayl had stayed by Alizebeth's side in the chapel.

Rassi had my runestaff, and was using it to stay upright.

'Get back,' I said to them all. 'Just get back... there's nothing we can do.'

'We fight...' gasped Rassi. 'We fight... the arch-enemy... in the name of the God-Emperor of Mankind... until we drop...'

He raised my runestaff and used it to amplify his weary mind. Psycho-thermic energy, manifesting far more powerfully than it had done through his cane, spat at the towering back of the great Titan. I don't know if he hoped to hurt it. I don't know if he was so far gone by that stage to believe he could. I think he was simply trying to distract it from the cutter.

Rassi's scorching arc of flame seemed so devastating as it swirled out of the runestaff beside me, so bright it hurt my eyes, so hot it singed my hair. But by the time it struck the Titan, its true scale was woefully revealed. It flared uselessly off the Titan's rear torso cowling.

But still he kept it going. The psychothermic fire turned green and then blue white. Haar started to fire his weapon. I think Kara did too.

Like kisses into the whirlwind, my old master Hapshant would have said.

Cruor Vult raked the cutter's wreck with blaster rounds. The first few instants of the merciless blitz ruptured the hull, twisting it, deforming it, dashing shards of metal up across the shore and out over the lake, peppering it with splash ripples.

The cutter seemed to writhe, as if it was trying to escape the bombardment. In truth, it was simply being shifted and jolted as the hurricane of shots hammered it from end to end and shredded it.

Then it exploded. A big, bright flash, a cudgelling boom and a rush of shockwave. The blast ripped a hole in the beach and sent a significant tidal wave back across the lake towards the far side.

Where the cutter had been – where Medea, Aemos and Dahault had been – was just a pit of leaping flame. Debris, water and pebbles rained down painfully like an apocalyptic cloudburst. The Titan virtually disappeared in a sudden outrush of steam.

Verveuk had been fifty metres from the wreck, stumbling inland, the last I had seen him. When I dared raise my head from the rain of shingle, there was no sign of him.

Its murder done, the Battle Titan turned on us.

I was knocked flat, and I struck my head so hard on a pre-fab wall I blacked out for a second. I discovered later that Begundi had taken me down into what little cover was available with a desperate flying tackle.

Cruor Vult had improved its aim.

The cold island air was full of mineral dust from the pebbles and rock that had been atomised by its blaster fire. Rassi and Haar simply didn't exist any more. They had been vaporised by the mega-grade military weapon. My runestaff, blackened but intact, lay on a wide patch of ground that had been transmuted to furrowed glass by the hideous alchemy of blaster fire. The only other trace of them was a small, broken section of Haar's lasrifle.

Kara Swole lay twenty metres away where the blast had thrown her. She was covered in blood, and I was sure she was dead.

And I was sure we were dead too. Thuring had won. He had killed my friends and allies in front of my eyes and now he had won.

I had nothing to left to fight him with. I had nothing that could take on the power of a Titan. I'd had nothing when this one-sided duel began, and I sure as hell had nothing left now.

I...

An idea came upon me, insidious and foul, wrenched into the light by the extremity of my position. I shook it off. It was unthinkable. The notion was revolting, inexcusable.

But it was also true. I did have something.

I had something more powerful than a Titan.

If I dared use it. If I had the audacity to unleash it.

Unthinkable. Unthinkable.

Cruor Vult thundered towards me through the ebbing steam.

I could hear the whine of the autoloaders in its massive gatling assembly connecting up fresh munition hoppers. I could see the beach pebbles at my feet, thousands of them, skipping slightly with every step it took.

'Bex...'

'Sir?'

'Get Kara and run. Go for the chapel.'

'Sir, I–'

Do it now, I willed and he sprang up, running fast.

I crawled over to the runestaff and grabbed its haft. It was hot to the touch, and sticky with blood.

Duclane Haar and Poul Rassi would have to serve as the sacrifice, I realised pragmatically, already disgusted with myself. There was no time, no opportunity to do anything more elaborate. As it was, I had scarcely any of the tools, devices, unguents, charms or wards that I would normally have believed necessary to undertake an action like this.

I caught myself. Until that very moment, I had never even considered undertaking an action like this, no matter the preparations.

Kneeling on the vitrified ground in the path of an oncoming Chaos Battle Titan, holding upright in both hands a runestaff slick with the blood residue of two beloved friends, I began the incantations.

It was hard. Hard to remember word-perfect the pertinent verses of the *Malus Codicium*, a work I had studied on and off for years in secret. These were writings I had been eager to learn and understand, but which filled me with dread all the same. After my first sabbatical to study the *Codicium*, just a few months after the execution of its previous owner Quixos, I had been forced into retreat to recover, and required counselling from the abbots of the Sacred Heart monastery on Alsor.

Now I was trying to remember the same passages. Driving myself. Struggling to repeat writings I had once struggled to erase from my mind.

If I got even a word wrong, a phrasing, a point of vocabulary, we would all be dead at the hands of an evil far worse than *Cruor Vult*.

SIX

Chaos against Chaos
The price
The consequence

A moment. A freezing classroom many years before. Titus Endor and myself, shivering in our seats at ebonwood desks eroded by the scratchings and carvings of a thousand previous pupils. We were merely eighteen days into our initial training as junior interrogators. Inquisitor Hapshant had stormed in, slammed the door, cast his stack of grimoires down on the main lectern – which made us both jump – and declared: 'A servant of the Inquisition who makes Chaos his tool against Chaos is a greater enemy of mankind than Chaos itself! Chaos knows the bounds of its own evil and accepts it. A servant of the Inquisition who uses Chaos is fooling himself, denies the truth, and damns us all by his delusion!'

On the lakeshore at Miquol, I was not fooling myself. I knew how desperate this gamble was.

* * *

*Commodus Voke, dead fifty years by then, had once said to me...
and I paraphrase for I did not record it word for word at the
time – "'Know your enemy" is the greatest lie we own. Never
submit to it. The radical path has its attractions, and I admit
I have been tempted over the years of my life. But it is littered
with lies. Once you look to the warp for answers, for knowledge to use against the arch-enemy, you are using Chaos. That
makes you a practitioner. And you know what happens to prac-
titioners, don't you, Eisenhorn? The Inquisition comes for them.'*

On that desolate beach, I felt sure I could sort truth from lies.
Voke had simply misunderstood the fineness of the line.

*Midas Betancore had once, during a late night of drinking and
Glavian rules regicide, said, 'Why do they do it? The radicals,
I mean. Don't they understand that even getting close to the
warp is suicide?'*

With the runestaff in my hands, on that frozen island on Durer,
I knew it wasn't suicide. It was the opposite.

*Godwin Fischig, in a grave-field shrine on Cadia, had once
warned me to stay away from any hint of radical sympathy. 'Trust
me, Eisenhorn, if I ever thought you were, I'd shoot you myself.'*

It wasn't that simple. Emperor damn me, it just wasn't that
simple! I thought of Quixos, such a brilliant man, such a
stalwart servant of the Imperium, so totally polluted by trea-
sonous evil because he had tried to understand the very filth
he fought against. I had declared him heretic and executed
him with my own hand.

I understood the dangers.

* * *

Cruor Vult thundered towards me. I uttered the last of the potent syllables and dipped my mind into the warp. Not the simmering warp-scape of the Titan's mind-link, but the true warp. Channelled by the runestaff and warded by the prayers I had ritually intoned, I flowed into a vaster, darker void. I reached across the fabric of space towards Gudrun, far away, an entire sub-sector away, towards a private estate on the Insume Headland.

I reached into it, into a secret oubliette that had been vacuum sealed, warp-damped, void-shielded and locked with thirteen locks. Only I knew the codes to break down those barriers, for I had set them myself.

It was crumpled in the middle of the floor, wrapped in chains.

I woke it up. I set it free.

I jerked out of my trance. The runestaff bucked in my hands as the unleashed daemon energy flared through it.

I fought to retain my grip and to enunciate precisely the words of command and the specific instructions.

Like a small sun dawning, the enslaved daemon poured out of the head of the runestaff. Its radiance lit up the dismal shore and cast a long shadow out behind the Titan.

'Cherubael?' I whispered.

'Yessss…?'

'Kill it.'

Lightning crackled. A freak storm suddenly erupted over the lake, swirling the heavens and driving rain down in sheets, accompanied by fierce winds and catastrophic electrical displays.

A ghastly white thing, moving so rapidly it could only be registered as an afterimage on the retina, surged out of my staff and went straight into the black bulk of *Cruor Vult*.

The Titan hesitated, mid-step, one foot raised. It shuddered. Its great arms flailed for a moment. Then its chrome skull-face cracked, crazed and shattered, blowing out in a burst of sickly green light.

Cruor Vult swayed, the rainstorm drenching off its creaking bulk.

A halo of light lit up the lake shore and the old PDF base. *Cruor Vult*, ancient enemy of mankind, exploded from the waist up in a globe of furious white heat. Nothing of its head, torso or arms survived the immolation.

The legs, one foot still raised, tottered and swayed and then collapsed, falling sideways like an avalanche and destroying the ruined remains of the station's dish.

Cruor Vult was dead. Feyde Thuring was dead.

And I was unconscious, hurled back by the death-blast.

And that meant Cherubael was free.

If it had fled then, it would have escaped. Indeed, it might have fled deep enough into the miasmic warp to evade me forever, even if I exhausted what was left of my life trying to summon it back. It was wary of me now, and knew my tricks.

Certainly, it might have escaped far enough to avoid my clutches for many years to come, and in that time have cost the Imperium dearly.

But it did not. The daemon was too consumed by rancor for that.

It came back to kill me.

I woke with a start, and realised instantly that Cherubael was free thanks to my loss of control. I looked around, but it seemed like I was alone on the beach. The sky was still swollen with storm clouds, and lightning formed crackling golden crowns around the peaks of the mountains.

The rain was easing, pattering across the glossy, wet pebbles and the steaming ruin of *Cruor Vult*. My skin prickled. I knew it was still here.

I had done the unthinkable, and now I had to undo it. Cherubael had to be bound again. It could not be allowed to remain free.

I picked up the runestaff. The rain was washing the filmy blood off its hard, polished form. I held it firmly in my left hand and drew Barbarisater. The blade twitched, tasting the daemon in the air.

'Gracious Emperor of Mankind, hallowed be your majesty, bright be your light everlasting, vouchsafe your servant in this hour of peril–'

'That won't save you,' said a voice. I switched around, but there was no sign of a speaker.

'Bright be your light everlasting, vouchsafe your servant in this hour of peril, so that I may continue to serve you, great lord, and purify your dominion of–'

'It won't, Gregor. The Benediction of Terra? It's just words, Gregor. Just words.'

'...continue to serve you, great lord, and purify your dominion of man, casting out all daemons and changelings of warpcraft–'

'But I have more than words for you, Gregor. I liked you, Gregor, of all men, you had a spirit I admired. I worked for you, I spared you more than once... consider that. All I asked in return was that you honour our compact and release me. And what did you do? You tricked me. You trapped me. You *used* me.'

The words seemed to echo all around me, but no matter how fast I turned, I could not see it. Its voice was in my head. I struggled to continue the repetitions, struggled to keep hold of the sense of the benediction, but it was hard. I wanted to answer its taunts. I wanted to rage at it that it had tricked me first. There had been no compact between us! It had used me to fashion its own escape from the enslaving charms Quixos had wrought around it.

I dared not. I focused on the repeats. Barbarisater shivered from hilt to tip, resonating with the psychic power that washed around me.

'...vouchsafe your servant in this hour of peril, so that I may continue to serve you, great lord–'

A star came out, over the lake. A hazy ring of white around a brilliant, gleaming centre. Almost fluttering, like a leaf on the wind, it eddied down towards me and settled a few metres away.

The pebbles beneath it turned to glass. The light was almost too bright to look at. Cherubael hovered in the centre of the glare. He was at his most deadly now, non-corporeal, a daemon spirit, raw and bare, unfettered by a fleshly host. I could not resolve any real details in the light. In truth, I had no wish to gaze upon the daemon's true form. It was not even man-shaped any more. I had always presumed white light to be pure and somehow chaste, to be noble and good. But this whiteness was unutterably evil, chilling, its purity an abomination.

'...hallowed be your majesty, bright be your light everlasting...'

'Shut up, Gregor. Shut up so I can hear myself kill you.'

My weapons, staff and sword, were useless physically. Cherubael had no host body to destroy. But they were strong psychically. I had banished Cherubael with the runestaff once before, and as far as I know obliterated his daemon kins Prophaniti. But my mind had been stronger in those battles, and psychic weapons are only as powerful as the will that directs them. Cherubael knew how tired and ill-focused I was. I could feel it trying to weaken me by teasing out the agonies I felt inside... Bequin, Medea, Aemos, Rassi, Haar... It wanted me to think about the deaths of those dear friends so that I would be weakened still further by grief.

But it was weak too. It had just expended huge reserves of power vanquishing a Titan.

The light surged forward, to test me, I think. I swung Barbarisater to deflect it and felt the electrical impact down my arm. It surged again and I swept the staff around, driving it back.

It circled me. I'd stung it. It knew it was in for a fight.

If that's what it wanted...

I lunged at it, Barbarisater keening. Cherubael blocked with a bar of luminous energy and convulsed out a pulse of pale radiance that blew me off my feet into the air.

I landed hard on the shingle, but sprang up fast, remembering every close combat move I'd been taught over the years by the likes of Harlon Nayl, Kara Swole, Arianrhod Esw Sweydyr, Midas, Medea...

It was coming right onto me, blinding bright. It was like fighting a star. I smashed at it with the head of my staff and then somersaulted out of its path, landing on my feet and sprinting away.

I ran under the smouldering arches of *Cruor Vult*'s fallen legs and then back up the tough slog of the beach towards the station. I could distinctly hear the air rush as it burned after me.

I feinted left, but it had guessed as much. The daemon-star was right on me. I swung my sword, leapt to the right, and vaulted over its next blade of light using the staff as a pole.

Cherubael laughed. Its cackling voice followed me as I sprinted up between two longhouses. The daemon-star chased after me, its psychic force scattering the beach stones behind it in a wake.

I heard a groaning, crashing sound and realised the walls were closing in. Cherubael was lifting both longhouses off their blocks and crushing them together with me in between.

I tore through the wall of the left hand prefab with Barbari-sater and leapt through as the juddering huts slammed into each other. Cherubael burned through the fibre-ply wall to get at me, and was greeted by my counter-attack of stabbing blade and staff.

I could drive it back, but I couldn't do any more than that. My mental reserves were just not strong enough.

My only chance was to bind him again. But how?

Dronicus came out of nowhere. I believe, or at least it is a notion I cling on to for the sake of my sanity, that the Emperor of Mankind provides help for his true servants in their hour of need, even in the strangest forms. Dronicus, old, insane Dronicus, had clearly been observing the day's dreadful events from hiding, and now he emerged because he had made a gravely mistaken apprehension. He had seen the white light of the daemon destroy the Titan. To him, therefore, the white light was a friend because it had vanquished a foe.

To him, the potent white light was the Emperor returned to save him.

He ran out of the shadows, calling the Emperor's name, praising him, piteously expressing his gratitude. He was an ancient, emaciated man dressed in dirt and rags. He should have offered no threat to the daemon whatsoever.

Except that, in the Emperor's honour, he had retrieved the fallen aquila altarpiece from the chapel and was holding it up in front of him.

Cherubael howled and backed away, tumbling like thistle-down along the dirt track between the longhouses. Perplexed,

Dronicus ran after it, offering words of worship to the Emperor that must have driven holy spikes into Cherubael's rotten soul.

I had a moment's respite from the assault.

I looked around. I knew I had to think fast.

Bastian Verveuk was still alive. He was a bloody, broken mess, his clothes and hair virtually burned off him from the cutter's death-blast. Though I loathed him for what he had done, I felt pity as I saw him. His eyes were still yearning. They seemed to light up with joy as they saw me approach. He reached out a bloody hand.

He thought I was coming to rescue him.

I confess here, now, that I hate myself for what I did. That I despised Verveuk does not excuse it. He was an odious wretch who had cost me more dearly than I could say, but he was still a servant of the Inquisition. And, damn him, he worshipped and trusted me.

But there was no alternative. I made the right decision. I had released Cherubael because *Cruor Vult* simply had to be stopped for the good of mankind. Now Cherubael had to be stopped, and I was forced to make a similarly hard choice. I will pay. In time. In the hereafter, when I come before the Golden Throne.

I knelt beside him. His yearning face looked up at me. Damn that yearning, puppy look!

'M-master...'

'Bastian, are you a true servant of the Emperor?'

'I... I am...'

'And you will so serve him in any way you can?'

'I will, master.'

'And are you pure?' Foolish question! Verveuk's damned purity had led to all his mistakes. His puritanical piety had made him a liability in the first place.

But he was pure. As pure as any man could be.

I placed my hand on his chest and made my fingers wet with his blood. Then I daubed certain runes and markings on his forehead and face, on his neck and his heart, muttering seldom heard imprecations from the *Malus Codicium*.

'W-what are you doing?' he wavered. Damned questions, even now!

'What must be done. You are doing the Emperor's work, Bastian.'

A scream howled out of the station and Dronicus appeared, running terrified towards the lake. His hands were on fire, dripping with white-hot, molten metal.

Cherubael had finally found the strength to melt the aquila.

Still screaming, the poor old man plunged into the icy lake, the water steaming and spitting around his agonised hands.

Cherubael's deadly star came shimmering down the beach towards me.

'Forgive me, Verveuk,' I said.

'O-of course, master,' he mumbled.

'F-for what?' he added, suddenly.

Bellowing the incantations of binding, the litany of servitus, the wards of entrapment, I met Cherubael head on, the runestaff glittering with power.

'*In servitutem abduco*, I bind thee fast forever into this host!'

'What in the name of hell happened here?' Fischig bellowed, his gun raised as he ran down towards me.

'Everything. Nothing. It's over, Fischig.'

'But... what is that?' he asked.

The daemonhost floated a few centimetres off the ground next to me. I had fashioned a leash from my belt, tied off around Verveuk's scorched, distended throat.

'I have trapped a daemon, Godwin. He is bound and cannot harm us now.'

'But... Verveuk?'

'Dead. We must honour him. He has given his all to the Emperor.'

Fischig looked at me warily. 'How did you know the means to bind a daemon, Eisenhorn?' he asked.

'I have learned much. It is an inquisitor's job to know these things.'

Fischig took a step back. 'Verveuk...' he began. 'He was dead before you used his body, wasn't he?'

I didn't answer. Three shuttles were powering in across the lake, preparing for landing. The reinforcements summoned by Alizebeth had finally arrived.

SEVEN

Taking leave of Miquol
Gudrun, sanctuary
Her heart's desire

I wanted nothing more than to be gone from the place. It had exhausted me and cost me.

My followers, well-drilled specialists all, deployed from the shuttles and took control of the area, rounding up the last of Thuring's dismayed accomplices. I was told that Menderef and Koth were on their way too, bringing with them units of militia and Inquisitorial guard.

I wasn't going to wait around for them.

There were things I wanted as few people as possible to see.

I issued instructions that would bite great holes out of my personal coffers. But I didn't care.

I sent Bequin away on a shuttle as fast as possible, with Nayl and Begundi guarding her.

Nayl was told to get her condition stabilised at the nearest general infirmary and then arrange passage for her off-world, to the Distaff's headquarters on Messina. They took Kara Swole with them too. Kara was alive, but seriously wounded.

I gave Fischig strict instructions to remain behind as my proxy. His heart didn't seem in it. I knew the daemonhost was troubling him more than he dared to say.

His brief was simple. Secure the island until the main Inquisitorial party arrived. See to it that a full statement was made and that the cache of dormant Chaos Titans was destroyed. Then formally close the Examination until further notice.

It didn't seem unreasonable. A senior inquisitor had just risked all and lost much stopping a Battle Titan. His withdrawal from the Durer Examination for recovery seemed utterly justified.

I would contact him later, and take it from there.

I was about to leave on another of the shuttles, with the silent, shrouded daemonhost, when the first piece of good news that day came to my attention.

Medea and Aemos had survived.

They were cut and battered, but she had dragged Aemos from the cutter crash and got him to cover before Verveuk had ejected. They had lain in cover, dazed and breathless.

They had seen everything.

I embraced them both. 'You're both coming with me,' I said.

'Gregor... what did you do?' Medea asked.

'Just get on the shuttle.'

'What did she mean?' Fischig asked.

I didn't answer him directly. I was too tired. Too afraid that my stumbling explanation would not satisfy him. 'See that things here are done properly. I will contact you in a month with instructions.'

I gave him my rosette badge of office so that his authority would be unquestioned.

It was gesture of the frankest trust, but it seemed to disturb him. Then I held out my hand, and he grasped it with a half-hearted grip.

'I'll do my job,' he said. 'Have I ever let you down?'

He hadn't, and I supposed that was his point. Fischig had never let me down, but perhaps now the reverse was not so true.

Two days later, we were ensconced in a suite of cabins aboard the far trader *Pulchritude*, en route to Gudrun in the Helican sub. A three-week passage, Emperor willing.

I slept for long periods during the voyage, the deep and thankfully dreamless sleep of the soul-weary, but my fatigue lingered. The work on Miquol had been draining, mentally and emotionally. Each time I woke, feeling rested, there was a moment of precious calm before I remembered what I had done. Then the anxieties returned.

Every day of the voyage, I made two visits. The first was to the ship's chapel, where I said my observances more dutifully and strictly than I had done in a hundred years. I felt unclean, violated, though the violation was self-inflicted, I know. I longed for a confessor. In better days, I would have turned to Alizebeth, but that was not possible now.

Instead, I prayed for her survival. I prayed for Swole's health to be restored. I made offerings and lit candles for the souls of Poul Rassi, Duclane Haar and poor Dahault, who had perished in the cutter crash.

I prayed for Bastian Verveuk's soul and craved absolution.

I prayed for Fischig's understanding.

In my service to the God-Emperor, I have always considered myself a dutiful and faithful soul, but it is strange how the everyday customs of worship become so easily neglected.

During that voyage, having stumbled closer to the path of heresy than at any time in my life, I felt, ironically, as if my faith was renewed. Perhaps it takes a glimpse over the lip of the abyss to truly appreciate the pure heavens above. I felt chastened and virtuous, as if I had survived an ordeal and emerged a better man.

During the moments of self-doubt and anxiety, and they were numerous, I wondered if that sense of spiritual improvement was simply subconscious denial. Had the events of Miquol really been an overdue wake-up call to steer me smartly back onto the puritan path, or was I deluding myself? Deluding myself like Quixos and all the others who had fallen into the abyss without even realising it.

The second daily visit was to the armoured hold where the daemonhost was secured.

The *Pulchritude*'s captain, a stern Ingeranian called Gelb Startis, had almost refused point blank to accept the daemonhost aboard his ship. Of course, he didn't know it was a daemonhost. Very few individuals in the Imperium would know how to recognise one, and besides I had draped the silent figure in hooded robes. But there was a tangible air of evil and decay around the shrouded monster.

I'd been in no mood to bargain with Startis. I'd simply established my credentials with my signet ring, given him my personal guarantee that the 'guest' would be properly monitored, and paid him three times the going rate for our passage. That had made the whole venture more appealing for him.

I'd chained the daemonhost in the hold, and spent ten hours inscribing the area with the correct sigils of containment. Cherubael was still zombie-like and dumb, as if entranced.

The severe trauma of its binding was still lingering, and for the while it was docile.

On each visit, I triple-checked the sigils and, where necessary, refreshed them. I used a quill and ink dye to permanently mark in the runes I had painted on its flesh in blood.

That was chilling work. Verveuk's body had healed and was now glossy and healthy. His eyes were closed, but his face was still that of the young inquisitor, though the boy's forehead was beginning to bulge with the vestigial nub-horns that were sprouting from the bone.

On the ninth day, it opened Verveuk's eyes. The blank wrath of Cherubael shone out. It had finally come through the terrible rigours of binding, rigours made worse by the crude and rudimentary way I had performed the rite.

'He wants you dead,' were the first words it spoke.

'Am I speaking to Bastian or Cherubael?'

'Both,' it said.

I nodded. 'Nice try, Cherubael. I know Verveuk is gone from that body.'

'He hates you though. I tasted his soul as he passed out of this body and I passed in. He knows what you did and he's taken that dread knowledge to the afterlife with him.'

'The Emperor protects.'

'The Emperor craps himself at the sound of my name,' it responded.

I slapped its face hard. 'You are bound, lord daemon prince, and you will be respectful.'

Floating off the dirty hold floor, wrenching at its securing chains, Cherubael began to scream obscenities at me. I left.

On each return visit, it tried a different tack.

On the tenth day, it was pleading, remorseful.

On the eleventh, sullen and promising grievous harm to me.

On the thirteenth, silent and uncooperative.

On the sixteenth, sly.

'The truth of it, Gregor,' it said, 'is that I've missed you. Our times together have always been exhilarating. Quixos was a cruel master, but you understand me. On that island, you called on me for help. Oh, we've had our differences. And you're a tricky so-and-so. But I like that. I think my existence could be an awful lot worse than being in your thrall. So, tell me... what do you have planned? What glorious work will you and I do together? You'll find me willing, ready. In time, you'll be able to trust me. Like a friend. I've always wanted one of those. You and me, Gregor, friends, working together. How would that be?'

'That would be impossible.'

'Oh, Gregor...' it chided.

'Silence!' I said. I couldn't stomach its silky bonhomie. 'I am an Imperial inquisitor serving the light of the Golden Throne of Terra, and you are a thing of filth and darkness, serving only yourself. You are everything I stand against.'

It licked its lips. Verveuk's canines were becoming ice-white fangs. 'So why did you ever decide to bind me, Eisenhorn?'

'I regularly ask myself the same question,' I said.

'Release me, then,' it whispered. 'Cut me free from these pentagrammic bindings and let me go. We'll call it even. I'll go, and we'll never bother each other again. I promise. Let me go and that will be the matter done.'

'Just how stupid do you think I am?' I asked.

He floated up a little higher, cocked his head on one side, and smiled. 'It was worth a try.'

I was at the door when he called my name again.

'I'm content, you know. Being bound to you.'

'Really?' I replied with disinterest.

It nodded gleefully. 'It gives me ample opportunity to corrupt you entirely.'

On the nineteenth day, it nearly got me. When I entered the hold, it was sobbing on the floor. I tried to ignore it, checking the sigils, but it looked up.

'Master!' it said.

'Verveuk?'

'Yes! Please, master! It's gone away for a moment, and I have control again. Please, cut me free! Banish it!'

'Bastian, I–'

'I forgive you, master! I know you only did what you had to do and I'm more grateful than you could know that you chose me as worthy for this desperate work! But please, please! While I have control! Banish it and release me from this torture!'

I approached it, gripping my runestaff. 'I can't, Bastian.'

'You can, master! Now, while there's a moment clear! Oh, the agony! To be locked in here with that monster! To share the same flesh! It is gnawing away at my soul, and showing me things to drive me insane! Give mercy, master!'

I reached out and pointed to a complex rune inscribed on his chest. 'You see this?'

'Yes?'

'That is the rune of voiding. It is an essential part of the binding transaction. It empties the host of any previous soul so that the daemon can be contained. In effect, it kills the original host. You are not Bastian Verveuk because Bastian is dead and departed from this flesh. I killed him. You mimick his voice well, as I would expect, because you have his larynx and palate, but you are Cherubael.'

It sighed, nodded and floated up again to the limit its chains would permit.

'You can't blame me for trying.'

I slapped its face again hard. 'No, but I can punish you.'

It didn't react.

'Understand this, daemon. Binding you, using you, that has cost me dearly. I hate myself for doing it. But there was no choice. Now I have you enslaved again, I am going to take no chances. The correct containment of you will now become my life's primary devotion. The history texts will not remember me as a man so driven to accomplish things he got lazy and slack. There is no escape from me now. I will not allow it. You are mine and you will stay mine.'

'I see.'

'Do you understand?'

'I understand you are a man of the highest piety and resolve.'

'Good.'

'Just one thing: how does it feel to be a murderer?'

Earlier, I remarked that very few citizens of the Imperium of Man would recognise a daemonhost or understand what one was. That is true. It is also true that the select group who would know included several of my followers. Those that had been with me on 56-Izar, Eechen, Cadia, Farness Beta.

Aemos and Medea certainly understood the concept of daemonhosting. I had briefed them myself. I felt that Medea, like Fischig, only vaguely understood what I had brought onto the *Pulchritude* with me, though they regarded it with shuddering suspicion.

Aemos knew, though. He knew damn well. As far as I could tell, he knew everything that it was possible to know without going mad. But he had been with me longer than any of them. We had been friends and companions for more years than I dared count. I knew I had his trust and that I'd have to err wildly before he questioned my methods.

I realised after a day or two of the voyage that he wasn't even going to mention it.

I couldn't have that. I wanted openness. So I brought the matter up myself.

It was late one night, perhaps the fifth night of the voyage. We were playing double regicide (two boards in parallel, one played backwards using militants as crowning pieces, the other played long with sentries wild and a freedom to regent-up on white-square takes after the third sequence of play... this was the only formation of the ancient strategy game that even began to test his mind) and sipping the best amasec Startis could provide.

'Our passenger,' I began, picking up a squire piece and then putting it down again as I contemplated my next move, 'what are your thoughts? You've been very quiet.'

'I didn't believe it was my place to remark,' he said.

I moved the squire to militant three and immediately regretted it. 'Uber, how long have we been friends?'

I could tell he was actually about to calculate. 'I believe we first met in the seventh month of–'

'I mean roughly.'

'Well, to say friends, perhaps several years after our first meeting, which would make it–'

'Could we agree that a rough estimate would be... a very long time?'

He thought about it. 'We could,' he said, sounding unconvinced.

'And we are friends, aren't we?'

'Oh, of course! Well, I hope so,' he said, promptly taking my dexter basilisk and securing a ruthless toe-hold into my second line. 'Aren't we?'

'Yes. Yes, we are. I look to you for answers.'

'You do.'

'Sometimes, I think those answers could come without me having to ask the questions first.'

'Hmmm,' he said. He was about to move his yale. He raised the bone-carved piece and studied it closely. 'I have always wondered about the yale,' he said. 'A heraldic beast, obviously, tracing its origins back into the ages before the Great Strife. But what does it represent? The analogies of the other pieces, given historic traditions and the structure of Imperial culture, are obvious. But the yale... of all pieces in regicide, that one puzzles me...'

'You're doing it again.'

'Doing what?'

'Procrastinating. Avoiding the issue.'

'Am I?'

'You are.'

'I'm sorry.' He put the piece down again, taking one of my raptors in a move I simply hadn't seen coming. Now he had my militant in a vice.

'Well?'

'Well?'

'What do you think?'

He frowned. 'The yale. Most perturbatory.'

I rallied and took his yale abruptly. It was a foolish move, but it got his attention.

'About the other matter. The passenger.'

'It's a daemonhost.'

'Yes, it is.' I said, almost relieved.

'You bound it into Verveuk's body on Miquol.'

'I did. I think you watched me do it.'

'I was concussed, drowsy. But, yes. I saw it.'

'What do you think about that?'

He made a guard piece a regent and crossed into my sinister field. The game would be over in another half dozen moves.

'I try not to, for what it's worth. I try not to imagine how a man I have followed and believed in for so long suddenly has the means and power to unleash a daemon, channel it and bind it again. I try not to think about the possibility that Bastian Verveuk was alive when the binding occurred. I try to believe that my beloved inquisitor hasn't crossed a line from where there is no crossing back.'

'Checkmate,' he added.

I conceded both boards and sat back. 'I'm sorry,' I said.

'For what?'

'For putting you through this.'

'Your questions are–'

'No. I don't mean that. In the course of my hunt for Quixos, I learned several dark things. Chief of those was the means to control a daemon. It is knowledge that I would have chosen never to use. But the Titan was too much. It couldn't be allowed to survive. I had nothing left in my arsenal except dark lore.'

'I understand, Gregor. Truly. This conversation wasn't even necessary. You did what you had to do. We survived... most of us anyway. Chaos was denied. That's the job, isn't it? No one ever said it would be easy. Sacrifices have to be made or the God-Emperor's work will never be done.'

He leaned forward, his augmetic eyes glittering in the fire-light. 'Honestly, Gregor... if I thought you had become some demented radical, would I be sitting here playing regicide with you?'

'Thank you, Uber,' I said.

* * *

Aemos had given me a harder time than I had expected. Medea, on the other hand, I was braced for, and her reaction surprised me too.

'Daemon-what? I don't care.'

'You don't?'

'Not really. Thuring is all I care about, and you used everything you had to to get him.'

'I did.'

'Well, good for you.'

We were sitting in amongst the plush cushions of the *Pulchritude*'s observation deck.

She peered at me, frowning. 'Oh, I get it. You're afraid that all of us will think that you've become some heretical psycho crazy.'

By 'all of us' she meant my staff.

'Do you?'

'Hell, no! Get over it, boss! If I could do what you can do, I'd have done the same! Screw Thuring any way you can!'

I sighed. 'I didn't do it for your father, Medea.'

'What?'

'I mean I did, but I didn't. I wanted to avenge Midas, of course, but I only unleashed the daemon because Thuring and his damned Titan threatened more than just us.'

'That planet, you mean?'

'That planet... and others.'

'Right.'

'What's the matter?'

She stroked her hair back off her face and reached for her drink. 'You're telling me that if the planet hadn't been in danger, you wouldn't have done the whole daemon thing?'

'No. I want you to understand this. I wanted Thuring dead. I wanted him to pay for your father's death. But I didn't release

Cherubael in vengeance. That would have been petty and small-minded. I could never have justified that, not even to myself. I released the daemon because Fayde Thuring had become more than just a personal enemy. He'd become an enemy of the Imperium. I had to stop him then, and I was out of options. What I mean is, it was a totally pragmatic decision in the end. Not a weak, emotional one.'

'Whatever. Thuring suffered, didn't he? He burned? That's all I care about. But you owe me, though?'

'I do?'

'You swore it. On your secrets. That I'd be there when–'

'You were!'

'No thanks to you! And not so I could play a part and make Thuring suffer. So you owe me. And I want that secret. Now.'

'What secret?'

'You choose. But it's got to be the darkest one you have. Since you brought it up, what about this... this Cherubael?'

And that was how I came to tell her everything about the daemonhost. Everything. I did it because of the honour of our oath. I also did it, I believe now, because I wished to unburden myself to a confessor and Bequin wasn't there. I did it and didn't even pause to think what might result from it.

God-Emperor forgive me.

I have always loved Gudrun, the old capital world of the Helican sub-sector. For a long time, I had made my main home on Thracian Primaris, a world crusted by cities, riddled with crime, lamed by overpopulation. But I had only lived there for the sake of convenience. It was the capital world after all, and the Palace of the Inquisition was sited there. I visit it as little as possible, for it depresses me.

But after the vile events of the Holy Novena, five decades

before, I had transferred my chief residence to the more relaxing climes of Gudrun. Returning there, I felt somehow safe.

We bade Startis farewell and offloaded our luggage onto a privately chartered shuttle. I had prepared a cargo pod for Cherubael, fully inscribed and warded, the accomplishment of which took many hours. I said the appropriate rites and chained it inside, adding a charm that would render it docile. The pod was loaded by mute servitors into the shuttle's hold.

We dropped planetwards.

From the ports of the passenger bay, I looked down at the green expanses of the world. The great stretches of wild land and forest, the blue seas, the tight order of the ancient cities. For many years it had been the sub-sector capital, until the bloated giant Thracian Primaris had commandeered that role. I knew from experience that evil and corruption lurked here as much as it did on any Imperial world. But this was the epitome of Imperial life, for all its vices and flaws, a singular example of the very culture I had devoted my life to safeguard.

We made a detour on the descent. I felt it prudent to secure Cherubael somewhere other than my residence, though I had previously stored it in the secret oubliette below the foundations. If there were any official consequences to the incident on Durer, my estate could be subject to all manner of unwelcome scrutiny.

I covertly owned a number of premises on Gudrun. They were not held in my name, so that they could be used as safehouses or private retreats. One was a semi-ruined watchtower in the wilds, three hundred kilometres south of my home, a lonely, remote spot that I had found conducive to meditation over the years.

Using the shuttle's servitors, I placed the warded cargo pod

containing the daemonhost in the tower's crypt, made the
necessary rituals of holding, and activated the simple but
efficient alarm perimeter I had installed in the tower when
I first purchased it.

It would do for the while. Later, I would be very thankful I
had made that decision.

My home was a dignified estate out on the Insume headland,
twenty minutes' flight time from the venerable lagoon city of
Dorsay. Called Spaeton after the feudal family that had built it,
it was an H-plan villa constructed of grey ouslite stone with a
green copper-tile roof. There were adjoining garages and stables, an aviary, a drone-hive, a famous landscaped garden
and maze laid out mathematically by Utility Krauss, a water
dock down on the private inlet and a perfect sulleq lawn. It
was surrounded to the north and east by untenanted woods,
fruit orchards and ample paddocks, and from the terrace it
had clear views over the Bay of Bisheen.

Jarat, my housekeeper, welcomed us back. It was late evening
and the residence was warm, clean and ready for occupation.
Plump and dressed in her trademark grey gown-robe and
white-veiled black cap, Jarat was very old by then. Alongside
her were Jubal Kircher, my head of security, and Aldemar
Psullus, my rubricator and librarian. Beside them, Eleena
Koi of the Distaff and the astropath Jekud Vance. The rest
of the house staff, thirty of them, maids, ostlers, gardeners,
cooks, sommeliers, eltuaniers and launderers, were lined up
in fresh-pressed white uniforms behind them, along with the
five black-armoured officers of the security detail. I greeted
each one personally. Jarat and Kircher had employed several
newcomers since I had last been there, and I made a point of

talking to them and learning their names: Litu, a perky junior chambermaid; Kronsky, a new member of the security detail; Altwald, a new head groundsman inheriting his job from his father, who had retired.

I wondered when Jarat would retire. Or Kircher, come to that. In the case of Jarat, probably never, I decided.

My first act was to open the stronghold oubliette in the basement. I shut down the shields and deactivated the locks, and then spent a long time obliterating all traces of what the oubliette had been used for. I used a flamer to scour the walls and burn away the runic inscriptions. The grisly remains of Cherubael's previous host form, now an empty husk, lay amid the slack chains, and I cremated that too. The host form had been a vat-grown organic vessel I had privately commissioned for use in the original summoning. At the time, it had been a hard enough decision just to use a synthetic body.

I thought of Verveuk and shivered. I burned everything.

Then I bathed, and stayed a long time in the hot water.

Two weeks I spent, recuperating at Spaeton. I had tried to rest, or at least recover, during the voyage home, but there is a tension in travel itself and my concerns about the daemonhost's rudimentary confinement had prevented me from relaxing.

Now, I could rest at last.

I took long walks around the headland's paths, or stood on the point watching the waves crash into the rocks at the fringe of the inlet. I sat reading in the gardens during the warm evenings. I helped junior staff members collect early windfalls into wicker drowsies in the orchards.

I went nowhere near the library, the maze or my office. Alizebeth was never far from my thoughts.

Aemos served as secretary during that period, a job that

Bequin would previously have undertaken. Around breakfast time every morning, he would inform me of the number
of communiqués received overnight, and I would tell him
to handle them. He responded to general letters, filed private ones for my later attention, and stalled anything official.
He knew there were only a few kinds of communiqué that I
would permit myself to be troubled with if they arrived: word
of Bequin, a direct communication from the Ordos, or anything from Fischig.

On a bright morning early in my third week there, with dawn
mist fuming off the lawns where the early sun caught it, I was
sparring with Jubal Kircher in the pugnaseum.

It was the third morning we had done so. Realising how out
of condition I felt, I had commenced a regime of light combat work to tone myself up. We were dressed in bodygloves
with quilted shield-sleeves, and circled each other on the mat
with scorae, basket-hilted practice weapons from Carthae.

Jubal was a weapons master but he was getting a little old,
and on peak form I had no trouble besting him. Where he
truly excelled me was in combat-lore and the techniques of
military science, which he had studied all his life. He used
those that morning, preying on my softness and slowness,
overwhelming my superior strength and speed with patient
expertise.

Three quarters of an hour, five rounds, five touches to him.
His old lined face was glowing with perspiration, but he was
five times the winner I was.

'Enough for today, sir?' he asked.

'You're going easy on me, Jubal.'

'Beating you five love straight is going easy?'

I hung my scorae over my belt and adjusted the straps of my

sleeve-shield. 'If I was one of your security detail in training, I'd have five bruises now to go with my five losses.'

Kircher smiled and nodded. 'You would. But an ex-Guard bravo or a slumboy trying to make my grade needs the bruises to remind him that work here isn't some well-paid retirement. I don't believe you need to learn that sort of lesson.'

'None of us are too wise to learn.' We both looked and saw Medea entering the pugnaseum. She wandered around the edge of the mat, one moment in the shadows of the wall panels, the next in the glaring yellow oblongs cast by the skylights. She looked at me.

'Just repeating one of your many aphorisms.'

I could tell something was up with her. Kircher shifted uncomfortably.

'Let me spar with him,' she said. I nodded to Jubal, who saluted, Carthaen style, with his scora and left the circular room.

Medea took off her father's cerise jacket and hung it on a window knob.

'What'll it be?' I asked, taking a sip of water from a beaker on the decanter stand.

She walked over to the armoury terminal and keyed on the screen, jump-cutting rapidly through the graphic templates the monitor displayed. She was dressed in a tight, semi-armoured bodyglove and her feet were clad in training slippers. She had prepared for this, I realised.

'Blades and power-bucklers,' she announced, stopping the menu and keying the authority stud.

There was a distant rattle and whirr as automated systems in the armoury under the floor processed the selected weapons from their racks and elevated them up into the ready rack in the wall next to the terminal. Two buckler modules. Two swords, matching, each the length of an adult human femur, single-edged and slightly curved with a knuckle-bar around the grip. She tossed one to me and I caught it neatly.

I walked over to join her, placing my scorae in the rack that would return it to storage. Then I took my buckler. It strapped around the left forearm, supporting a round, machined emitter the size of a pocket watch. Engaged, it projected a disc of shield energy the size of a banquet plate above the back of my hand and forearm.

'Attention, you have selected weapons of lethal force. Attention, you have selected weapons of lethal force...' The terminal issued the notice in soft but urgent repeats.

I shut it off with a key-press.

'We can use full body shields, if you're worried,' she said.

'Why would I be worried? This is just sparring.'

We engaged our power-bucklers and faced each other across the centre of the mat, slightly side on, shield towards shield, our blades held low in our right hands.

'Signal cue,' I said.

'Three,' said the terminal speaker, 'two, one... commence.'

Medea had been practising.

She swept round with her blade, and simultaneously parried my first approach with her buckler which squealed and sparked off mine as their fields met and repulsed.

I undercut defensively, gathering her blade in towards our shields so that for a moment all four weapons were locked in a protesting knot of spitting electrical energy.

We broke, and circled.

She came in again, leading with her sword. I fended it away with my buckler, then again, and then for a third time as we continued to go around.

She was canny. Sword and buckler work was as old as all the worlds, and the trick to staying alive was to use the shield more than the sword. The trick to winning, however, was to use the sword more than the shield.

I kept my buckler to the front but, by seeming to be unguarded with her own force shield lagging back as if casually forgotten, she was inviting me to overstep or make a badly judged lunge.

I left my blade well alone, keeping it where she could see it, and using my shield as Harlon Nayl had schooled me. The buckler was a weapon. Not only could it block, it could lock or even break a blade. I had heard of some duels where the small shield's solid-energy edge had actually delivered the killing stroke to an unprotected windpipe.

Medea rotated suddenly, driving my buckler aside with a swipe of her own, and lashed in with her blade, dancing across the mat. I was forced to parry with my sword, and then rally hard as she kept up the pressure.

Her blade sliced to within a handsbreath of my face and I cross-guarded desperately with both blade and buckler.

She drove her own shield in under my guard and her own locked sword and doubled me up with a punished strike to my midriff.

I fell onto the mat.

'Enough?' she asked.

I got up. 'We'll go again.'

She came at me again, leading with the blade as I had expected. I ducked, swung round and feinted in time for her buckler to swing in to parry my blade.

The spitting electrical dish tore the sword from my hand, stinging my fingers.

Just as I had intended.

Her eyes were on my sword, distracted as it flew aside. With my now free right hand, I grabbed her buckler arm above the elbow and pulled it down so that her own power shield locked with her sword as she brought it up. She stumbled. I smashed her across the extended shoulder with the flat of my buckler and knocked her down.

I could have used the edge. I could have aimed for her exposed face. But we were sparring.

'Enough?' I asked.

She said nothing.

'Medea?'

She extinguished her buckler and pulled the strapping off.

'What's on your mind?'

Medea looked up at me. 'I never wanted revenge,' she said.

'You told me you did.'

'I know. And I suppose I did. Part of me. Revenge... it doesn't feel...'

'Satisfying?'

'Like anything at all. Just empty. Stupid and empty.'

'Well... I could have told you that. In fact, I think I did.'

I helped her up. We didn't speak for a minute or two as we put the weapons back in the rack and returned them to the underfloor store bay.

Then we took beakers of water from the stand, opened the pugnaseum's side doors and went out onto the sunlit terrace.

It was going to be a hot day. The sky was cloudless and the light white. The shade of the woods seemed gloriously dark and inviting. The distant inlet was hazy with glare and the sea glinted like diamonds.

'Ever since I was old enough to understand what Fayde Thuring did,' she said, 'I've wanted something. I've always presumed it was revenge.'

'Revenge is a disguise for other, more valid emotional responses,' I said.

She looked at me sourly. 'Stop trying to be my father, Eisenhorn.'

She might has well have slapped me across the face. I had never thought of it that way.

'I only meant–' I began.

'You're a very wise man,' she said. 'Very clever. Learned. You give people the most profound advice.'

'I try.'

'But you don't *feel*.'

'Feel, Medea?'

'You know things but you don't feel them.'

Birds twittered in the edges of the woods and the orchards. Two of the junior groundstaff were pressing the lower lawns with a heavy roller. I wasn't quite sure I knew what she meant.

'I feel–'

'No. You don't feel the content of your advice, most of the time. They're just wisdoms, without heart.'

'I'm sorry you think that way.'

'It isn't a criticism. Well, not really. You are just so driven to do what is... right, that you forget to wonder why it's right. I mean–'

'What?'

'I don't know.'

'Try.'

She sipped her water. 'You fight the way Kircher tells you to fight because he says that's the best way to do it.'

'It usually is.'

'Of course. He's an expert. That's why you defeated me. But why is it the best way to fight? Using those weapons, for example?'

'Because–'

'Because he told you? He's right. But why is he right? You

never wonder about that sort of thing. You never wonder what mistakes or decisions were made to arrive at that right way.'

'I'm still not sure I follow you...'

She smiled and shook her head. 'Of course you don't. That's my point. You've spent your whole life learning the best way to do everything. Learning the best way to fight. The best way to investigate. The best way to learn, even. Did you ever wonder why those are the best ways?'

I put my glass down on the low wall at the edge of the terrace. 'Life's too short.'

'My father's life was too short.'

I said nothing.

'My father died and I wanted something, and you told me that it wasn't revenge. And you were right. Revenge is trash. Worthless. But why? What was it I needed instead?'

I shook my head. 'I was only trying to spare you the effort. Revenge is a waste of time and–'

'No,' she said, looking at me directly. 'It's a displacement activity. It's something you can lock on to and do because you can't do the thing you really want to do.'

I had grown impatient. 'And what might that be, Medea? Do you know?' I asked.

'I do now,' she said. 'Thuring killed my father. I needed something, and it wasn't payback. It was what he took from me. I needed to know my father. If I'd ever had that, then I'd never have given Thuring another thought.'

She was right. It was so obvious, it chilled me. I wondered how many other, similar, obvious mistakes I had made in my life with my head so full of certain knowledge and my heart so numb.

I looked back at the pugnaseum, and saw Midas's cerise jacket handing where she had left it, draped against the inside of one of the windows like a trapped butterfly.

'I can give you what you want,' I said, 'in part, at least. If you really want it.'

I summoned my astropath, Vance, and requested that he made the preparations. He suggested that evening might be a good time, when things were quieter, and so I asked Jarat to serve a light dinner early to leave the evening clear, and to leave out a cold supper in case we were hungry once we were done.

At seven, Medea and I went to the reading room above the house's main library. I gave Kircher specific instructions that we were not to be disturbed. Most of the household had retired early to private study or relaxation in any case.

Psullus, the rubricator, was in the library, repairing some bindings that were fraying at the spines.

'Give us a while,' I said to him.

He looked unnerved. Infirm with a progressive wasting disease, he virtually lived in the library. It was his private world and I felt cruel ousting him from it.

'What should I do?' he asked cautiously.

'Go sit in the study, watch the stars come out. Take a good book.'

He looked around and sniggered.

My library was at the heart of Spaeton House, and occupied two floors. The lower level was divided by alcoves of shelves and the upper gallery was supported by those alcoves, giving access to further shelving stacks lining the gallery walls. Soft glow-lamps hung from slender ceiling chains and cast a warm, golden light all around, and the panelled reading lecterns along the centre of the ground floor were fitted with individual reading lamps that generated little pockets of brighter blue luminescence.

The place was comfortably warm, its atmosphere carefully controlled to guard against any excess humidity that might damage the stored books. There was a smell of wood polish, chemical preservatives, and the ozone whiff of the stasis fields that protected the oldest and most fragile specimens.

Once Psullus had gone, taking with him a copy of Boydenstyre's *Lives*, I led Medea up the brass staircase to the upper gallery and along to the heavy door of the private reading room at the far end.

At the door, Medea paused and took a Glavian needle pistol from her pocket.

'I brought this,' she said. 'It was also my father's, one of the pair made for him.'

I knew that well enough. Medea still carried the matched pistols in combat.

'Leave it outside,' I told her. 'It's never a good idea to attempt connection through weapons. Even friendly heirlooms like that. The sting of death attaches itself to them and you'd find that unpleasant. The jacket will be fine.'

She nodded and left the gun on a bookshelf near the reading room door. We went inside and found Vance waiting for us. The small chamber was candle lit, with three chairs arranged around a cloth-covered table. The last rays of sunset were glimmering in through the stained glass skylight.

We took our seats. Vance, a tall, stooping man with kindly, tired eyes, spread Midas's cerise jacket on the tablecloth. He had already been meditating enough to put him near to the trance state, and I gently guided Medea to a receptive calmness.

The auto-seance began. It is a simple enough psychic procedure, and one which I have used many times for investigation and research. Vance was the conduit, channelling the power of the warp. I focused my own mind-strength to keep us centred. From the point of transition, the room took on a cold, frosty light. Solids became transluscent and fizzy. The dimensions of the little reading room stretched and shifted impatiently.

Midas's jacket, now a wisp of turquoise smoke, was swathed in the aura it had accumulated over time, the echoes of its contact with human hands, human minds.

'Take it,' I said. 'Touch it.'

Medea reached out her hand warily and brushed her fingers against the edge of the aura, which bloomed and fluffed up at her touch.

'Oh,' she said.

We teased apart the psychic memories clinging to that garment until we found her father. Midas Betancore, pilot, warrior, my friend. We coaxed his phantom out of hiding.

It was no ghost, just the after-image he had left behind. An impression of him, his looks, his voice, his emotions. A distant hint of his rich chuckle. The faint odour of the lho-sticks he liked to smoke and the cologne he chose to wear. We saw him young, little more than a boy. We saw him in virile middle age, just a few years from his untimely death. There, at the helm of the gun-cutter, itself now just a ghost too, the Glavian circuitry inlaid into his hands marrying him profoundly to the craft's controls. There, steering a long-prow. There, watching the suns rise over the Stilt Hills of Glavia.

We tasted his grief at the death of Lores Vibben, but I had Vance pass along quickly to spare us the empathic pain. We clung to him through several exhilarating dogfights, sharing the joy of virtuoso manoeuvres and expert kills. We watched as he saved my life, or the lives of my companions, over and again.

We listened at a dinner table while he made the company roar and clap with an outrageous tale well told. It made all three of us laugh out loud. We saw him, in silence, studying a regicide board and trying to fathom out how Bequin had managed to beat him again. We watched him, through a blizzard of coloured streamers, take his bride to the altar of the High Church at Glavia Glavis. I glimpsed myself, alongside Fischig, Alizebeth and Aemos, in the front pew, cheering and ringing our ceremonial bells with the rest of the congregation.

'That's my mother!' Medea whispered. The veiled woman on Midas's arm was stunning, exquisite. Jarana Shayna Betancore. Midas always did have such good taste. Jarana lived still, far away on Glavia, a distinguished widow and director of a shipwrighting firm. 'She looks so young,' Medea added. There was a note of sadness in her voice. She hadn't been back to Glavia to visit her mother for many years.

Then, almost as if we were intruding, we saw Midas and Jarana embracing on the shores of Taywhie Lake. Midas was beside himself with happiness and excitement.

'Really? Really?' he kept asking.

'Yes, Midas. Really. I'm really pregnant.'

I looked at Medea, saw the tears in her eyes.

'We should stop now, I think,' I said.

'No, I want to see more,' she said.

'We should,' I advised. I could tell that Vance was getting tired. And I knew it wouldn't be long before we stumbled into memories of Fayde Thuring and the last hours. 'We should stop. We–'

I was cut off by the sudden shrilling of my communicator. I cursed loudly. Kircher had been told: no interruptions.

The sound shattered the seance at once. The blue light flashed and vanished, and the room returned to normal with a sudden lurch that blew out the candles and cast us painfully out of the warp. Vance slumped forward, breathing hard, in distress. My head ached with a sudden piercing pain. Medea pulled the jacket towards her across the table and buried her head into its silk folds, sobbing. The walls were sweating.

Damn Kircher. Seances shouldn't be broken like that. Any one of us could have been badly damaged by the abrupt termination. As it was, we were all emotionally dazed.

I got up. 'Stay here,' I said to them both. 'Take a moment to recover.' Vance nodded feebly. Medea was lost in her own storm of feelings.

I went outside and pulled the door closed, breathing hard. Yanking the little hand vox from my pocket, I keyed the 'respond' rune.

'This had better be good, Jubal,' I said hoarsely.

Static crackled back.

'Jubal? Jubal? This is Eisenhorn.'

Nothing. Then a quick blurt of frantic words I couldn't make out. Then static again.

'Jubal?'

From somewhere distant, on the other side of the house, I heard a trio of muffled cracks.

Las-fire.

I snatched up Midas's needle pistol from the shelf where Medea had left it and ran for the library door.

EIGHT

The fall of Spaeton House
For our lives
Sastre, loyal Sastre

The halls of the house were quiet, with the lights dimmed, but I could smell burning. I hurried down a carpeted crosswalk, arming the needle pistol. Thirty rounds and a fully charged cell. I had no reload.

Tiny red lights were winking on the security monitor dials recessed into the walls at regular intervals. I went to the nearest one, opened the cover and was about to press my signet ring into the reader when I heard movement.

I raised the gun.

Two maids and a houseman ran into view and yelped when they saw me.

'Steady, steady!' I cried out, lowering the gun. 'This way, come on!'

They ran up to me and cowered behind some ornamental plant stands.

'What's going on?'

They were too scared to answer at first. I saw that the youngest of them was the new girl, Litu. She looked up at me with terrified, tear-pink eyes.

'Litu? What's going on?'

'Raiders,' she said, her voice breathy with panic. 'Raiders, sir. Just minutes ago, there was suddenly this great big bang from upstairs, and then shooting. Men running around, with guns. I saw a man dead. I think it was Urben. I think.'

Rocef Urben. One of my security detail.

'He had all blood coming out of his face,' she stammered.

'The raiders, Litu. From which direction?'

'From the west, sir,' said the houseman, Colyon. 'From the main gate, I think. I heard Master Kircher say they were coming from the stable block too.'

'You saw Kircher?'

'It was a bit mad, sir. I heard him as he ran past.'

I looked around. The smell of burning was getting stronger and I could hear more shots.

'Colyon,' I said, 'do you have your house keys?'

'I'm never without them, sir,' he said.

'Good man. Go along here to the east porch and then get yourself and these women into the gardens. Head for the orchards. Hide. Got a comm?'

'Yes, sir.'

'If you don't hear from me in the next twenty minutes, try and get all three of you off the property. Look after them, Colyon.'

'I will, sir.'

They ran off. I fitted my ring into the monitor and authorised access. The little wall unit lit the air with a small diagnostic hologram. Incredibly, it stated that all security systems, all detectors, all perimeter shields, were shut down. They'd been shut down at source, using an authorised command code.

How in the name of hell?

'Jubal?' I tried the vox again. 'Anybody? This is Eisenhorn. Respond.'

The hand vox answered this time. A man's voice, hard like stone. 'Eisenhorn. You are dead, Eisenhorn.'

I went down through the staff quarters. It seemed like everyone had fled. Doors were open and a few chairs were overturned. Half drunk cups of caffeine, still steaming. A half-finished game of regicide in the butler's pantry. A pict-unit still playing a live broadcast from the arena at Dorsay. A fallen lho-stick burning a patch in the carpet.

I stamped out the embers.

Through a door into the west landing I found Urben. He was dead all right. He was sprawled with his back arched in the doorway. Laser fire had blasted him open.

I was bent over him when I heard footsteps.

Three men came in through the other side of the landing, but I only saw two of them. They were moving fast, with the fluid confidence of trained killers. They were wearing combat armour made of rubberised mesh, their faces hidden behind grotesque papier-maché masks, the kind you can buy in Dorsay's market for the carnivals. They had cut-down lasrifles.

They fired as soon as they saw me, their shots striking the doorframe. I barely had time to dive into cover. I heard the pip and chatter of their microbead communicators.

One, sporting a gilded carnodon mask, moved in, running low, as another in a mermaid mask gave cover.

From the doorway, I fired the needle pistol twice and put two tiny holes through the carnodon leer. The raider folded up and crashed to the floor, his knees buckling under him.

The mermaid fired again, repeatedly, and I switched to the other side of the doorway.

Cease! I commanded, using my will. No reaction. They were psy-shielded.

Someone had prepared.

I crouched and fired up at the chandelier. When it came crashing down, the mermaid dived to the side and I caught him squarely with three needles, any of which would have been a kill shot. The mermaid thumped backwards heavily and brought a console table over as he fell.

I moved through the door, not realising the third one was there. His shots grazed my shoulder and knocked me down hard.

There was a very loud bang.

I looked up.

'Gregor?'

It was Aemos.

'Gregor, I think I've jammed your bloody gun,' he said.

I got up. Aemos was standing in a nearby doorway, fiddling with my bolt pistol. The third, unseen raider had made a clotted dent in the plasterwork.

'Give it to me,' I said, snatching the bolt pistol and freeing the slide.

'Thank you, Aemos,' I added.

He shrugged. 'It's most perturbatory,' he said. 'Guns and me, we don't seem to get on and I always–'

'Aemos, hush! What the hell's going on?'

'We're under attack,' he said.

'I need a little more than that, old friend.'

'Well, I know little more, Gregor. Boom, we're under attack. No warning, no nothing. Men everywhere. Lots of running around and shooting. We thought you were dead.'

'Me?'

'They hit the study first. A grenade or something.'

'Damn! Come with me. Stay close.'

We went upstairs. Skeins of smoke drifted through the air. I had the needle pistol in one hand and the boltgun in the other. At the top of the stairs we found two members of my house staff. They had been shot against a wall.

'Oh, that's terrible...' Aemos murmured.

It was. Someone would pay dearly for this outrage.

The door to my study was open and the smoke was issuing from inside.

'Stay back,' I whispered to Aemos and lunged in through the door.

The room was a mess. A missile or ram-grenade fired from the lawns had blown out the main windows and turned the desk and chair into kindling. Cold night air breezed in through the shattered casement and wafted the smoke from the burning rug and shelving into the house.

There were three more raiders inside, ransacking the bookshelves and trying to force open the file store. A man with a clown mask was raking precious manuscripts, slates and scrolls out of a climate-controlled case into a sack. Another in a serpent mask was repeatedly kicking the display case in which Barbarisater was stored, trying to rupture it. A third, sporting a grinning sun, was attacking the armoured sleeve of my file bureau with a crowbar.

They all turned, reaching for their weapons.

Throne, they were fast! I had the drop, but they moved like lightning. The serpent actually managed to loose a burst at me that went over my diving head before I felled him with a bolt-round. His body hit the armour glass cover of the sword case and left a streak of gore down it as it slid off. The clown was slower, and his torso was punctured by needle rounds before he'd dropped the sack. He just fell over, his mask crumpling as it struck first one shelf edge, then another, then another on its way down to the floor.

The sun face threw the crowbar aside, and dived behind the ruins of the desk even as I was rolling out of the end of the dive and re-aiming.

His blurt of las-fire met my hail of bolts and needles. I swear that at least two of my bolt rounds were exploded in mid-air by his laser shots. But the needles went clean through the desk and clean through him. He lolled back, dead.

I got up and walked towards the destroyed end of my study.

That's where I found Psullus. I'd sent him here just a few hours before. The burning pages of Boydenstyre's *Lives* were littered around. He'd been sitting at my desk when the missile had taken out the window bay.

'Dear Emperor... Aldemar...' Aemos was bitterly shocked at the ghastly sight.

I was simply furious by then. I pushed the needle gun, now virtually spent, into my pocket and grabbed more bolt clips from the shelf by the window.

'We have to get out of here, Aemos,' I said.

He nodded dumbly. I picked up the sack that the clown had been filling and handed it to Aemos. 'Fill it,' I said. 'You know what's valuable.'

He hurried to obey.

I typed security codes into the cases containing Barbarisater and the runestaff. The armour glass covers purred open.

Outside, there was a shrill whining noise and the beams of searchlights crossed the lawns and the orchards. My attackers had air cover.

One final necessity. I opened my encoded void-safe and took out the ancient, wretched copy of the *Malus Codicium*. I tucked it into my coat, but Aemos had seen it.

'Come on!' I said.

'One moment,' Aemos replied, tugging a last few scroll cases into the sack and then hoisting it onto his back.

'Now, I'm ready,' he said.

I went to the door, boltgun in one hand and Barbarisater in the other. The staff was slung across my back. I could hear a fierce bout of shooting from below, a serious firefight.

My loyal friend Jubal Kircher wasn't going without a fight.

'Follow me,' I told Aemos.

It had only been a few minutes since the comm-alarm that had disrupted the auto-seance. Already that tranquil encounter with the shade of Midas Betancore seemed like ancient history.

The house was on fire. From the east wing, flames leapt up into the cool night and filled the air with fluttering ashes and cinders. We cowered behind a wall in the yard outside the kitchen, and got a look out across the back lawn. Three heavy speeders had landed there, crouching like glossy black insects on their extending landing claws. Their side hatches were open and cabins empty. A fourth, and then a fifth, passed low overhead, searchlights sweeping down as they riddled the back of the house with cannon fire.

Five fliers. Each one was capable of carrying a dozen armed men. That meant a small army was assaulting Spaeton House. Someone wanted me and my staff eradicated. Someone wanted my precious secrets and trinkets looted. And someone had enough money and influence to make those things happen.

In truth, the house's auto-defences should have easily held off the attack, even an attack of this magnitude. Inquisitors make enemies. A fortified residence is an occupational necessity.

But Spaeton House had been broken wide open. Its screens,

void shutters, lock-outs, motion detectors, sentry servitors, gun-pods... everything had been inert when the attackers arrived.

They were mercenaries, I was sure of that. Highly trained, highly motivated, utterly ruthless. But who had bank-rolled them, and why?

Answers later, I decided, as another series of explosions rippled across the estate and lit the sky.

The stable block, which I used as a hangar and garage, had just gone up.

'What about one of their vehicles?' Aemos whispered, gesturing the fliers on the lawn.

It was too risky. We'd be out in the open and the speeders were likely to be guarded. I shook my head.

'The water dock then?' he suggested. 'Maybe they haven't got to the boats?'

'No, they had everything else covered. They knew the layout, knew to hit the stables. They were briefed about this place inside and out.'

We went back inside, through the kitchen and across the little walled herb garden into the scullery behind the dining hall. Smoke fumes strung the air like silk hangings. I had one last means of escape, one I believed they didn't – couldn't – know about.

Barbarisater twitched and I knew someone was coming. I pushed Aemos back behind me.

Two figures came into view. One was Eleena Koi, the untouchable assigned to the house. She was supporting Xel Sastre, one of Kircher's men. He had been wounded in the arm and shoulder.

'Eleena!' I hissed.

'Lord! Thank the Emperor! We thought you were dead!' Her

narrow face was taut with panic and Sastre's blood was all over her brushed epinchire gown.

I took a quick look at Sastre's wounds. They were bad, but he'd live if we could get him to an infirmary.

'Have you seen any others? Kircher? Have you seen him?'

'I saw him die,' said Sastre. 'They were driving us back, and he stayed to hold the main hall. Took on twenty of the bastards.'

'You sure he's–'

'They blew him apart. But not before he'd finished a good half dozen. He told me... told me Kronsky let them in.'

'What?'

'Kronsky. The new guy hired last month. He betrayed the whole house. Shut down the defence system.'

An inside job, as I had feared. Kircher had employed this Kronsky in good faith, and no doubt scrupulously vetted his background and subjected him to a mind-search. And I had welcomed Kronsky to my house. My respect for the resources, skill and preparation of my unknown enemy grew.

A speeder howled by close outside, and the sound of its sporadic fire shook the windows in their frames.

'Can you keep up?' I asked Sastre and Eleena. They nodded. 'Where are we going?' asked Eleena.

'Out through the dining hall, then quickly across the lawn of the rose garden into the orchard behind the maze. After that, we swing south, make our way to the front fence and then over the main road into the woods.'

I was describing a journey of over two kilometres, but no one balked. Staying put was suicide.

I wanted to try my vox again and try to raise Medea, but knew it was pointless. The raiders had all channels covered. Instead, I reached out with my mind.

Medea... Medea...

To my amazement, I was answered almost at once. It was Vance.

We're just outside the pugnaseum. Medea's going to try and take one of their fliers.

No! Stop her, Jekud. They're too well guarded. Tell Medea 'The Storm Oak.' She'll know what it means. If we get there first, I'll wait as long as I can.

The dining hall was in darkness and the buffed wood floor was littered with glass. The windows had been blown in and the drapes rustled in the night breeze.

We made our way across to the windows. Outside, the rose garden was quiet and gloomy. The light of the fires cast long shadows across the immaculate lawn.

We ducked back inside as a flier flew over. It paused above the lawn, engines wailing, its downjets rippling the surface of the lawn. It was so close I could hear the crackle and sputter of the cockpit intervox. The searchlamp swung towards us, suddenly blinding, jabbing beams of frosty white light into the dining hall. The glass litter glittered like a constellation.

Then the speeder moved off again, thundering around towards the back of the house.

'Go!' I hissed.

We ran across the lawn. Aemos was surprisingly spry, but Eleena struggled with Sastre. I dropped back and helped her with him. He kept apologising, telling us to leave him.

He was a good man.

We reached the edge of the orchard and lost ourselves in the shadows of the arbors, following the back of the maze. The air was richly scented with the maze's pungent privet and the sweet, acid smell of the ripening fruit. Moths and nocturnal insects fluttered in the half light.

Well into the orchard, seventy metres from the house, we stopped for breath. Weapons fire and shouting still echoed from the residence. I looked around, trying not to look at the brilliant blaze of the buildings so I could adjust to the gloom under the trees. They were low, graceful apple, tumin and ploin, planted in orderly rows. The white bark of the tumin trees shone like snow in the dimness, and some of the early ploin clusters had been carefully bagged against scavenging birds. Scant days before, I had been out here with the junior staff, joking as we gathered up the first tumin crop. Altwald had been with us, taping the bags around the dark, swelling ploins. That night, Jarat had served a glorious tumin tart as dessert.

Jarat. I wondered what had become of her in all this.

I never did find out.

Sastre stiffened and brought up his laspistol at a movement nearby, but it was just a garden servitor, moving along the aisle of fruit trees, spraying pesticide. Oblivious to the carnage nearby, it was simply obeying its nightly programming.

We started forward again, but when I looked back, I saw several figures coming out of the dining hall windows and spreading out across the rose garden.

I bade the other three move ahead and crept back, staying as concealed as possible, in case they had night-vision lenses or motion detectors.

I came upon the slow-moving servitor from behind, opened a back panel as it trudged monotonously forward, and keyed in new instructions. It moved off towards the rose garden, adjusting its route only to avoid trees. I had increased its pace.

I was already on my way back to rejoin the others when I heard the first few shots: the raiders, surprised by the sudden appearance of the servitor. With any luck, it would delay or distract them. If they had been following our movement, then maybe the servitor would convince them that was all they had detected.

We kept going until we were well clear of the maze and had left the orchard behind. We crossed dark, overgrown paddocks, fumbling blindly. The only light came from the haze in the sky behind us where Spaeton House blazed.

We turned south, or a rough estimation of south. This was still my estate – indeed the land I held title for stretched for several kilometres in all directions – but this was uncultivated wood and scrubland. I could hear the sea, tantalisingly out of reach beyond the headland behind us.

I wondered how far we could get before the raiders finished their quartering of the house and realised I had slipped through their fingers.

We hurried on for another twenty minutes, passing through glades of scrawny beech and wiry fintle. The ground was lush with nettles. We reached a waterlogged irrigation ditch, and it took us several minutes to manhandle Sastre across.

I could see the perimeter fence and the road beyond. On the far side of that, the rising mass of the wild woodland, the heritage forests that still covered two thirds of Gudrun, untouched and unmolested since the first colonies were built there.

'We're almost there,' I whispered. 'Come on.'

Tempting fate, as always, Eisenhorn. Tempting fate.

Las-bolts slashed the air over our heads. A few at first, then more, from at least four sources. They lowered their aim and the bright orange shots ripped into the nettles, kicking up mists of sap and pulp. Two young larches by the fence ditch were splintered. Dry gorse and fintle shuddered and burst into flames.

A flare went up, bursting like a star, and damning us all with its invasive light.

'The fence! Come on!' I cursed.

Behind us, by the light of the flare, I could see dark figures wading through the nettles and emerging from the trees. Every few moments, one of the figures would halt and raise his weapon, spitting dazzling pulses at us.

Further away, back at the bright pyre of Spaeton House, I saw two white blobs of light rise and disengage themselves from the fireglow. Speeders, called in, heading this way, chasing their beams across the paddocks and woods.

We were at the fence. I channeled my fury into Barbarisater and slashed open a hole two metres wide.

'Get through!' I yelled. Aemos went through the gap. Sastre stumbled and fell, losing his grip on Eleena's arm. I pushed her through the gap too and went back for the wounded man.

Sastre had trained his pistol at the advancing killers, and was firing. He was sitting down, leaning his back against the fence. He made two kills as I remember, cutting down figures struggling forward in the weeds and undergrowth fifty metres away.

'Go, sir!' he said.

'Not without you!'

'Go, damn it! You won't get far unless someone slows them down!'

A rain of las-fire fell around us, puncturing the fence and throwing up wet clods of earth. I was forced to turn and use Barbarisater to deflect several shots. The blade hummed as it twitched and soaked up the power.

'Go!' Sastre repeated. I realised he had been hit again and was trying to hide it. He coughed blood.

'I can't leave you like this–'

'Of course you can't!' he snapped. 'Give me a bloody weapon! This damn las-cell is nearly spent.'

I crouched beside him and handed him my boltgun and my spare clips.

'The Emperor will remember you, even if I don't live to,' I told him.

'You damn well better had, sir, or I'm wasting my efforts.'

There was no time for anything further, no time even to take his hand. As I clambered through the fence, I heard the first roaring blasts of the boltgun.

Eleena and Aemos were waiting for me on the far side of the road in the fringes of the wild woods. I gathered them up and we ran into the darkness, stumbling over gnarled roots, clambering up loamy slopes, surrounded by the midnight blackness of the primordial forest.

The boltgun continued to fire for some time. Then it fell silent.

May the God-Emperor rest Xel Sastre and show him peace.

NINE

The Storm Oak
Going back
Making Midas proud

For almost an hour, we plunged into the great darkness of the forest, blind and desperate. In what seemed an alarmingly short time, we lost all sight of the great conflagration we had left behind. The woodland, dense and ancient, blocked it out.

'Are we lost?' Eleena mumbled in a faltering voice.

'No,' I assured her. Kircher, Medea and I had spent many hours hunting and tracking in the wild woodlands, and I knew these fringes well enough, though in darkness, there was an unhelpful depth of mystery and unfamiliarity.

Once in a while, I noticed a landmark: a jutting tooth of stone, an old tree, a turn in the terrain. Usually, I recognised such things once we were right on them, and took a moment to adjust our bearings.

Twice, speeders passed overhead, their stablights backlighting the dense foliage. If they'd possessed heat trackers, we would have been dead. But they were hunting by searchlight alone. At last, I privately rejoiced, the enemy has made an error.

We reached the oak.

Medea had named it the Storm Oak. It had been hundreds of years old when lightning had killed it and left it a splintered, leafless giant, like a shattered castle turret. The bark was peeling from its dead wood, and the area around it was crawling with grubs and rot-beetles. It had grown in a hollow, sprouting from the dark soil overhang of a scarp twenty metres high. The oak itself was fifty metres tall from its vast, partly exposed root mass to its shattered crown, and fifteen metres across the trunk.

I scrambled down into the hollow beneath its roots. When the lightning had struck it, ages past, it had partially ripped the massive tree from the ground, creating a cavern under its mighty foundations. The dank hole was like a natural chapel, with roots serving as the crossmembers for the ceiling. The previous owners of Spaeton House had, I had been told, used it as a chancel for private ceremonies.

Medea and I had decided to use it as a hangar.

No one else knew about this, except Kircher. We had all agreed it was a dark, secret place to stow a light aircraft. A bolt hole. I don't think we ever really imagined a doom falling on Spaeton House like the one that overwhelmed it that night, but we had played along with the idea it might be wise to keep one transport tucked out of sight.

The transport in question was a monocoque turbofan flier, handmade on Urdesh. Light, fast, ultra-manoeuvrable. Medea had purchased it ten years before when she was bored, and had stored it in the main hangar at Spaeton until one notorious night while we were away on a case when several junior staff members had decided to take it for a spin, it being so much more racey than the house shuttles and bulk speeders.

They'd had the damage repaired by the time we got home, but Medea had noticed. Reprimands had followed.

Weeks later, when we found the Storm Oak during a hunting trip, and devised the notion of a last ditch transport, Medea had moved the craft here. We never actually thought we'd have to use it for escape. It was just an excuse to park it away from the envious juniors.

I stripped off the tarp and popped open the hatch. The cabin interior smelled of leather and the faint dampness of the forest.

Six metres long and finished in slate grey, the craft had a wedge-shaped cabin that tapered to a short, V-vaned tail. There were three turbofan units, one fixed behind the cabin under the tail for main thrust, the other two mounted on stubby wings that projected from the cabin roof on either side. The wing units were gimbal-mounted for lift and attitude control. The cabin was snug, with three rows of seats: a single pilot's seat in the nose, with two high-backed passenger seats behind it and a more functional bench seat behind them against the cabin's rear partition.

I strapped myself into the pilot's seat and ran a pre-flight to wake the systems up as Eleena and Aemos installed themselves in the pair of seats behind me. The instrument panel lit up green and there was a low sigh as the fans began to turn.

Eleena closed the hatch. The leaf-litter in the root cave began to twitch and flutter.

We'd heard nothing from Vance since we entered the wild woodland. I reached out with my mind, urging them to hurry up. There was no answer.

The plane's power cells showed about seventy-five per cent capacity. There were no alert or disfunction runes on the diagnostic panel. I went through a final check. The craft was armed with a light las-lance, fitted discreetly under the nose in a fixed-forward mount. We'd never used it, and the instruments showed it was off-line. I entered a code to activate it, and the screen told me it was stowed for safety and non-functional.

With the fans still idling, I got back out and went round to the flier's nose, crouching down to look beneath. The lance, little more than a slender tube, was capped with a rubberised sleeve to muzzle the weapon and keep dirt out of the emitter. I fumbled with the sleeve and removed it. Pulling the safety sleeve off broke a wire clasp that allowed a small pin to be yanked out. The lance was enabled.

I climbed back into the cabin, slammed the hatch and checked the instruments. The weapon was now showing as on-line and I activated the power-up function to charge its firing cells.

I'd just about finished when I felt it.

'Sir, what's wrong?' Eleena cried out as I gasped and lurched forward.

'Gregor?' said Aemos, alarmed.

'I'm okay... it was Vance...' A quick, terrible psychic shriek from the direction of the estate. A psyker in pain.

I tried to raise him again, but there was nothing except a blurry wall of background anguish. Then I heard, for a second, his mind urging Medea, urging her to run, run and not to look back.

Again I gasped as a second jolt of agony rippled through the mental spectrum.

'God-Emperor damn it!' I cursed and threw the plane forward. The fans wailed. We were instantly surrounded by a maelstrom of leaves and dead twigs which rattled and pinged off the fuselage and windows. I nursed out just a few centimetres of lift to clear the ground, with the wing fans angled straight down, and we edged forward out of the Storm Oak's root cave on minimum thrust.

I kept one eye on the proximity scanner, which was throbbing red as it detected the structure enclosing us. As soon as it signaled that the tail boom had cleared the overhang of the root ball, I keyed in more lift and we rose, swirling the leaves of the clearing around us in a whirling eddy.

We hovered and turned slowly, once, twice, as I let the auspex's terrain tracker scan the area. Then I lined up.

'Uhm, Gregor?' Aemos said, leaning forward and pointing over my left arm at the illuminated compass ball. 'We're heading north.'

'Yes.'

'It, uhm, goes without saying north is the direction we came from.'

'Yes. Sorry. We're going back.'

I put the nose down, the wing jets whirred round to an aft three-quarter thrust in their socket mounts, and the craft raced off into the darkness.

I swept us through the forest at something like twenty knots, lights off. Visibility was virtually zero, so I flew using a combination of the auspex and the proximity scanner, reading the green and amber phantoms of tree boles and branches as they loomed, steering around and under. Every now and then I cut it too fine, and the collision alert sounded as something swept across the screen in vivid red. There were plenty of near misses, but only once did I hit something – a small branch that snapped away, thankfully. Aemos and Eleena both cried out involuntarily.

'Relax,' I urged them.

We'd have made better – and safer – progress above the forest canopy, but I wanted to stay concealed for as long as possible.

In vain, I reached out to find Vance's mind.

Barely avoiding a massive low branch, we came down a long slope under the trees, and the auspex showed me that we'd reached the edge of the woodland. The road was just ahead.

Through the tree-line, I could see light, pulsing white. Another flare. I cut the forward thrust, and crept forward on down-angled jets, just a drifting hover.

I could see out over the road and the fence into the paddocks and scrub south of Spaeton House we had toiled through on foot to make our escape. The whole area was bathed in a cold, grey luminosity, a wobbling flicker cast by the dying flare. Black shapes, dozens of them, scrambled through the grasses and weeds, spread in a line, searching.

Medea, I willed. She couldn't answer. She was a blunt. But I prayed she could hear.

Medea, I'm close.

There was a sudden surge of activity to the north-east, around a spinney of fintle trees. The flash of las-fire. Two fresh flares banged up, making everything harsh black and white. The raiders were moving towards the spinney.

They had someone cornered, pinned down. I knew in my gut it was Medea.

With my lights still off, I gunned the flier forward, going low over the road and fence and across the paddock reaches. The downwash sliced a wake in the grasses. Figures turned as we swept over them. By the flarelight, I glimpsed carnival faces.

I hugged the ground, scattering some of the raiders, and powered towards the spinney. Las flashes were coming my way now.

My thumb flipped the safety cover off the control stick's firing stud. There was no aiming mechanism for the fixed lance except the craft itself. If the flier was pointing at something, then the lance was too.

I squeezed the stud.

The lance fired a continuous beam for as long as I held down the trigger. It had no pulse or burst option. A line of bright yellow light, pencil thin, sliced out from under the nose and ripped into the scrub by the spinney. I saw mud and plant debris spray up from the furrow it cut. The plane's nose was dipped. I was falling short. I nudged the flier's snout up and fired again.

Two raiders collapsed, sliced through by the beam. Several saplings and a mature fintle at the edge of the spinney came down in a shower of leaves. With the plane moving, it was damn hard to aim at all.

Twenty metres short of the trees, I pulled up in a shallow hover. Serious fusillades were zipping at us now. The craft wobbled as shots struck the lower hull.

I fired for a third time, holding the flier level and gently rotating her right to left as I held the trigger down. Raiders threw themselves flat to avoid the lethal beam of light passing over them. Several didn't make it. The lance simply sectioned them, clean through flesh, bone and armour. I must have hit a power pack or a grenade, because one exploded in a sheet of flame.

More shots thumped into the fuselage from the rear. I surged forward again, sweeping around the west side of the trees.

I saw Medea on the auspex. She was running clear of the spinney at the north end, breaking cover. It took me a moment to find her by eye. Just a dot in the long weeds. A bright dot. She was wearing her father's cerise jacket. I realised she must have come out into the open to give me a chance to set down and reach her. The thin trees in the spinney were far too tightly packed.

Las-bolts chased her. She turned and fired back with a handgun, still running.

You're clear! Get down!

I saw her turn, seeing where I was. Then she was hurled face first into the grass by a las-shot.

'Medea!' I accelerated hard, pushing us back into our seats. 'Aemos! Get ready with the side hatch!'

I got as close in to the patch of weeds where she had fallen as I dared. The down-thrust of the plane could cause serious injuries. We jolted hard as I set down, throwing the throttles to idle. Aemos was opening the hatch, but he was old and slow and scared. Eleena couldn't reach over because he was blocking her.

I leapt out, pushing Aemos back into his seat, and thumped down into the wet nettles and burry fex-grass. The night air was sudden and cold. Another flare bloomed above us, and I realised the echoing spit I could hear was the enemy guns discharging in my direction.

I ran forward, searching for her.

'Medea! Medea!'

Now I was on the ground, it was nigh on impossible to tell where in the thigh-high grass she'd fallen.

'Medea!'

A las-round stung the air to my left. The closest of the raiders, running across the paddock, was only a few dozen metres away.

I realised I was unarmed. I'd given my boltgun to Sastre, and Barbarisater and the staff were stowed in the flier behind me.

No, I had Medea's Glavian needle pistol. It was still in my

coat pocket. I dragged it out and fired, aiming it with both hands.

My first shot hit the nearest raider and he fell over into the grass. My second shot winged another and he too disappeared into the rough scrub.

I glanced at the needler's mechanical dial. Two rounds left.

Bending low, I searched the grass with increasing frenzy as shots whined in close.

'Medea!'

And there she was, face down in the thick scrub. There was a bloody, burned hole in the back of her silk jacket.

I dragged her up and threw her limp body over my shoulder. The autopistol she had been using slipped heavily from her slack hand.

I stooped and grabbed it. The clip was half-full.

I swung round, trying to keep her from falling, and fired the autopistol wildly at the advancing enemy, relishing the satisfying roar and recoil of the hefty solid-slug weapon. Needle guns were elegant and deadly, but you barely knew you'd fired them.

This thing, chrome and square-nosed, kicked like a yurf, and spent brass cases rang as they flew from the pumping slide.

I started to run back to the plane, expecting a shot in the back any moment. I heard las fire, but it wasn't coming from behind me. Eleena Koi was braced in the open side hatch of the flier, laying down covering fire with a laspistol I hadn't realised she was carrying. Aemos had got into the back, onto the bench seat, giving Eleena access to the door.

Aemos reached out and gathered Medea in his arms. Eleena seized her too and the three of us bundled the girl into the rear beside Aemos.

I was wishing so hard she wasn't dead.

Eleena fired one last time and fell back into the passenger seats. I jumped in, yelling at her to slam the hatch.

There was no time to strap in. Multiple shots slammed against the aircraft's flank. A window panel burst. Dents appeared in the inner skin, spalling fragments off the hull.

I hoisted us off the ground, and spun us to face the charging raiders.

I think, although I can't be sure, I said something singularly unedifying as I pressed the trigger. Something like: 'eat this, you bastards.'

I don't believe I actually hit any of them but, by the Golden Throne, they took cover.

'Sir!' Eleena yelled over the scream of the turbofans.

A ball of light was approaching from the other side of the spinney. I couldn't see the speeder, just its stablight shining like a white dwarf against the night sky.

Time to go.

I kept it low, but pulled away south across the paddock at full thrust, accelerating all the time. We were doing forty, forty-five knots by the time we reached the road. The woods loomed.

In an instant, I weighed my options. Go high, over the trees, and be a clear target for any pursuer. Go through, lights off, and drop speed dramatically to avoid collision. Go through, lights on.

I picked the third way.

The flier's lamps kicked on, lighting a cone of space ahead of us. Even with the lights, and the auspex and the proximity alarm, this course was borderline suicide. Within a few seconds, having only just avoided a head-on smash with a mature spruce, I had to drop the speed to thirty.

'You're... you're gonna get us killed!' Eleena wailed.

'Be quiet!' The black shapes of tree trunks whipped past on either side, forcing me to turn and bank hard, repeatedly, jagging left, then right, then left again. Branches, some as massive as trees in their own right, swept over us like arches or under us like bridges. Several times, we exploded through sprays of canopy, the engine-out alarm pipping as the fans fought to clear away the leaf debris choking them. The phantoms on the scanner screen were almost constantly red.

Eleena started to say an Imperial prayer.

'Say one for us all,' I barked. 'Aemos! What's Medea's condition?'

'She's alive, thank the stars. But her breathing's not right. Perhaps a collapsed lung, or internal cauterisation. She needs a medic, Gregor.'

'She'll get one. Make her as comfortable as you can. There's a medi-pack in the locker behind you. Patch her wound.'

Apart from being an insane death wish, flying at speed through dense, ancient forest at night was baffling. Simply avoiding collision required such concentration, I kept losing my bearings. A few forced turns to the left, say, pointed us east. Correcting that, and evading an oak to the right, and we were turned west. We were zig-zagging through the wild woodland, and a zig-zag is not the fastest route of escape.

At least four of the five speeders I had seen during the raid were after us. Two were following us directly through the trees, about five hundred metres behind us. The other two had gone up and over the tree cover, making much better time, chasing hard to pass over us and get ahead.

They were ex-military models; I'd seen that much from the glimpse I'd got of them parked on the lawns. Bigger power plants than this nimble Urdeshi turbofan; bigger, and better armoured. And their cannons, mounted on racks in the doorframes, meant they could, essentially, fire in any direction. They didn't have to be pointing at their target.

The auspex started to chime and I saw hard light flash down through the leaf cover above us, breaking through in shafts like a sun breaking through low cloud. One of the fliers above the forest was matching us for speed.

I jinked and evaded, not so much to lose him as to avoid instant obliteration against the bole of a tree. I saw the forest floor convulse and ripple as the door gunner fired down at us.

So I banked hard, one wing down, right around a colossal fanewood, and shot off in a westerly direction. The overhead lights disappeared for a moment, but then reappeared, travelling fast, parallel to us, to the left. A tree, flashing past to my right, lost its bark in a blitz of diagonal crossfire.

Damn them. I was fairly certain they had no heat or motion tracking instruments. They were following the glow of my lamps underlighting the canopy.

I killed the lights but unfortunately didn't kill my speed. The proximity alarm squealed, and though I yanked on the stick, we struck a trunk a grazing blow.

We wobbled hard. The engine-out alert shrilled a continuous note. The starboard fan had stalled.

I went to hover, and pressed restart on the starboard unit, hoping that it had simply been jolted dead by the impact. If the casing or the fan itself were buckled, restarting might be very messy indeed for all of us.

The dead fan turned over and coughed. I tried again. Another mewling wheeze. Twenty metres behind us, the forest was coming to pieces in a deluge of wood pulp, bark scraps and pulverised foliage as the flier high above tried to smoke us out with a sustained salvo.

The starboard fan whipped into life on the third attempt.

Staying at hover, I played the stick back and forth and side to side, pitching and yawing the craft, dropping its nose and then its tail, dipping the stubby wings, just to make sure I hadn't lost any attitude control. It seemed alright.

I looked over my shoulder and saw Eleena staring at me, her face corpse-pale. Aemos was cradling Medea.

'Are we all right, Gregor?' he whispered.

'Yes. I'm sorry about that.'

The glade to our left suddenly lit up with vertical shafts of light and was pummelled by cannon fire. They were still searching blindly.

I had a sudden moment of recall. A void duel. Seriously outnumbered. Midas flying by the seat of his well-tailored pants. I remember him glancing at me from the controls of the gun-cutter, and saying: 'Mouse becomes cat.'

Mouse becomes cat.

Still hovering, I rotated the flier towards the blitzed glade and then raised the nose slowly, pointing it at the light source above the trees. Aiming it at the light source.

I squeezed the toggle, just for a second.

The lance beam seared up into the backlit canopy. There was a brief flash and then a nine tonne metal fireball that had once been a speeder simply dropped down into the clearing, smashing through the branches, ripping apart and hurling flaming debris in all directions.

'Scratch one,' I said, smugly. Well, it's what Midas would have said.

There were lights behind us, zooming closer through the forest. Keeping the lamps off, I nudged us away from the wreckage inferno and turned in behind a twisted antlerbark that had slumped sideways in old age. Curtains of moss draped from its weary branches.

I watched the lights approach, easing the nose around to follow the nearest one. They had slowed down, hunting for signs of us. The nearest lights were tantalisingly close, but obscured by a line of fat oaks.

The other one zipped in towards the blazing crash site.

I swung us up, leading the flier's nose towards the coasting speeder.

It came into view, stablights sweeping the woodland floor.

I fired again.

The shot was pretty good. It sheared the tail boom off the speeder. With its rear end discharging blue electrical arcs, it spun out of control, end over end. It made a mess of a giant fanewood, and vice versa.

The other speeder came out from the cover of the oaks, firing right at us. The shots rent aside the curtains of moss.

I realised someone had had the sense to bring night vision goggles. They could see us.

I tried one shot, missed and then turned tail, kicking in the floods and raising the speed as high as I dared. The proximity alert screen was just an overlapping red blur now, and we were all thrown around by the violent turns I was forced to make.

The pilot of the speeder chasing us was good. Distressingly good. Like the merc foot troops, he was clearly the best of his kind money could buy.

He stuck to my tail like a leech.

Pushing thirty-eight knots, I caroomed through the dense trees, pulling gees sometimes when the turns demanded it. He raced after me, following my lead and enjoying the gain of my turbowash slip stream

The chase was verging on balletic. We snaked and

criss-crossed between trees, banked and looped like dancing partners. Several times I stood on a wingtip coming round one side of a big tree and he mirrored the move coming round the other. Fans screaming, I pulled a hard turn to the north, and then rolled, reversing, turning south. He overshot, but was back a moment later, accelerating fast onto my tail. Tracer rounds winked past me.

Two hard jolts came in quick succession, and the instruments confirmed what I suspected. We'd been hit. I was losing power: not much, but enough to suggest a battery had been ruptured or disconnected. He was firing again. Stitching lines of tracer shells spat past the cockpit. Now I had distress runes lighting up on my control panels.

Something drastic was needed, or we'd be his latest cockpit stripe. I thought about cutting the fans and dropping to make him overshoot, but at the speed we were going, we'd crash and burn.

'Hold on!' I yelled.

'Oh shit,' said Eleena Koi.

I killed the thrust and went vertical.

We exploded up through the canopy into the sky, shredding branches around us. The speeder shot by underneath. Astonished, he tried to bank round to re-engage, but my manoeuvre had flummoxed him. Just for a moment, but long enough.

He didn't trim his thrust as he tried to make the turn. A tree took one stabiliser wing clean off and that was the last I saw of him except for the series of impact explosions he made under the trees below us.

I was shaking, my hands numb. Exhaustion punched into me. The concentration had been so terribly intense.

But Midas, I was sure, would have been proud of me. He'd forever been trying to teach me his skills, and he'd declared on more than one occasion that I'd never make a combat pilot.

In his opinion, I had the essential reflexes and strength, but I never saw the big picture. And it was always that last, over-looked detail that got you killed.

That last, overlooked detail came in from the north, across the treetops, autocannons flashing.

TEN

Down
Doctor Berschilde of Ravello
Khanjar the Sharp

It was the fourth speeder that had been hunting us. Before I could even let out a curse, its streaming cannon fire had severed our tail boom and mangled the aft fan, shredding off its cover and twisting the still-spinning props.

We started to rotate violently. The cabin vibrated like a seizure victim. Eleena screamed.

I wrestled with the controls, fighting the bucking stick. I cranked the wing fans to vertical and throttled up to break the drop. The flier crunched down through upper branches, glanced off a main bough, and nose dived.

I stood on the rudder and yanked back the stick.

'Brace!' I yelled. That was all I had time to say.

We side-swiped a fanewood's trunk, a collision that ripped off the port fan and stripped the monocoque's hull paint down to the bare metal and bounced once off a peaty ridge of moss and leaf mould. Then we rose again, yawing to the left as the remaining turbofan screamed to the edge of its tolerance trying to gain some sort of lift. The engine-out alarm shrilled as the fan stalled, overcome by the pressure. We fell then, sideways, survived a headlong impact with an oak that crazed the windshield and slammed into the loamy earth, slithering a good fifty metres before we rocked to a halt on our side.

I didn't black out but the long silence following the crash made it feel like I had. I blinked, lying on my shoulder against the side hatch. Eleena moaned and Aemos started coughing. The only other sound was the tinkling patter of the shattered windscreen scads gradually collapsing into the cabin.

I got up and clambered over the seats.

'Eleena? Are you hurt?'

'No, sir... I don't think so...'

'We have to get out. Help me.'

Together we dragged the coughing Aemos clear and went back for Medea who was still, mercifully, unconscious.

The searchlights of the speeder lanced down through the hole we had made in the canopy, poking around.

Any moment now...

Eleena and I dragged the other two into the shelter of a hollow a good distance from the downed aircraft.

'Stay here,' I whispered to her. 'Give me your weapon.'

Silently, she offered me her stubby laspistol.

'Stay down,' I advised and ran back to the wreck, retrieving my staff and my sword. I tossed the runestaff into the undergrowth to keep it out of sight and drew Barbarisater.

The speeder was coming down through the upper branches, trying to pick out the flier with its stablight. I tucked the sword and pistol into my belt and lunged up into the lower branches of the gros beech that overlooked our crash site.

The tree was huge and gnarled. Grunting, I swung myself up into the main boughs and then further up into the web of thinner branches.

The speeder hovered into view, crawling slowly towards the smoking wreck, its searchlight playing back and forth. I could see the masked side-gunner in the open door, one hand on the yoke of the pintle-mounted autocannon, the other on the bracket of the lamp.

The speeder descended. I climbed higher, up into the lofty reaches of the beech, until I could climb no further and the hovering speeder was directly below me.

The pilot said something. I distinctly heard the crackle of his intervox. The door gunner replied and let go of the lamp, setting both hands on the cannon's grips, turning it to aim down at the crumpled flier.

The glade below me filled with flashes and booms as he riddled the airplane with his cannon fire. The valiant little Urdeshi craft shredded like tinfoil.

The door gunner stopped shooting and called down to his pilot.

Now or never.

I let go of the branches and dropped straight onto the roof of the speeder. It rocked slightly beneath me. I steadied myself, crouched down, gripped the upper frame of the door hatch and swung in, boots first.

The gunner was bent over with his back to the hatch, getting a fresh ammunition box from the wall rack. My boots connected with his lower back and shunted him face-first against the cabin wall. I landed beside him as he staggered backwards, his hands clutching at his broken face, grabbed him by the arm and propelled him backwards out of the hatch. We were ten metres up.

The pilot gave a muffled grunt as he looked round and saw me. A second later, the muzzle of the laspistol was pressed against the corner of his jaw.

'Set down. Now,' I said.

I prayed I was dealing with a mercenary and not a cultist. A merc would know when to cut his losses, and bargain to live for another day and another paycheck. A cultist would fly us into the nearest tree, gun or no gun.

Making his motions very slow and clear so I could be sure to read them, the pilot cut the speeder's main thruster, and sank us to the forest floor.

'Shut us down,' I said.

He obeyed, and the lift units hummed to a halt. The dashboard went blank apart from a few orange standby lights.

'Unstrap. Get out.'

He unbuckled his harness and slowly pulled himself up out of the pilot's seat as I covered him with the pistol. He was a short but well-built man in ablative armour and a grey flight helmet with a breathing visor.

He jumped down from the speeder's side hatch and stood with his hands raised.

I got down next to him. 'Take off the helmet and toss it back into the speeder.'

The pilot did as he was told. His skin was pale and freckled, his thinning hair shaved close. He regarded me with edgy blue eyes.

'Unzip the suit.'

He frowned.

'To the waist.'

Keeping one hand raised, he drew the zipper of the ablat-suit down, revealing an undervest and shoulders marked with old, blurry tattoos. The psi-shield was a small, disc-shaped device hung round his neck on a plastic cord. I snapped it off and tossed it into the undergrowth. Then I used my will.

'Name?'

'Nhh...' he growled, grimacing.

'Name!'

'Eino Goran.'

I nudged my mind against his. It was like rubbing up against something sheathed in plastic.

'Right, we both know that's an emplated identity. A rush job from the feel of it. Real name?'

He shook his head, his teeth clenched. Emplate IDs were cheap enough to buy on the black market, especially a fairly poor quality one like this. They were fake personalities, usually sold with matching papers, psi-woven over the subject's persona like a fitted dust cover on a piece of furniture. Nothing fancy. If you had the money, you could buy fingerprints and retinas to match. If you really had the money, a new face too.

This one was like a false wall erected in a hurry to ward off casual minds. It lacked any sort of real history, not even vague biographical engrams. A mind mask as cheap and unrealistic as the carnival faces his comrades had worn.

But, though poor, it had been put in place with great force. I tried to shift it, but it wouldn't budge. That was frustrating. It was obviously false, but I couldn't get past it.

There was no time to worry at it now.

Out! I willed, and he collapsed unconscious.

'Eleena! Aemos! Come on!' I shouted, dragging the limp man back into the speeder. I checked him for weapons – there were none – and then lashed his hands behind his back with a length of cable from the speeder's pulley spool. By the time Eleena and Aemos reached me, carefully bearing Medea, I had the pilot gagged and blind-folded, and tied to one of the speeder's internal cross-members.

We got everything aboard – the items we had rescued from my study, the runestaff, all of it – and secured Medea in a pull-down cot in the aft of the speeder's crew bay. Then I got into the pilot's seat and, once I'd made sense of the control layout, got us airborne.

I edged up just above the treetops, running unlit. The moon was up and the night was clear, apart from a brown smudge against the stars away to the north. The smoke from my burning estate, I had no doubt. There was no sign of anything else in the air. Hugging the tips of the trees, I turned us south.

Once we were underway, I checked out the cockpit. It was clearly an ex-military flier, bought for the purpose in my opinion. Insignia mouldings had been chiselled off, service numbers erased with acid swabs. Apart from the basic controls, the cabin was provided with several socket racks where optional instrument modules could be bolted in. Only a vox-set had been fitted. There were gaps where an auspex, a terrain-reader and night vision displays might have gone, and also slots for a navigation codifier and a remote fire control system that would have slaved the door weapon to the pilot and done away with the necessity of a separate gunner. Whoever had supplied the mercenaries with their vehicles had provided only the most basic package. An armed troop-lifter with an old model vox-caster comm. No automated systems. No clue to origin or source.

But it had decent power and range – over a thousand kilometres left in it before it would need a recharge. Something to get them in, lay down cover and get them out again.

The forest flickered by beneath us. The vox burbled

intermittently, but I had no idea of the codes or cant they were using, and little desire to let anyone know the flier was still operational.

After a while, it shut off. I unplugged it, pulled it out of its rack and told Eleena to toss it overboard.

'Why?' she asked.

'I don't want to risk it having a tracker or transponder built into it.'

She nodded.

I tried to get our bearings manually, using the basic instrumentation, working to reconstruct a map of the area in my head. It was pretty much guesswork. Dorsay, the nearest main city, was perhaps a hour west of us now, but given the scale of the operation mounted against me, I felt going there would be like flying into a carnodon's den.

There were small fishing communities and harbour towns on the east side of the Insume headland, the closest now more than two hours away. Madua, a chapel town in the south-east, was in range. So was Entreve, a market city on the fringe of the wild woodland. So were the Atenate Mountains.

I thought about calling the Arbites on the vox, but decided against it. The attack on Spaeton House must surely have been noted by sentries at Dorsay, especially once the main fires started, but no emergency support units had come. Had the Arbites been paid to turn a blind eye? Had they been more complicit still in the raid?

Until I understood who and what my enemies were, I could trust no one, and that included the authorities and even the Inquisition itself.

Not for the first time in my life, I was effectively alone.

I headed for the mountains. For Ravello.

* * *

Ravello is a hill town in the flanks of the western Atenates, situated at the foot of the Insa Pass, on the shores of a long freshwater lake that forms the headwaters of the great Drunner. It has a small but distinguished universitariate specialising in medicine and philology, a brewery that exports its lake-water ale all over Gudrun, and a fine chapel dedicated to Saint Calwun, which houses to my mind some of the best religious frescoes in the sub-sector.

It is a quiet place, steep and densely packed, its old buildings lining narrow hill streets so tightly their green copper roofs overlap like plate armour. From the air, it looked like a patch of dark moss clinging to the blue slopes of the Itervalle.

The sun was rising as we approached from the north. The air was clear, a baking blue. We had left the wild woodland in the first touches of dawn, and climbed up into the foothills, following the line of the Atenate Minors up into the higher altitudes. The Itervalle was high enough to have cloud cover round its peak, but across the lake, the first of the great giants rose: Esembo, ragged like a tooth; Mons Fulco, a violet triangle stabbing the sky; snow-capped Corvachio, the sport and bane of recreational climbers.

We were nearly out of power and the speeder was getting sluggish. I dropped us to road level and came in through the western gate. There were no traffic and no pedestrians. It was still early in the morning.

The streets were paved with the same blue-grey ouslite that the buildings were constructed from, bright in the sunlight, dank in the shadows of the narrow streets. We passed through a square where a student lay sleeping off a night's drinking on the lip of a small fountain, along a wider avenue where ground cars and civilian fliers were parked in a herringbone, and then turned up a narrow street and climbed the hill out of the glare of the sun. I opened the speeder's windows and breathed in the fresh, clear air. The muted sounds of the flier's engines washed back at me, reflected oddly by the tall, shuttered faces of the dwellings on either side of the steep, paved lane.

It had been a long time, but I still knew my way around.

We parked in a cul-de-sac alley just off the lane, little more than a blunt courtyard where a mountain spurra struggled to grow against the face of a wall. The spurra, or at least its little yellow spring flowers, was the emblem of Saint Calwun, and votive bottles and coins littered the little stone basin the tree was growing from.

A first floor shutter twitched at the sound of our engines, and I was glad I had asked Aemos to stow the door gun during our flight. At least we resembled a private transport.

'Stay here,' I told Eleena and Aemos. 'Stay here and wait.'

I walked back down the street in the quiet morning. I was still wearing the boots, breeches, shirt and leather coat I had put on before the auto-seance the night before, but Aemos had lent me his drab-green cloak. I made sure I was displaying no insignia or badge of office, except my signet ring, which would pass notice. Medea's autopistol, reloaded with shells from a box magazine we found on the speeder, was tucked into the back of my belt.

A stray dog, coming up from the town centre towards me, paused to sniff my cloak hem and then trotted on its way, uninterested.

The house was as I remembered it, halfway down the lane. We had passed it on the way up, and now I made certain. Four storeys, with a terrace balcony at the top under the eaves of the copper-tiled roof. The windows were shuttered and the main entrance, a pair of heavy panelled wooden doors painted glossy red, were bolted shut.

There was no bell. I remembered that. I knocked once and waited.

I waited a long time.

Finally, I heard a thump behind the doors and an eyeslit opened.

'What is your business so early?' asked an old man's voice.

'I want to see Doctor Berschilde.'

'Who is calling?'

'Please let me in and I will discuss it with the doctor.'

'It is early!' the voice protested.

I raised my hand and held my signet ring out so its design was visible through the eyeslit.

'Please,' I repeated.

The slit shut, there was a rattle of keys and then one of the doors opened into the street. Inside was just shadow.

I stepped into the delicious cool of the hall, my eyes growing accustomed to the gloom. A hunched old man in black closed the door behind me.

'Wait here, sir,' he said and shuffled away.

The floor was polished marble mosaic that sparkled where scraps of exterior light caught it. The wall patterns had been hand-painted by craftsmen. Exquisite, antiquarian anatomical sketches lined the walls in simple gilt frames. The house smelled of warm stone, the cold afterscents of a fine evening meal, smoke.

'Hello?' a voice filtered down from the stairs above me.

I went up a flight, onto a landing where shutters had been opened to let the daylight stream in.

'I'm sorry to intrude,' I said.

'Gregor? Gregor Eisenhorn?' Doctor Berschilde of Ravello took a step towards me, registering sleepy astonishment.

She was still a very fine figure of a woman.

I think she was about to hug me, or plant a kiss on my cheek, but she halted and her face darkened.

'This isn't social, is it?' she said.

I went back to the speeder and flew it round to the private walled courtyard behind her residence where it was screened from view. The doctor's old manservant, Phabes, had opened the ground floor sundoors, and stood ready with a gurney for Medea. Eleena, Aemos and I followed them inside. I left the pilot, still in his will-induced fugue state, tied up in the flier.

Crezia Berschilde had put on a surgical apron by then, and met us in the ground floor hall. She said little as she examined Medea and checked her vitals.

'Take her through,' she told her man, then looked at me. 'Anybody else injured?'

'No,' I said. 'How is Medea?'

'Dying,' she said. All humour had gone from her voice. She was angry and I didn't blame her. 'I'll do what I can.'

'I'm grateful, Crezia. I'm sorry I've troubled you with this.'

'She ought to go to the town infirmary!' she snapped.

'Can we avoid that?'

'Can we make this unofficial, you mean? Damn you, Eisenhorn. I don't need this!'

'I know you don't.'

She pursed her lips. 'I'll do what I can,' she repeated. 'Go through into the drawing room. I'll have Phabes bring some refreshment.'

She turned on her heel and disappeared into the house after Medea.

'So,' said Aemos quietly, 'who is this again?'

* * *

Doctor Crezia Berschilde was one of the finest anatomists on the planet. Her treatises and monographs were widely published throughout the Helican sub-sector. After years of practice in Dorsay and, for a period, off-world on Messina, she had taken up the post of Professor of Anatomy here at Ravello.

And, a long time ago, I had nearly married her.

One hundred and forty-five years earlier, in 241 to be exact, I had lost my left hand during a firefight on Sameter. The details of the case are unimportant, and besides, they are recorded elsewhere. I was fitted with a prosthetic, but I hated it and never used it. After two years, during a stay on Messina, I had surgeons equip me with a fully functioning graft.

Crezia had been the chief surgeon during that proce-dure. Becoming involved with a woman who has just sewn a vat-grown clone hand onto your wrist is hardly a way to meet a wife, I realise.

But she was quick-witted, learned, vivacious and not put off by my calling. For years we were involved, on and off, first on Messina, then at a distance, and then on Gudrun once she had moved back to Ravello to take up her doctorate and I had based myself at Spaeton House.

I had been very fond of her. I still was. It is difficult to know if I should use a word stronger than 'fond'. We never did to each other, but there are times I would have done.

I had not seen her for the best part of twenty-five years. That had been my doing.

We sat in the drawing room for over an hour. Phabes had opened the windows and the day's brilliance blasted in, turn-ing the tulle window nets into hanging oblongs of radiant white. I could smell the clean, fresh chill of mountains.

The drawing room was furnished with fine old pieces of

furniture, and filled with rare books, surgical curios and display cases full of immaculately restored antique medical apparatus. Aemos was quickly lost in close study of the items on display, murmuring to himself. Eleena sat quietly on a tub chair and composed herself. I was fairly sure she was inwardly reciting the mind-soothing exercises of the Distaff. Every few minutes she would absently brush a few strands of brown hair off her slender face.

The doctor's man returned with a silver serving cart. Yeast bread, fruit, oily butter and piping hot black caffeine.

'Do you need anything stronger?' he asked.

'No, thank you.'

He pointed to a weighted silk rope by the door. 'Ring if there's anything you need.'

I poured caffeine for us all, and Aemos helped himself to a hunk of bread and a ripe ploin.

Eleena tonged half a dozen lumps of amber sugar crystal into her little cup. 'Who did it?' she asked at length.

'Eleena?'

'Who... who raided us, sir?'

'The simple answer? I have no idea. I'm working on possibilities. It may take us a while to find out, and first we have to be secure.'

'Are we safe here?'

'Yes, for the time being.'

'They were mercenaries,' said Aemos, dabbing crumbs from his wrinkled lips. 'That is beyond question.'

'I thought as much.'

'The pilot you captured. You saw the tattoos on his torso.'

'I did. But I couldn't read them.'

Aemos sipped his hot, sweet drink. 'Base Futu, the language of the Vessorine janissaries.'

'Really? Are you sure?'

'Reasonably so,' he said. 'The man has a repatriation bond written on his skin.'

I considered this news. Vessor was a feral world on the rimward borders of the Antimar sub-sector that bred a small but hardy population famous for its vicious fighters. Attempts had been made to form a Guard regiment there, but the Vessorine were hard to control. It wasn't that they lacked discipline, but they found loyalty to Terra too cerebral a concept. They were bonded into clan families, understanding simply the material wealth of land, property, homestead and weapons. As mercenaries, therefore, they excelled. They would fight, peerlessly, savagely and to the death, in the Emperor's name, provided that name was stamped on high denomination coinage.

No wonder the attack on Spaeton House had been so direct and efficient. In hindsight it was remarkable any of us had got out alive. I was glad I hadn't known who they were at the time. If I'd been told I was facing Vessorine janissaries, I might have frozen up... instead of charging them head on to rescue Medea.

I took off the cloak Aemos had lent me, and also my leather coat, and rolled up the sleeves of my shirt. The sun was warming the drawing room. I had just taken the pistol out of my belt to check it when Crezia came into the room. She was peeling off surgical gloves and when she saw the gun in my hands, her already sour look became fiercer. She pointed sharply at me and then gestured outside.

'Now,' she said, curtly.

I pushed the weapon into the folds of the cloak on the table and followed her out, across the hall into a sitting room hung with oil paintings and hololithic prints. The shutters in here were still shut and she made no attempt to open them. She turned up the lamp instead.

'Shut the door,' she instructed.

I pushed the door shut. 'Crezia–' I began.

She held up a strong, warning finger. 'Don't start, Eisen-horn. Just don't. I'm this damn close to throwing you out! How dare you c–'

'Medea,' I interrupted firmly. 'How is she?'

'Stable. Just about. She was shot in the back with a laser weapon and the wound was left untreated for several hours. How do you think she is?'

'She'll survive?'

'Unless there are complications. She's on life support in the basement suite.'

'Thank you, Crezia. I'm in your debt.'

'Yes, you damn well are. You're unbelievable, Eisenhorn. Twenty-five years. Twenty-five years! I don't see you, I don't hear from you and then you turn up, unannounced, uninvited, armed and on the run, so it would appear, with one of your party shot. And you expect me just to take this in my stride?'

'Not really, I know it's a terrible imposition. But the Crezia Berschilde I knew could cope with an emergency now and then. And she always had time for a friend in need.'

'A friend?'

'Yes. You're the only person I can turn to, Crezia.'

She snorted scornfully and tugged off her apron. 'All those years, I was happy to be the one you could turn to, Gregor. And you never did. You kept me at arm's length. You never wanted me involved in your business. And now...' She let the words trail off and shrugged unhappily.

'I'm sorry.'

'You bring guns into my house–' she hissed.

'I probably shouldn't tell you about the mercenary tied up in my speeder then,' I said.

She snapped round to look at me, incredulous, and then shook her head with a grim smile. 'Unbelievable. Twenty-five years and you roll up at dawn, bringing trouble with you.'

'No. No one knows I'm here. That's one of the reasons I came.'

'Are you sure?'

I nodded. 'Someone raided my residence last night. Razed it. Murdered my staff.'

'I don't want to hear this!'

'We barely got out alive. I needed sanctuary and medical help for Medea. I needed to find somewhere I knew would be safe.'

'I don't want to hear any more!' she snarled. 'I don't want to be tangled up in your battles. I don't want to be involved! I have a nice life here and–'

'You do need to hear it. You need to know what's going on.'

'Why? I'm not going to get involved! Why the hell didn't you go to the Arbites?'

'I can't trust anyone. Not even the authorities, right now.'

'Damnation, Eisenhorn! Why me? Why here?'

'Because I trust you. Because my enemies may have every known associate of mine on the planet under observation, every Arbites precinct, every office of the Ministorum and the Imperial Administratum. But our relationship is secret. Even my closest friends don't know we were ever associated.'

'Associated? Associated? You know how to flatter, you pig!'

'Please, Crezia. There a few things I need to do. A few things I need to arrange. A little help I need to ask of you. Then we'll be gone and you'll never have to worry about this again.'

She sat down on a chaise and rubbed her hands together anxiously.

'What do you need?'

'To begin with, your forbearance. After that... access to a private vox-link. I'll need you to summon an astropath, if that's in any way possible, and also have your man purchase clothes and other items for us.'

'The town tailors will be closed today.'

'I can wait.'

'There may be clothes here.'

'Very well.'

'There's a vox-link in my study.'

I went to look in on Medea, who was sleeping peacefully in the scrubbed medical suite built into the basement of Crezia's town house, and then retired to the room Phabes had prepared for me. Eleena and Aemos were in adjoining rooms, resting.

I bathed and shaved, doing both activities on automatic as my mind worked things through. I discovered my body had acquired several new bruises since the day before and a las-graze across the thigh I hadn't even noticed. My clothes were dirty, torn and smoke-damaged, and the breeches were covered in burrs and sticky grass seeds.

Phabes had laid some clothes out in my room, several changes of male attire. I recognised they were my own. I'd kept clothes here over the years, mostly soft, informal wear to change into when I visited. Crezia had stored them. I didn't know whether to be delighted or alarmed. All these years, and she hadn't thrown out the possessions I'd left in her territory. They were fresh too, as if aired or laundered regularly. I realised that Crezia Berschilde had always expected me to return one day.

Perhaps it was the manner of my return that had upset her – that I came back for her help and not simply for her. I couldn't blame her for that. I wouldn't be pleased to see me now, considering the trouble I was in. And not if I had broken all links of friendship two and a half decades before.

The chapel bells were ringing in the town below, calling the faithful for worship. Lakeside inns were opening up, and the smells of roasting and herbs were carried on the breeze.

I chose a dark blue cotton shirt with a thin collar, a pair of black twill trousers and a short flat-fronted summer jacket of black suede. The boots I had been wearing the night before would have to make do, but I scrubbed them clean with a cloth. I wanted to tuck the pistol into my jacket, but I knew how Crezia felt about guns, so I left it, with Barbarisater and the runestaff, under the mattress of my bed. The sacks of scrolls and manuscripts Aemos and I had rescued from Spaeton were with him in his room.

I had little else with me: my signet ring, a short-range hand vox, some coins and my warrant of office – a metal seal in a leather wallet. It was the first time since Durer that I missed my rosette. Fischig still had that, wherever he was.

As I hung my leather coat up in the wardrobe, I felt a weight in it and remembered I did have something else.

The *Malus Codicium*.

It was an infernal book, thrice damned. I knew of no other copy in existence. One half of the Inquisition would kill me to get their hands on it, the other half would burn me for having it in my possession.

Quixos, the corrupt veteran inquisitor I had finally brought to account on Farness Beta, had built his power upon it. I should have destroyed it when I destroyed him or at least surrendered it to the ordo. I had done neither. Using it, secretly studying it, I had increased my abilities. I had captured and bound Cherubael using its lore. I had broken open several cult conspiracies thanks to the insight it had given me.

It was only a small thing, fat, soft-covered in simple black hide, the edges of its pages rough and hand-cut. Innocuous.

I sat down on the corner of the bed and weighed it in my hands. Splendid mid-morning sunlight shone in through the casement, the sky was blue, the slopes of the Itervalle visible from the rear of the house a soft lilac. But I felt cold and plunged into darkness.

I'd never really thought about why I had saved that hideous work for my own ends. Knowledge, I suppose. Curiosity. I had encountered prohibited artefacts many times in my life, the most notorious being the accursed Necroteuch. That loathsome thing had possessed a life of its own. It stung to the touch. It lured you in and coerced you into opening it. Just to be near it was to poison the mind.

But the *Codicium* was silent. It always had been. It had never seemed alive, like the other toxic, rustling volumes I have encountered. It had always been just a book. The contents were disturbing, but the book itself...

I wondered now. The moment it had come into my possession, things had started to change. Starting with Cherubael and on, on to the bleak events on Durer.

Maybe it was poisoning me. Maybe it was twisting my mind. Maybe I had crossed far too far over the line without realising it, thanks to its baleful influence.

Perhaps that was a measure of how evil it was. That it was painless. Invisible. Insidious. The moment you touched the Necroteuch, you knew it was a vile thing, you knew you had to resist its seductive corruption. You knew you were fighting it.

But the *Malus Codicium*... so infinitely evil, so subtle, seeping slowly into a man's soul before he even knew it.

Was that how a servant of the Emperor as great as Quixos had become a monster? I had always wondered why he had never seen what he was becoming. Why he was so blind to his own degeneration.

I opened the drawer of my night stand and put the book inside. As soon as we were clear of Ravello, I would have to deal with it.

I went down to Crezia's study and found the vox-link. There was a hololithic pict unit too, and I tuned that in. Morning broadcasts, weather, planetary news. I watched for some time but there was no mention of any incident in the Dorsay region. I had anticipated as much, but it was still unnerving.

I used the vox and listened in to the Imperial channels, eavesdropping on Arbites frequencies, PDF transmissions, Ministorum links. Nothing. Either no one knew what had happened the night before at Spaeton House, or they were staying ominously silent.

I needed an astropath. If I was going to contact anyone, it would be off-world. I had no choice.

I really couldn't trust anybody on the planet.

The flier was still parked in the back courtyard. Phabes had been good enough to run a power cable from the house and the craft's batteries were recharging.

It was hot in the yard. Insects buzzed in the thick spill of flowering bucanthus that covered the side wall.

The mercenary was awake. He twisted his head from side to side as he heard me approach, blind and dumb.

I tore the tape from his mouth and then filled a dish-cup with water from a bottle I had borrowed from the kitchen. I held it up to his mouth.

'It's just water. Drink it.' He pursed his lips and turned his head away.

'You'll dehydrate in this heat. Drink.'

He refused again.

'Look, if you dehydrate, you'll become weak and far more vulnerable to my questions and mind probes.'

He paused and swallowed, but then shied away from the cup again as I brought it up.

'Have it your way,' I said and put the dish down. The Vessorine were famously hardy. It was said they could go without food or water for days when battle demanded it. If he wanted to show off, it was fine by me.

I rose and went over the body of the speeder carefully. I had borrowed a scanner wand from Crezia's study, and set it to detect high and low band signals... transponders, beacons, codes. I found nothing. For good measure. I swept the Vessorine too. Both flier and prisoner were clean. If the mercenaries were looking for us, they wouldn't find us because of the craft or pilot.

It had taken me half an hour to sweep the vessel. I went back to the pilot. The mid-morning sun was now high enough to throw sunlight in through the flier's side hatch, and he was obviously feeling the heat because he'd drawn his legs up into what shade remained.

I offered the water again. No response.

'Tell me your name,' I said.

His jaw clenched.

'Tell me your name,' I repeated, using the will now.

He shuddered. 'Eino Goran.' His voice was dry and slurry.

'And before it was Eino Goran, your name was what?'

'Nngh...'

His resolve was strong. The Vessorine were a blunt race, with a high frequency of untouchables. Part of their martial training was to learn methods of resisting interrogation, and at first I thought he might have some well-developed mind-trick to wall out psychic impulses.

But as I questioned him further, I began to suspect it was more to do with the emplated identity he was wearing. I'd tried to pick it away, but it still wouldn't budge. Crude and simple it may have been, but it was psychically riveted into place. Part of that profound fixture, I was sure, was acting as a screen. It wasn't that he wouldn't answer. He couldn't.

'Gregor?'

I looked out of the hatch and saw that Crezia had come out into the yard. 'Gregor, what the hell are you doing?'

I got out of the flier and drew her back towards the garden doors. The Vessorine had undoubtedly heard her use my name. It couldn't be helped.

'That man's tied up like damn cygnid!' she said.

'That man would kill me given the chance. He's tied up for all our sakes. I have to ask him questions.'

She glared at me. She had changed into a long gown of blue satin with an epinchire trim. Her straw-blonde hair was tightly braided behind her head and held up by two golden pins. She was beautiful and haughty, just as I remembered her. Crezia had high cheekbones, a generous mouth, and pale brown eyes given to expressions of passion and intelligence. The only passion I had seen in them since my arrival had been fury.

'Like a cygnid,' she repeated. 'I won't have it. Not in my house.'

'Then what do you suggest? Have you a secure room, one that can be locked from outside?'

'Provide you with a cell for him? Pah!' she scoffed.

'It's that or the flier.'

She thought about it. 'I'll have Phabes clear out a box room upstairs.'

'No windows.'

'They all have damn windows! But the room I'm thinking of has just a small vane-light. Not big enough for anyone to get through.'

'Thank you.'

'I want to check him over.'

It was no good arguing. She inspected the man carefully.

'Don't be alarmed. I'm Doctor Cr–'

'He really doesn't need to know your name. Or mine. Think about it.'

She drew a deep breath. 'I am a doctor. I'm only going to check on your health. Do you have a name?'

He shook his head.

'He's using the name Eino Goran.'

'I see. Eino, this situation is unpleasant, but if you co-operate with me, and with Gr... with my associate here, it will work out for the best. Soon.'

Associate. I could feel the spiteful relish she put into that word.

Crezia looked at me disapprovingly. 'He needs to drink and eat. Drink particularly, in this heat.'

'Tell him, not me.'

'You need to drink, Eino. If you don't drink, I'll have to put you on a fluid drip.'

He allowed her to feed him the dish, and sipped slowly.

'Very good,' she said. Then to me, 'His bonds are far too tight.'

'That's not going to change.'

'Then get him up and walk him round a little. Tie his hands the other way.'

'Later perhaps. If you knew what he was, what he has done, you wouldn't be so humane.'

'I'm a officer of the Medicae Imperialis. It never matters what they've done.'

We went back into the drawing room.

'His identity is emplated. I need to get past the barriers.'

'To find out who he really is?'

'To find out who he's working for.'

'I see.' She sat down and bit at a fingernail. She always did that when she was troubled.

'You have medical stocks here. Zendocaine? Vulgate oxybarbital?'

'You're joking?'

I shook my head and sat down opposite her. 'Deadly serious. I need a psychoactive or at least an opiate or barbiturate to loosen his will power.'

'No. Absolutely no way.'

'Crezia...'

'I will not be party to torture!'

'It is not torture. I'm not going to hurt him. I just need to open his mind.'

'No.'

'Crezia, I am going to do it. I have the mandate of the Holy Inquisition to perform interrogation, and these circumstances permit me an even greater latitude of emergency powers. Wouldn't you rather it be done under your expert supervision?'

In the latter part of the afternoon, we brought the Vessorine inside, and put him in the box-room Phabes had cleared. There was nothing in the room but a bedframe and mattress. I removed his blindfold and then covered him with the autopistol as Aemos removed his bindings.

Crezia looked on, pointedly saying nothing about the weapon.

'Unfasten your tunic again,' I said.

Crezia started to say something but I cut her off. 'You'll need to get at his arm, won't you, doctor?'

There was another reason for getting him to disrobe. Aemos carefully studied the man's tattoos, making notes. The Vessorine just stood there, stripped to the waist, sullen. He refused to make eye contact.

I noticed he was slender but whipcord tough. The marks of old scars dotted his torso. I'd taken him to be a reasonably young man, but either he was older than he looked, or his short life had been barbarically tough.

Aemos finished. 'I'll get it translated properly. But it's what I thought it was.' He turned to go downstairs. I stopped him and passed him the pistol.

'Cover him, please.'

Aemos waited while I re-tied the merc's hands. I tied them in front of his body now, and then lashed his ankles together and tied off the end of that cord to the bedstead.

'Sit down,' I told him. He sat. I took the weapon back from Aemos, tucked it into my belt and sent him on his way.

'If you will, doctor?'

She looked at me. 'Just like that? Don't you want to give him the chance to volunteer first?'

There was no point, but I wanted to keep Crezia on side.

'Tell me your name,' I said.

'Eino Goran.'

'Tell me your real name.'

'Eino Goran.'

I shot a warning look at Crezia and used the will. I focused it in the Vessorine's direction so she would be spared, but it still made her shiver.

He gurgled a non-verbal response.

'Now, please.'

Crezia quickly injected twenty millilitres of zendocaine into the man's upper arm and drew back. Zendocaine is a psychoactive, a synaptic enhancer that causes a flurry of cortex activity disguised by a soothing opiate. The man coughed, and after a few moments his eyes took on a glassy sheen.

Crezia checked his blood pressure.

'Fine,' she said.

I placed my hand on the man's temple, and eased my mind into his. He was relaxed and offered no resistance, but his mind was lively. An ideal balance if I was going to prise off his emplated identity.

I tried a few test questions, both verbally and mentally. His answers were slurred.

'What is your name?'

'Eino Goran.'

'What is your age?'

'Forty sstannard.'

'What is your height?'

'Two anna third kwen.' That was a good sign. I had no idea what a 'kwen' was, but I'd take a bet it was a Vessorine measure.

'Where are we?' I continued.

'Inna room.'

'Where is the room?'

'Inna house. Dunno.'

'On what world?'

'Gudrun.'

'What colour is the sky?'

'Hnn, this sky?'

'Yes. What colour is this sky?'

'Blue.'

'What other sky might I have meant?'

'Dunno.'

'What is my name?'

'Gregor.'

'How do you know that?' I asked, without reacting.

'She call it you.'

Crezia glanced at me nervously.

'Who does that make me?'

'Dunno.'

'Who might I be? Who do you suppose?'

'Eisssnhorn.'

'Why do you know that name?'

'Job.'

'What job?'

'Be merc work. Pay job.'

'Tell me more about that.'

'Dunno more.'

'What is your name?' I asked the mercenary again.

'Tol' you. Eino Goran.'

'Where are you from?'

'Hesperus.'

'What colour is the sky?'

'Blue. Defn'ly.'

'What is your name?'

'Eino. Goran. Eino Goran. Eino Goran.'

The words came out like a mountain stream, overlapping, light, without any meaning.

'Where are you from?' I went on.

'Hesperus... uh. Dunno.'

'What does the tattoo on your upper body signify?'

'Bond.'

'In what language?'

'Dunno.'

'Is it a repatriation bond?'

'Uh huh.'

'That's a mercenary custom, isn't it?'

'Uhm.'

'It states, for any captor to see, that if you are returned to your home world, or an agency of your home world unharmed, a bond will be paid. Is that correct?'

'Yeah.'

'Are you a mercenary?'

'Yessss.'

'What colour is the sky?'

'Blue. No, yes... blue.'

'What is your name?'

'Uh...'

'I asked you, what is your name?'

'Wait... I know this. Be hard to think...' His eyes rolled in their sockets.

'What is your name?'

'Dunno.'

'Are you a mercenary?'

'Yeah...'

'Was I your target last night?'

'Yeah.'

'Who was your target last night?'

'Eisenhorn.'

'Am I Eisenhorn?'

'Yes.' He looked at me, but his eyes remained glassy, unfocussed.

'What were your orders?'

'Chill 'em all. Burn the place.'

'Where did the orders come from?'

'Clansire Etrik.'

'Is clansire a rank?'

'Yeah.'

'Is Clansire Etrik a Vessorine janissary?'

'Yes.'

'Are you a Vessorine janissary?'

'Yes.'

'What is your name, janissary?'

'Sire! Vammeko Tarl, sire!'

He paused and blinked, not sure what he had just said. Crezia was staring at me.

'You're doing very well, Tarl,' I said.

'Uh huh.'

The emplate was shredding away from his mind like damp paper now. I went in for the kill with my full willpower now his mind was open.

'Where were you hired?'

'Twenty weeks ago. Nnngh. Twenty weeks.'

'Where was that?'

'Heveron.'

'What were you doing there?'

'Looking for work.'

'Before that?'

'Gnnh... be hired for a border war. Local governor hired us. But the war fizzled out.'

'And you found a new client?'

'The Clansire did. Good pay, for a longterm hire. Off-world, transit paid.'

'To do what?'

'They didn't tell us. Shipped us off to someplace.'

'Where?'

'Gudrun?'

'Was it Gudrun?'

'Yeah...' A shudder went through him.

'And the job, in outline?'

'Hardware and fliers provided by client. Told to hit this place on a headland. Chill everyone.'

'Whose place was this?'

'Be someone called Eisenhorn.'

'How many men were hired?'

'All of us. The entire clan.'

'And how many men is that?'

'Eight hundred.'

I paused. Eight hundred?

'All for this job on Gudrun?'

'No. Be seventy of us for that. The rest for other jobs.'

'What other jobs?'

'Wasn't told. Gah... my head aches.'

Crezia touched my sleeve. 'You must stop,' she whispered. 'He's beginning to hyperventilate.'

'Just a few more questions,' I hissed back.

I looked at Tarl. He was sweating and rocking slightly in his seat as his breaths came quick and fast.

'Where did you stage before the raid?'

'Nnh... Piterro.' A small island in the Bay of Bisheen. Interesting.

'What was the name of the ship that brought you here?'

'The *Beltrand*.'

'What was the name of your client?'

'Dunno.'

'Did you ever meet him?'

'No.'

'Did you ever meet any of his agents?'

'Yeah... uhhnn! It hurts!'

'Gregor!'

'Not yet! Tarl, who was the agent?'

'Woman. Psyker. She came to emplate us the night before the raid.'

'She personally fixed your identity veils?'

'Yes.'

'What was her name?'

'Call herself Marla. Marla Tarray.'

'Picture her in your mind, Tarl,' I ordered. I got a brief but vivid flash of a sharp featured woman with long, straight black hair. Her eyes were what I remembered most. Kohl-edged, large and green like jade. She seemed to look into my head. I snatched back.

'Are you all right?' Crezia asked.

'Yes, I'm fine.'

'We're going to stop now,' she told me straight. 'Right now.'

'Right now?'

'That's what I said.'

The janissary had sunk back on the bed, his skin puffy and damp. He closed his eyes and moaned.

'He's coming down. Now he's feeling the disruptions of your mind probe.' I could see she was shaking slightly. She'd felt them too, second hand.

'One last question.'

'I said we were stopping now and I meant it. I have to stabilise him.'

I held up my hand. 'One more. While he's still open. We come back later or tomorrow and he'll have closed up. And you don't want to do this again, do you?'

'No,' she relented.

'Tarl? Tarl?'

'Go 'way.'

'What was the name of your client? What was the name of Marla Tarray's boss?'

The Vessorine murmured something.

'What was that?' whispered Crezia. 'I didn't catch it.'

I had. Not verbally, but in my mind. Something blocked out, something he hadn't been able to say even before if he'd wanted to. As he collapsed into psi-fugue, the last shreds of his emplated veil melted away and the final name tumbled out.

'He said Khanjar,' I told her. 'Khanjar the Sharp.'

ELEVEN

Adept Cielo
Death notices
Dangerous kindness

I woke before dawn. It was still twilight outside, and the curtains of my room swayed in the cold breeze.

I got dressed, and went downstairs. On the way, I checked on Tarl. He was profoundly asleep, curled on his bed. Crezia had made sure he was alright, given him a secondary, mild opiate to reduce his trauma and covered him with a blanket. He'd been out for the best part of fourteen hours. Crezia had almost flipped out with fear when she discovered the captive in her box room was a Vessorine janissary.

I checked Tarl's bindings, and he groaned softly as I disturbed the blanket.

Aemos was already up. Drinking caffeine he had brewed himself, he sat in Crezia's study, listening to the early morning vox broadcasts.

'Couldn't you sleep?' I asked.

'I slept fine, Gregor. But I never sleep for long.'

I fetched another cup and poured caffeine from his pot.

'There's nothing about us,' he said, gesturing to the vox.

'Nothing?'

'It's most perturbatory. Not a word, not even on the Arbites band.'

'Someone managed to hire eight hundred Vessorine killers, Uber. They have clout. The news has been withheld. Or censored.'

'The others will know.'

'How do you mean?'

'Fischig, Nayl. The moment they don't get a response from Spaeton House, they'll know something is up.'

'I hope so. What did you make of our friend's tattoos?'

'Base Futu, just as I supposed. I cross-checked it using the doctor's cogitator.' He took out a note-slate and adjusted his eye-glasses. 'This mark bears witness that Vammeko Tarl, a janissary, is owned by the Clan Etrik, and a bond of ten thousand zkell will be paid for his repatriation. He is of flesh made and his flesh speaks for him.'

Aemos looked up at me. 'Strange practice.'

'Totally in keeping with the Vessorine mindset. Janissaries are objects. Material items. You might as well keep a cannon or a tank as a prisoner of war. They have no political affiliation, no loyalties within the particular frame of whatever conflict they're involved with. No use as a hostage. Putting that little incentive on each one makes things clear and simple. Puts a simple price on the matter and dissuades a captor from simply killing them.'

'How much is ten thousand zkell, then?'

'Enough, I should think.'

'What do we do with him when we leave?'

Now there was a question.

I went into the kitchen to brew more caffeine and hunt for bread, and found Crezia juicing ploins and mountain tar-berries in a chrome press. Her hair was loose and she was wearing a short, cream silk houserobe.

'Oh!' she said as I walked in.

'I'm sorry,' I said, retreating.

'Oh, don't bother, Gregor. You've seen me in a lot less.'

'Yes, I have.'

'Yes, you have. Fruit juice?'

'I was looking for caffeine, actually.'

'How could I forget? Breakfasts on the terrace... me with my fruit and grain-cakes, you with your caffeine and eggs and salt-pork.'

I filled a pan from the sink pump and lit the stove. Then I rinsed out the pot. 'I suppose now's your opportunity to tell me "I told you so",' I said.

'What do you mean?'

'You always said fruit and grain-loaf was the path to a healthy life, remember? You used to go on about diet and fibre and all sorts. Told me my intake of caffeine and alcohol and red meat would kill me.'

'I take it back.'

'Really?'

'It won't be your diet that kills you, Gregor,' she said, suddenly biting at a fingernail.

'You were right, of course. Look at you.'

'I'd rather not,' she said, crushing a ploin with excessive force.

'You're as lovely as the day I first met you.'

'The day you first met me, Gregor Eisenhorn, you were half-comatose with anaesthetic and I was wearing a scrub mask.'

'Ah. How could I forget?'

She looked at me witheringly.

'Still,' I said. 'I'm not lying. I treated you badly. I'm still treating you badly. Someone like you doesn't deserve that.'

She tasted her pulpy juice drink. 'I won't argue with any of that. But... it's nice to hear you admit it.'

'It's the truth. So's the fact you're still lovely.'

She sighed. 'Juvenat programs are all easy to administer. I look this way thanks to Imperial science, not fruit juice.'

'I still believe in fruit juice.'

She grinned. 'You don't look so bad yourself, red meat and caffeine considered.'

The pan began to boil. 'I feel about a thousand years old next to you. Life has not treated me kindly.'

'Oh, I don't know. There's a nobility about your scars. Something very masculine about the way you wear your age well.'

I started to look in cupboards for the ground beans.

'That canister there,' she said. 'The chicory blend you always used. I've never lost the taste for it.'

I took the tin canister and spooned out several measures into the pot. 'Crezia,' I said, 'you should have let go of me a long time ago. I was never any good for you. I was never any good for anyone, truth be told.'

'I know,' she said. 'But I can't. That's just the way of things.'

I poured the boiling water into the pot and let it stand.

'How's Alizebeth?' she asked suddenly.

I had been sort of waiting for that. I had broken my long relationship with Crezia Berschilde in the end because of

Bequin. Even though I knew Alizebeth and I could never be together in any way except friends, I knew I would never get past my love for her. It was too much in the way, and that could never be fair on Crezia.

Twenty-five years before, in that very house, I had told her as much. And walked away.

'She's dying,' I said.

Crezia put her glass down suddenly. 'Dying?'

'Or already dead.' I told her what had happened on Durer.

'Oh, God-Emperor,' she said. 'You should go to her.'

'What could I do?'

'Be there,' she said firmly. 'Be there and tell her before it's too late.'

'How do you know I haven't already told her?'

'Because I know you, Gregor. Too well.'

'I... well...'

'The two of you never... I mean?'

'No. She's an untouchable. I'm a psyker. That's the way it works.'

'And you never told her?'

'She knows.'

'Of course she knows! But you never told her?'

'No.'

She embraced me. I pulled her close. I thought of all the things I had never done, or never started, or never finished. Then I remembered all the things I had done and could never undo.

'The last thing you want is me, Crezia,' I whispered into her hair.

'I'll be the judge of that.'

The kitchen door burst open and Aemos limped in. Crezia and I let each other go.

We could have been doing anything for all Aemos cared. 'You have to come and hear this, Gregor,' he said.

He had been listening to the Sub-sector Service on the vox, news from all around the Helican sub, some of it days or weeks old. By the time we were standing around the old set, the news had moved on to stock reports and shipping forecasts.

'Well?' I asked.

'A report from Messina, Gregor. The upper levels of spire eleven of Messina Prime were destroyed twenty-four hours ago by what was cited as a recidivist blast.'

I went cold. Spire eleven, Messina Prime. That was the location of the residence I had leased for the use of the Distaff. Nayl and Begundi had taken Alizebeth and Kara there. For safety.

'The report said that over ten thousand lives had been lost,' Aemos murmured. 'The Messina Arbites are hunting for suspects, but it's been attributed to a radical free Messina outfit.'

I sat down, trembling. Crezia crouched beside me, hugging me. The Distaff... gone? Bequin... Nayl... Kara Swole... Begundi?

It was too much.

I realised why Khanjar the Sharp had hired so many Vessorine janissaries. Multiple strikes, multiple worlds. What else had this Khanjar hit? What other pain had he already caused me?

Who else had he killed?

'What's going on?' Eleena asked, coming in, rubbing her sleepy eyes.

I paced the house and the courtyard garden. Two or three times, I started up towards the box room, the autopistol in my hand. Damn the bond! I would have vengeance!

Each time, I turned back. I'd counselled Medea against vengeance, and so I should listen to my own good advice. Killing Tarl would be like breaking a sword. What was it Medea had said? *It's a displacement activity. It's something you can lock on to and do because you can't do the thing you really want to do. I needed something, and it wasn't payback.*

So what was it? I needed to get back in the game. I needed to round up my allies. I needed to discover who Khanjar the Sharp was.

And then, damn the advice I had given Medea, I needed to destroy him.

At nine sharp, Adept Cielo arrived with his clerk, having been summoned the day before. Both were hooded and cloaked, which I suppose was their idea of subtlety.

I met with them in the drawing room, with Crezia in attendance. She had dressed in a trouser suit of beige murray.

Adept Cielo was an elderly, experienced astropath, one of the best the Guild House in Ravello had to offer.

'I take it, sir, this is a private matter?'

'It is.'

'Are you purchasing my services in cash?'

'No, adept, by direct fund transfer. I have a confidential message service which I wish to use. I expect the utmost discretion.'

'You have the guarantee of the Guild, sir,' said Cielo. His clerk opened a data-slate and offered me the thumb-print scanner.

I pressed my thumb against it and then entered my code.

'Ah,' said Cielo, as the slate chimed and displayed a readout. 'That's all sorted out. Your accounts have released the funds. Everything's in order, Mr Eising. Let us proceed.'

* * *

Of course, I wasn't using any accounts that were connected with the person of Gregor Eisenhorn. I had good reason to suspect my finances were under observation, if not frozen. But I wasn't even going to try, because that would let my enemy know that someone with the authority to access Gregor Eisenhorn's accounts was still alive, and it would be comparatively simple to trace that access.

As with the various properties I owned, I had resources under other identities. 'Gorton Eising' had several holdings with the Imperial Thracian treasury, with enough funds for my current needs.

I had set up the confidential message service many years before so that I could send and receive messages without using my real identity. It was essentially an automatically maintained mailbox account that I could access, using an astropath, from any location. I could send messages through it, and read any communiqués that had been posted to it. The service was registered under the name 'Aegis'.

When Cielo accessed the Aegis account, there were no communiqués waiting to be read. Composing the contents in Glossia, I had Cielo send warning messages to Fischig on Durer, to Messina, to agents of my organisation on Thracian Primaris, Hesperus, Sarum and Cartol. I used the signature 'Rosethorn'. I also sent a private, coded, anonymous transmission to a friend outside the Helican sub-sector. It was a single word message that read 'Sanctum'.

I would wait for responses before I contacted my Lord Rorken. I wanted to take things one step at a time. Not for the first time in my career, I wanted to stay out of sight, except to friends.

Of course, even sending communiqués in another name was risky. Many or all of the people I was trying to contact might be under surveillance themselves – if they hadn't already been eliminated. But Glossia was a private code. Even if my messages were intercepted, they would be impossible to decipher.

The first responses arrived by noon the next day. Cielo's clerk came up from the Guild House to deliver them.

One was a message from Fischig, in Glossia, that essentially told me he was already en route from Durer and would arrive at Gudrun in about twenty days. I dispatched a reply that emphasised caution and told him to contact me when he was close.

The message 'Sanctum' had been answered with the words 'Sanctum arising, in fifteen'. There was no ident on the communiqué, and the source was deep space.

The clerk then passed me a data-slate. 'The communiqués to Messina, Thracian Primaris, Hesperus and Cartol have all been returned as undeliverable. That is strange. The message from Hesperus has a statement from the local Arbites attached, recommending you get in touch with them directly. There has been no response from Sarum.'

After the clerk had left, I discussed it with Aemos. He was as alarmed as I was. 'Undeliverable? Most perturbatory. And the interest of the Arbites is disturbing.'

'What progress with the names?' I asked. He had been at work on Crezia's codifier all morning.

'Nothing. No listing for a Marla Tarray and nothing on any Khanjar the Sharp. A khanjar is a blade weapon, of course. A curved dagger from ancient Terra. The word is occurs in several Imperium cultures.'

'Can you resource further?'

'Not using this machine. But your doctor friend is going

to walk me to the universitariate this afternoon and get me access to their main data engines.'

He was gone for hours, until late in the evening. Crezia had teaching duties to perform, and Phabes was all but invisible. I was left alone with Eleena.

I checked the prisoner. He was awake but unresponsive. Crezia had left him a tray of food and some water before leaving, but it was untouched. I tried a few questions but he didn't stir. He was zoned out in a post-interrogation stupor.

Medea was still sleeping, but her life signs was good and there was no trace of post-operative infection. I kissed her forehead gently and went back to the kitchen.

Eleena was seated at the refectory table, one third down a bottle of fine Hesperean claret. Without asking, she fetched me a glass and poured me some.

I sat down with her. The kitchen doors were open, affording us a cool evening breeze and a fine view out over the courtyard to the Itervalle. The mountain was ochre in the setting sun, and even as we watched it gently shifted colour, becoming russet, then almost scarlet, then ultramarine.

'Have you eaten?' Eleena asked.

'No. Have you?'

'I'm not very hungry,' she replied, and drank a mouthful of wine.

'I'm sorry, Eleena,' I said.

'Sorry, sir? Why?'

'Sorry that you should be in the middle of all this. It's an unpleasant business and costing us all dear.'

She smiled. 'You got me out of Spaeton alive, sir. For that I'm thankful.'

'I only wish I could have got everyone out alive.'

She shrugged. I could tell she was haunted by the killing she had seen. Sastre's brave sacrifice in particular had scarred her. Eleena Koi was only about twenty-five, just a girl, and a new recruit to the Distaff. She'd not seen any active service in the field yet. She'd been posted to Spaeton as resident untouchable – something the Distaff regarded as an easy job – to get her acclimatised to the work. Some acclimatisation.

'If you'd like to leave, I think that would be all right. I could arrange some adequate papers, some money. You could get off-world, to safety.'

Eleena looked almost offended. 'I am a contracted untouchable in the pay of the Distaff, sir. Perhaps, Emperor bless me, the last one alive. I knew service to an inquisitor would be dangerous when I started. I'm under no illusions.'

'Even so–'

'No, sir. I'm strong enough for this. It may be extreme, but it's what I was hired to do. Besides...'

'Besides what?'

'Well, for one thing, we know that the enemy has at least one powerful psyker in his pay. That means you'll need an untouchable.'

'True.'

'And... I think I'd feel safer sticking with you, sir. If I went off on my own, I'd be looking over my shoulder for the rest of my life.'

'Thank you, Eleena. You could stop calling me "sir" now, though. If what we've been through these last few days can't be counted as a bonding process, I don't know what can.'

'Right,' she smiled. It was a change to see a smile on her face. She was tall and overly thin, in my opinion, always seeming edgy and nervous. The smile suited her.

Neither of us said anything for a few moments.

'So, what should I call you?' she asked eventually.

We chatted idly for a while longer, until the Itervalle had become black and the sky Imperial blue. The stars were out.

'Do we have a plan?' she asked.

'Theoretically, we find out who is set so murderously against us and hunt him down. Practically, that means staying here, out of sight, for a while at least, then getting off planet.'

'How long for that, do you think?'

'My preferred means of planet exit will be available in fifteen days.'

She refilled our glasses. 'I like that. I like it when you sound like everything's under control.'

'So do I,' I chuckled.

'So... once we're off-planet, what then? Practically speaking?'

'It depends on a few things. What we manage to turn up in the next two weeks. Whether I dare correspond with the ordos.'

'You don't think the Inquisition is involved, do you?'

'Not at all,' I replied. It wasn't a lie, because I was sure we weren't in conflict with any external agency, but it wasn't entirely the truth either. I had been in the job long enough to know that nothing is out of the question. But there was no point alarming her. 'It's simply that I think our enemy is so well co-ordinated, so well provided, that he's watching everything. If I contact the Inquisition, it could betray us.'

I took up my glass and drank a good measure of the fine red wine. 'So, if nothing turns up, when we leave here... it's open. There are places we could run to find security, friends I could call upon. Our best bet might be to disappear and stay hidden until our plans are formalised. But I'm torn. I'd like to head to Messina. If there's a chance any of them are alive...'

Apart from roaming field agents engaged on diverse tasks, the Distaff headquarters on Messina represented my only other base of operations. If it was gone, and Spaeton House too, I was cut adrift.

'I had many friends at the Distaff Hall. I hope they're all right.' She looked at the table and fiddled with her glass. 'I suppose you're most concerned about Madam Bequin.'

'Well–' I began.

'She being such an old friend and colleague of yours, I mean. And that she was badly hurt on Durer. And everyone knows...' She stopped suddenly.

'Knows what, Eleena?'

'Well, that you love her.'

'Everyone knows, do they?'

'You can't hide something like that. I've seen you together. You adore each other.'

'But–'

'You're a psyker and she's one of us. I know, I know. That doesn't mean you don't love her, all the same.'

She looked at me and blushed. 'This wine!' she said. 'I've said far too much, haven't I?'

'No, Eleena,' said Crezia. Neither of us had heard her come in. 'Talk some sense into him, will you? He has to go back and see her. It's the right thing.'

Crezia was dressed in her formal tutorial robes. She took a glass from the rack, came to the table and, finding the bottle was empty, set about opening another.

'How was your day?' I asked, trying to change the subject.

'I spent four hours lecturing the sophomore class on the principles of thoracic palpation. I've never seen such a crowd of ill-prepared dolts. When I got one fellow up for a practical, he took hold of the volunteer subject's thigh. How do you think my day was?'

She sat down with us at the table. 'I looked in on our guest.

I'm concerned about his condition. He hasn't taken any food or drink, and he's only marginally responsive. I think you may have damaged him with your mental probings.'

'Either that,' I said, 'or he's having an adverse reaction to the drugs.'

'Possibly. If he's the same in the morning, I'll run some bloodwork on him. Whatever, he's not well and he's not comfortable. There's severe lividity in his hands and feet. You tied those bonds so damn tight.'

'As tight as they needed to be, Crezia. He's a Vessorine janissary paid to murder me, don't forget.'

'Shut up and pour me a drink.'

The moment Aemos came in, past ten o'clock, I could tell something was wrong. He was carrying a small pile of data-slates and accepted a drink from Eleena without question, which was unusual for him.

His hand was trembling as he raised the glass to sip. Even Crezia could see this was not like him.

'Well, old friend?' I asked.

'I spent hours resourcing those names, Gregor. Still nothing on this Khanjar, though I assembled a list of planets that still use the word.' He slid a slate across to me.

'Marla Tarray... a little more success there. A Marla Tari was arrested by the Arbites on Hallowcan five years ago for participating in cult activity. She was pending trial when she escaped custody. She turned up twice more: on Felthon, where she was a known associate of the cult leader, Berrikin Paswold; and on Sanseeta, where she was wanted in connection with the murder of Hierarch Sansum and five Ministorum clerics. The Inquisition also has a warrant out for her restraint as a suspected rogue psyker.'

'So, an active participant in cult activity, then?' I looked at the extracts Aemos had put on a slate. They didn't tell me much more. If I contacted the Inquisition, they'd have a more complete file. Despite the risks, I felt inclined to get in touch with Rorken.

'If it's the same woman,' he replied.

There was no picture, but the physical description matched my mind's retrieved image.

'What's her background?'

'There's nothing on that... except that when questioned during her detention on Hallowcan, she claimed to be thirty-seven and stated her birthworld was Gudrun.'

'Interesting...' I said. 'We should check her details against the planetary census and–'

'I believe you pay me to be thorough, Gregor,' said Aemos, churlishly. 'I've already done that. There is no record of her here. In fact, there is no one on Gudrun with the surname Tarray or Tari. The surname does, however, occur on other worlds. Too many, in fact, to be of any help.'

'So, savant,' said Crezia, 'what's really troubling you?'

Aemos took another glug of wine and pushed a slate into the centre of the table. 'I was running out of options with the names, so I turned to something else. I inspected the news registers from across the sub-sector, hunting for key words. You won't like it.'

I read down the slate, my heart turning to cold stone. It showed me bulletin reports of incidents from several planets in the sub. Just little items, most of which wouldn't even have made column space beyond the regional news wires. Certainly, the events reported wouldn't have been planetary news, and definitely not interplanetary. Aemos had only found them because he had been specifically looking, and trawling the Imperium's news wire data compendium.

The first report was of the explosion on Messina. Messina Prime, the main hive, spire eleven. The blast had occurred at ten fifty, local. That was chilling. By my estimation, the raid on Spaeton had commenced at precisely the same time, given sidereal adjustments. The explosion had incinerated the uppermost ten levels of the spire. The death toll was put at eleven thousand six hundred. The Lord Governor had declared a state of emergency.

There was a long appended list of properties and business destroyed. Amongst them halfway down the second page, was the Thorn Institute, the name by which the Distaff had been publically known.

No survivors. I supposed it could have been a coincidence, but I didn't believe in them. Which meant that my foe, this Khanjar the Sharp, had not hesitated to exterminate thousands of civilians just to take out the Distaff.

The news file stated that a proscribed movement calling itself the Scions of Messina had claimed responsibility. That group, it said, struck for Messina's independence from the Imperium.

Which was frankly rubbish. Messina was as Imperial as a planet-culture got.

The second report listed on the slate was filed from Cartol. A family touring Kona Province on vacation had been found murdered by unknown gunmen. Two men and three women. Identities were to follow as soon as they had been established. Authorities on Cartol estimated the time of death at between ten and midnight, two days back.

I had sent my agent Leres Phinton, along with Biron Fakal, Loys Naran and two untouchables, to Cartol five months earlier, to gather evidence concerning a death cult in the Kona region. They had reported back regularly. Dear God-Emperor...

I scrolled to the next item. From Thracian Primaris. A private residence in Hive Sixty-Two had been firebombed just before midnight. Eight dead, unidentified. The location was listed as Sixty-two, Up-Hive, level 114, 871... which was the address of the subsidiary office I maintained on the capital world of the Helican sub-sector. Barned Ferrikal, who had been with me for thirty years, ran that place with a staff of seven.

The next. Hesperus. Two men killed in a firefight with juve-gangs. Just before midnight a week ago. They had wandered into the wrong part of town, an Arbites spokeman said.

Lutor Witte and Gan Blaek, two of the most capable undercover agents I ran, had been operating on Hesperus for a year, seeking to uncover a Tzeentchian cult that was preying on the juve population of the underhives.

Next, Sarum, capital world of the Antimar sub. One of my most promising pupils, Interrogator Devra Shiborr, had gone there under my instruction eight months prior to infiltrate and expose a chaotifiliac ring in the central university. She had posed as Doctor Zeyza Bajj, a historian from Punzel.

The news item recorded the death, apparently by suicide, of the promising academic Bajj. Her body, dead for about eight hours, had been discovered in her bathroom at choir bell this same morning.

And then the last, the most shocking. From the Sameter Global News Wire, posted a week ago. The residential home of Inquisitor Nathun Inshabel had been attacked by an unidentified enemy and obliterated. Inshabel was listed amongst the dead.

* * *

I sat back. They were all looking at me. Aemos was leaning his chin on his hands and the two women were staring with anxious patience.

'They're all dead,' I said. 'Everyone. Every thread of my staff operation. My home here, the Distaff headquarters, and all the agents I had on active work in the field. Every one, everything. All hit at effectively the same hour on the same day of the week.'

My voice tailed off. I was too deeply shocked. Crezia poured me a glass of amasec and took one herself.

All of it, gone. The operation I had spent decades building up, the friends and allies I had drawn together... destroyed in one night. All my visible resources had been identified, targeted and eliminated. Apart from dear Fischig, slogging his way back to meet us, we were all that was left.

I felt disconnected more than anything else. The network of intelligence and active personnel I had built up since the start of my career had been brutally taken from me.

I was alone.

I wanted nothing... nothing more than to see this Khanjar the Sharp face to face and make a reckoning.

I went to bed, the amasec untouched, and slept fitfully. In the small hours, I woke painfully from a dream I couldn't quite remember at first. As I lay in the darkness, the details slowly returned to me. I had been dreaming about the escape from Spaeton. Medea and Jekud Vance had been calling out to me, begging to be rescued. I remembered the sensation of taking Medea's hand, and clutching out at Vance, who couldn't quite reach me. The janissaries shot him down, cutting his body apart with las-fire. His psychic death scream had cut into my mind like a hot wire, and that's what had woken me.

Hadn't it?

* * *

I woke again at four. The night was quiet except for the click of the mountain crickets.

Something was wrong. I got up, slid the autopistol out from under the mattress and crept out into the landing.

I could hear Aemos snoring in his room, and the distant sighs of Crezia in slumber.

Eleena's door was open.

I looked in. The bed was empty and the quilt cast off onto the floor.

I edged down the corridor with my back to the wall and my weapon raised in both hands, almost as if I was praying. There was a light shafting out from under the next door. The bathroom.

I heard water gurgle and light suddenly flooded me as the door opened.

I aimed the gun.

'Oh god! Golden Throne, sir! What the hell are you d–'

I slapped my hand across Eleena's startled mouth and pulled her into the shadows.

'You scared the hell out of me,' she whispered once I relaxed my grip.

'Sorry.'

'I was just going to the bathroom.'

'Sorry. Something's wrong.'

'Gregor? What's the noise?' Crezia's voice floated down the landing.

'Get back in your room!' I hissed.

In a typically Crezia Berschilde manner, she did the opposite. She was pulling on her silk robe as she padded down to join us.

'What is damn well going on?'

'For once, just shut up, Crezia,' I snapped.

'Well, excuse me all to hell.'

I pushed them both behind me and crept down towards the door of the box room.

'Nice rump,' said Crezia. I was only wearing a wrap.

'Will you be serious just for a minute?' I snarled back.

'Please, doctor,' urged Eleena. 'This is serious.'

The box room door was shut and dark.

'See?' said Crezia. 'No problem.'

I felt the doorknob and realised it was loose. Crezia jumped as I kicked the door in, and aimed my gun at the bed.

The empty bed.

Eleena turned on the light. The wispy, fraying strands of Tarl's bindings were still tied to the bedstead. He'd bitten through them or tugged them off.

'Golden Throne, he's gone!'

'Oh no...' Crezia murmured. 'I only loosened his bonds a little.'

'You did what?'

'I told you! I told you I was worried about the constriction. The lividity in his hands and his–'

'You didn't tell me you'd slackened them off!' I raged.

'I thought you'd understood what I meant!'

I ran downstairs. The unlit hall was pale with moonlight that slanted in through the half-open front doors.

'He can't have gone far! What does it matter any way?' Crezia called after me.

I stepped out into the street. There was no sign of any one or anything. The cool shadows of the night spread fluidly across the flagstones.

Tarl, I was sure, was long gone.

I went back inside and Crezia turned on the hall lights.

And screamed.

Phabes was bent over in the corner, like a man who has

fallen asleep sitting up. But he was very dead. His throat had been slashed. A wide pool of blood was leaking outwards slowly from his hunched form.

'Do you see now, Crezia? Do you?' I yelled up at her.

Tarl was loose. He knew who I was and where I was. We had to leave.

Fast.

TWELVE

Into the night, into the mountains
The Trans-Atenate Express
A prompt from the dead

'No,' said Crezia. 'No. No way. No.'

'This isn't up for debate, Crezia. It's not a suggestion, it's a... an instruction.'

'How dare you order me around like one of your staff lackeys, Eisenhorn. I am not leaving!'

I opened my mouth, then closed it again. The brutal murder of her man Phabes was causing her great distress. Getting through to her would be hard.

I turned to Aemos and Eleena. 'Get dressed. Collect up everything and stow it in the flier. I want to be away from here in under half an hour.' They both hurried away.

It was difficult to know how long the janissary had been gone. Phabes, whose body Aemos had covered with a sheet, was still quite warm, so I reckoned Tarl only had an hour's head start, ninety minutes worst case. Given his Vessorine pragmatism, I figured he had headed straight for a vox-station to report our location to his brethren. That's what I'd have done in his position. He could have tried to kill me himself, but by then he knew not to underestimate my abilities. There was a decent chance I'd have taken him down, in which case the secret of my location would never have got out.

No, he'd gone to find means of sending the message. It was impossible to know how close elements of his party were, but if we were still here in sixty minutes' time, I didn't much rate our chances.

It also occurred to me that once he'd got his message off safely, he'd be clear to come back and have a try at me himself.

I took Crezia by the hand and led her back upstairs. Her eyes were puffy and red, and she was a little vacant with shock. She sat on the end of my bed as I got dressed.

'If I could just go, Crezia, I would,' I said softly, finding a fresh shirt. 'If it was just a matter of walking away and removing all my crap from your life, that's what I'd do. But that's not what's going to happen. Mercenaries will be heading this way. They will be arriving soon, probably before dawn. They will question and kill anyone they find. You won't be able to tell them you don't know where I've gone. They will... well, they're Vessorine janissaries and they're being paid well. I can't leave you here.'

'I don't want to go. This is my home, Gregor. My damn home, and look what you've done.'

'I'm sorry.'

'Look what you've damn well done to my life!'

'I'm sorry. I'll make amends.'

She got up, the anger coming back and eclipsing her sorrow. 'How? How the hell can you make up for this? How the hell can you make up for all the pain you've ever caused me?'

'I have no idea. But I will. And you have to stay alive so I can. I've got the ruination of your nice comfortable existence on my conscience, Crezia. I will not add your death to that.'

'Fine words. I'm not coming. I'm going back to bed.'

I grabbed her by the arm and stopped her. I had to find a different tack. As a medic, she was almost professionally self-less. Appealing to her sense of self preservation was futile.

'I need you to come. That's the truth of it. I've got to take Medea with me. I can't leave her here, and I don't think she's in a position to travel.'

'Of course she isn't!'

'So she'll die?'

'If you move her now? In her state?'

'Better she travelled with a doctor then, don't you think?'

She shook off my hand. 'I will not allow you to jeopardise the health of my patient, Eisenhorn,' she warned.

'Then consider the prognosis, doctor. If she stays here, she'll be dead by morning. They will kill her when they find her. If she comes with me without you, she'll likely die too. I think what's really in question here is your medicae oath to pre-serve life.'

I hated being so manipulative... well, with her anyway. She regarded me with venom, knowing that I'd cornered her.

'You bastard. You clever, clever bastard. I don't know why I ever loved you.'

'I don't know why either. But I know why I loved you. You always cared. You always did the right thing.'

She turned and walked out of my room.

I finished dressing, and tucked spare clothes and Barbari-sater into a leather grip I found on top of the wardrobe. Then I picked up the rune staff and–

–stopped in the doorway.

The *Malus Codicium* was still in the drawer of the nightstand.

I wrapped it in a pillow case and tucked it into the grip. How could I have nearly forgotten it?

The first answer that occurred to me was strange and unnerving. Perhaps it wanted to be forgotten.

The flier's interior lights illuminated a patch of the little court-yard. Aemos and Eleena had stowed everything – clothes for each of them, and the manuscripts and books we had res-cued from Spaeton House. I put my own stuff aboard and ran a pre-flight. The flier was charged to optimum.

'Help me, damn you all!' Crezia said.

She was dressed in a dark green utility suit and a quilted coat, and had two travel bags with her. Medea lay on a grav-gurney, strapped in place with a resuscitrex unit and a narthecium full of supplies magnetically anchored to the underside of the gurney. Crezia had slaved two med-skulls to our patient, and they hovered in the air behind the stretcher.

We got Medea aboard and then clambered in ourselves. Crezia sat beside Medea, saying nothing. She didn't even look back at the house as we rose into the night and powered away.

We flew south, towards the main Atenate range, a massif of gigantic peaks that split the centre of the continent for three and a half thousand kilometres. The Itervalle and its neigh-bours were just foothills compared to this great geological structure.

I didn't want to stay in the air for too long. Tarl knew we had a flier and would have informed his comrades. This was just a short hop to get us going. I studied a chart-slate and began to compose a route.

* * *

By dawn, we were about ninety kilometres to the south-west and several hundred metres higher, in the base valleys of the ragged-edged Esembo. It was a soaring black shape in the early light, with a glinting wig of ice. Its mighty neighbours lurked behind it.

We set down at a town called Tiroyere, a small place that thrived as a logging centre and a waystation for travellers heading to the resorts at the top of the Esembo Pass. I parked the flier on the edge of the town under a brake of firs that would shield it from aerial observers.

No one had said much. The air was briskly cold and I turned the cabin heater to maximum for Medea's benefit.

'We should eat,' Eleena said. 'I'd go and get something... but...'

None of us had any money.

Crezia pulled off her gloves and produced a wallet from her coat. 'Am I the only person who thinks practically?' she commented sourly.

Eleena took a credit bar from Crezia and walked down through the trees into the town. She came back fifteen minutes later carrying a styrene box in which were four tall, sweet caffeits in disposable flasks, hot pastries in waxed paper wraps, a loaf stick and some vacuum-sealed sausage meats.

She'd also bought a mini data-slate loaded with a touring guide of the region. 'I thought it might be useful,' she said.

'Great,' said Crezia. 'Now we can pick the best spots to ski.'

While Eleena had been gone, I had spent considerable time and effort freeing the flier's side hatch. It had been bolted open in military style for the permanent gunner position. With the weapon stowed and a fragile human cargo, I wanted the cabin sealed. It would pull to but the latch wouldn't engage. I tried brute force, but I don't think it had ever been closed in its entire service life.

We ate and drank in silence, and the med-skulls administered sustenance for Medea via the fluid drips.

I watched the sky and the long arc of the road into the town. There wasn't much traffic. A few utility vehicles and mobile dromes, the occasional fast speeder. All tourists heading for the resorts.

While I ate, I scrolled through the guide Eleena had bought.

We left Tiroyere at nine thirty, and spent the rest of the day flying further west, around the shoulders of the Esembo, over the mirrors of the high lakes and on towards the northern resort of Gruj. For a long time, I was convinced we were being followed by a small, yellow speeder. I became so concerned that I diverted east, around a tract of mountain pasture and steep forest.

I lost sight of the yellow craft, but about thirty minutes later picked up a black one that shadowed us steadily at a distance of five kilometres. My anxieties returned again.

In the late afternoon, as we flew in towards Gruj, the black flier turned south on a route that would take it to the spa resort of Firiol on the southern face of Mons Fulco.

I had been jumping at phantoms.

At Gruj, I landed the speeder in the cover of some pines south-west of the old city wall. I took Crezia's credit bar and walked into the town alone.

Gruj was an old town with a meandering plan like Ravello, but it was far less picturesque. Slot bars and dance parlours occupied the main thoroughfares and there was a busy stream of young, vacationing Gudrunites on every street.

I found the local chambers of the Adeptus Astra Telepathica, a tall, black windowed structure on the corner of the main square, and went inside.

A careworn female adept called Nicint debited my credit bar and provided me with access to the Aegis account. I wanted to check if anything had come in during the last day or so.

I was in for a surprise.

There was a communiqué from Harlon Nayl.

He had survived.

His message was quite long, and written in Glossia. The gist of it was that he had left Messina two weeks earlier, suspecting, for reasons that he didn't go into, that something bad was afoot. That didn't surprise me. Nayl had a nose for trouble. That he, of all my poor, lost agents, had been forewarned of the danger was easy to believe. He was, at the time of sending, just three days shy of Gudrun.

I had the adept send a reply, also in Glossia, telling Nayl to head for the southern capital New Gevae and, once there, to arrange passage off planet. I asked him to confirm and told him I would send again when I was close. Four days was my estimate. Four days and we would be with Nayl at New Gevae and heading off-world.

The snow-trak was essentially a luxury recreational vehicle. A well upholstered cockpit and adjoining cabin housed in a sleek grey hull and carried on a main track power unit with thick forward wheels for steering.

The rental agent was in full flow, singing the machine's praises, when I cut him off.

'I'll take it.'

'A sound choice, sir.'

'Two weeks' rental. I'm driving to Ontre, and I'll be leaving it there.'

'That's fine, sir. Deliver it to our offices in Ontre. There's a little paperwork to fill out. You have means of identity?'

Crezia's credit bar soaked up the cost of the deposit. I
wanted to keep the transaction fairly anonymous.

I used the rental agent's palm reader to rouse another of
my slumbering fake identities. Torin Gregori, a vacationing
Thracian businessman with ample funds. The dealer seemed
satisfied.

The snow-trak was a hefty brute with a surprising kick in its
heels. I drove it back out of the town towards the flier, stopping on the way to stock up from a grocery market.

My friends at the flier regarded my approach with caution.
I discovered later that Eleena had had her laspistol drawn
and ready.

I leaned out of the cab and waved at them. 'Get yourselves
aboard. We're switching vehicles.'

We left the empty speeder under the trees, and as soon as
Medea was safely positioned in the plush, leather-padded
cabin, I headed out towards the pass road.

I didn't tell the others about Nayl. I didn't want to get their
hopes up.

By nightfall, we were powering up the snow-dusted high-
way over the pass towards Ontre. Gruj fell away behind us. I
thought I saw a small yellow flier approaching the town as
we left, but it was too far away to be sure.

We drove through the night, taking turns at the wheel. The
weather was clear, and the cockpit vox was tuned to the
climate-casts to catch snow advisories.

Crawling up the northern hem of Mons Fulco, we ran
through steady squalls of snow, and had to drop speed and
use the main lamps. Crezia was driving at that point. She'd
lived in the mountains for long enough to know what to do.

I napped in the cabin, resting out on the long bench seat

opposite the still sleeping Medea. I dreamed about her again, dreamed about saving her. Jekud Vance was in my dream too, desperate for my help. He screamed, bawling out a spear of sound and psi-pain that woke me.

I blinked over at Medea, but she was still stable. Eleena was asleep nearby.

The cabin rocked and vibrated with road noise and snow ghosts fluttered past the windows.

'Are you all right, Gregor?' Aemos asked.

He was sitting on the bench seat at the back of the cabin, surrounded by data-slates.

'A dream, that's all, Uber. It woke me last night too.'

I paused and sat up. The previous night I had assumed I had been woken by the sounds of Tarl's escape. But now it had happened again. The dream had woken me. Woken me both times. Jekud Vance's terrible death-scream of pain and rage and frustration.

We rumbled into Ontre in mid-afternoon the following afternoon. Heavy snow had slowed us down, and ice caked the copper roofs of the famous resort. But heavy snow had also brought the winter sports crowd into town in great numbers. The place was buzzing with activity, the roads sluggish with vehicles, the skies flecked with arriving speeders.

I drove the snow-trak into the parking lot of the Ontre Transcontinental Station, and found a place. Aemos and I went up to the concourse building where Torin Gregori purchased tickets for three connecting sleep berths. The express was due in an hour we were told.

Just as the mighty Atenate Range creases the centre of Gudrun's largest continent, so the Trans-Atenate Express runs like an artery along it. The railway is famously romantic. Most who ride it do so because of the ride, vacationers who would rather travel than arrive. The young flock to centres like Gruj and Ontre to use them as a base for skiing and ice-surfing, but the wealthy choose the Trans-Atenate, where they can sit in coddled luxury and watch Gudrun's most spectacular scenery slip by outside the window.

The great, chrome, promethium-fuelled locomotive pulled into Ontre at five, pulling a string of ten double-decked carriages. Porters helped us to manoeuvre Medea aboard.

Our cabins, on the top deck of car three, a wagon-lit, were first class and spacious. We put Medea in one of them, with Eleena to one side of her and Crezia to the other. Uber and I shared a fourth. There were communicating doors between the suites and everything was finished in polished maple.

The express hooted its siren and panted out of Ontre, muscularly taking the gradient into the Fonette Pass. The huge silvery beast could reach one hundred and seventy kilometres an hour on flat sections.

I regarded the timetable. Overnight to Fonette, then a short stretch to Locastre, followed by a high speed, uninterrupted run all the way down through the Atenate Majors, across the Southern Plateau to the coast.

We would be in New Gevae in just under three days.

There was barely any sense of motion: a slight, rolling vibration that one swiftly became oblivious to. The cars were robust, thick skinned, heated and insulated against the Atenate chill, but the side effect of this was to virtually eliminate exterior sound. The massive engine, deafening from the vantage of the platform concourse at Ontre, was virtually inaudible. Only when the express hammered down a cutting or a gorge and the engine noise was compressed and channeled backwards by the steep sides, did we catch a whisper of it at all.

With the cabin blind down, I might have been at home in a comfortable parlour.

While daylight remained, I kept the blind up and was afforded panoramic views of the pass, the snowfields, pink and soft in the sunset, the hard-shadowed scarps of rising ice broken at the folds by knuckles of black rock. Once in a while, beige smoke from the engine streamed past the windows and obscured the view.

On slow turns, it was possible to lean across to the window port itself and see the foreshortened flanks of the cars and train ahead, segmented like a great snake, the chrome and blue-and-white livery catching the last of the sun. Twice, a long, jumping shadow of the train ran along side us across the snows.

Night fell and the views outside vanished. I drew the blind. Aemos was snoozing, so I thought I might walk the length of the train and get to know the layout.

The communicating door opened and Crezia came in. She was dressed in a grey satin robe with tightly laced pleating that ran from the high throat right down to the top of the gathered skirt. A fur wrap was draped over one arm, and she had put her hair up.

I rose from my seat almost automatically.

'Well?' she enquired.

'You look... stunning.'

'I meant "well" as in, isn't it time you escorted me to dinner?'

'Dinner?'

'Main meal of the day? Usually found somewhere between lunch and a nightcap?'

'I am familiar with the concept.'

'Good. Shall we?'

'We are fleeing for our lives. Do you think this is the time?'

'I can think of no better time. We are fleeing for our lives,

Gregor, on the most exclusive and opulent mode of travel Gudrun has to offer. I suggest we flee for our lives in style.'

I went into the bathroom and changed into the most presentable clothes I had with me. Then I linked arms with her and we strolled back along the companion way to the dining van three cars back.

'Did you bring these clothes with you?' I asked quietly as we wandered down the softly lit, carpeted hallway, encountering other well-dressed passengers walking to and from the dining van.

'Of course.'

'We left in haste, and you packed a gown like that?'

'I thought I should be ready for anything.'

The dining salon was on the upper deck of the sixth car. Crystal chandeliers hung from the arched roof, and the roof itself was made of armourglas. It doubled as an observation lounge, though just then it simply provided a ceiling of starry blackness.

A string quartet was playing unobtrusively at one end, and the place was filling up. The air was filled with gentle music, clinking silverware and low voices. Discreete poison snoopers hovered like fireflies over each place setting. A uniformed steward showed us to a table by the portside windows.

We studied the menus. I realised how hungry I was.

'How many times, do you suppose?' she asked.

'How many times what?'

'Years ago, when we were together. You would come to visit me in Ravello, secretive as is your manner. How many times did I suggest we took the express through the mountains?'

'You mentioned it, yes.'

'We never did, though.'

'No, we didn't. I regret that.'

'So do I. It seems so sad we're doing it now out of necessity.

Although I might have guessed I'd only get you on a romantic trip like this if you had to do it.'

'Whatever the reason, we're here now.'

'I should have put a gun to your head years ago.'

We ordered potage velours, followed by sirloin of lowland
runka, roulade with a macedoine of herbs and forest mush-
rooms affriole, and a Chateau Xandier from Sameter that I
remembered was a favourite of hers.

The soup, served with mouthwatering chapon and a swirl of
smitane in wide-lipped white dishes delicately embossed with
the crest of the Trans-Continental company livery, was vel-
vety and damn near perfect. The runka, simply pan-seared in
amasec, was saignant and irreproachable. The Xandier, astrin-
gent and then musty in its finish, made her smile with fond
memories.

We talked. We had decades to fill in. She told me about her
work and her life, the interest in xeno-anatomy she had developed, the monographs she had composed, a new procedure
for muscle grafting she had pioneered. She had taken up the
spinet, as a means of relaxation, and had now mastered all
but two of Guzella's Studies. She had written a book, a trea-
tise on the comparative analysis of skeletal dimorphism in
early human biotypes.

'I almost sent you a copy, but I was afraid how that might
be misconstrued.'

'I own a first edition,' I confessed.

'How loyal! But have you read it?'

'Twice. Your deconstruction of Terksson's work on the
Dimmamar-A sites is convincing and quite damning. I might
take issue with your chapters on Tallarnopithicene, but then
you and I always did argue over the "Out of Terra" hypothesis.'

'Ah yes. You always were a heretic in that regard.'

I felt I had so much less to give back. There was so much about my life in the last few years I couldn't or shouldn't tell her. So I told her about Nayl instead.

'This man is trustworthy?'

'Completely.'

'And you're sure it's him?'

'Yes. He's using Glossia. The beauty of that code is that it's individually idiomatic. It can't be broken, used or understood by outsiders. You'd have to be in my employ for a long time to grasp the fundamentals of its mechanism.'

'That bodyguard. The one who betrayed your household.'

'Kronsky?'

'Yes. He was in your employ.'

'Not for long. Even with the basics he'd grasped, he couldn't dupe me for long using Glossia.'

'So we're going to be rescued?'

'I'm confident we'll be able to get off-planet.'

'Well, Gregor, I think that good news calls for an indulgent dessert.'

The steward brought us ribaude nappé, sticky and sweet, followed by rich black Hesperine caffeine and digestifs, an oaky amasec for me and a thimble of pasha for her.

We were laughing together by then.

It was a fine dinner and a good night spent in delightful company. I have not known its like to this day.

I was woken by the jar and a thump of a halt just after dawn. Outside, a whistle blew, muffled by the car's hull, and there came the distant mutter of men's voices.

Slowly, I slid out of bed, doing my best not to disturb Crezia. She was still deeply asleep, though she rolled over and reached, murmuring, into the cooling space I had just vacated.

I tried to find some clothes. They were strewn on the floor, and with the blind down, it was a matter of touch.

I prised back the edge of the blind with one finger and peeked out. It was already light, frosty and colourless. There was a station outside, and people milling on the snowy platform.

We had reached Fonette.

I got dressed, shivering. Now the train was halted and idling, the wall vents issued a cooler wash of air.

I opened the door and slipped out, casting one last look behind me. In her sleep, Crezia had curled up into a ball, cocooning herself in the bedsheets, shutting out the cold and the world.

Outside, it was near-freezing and very bright. The wide platform was busy with passengers leaving or joining the express, and servitor units conveying pyramids of baggage.

Snow was lightly falling. I hugged myself and stamped my feet. Several other travellers had got down from the train to stretch their legs.

Fonette station occupied an elevated area above the town, shadowed to the north by Mons Fulco and to the south by the Uttes, Minor and Major, and then the weather-veiled bulk of the Central Atens.

'How long do we stop?' I asked a passing porter.

'Twenty minutes, sir,' he replied. 'Just long enough for change over and for the tender to take on water.'

Not long enough to run down into the town, I figured. I stayed on the platform until the boarding whistle sounded and then stood in the carriage hallway leaning out of the doorway window as we slowly pulled out of town.

The station building slid by, revealing a view of the town

below that had not been visible from the platform. Steep roofs iced with snow, a Ministorum chapel, a sturdy Arbites block-house. A landing field, just below the station causeway, filled with berthed and refuelling fliers.

One of them was small and yellow.

I went back to Crezia's cabin, took off my coat and boots and lay beside her until she woke. She rolled over and kissed my mouth.

'What are you doing?' she asked, sleepily.

'Checking the timetable.'

'I don't think there are any changes on this line.'

'No,' I agreed. 'We'll be at Locastre in about four hours. There's a longer halt there. Forty-five minutes. Then the long run to New Gevae.'

She sat up, rubbing her eyes. Drowsy, unguarded, she was more beautiful than ever.

'So what?' she asked.

'I'll check the astropathic account there. There'll be time.'

There was a knock at the door. It was the cabin-service stew-ard with a laden trolley. The last thing we had done the night before was to order a full, cooked breakfast.

Well, not quite the last thing.

Eleena and Aemos were up, taking breakfast together. Crezia pulled on her robe and checked on Medea, who was still sta-ble and sleeping deeply.

'The signs are good,' she told me on her return. 'Tomorrow, perhaps the day after, she should be back with us.'

We ate together in her cabin, picking up our conversations from the night before. It was all familiar and relaxed, as if we had adjusted our clocks by twenty-five years. I realised how much I had missed her company and vitality.

'What's the matter?' she asked. 'You seem preoccupied.'

I thought about the yellow speeder.

'Nothing,' I said.

During the long, slow climb up through the Uttes to Locastre, I went through the data-slates of material Aemos had compiled since the attack on Spaeton House. I paid particular attention the name Khanjar the Sharp. Aemos had compiled a list of planet cultures where the word 'khanjar' was still in parlance. Ninety-five hundred worlds, and I went down the list systematically, even though I knew Aemos, with his greater knowledge of trivia, had already done so. Any one of them might hold the key. A khanjar was a ceremonial oathing dagger on Benefax, Luwes and Craiton. It was the slang term for a gang-lord on distant Mekanique. It was the common word for a pruning knife on five worlds in the Scarus sector alone. It was a hive-argot adjective for sharp practice on Morimunda. On three thousand worlds, it was simply the word for knife.

A knife cutting me to the quick. Who was Khanjar the Sharp? Why was he diligently seeking my destruction and the destruction of my entire operation?

I turned to consider the slate listing the injuries he had dealt against me, the deaths he had, I'm sure, ordered. They were all still shocking to me. The sheer scope of his murderous efforts astounded me. So many targets, so many worlds... and all struck at the same sidereal moment.

I found that I kept coming back to the notice of Inshabel's death. It was, simply, the odd one out. Every other victim or location target had been a specific part of my personal organisation. But Nathun Inshabel was not. He was – had been – an inquisitor in his own right. During my campaign against the heretic Quixos, almost fifty years earlier, Inshabel,

DAN ABNETT

then holding the rank of interrogator, had been part of my team. He had joined my fold after the death of his master, Inquisitor Roban, during the atrocity on Thracian Primaris, and had continued to aid me devotedly until after the purge of Quixos's stronghold on Farness Beta. After that, with my sponsorship, he became an inquisitor and began his own work.

Since then, we had been in contact only a few times and, apart from our old friendship, there was no connection between us. Why had he been marked out for destruction too? Coincidence was not a good enough answer.

What connected us? Who connected us? The obvious name was Quixos, but that led nowhere. I had eliminated Quixos myself.

I ran through the list of worlds again, trying to discern a link.

One of the planets named on the list was Quenthus Eight.

That name snagged me like a protruding claw. Quenthus Eight. A margin world. I had never been there. But I'd once been told about it.

Running on instinct, I cross-checked Quenthus Eight with the vast list of worlds on which Tarray or Tari was a registered surname. Aemos had already cross-referenced the lists of worlds using 'khanjar' with worlds owning the surname 'Tarray', and had come up with seven hundred possibles. Now I was able to add sense to one of them.

There it was. 'Khanjar' was the word for a war knife on Quenthus Eight, and Tarray was a clan name from that world. Nearly three hundred and fifty years before, one of the most vile sociopaths in the Imperium had started his career on Quenthus Eight. Marla Tarray's reported claims to have been born on Gudrun had been discounted by Aemos, who had checked the census and found no sign of the name.

He hadn't gone back far enough. He hadn't gone back three

and a half hundred years. I did, and found that Tarry had been a peasant name on Gudrun until that time. The family tree ended right there.

I knew who it was. I knew who my enemy was.

THIRTEEN

Locastre
Full stop
End of the line

We arrived at Locastre over an hour behind schedule. Unseasonal blizzards had swept up from the east into the Uttes, and the express had been forced to reduce speed to a crawl. On steep gradients through the passes, there was a danger of back-slip, and we could feel the frequent jerks as the car bogies hunted over the ice-caked rails. There was a ten minute stop on a straight section on the west of Utte Major as the train's engineer gangs got out and winched the locomotive's nose plough into place. The blizzard was around us then and everything outside the windows was a colourless swirl.

I went down to the end of the car and peered out through the van windows. Black blobs were moving in the white haze, some lit by fizzling flares of green and red. I felt several jolts and metallic clunks shiver through the deck beneath me.

The intercar tannoy softly informed us that we would be on our way soon, reassured us that the weather was no hazard, and soothed us with the news that complimentary hot punch was now being served in the dining salon. Unnecessarily muffled in furs or expensive mountainwear, other passengers came to peer out of the mush-flecked ports, grumbling and what if-ing.

I returned to the cabin I shared with Aemos, locked the doors and sat down with him. I ran through my theory.

'Pontius Glaw...' his old lips spat the name. 'Pontius Glaw...'

'It fits, doesn't it?'

'From what you tell me, Gregor. Though of course, I know little of what passed between you and that monster on Cinchare.'

We had first tackled the villainy of Pontius Glaw and his poisonous brood right there on Gudrun back in 240, an age ago as it seemed. At the time, Glaw himself, a notorious heretic, had been dead for two centuries, his obscene activities curtailed by Inquisitor Angevin.

But Glaw's intellect and engrammed personality had been preserved in a psipathetic crystal by his noble family. We thwarted the attempts of House Glaw to restore him to corporeal life, and afterwards I had the crystal placed for safekeeping with my old ally, Magos Geard Bure of the Adeptus Mechanicus.

A century later, in 340, I had revisited Bure's remote fastness on the mining world Cinchare during the Quixos affair, in order to obtain arcane information concerning daemonhosts from his prisoner. Without Pontius Glaw's dark advice, I would never have been able to vanquish Quixos or his slaved daemons Prophaniti and Cherubael.

But I had been forced to deal with Glaw. Make it worth his while. The lure I dangled was that in return for his help, I would commission Bure to manufacture a body for him to inhabit.

And, because I was an honourable man, I kept my word, believing that even if Glaw was given mobility, he would never escape Geard Bure's clutches.

It seemed I had been wrong about that.

During those private interviews on Cinchare, Glaw had confessed to me the event that had driven him, the accomplished scion of one of Gudrun's most respected noble houses, into the worship of the warp.

It had happened on Quenthus Eight in 019. Glaw had been visiting the Quenthi amphitheatres, purchasing gladiators for his pit-fighting hobby. Even before his fall, he was a cruel man. He bought one brute, a warrior from a remote feral world... Borea, I seem to recall. Anxious to please his new master, the warrior had given Glaw his torc. It was an ancestral relic from the feral world, and neither the warrior nor Glaw realised it was tainted with the foulest Chaos. Glaw had put it on and immediately had fallen into its clutches. That one simple act had sealed his fate and transformed him into the idolatrous fiend who had plagued the Helican sub-sector for nearly two decades.

I gave Aemos the gist of this.

'The matter seems to fit together. You believe, I take it, that Pontius Glaw has escaped from his prison on Cinchare, built up his forces, and is now targetting you for revenge?'

'Revenge? No... well, indirectly, perhaps. He certainly would want to have his revenge on me, but the scale of his attack, the effort, the comprehensive scope... every element of my operation, and Inshabel too.'

Aemos shrugged. 'Inshabel was with us at Cinchare.'

'That's my point. Pontius is trying to destroy everyone who might know he exists. Most of the Imperium believes he is long dead. We pose a threat to him just by knowing about him.'

I could tell Aemos had something on his mind that he didn't want to say.

'Aemos?'

'Nothing, Gregor.'

'Old friend?'

He shook his head.

'Say it. Pontius Glaw's existence is only a secret because I never informed the ordos that he was still sentient. Because I never delivered his engram sphere into the custody of the Ordo Hereticus as I should have. And he's only free now because I had a body built for him.'

'No.' He got to his feet and squinted out of the car window, trying to see something, anything, in the blizzard. 'We've had this conversation before, or at least one like it. About Cherubael.'

He turned to look at me. He was so very old. 'You are an inquisitor of the Glorious Imperium of Mankind. You are dedicated to the destruction of evil in any facet of its three classic forms: Xenos, Malleus, Hereticus. You face unimaginable hazards. Yours is the most arduous task undertaken by any Imperial servant. You must use every weapon at your disposal to protect our culture. Even the arsenal of the enemy. And you know full well that sometimes such uses have consequences. We may now regret your actions with Pontius Glaw, but without those, Quixos would not have been brought down. We can play the "if only" game all day. The simple truth is that victory comes at a price, and we are paying that price now. The true measure of your character is what you do about it.'

'I correct my mistakes. I bring down Pontius Glaw.'

'I have no doubt of that.'

'Thank you, Aemos.'

He sat down again. 'This Tarray woman. How does she fit in?'

I showed him the census record. 'The Tarrays were a low caste family on Gudrun during Glaw's organic lifetime. Then the line stops abruptly, but reappears on Quenthus. I think the Tarrays, or at least a Tarray, was amongst Glaw's retinue, and he took them to Quenthus. I need you to look into that at Locastre.'

'Locastre? But we're only going to be stopping there for forty-five minutes.'

I gestured to the window. 'It'll probably be longer given the weather, but you'll have to move fast. I'm going to use the time to access the Aegis account.'

The handle of the locked connecting door ratcheted back and forth.

'Gregor?' It was Crezia.

'What are you doing locked in there?' she called through the door.

'Just discussing things with Aemos.'

'They're serving hot punch in the salon. I thought we might mingle.'

'In a minute,' I called out in reply. There was a lurch and the train started to move again.

I looked at Aemos. 'The things we've spoken about... they don't go any further. Not yet. Crezia doesn't need to know, neither does Eleena, come to that.'

'My lips are sealed,' he said.

We came out of the blizzard and down a comfortable gradient into Locastre. It was nearly midday. The bad weather lurked like a grey wall behind us, veiling the Uttes, but reports suggested it was moving into the valley.

At Locastre, the porters announced a ninety minute stop.

I told Eleena to make sure the express didn't leave until Aemos and I were safely back.

Locastre occupies a cleft valley gouged by glaciers. The old buildings are dark grey – granite stands in for the traditional Gudrun ouslite used in the lowlands – and the altitude and climate is such that pressurised, heated tunnels of armourglas sheath the streets. I hired a servitor litter and had it scurry me through the warm, damp street tunnels, as ominous squalls of snow peppered the transparent roof above.

Outside the office of the Astropathic Guild, I told it to wait and left my credit bar locked into its fare-meter as good faith. It settled low on its spider-limbed chassis, venting steam from its hydraulics.

There was a message from Nayl waiting for me in the Aegis account. He had made good time, and was already in New Gevae. Passage off-world had been arranged with a freighter called the *Caucus*. He was eager to see me.

Nayl's communiqué was in Glossia and I phrased my reply the same way. Weather permitting, we would be in New Gevae in two days. On arrival, I would arrange a meeting with him.

'Is that all, sir?' asked the adept attending me.

I remembered Crezia's comments over dinner about Nayl being trustworthy. I added another line, suggesting that the situation reminded me of the tight spot we'd been in on Eechan, years before, facing Beldame Sadia.

'Send it, please,' I said.

Up at the station, the express sounded its horn.

The express rumbled up into the Central Atens, chased by the weather. Despite the fact that we were now scaling some of the steepest and longest gradients in the route, the locomotive was running at full power, trying to outpace the snows for as long as it could.

The main range of the Atens, through which we now travelled, included the greatest mountains on Gudrun: Scarno, Dorpaline, The Heledgae, Vesper, Mount Atena. Each one dwarfed the peaks like Mons Fulco that we had encountered earlier. They seemed as dark and cyclopean as tilted continents.

They were also beautiful. Peerless tracts of blue-white ice, unblemished leagues of snow, sharp sunshine that almost twinkled like starlight in a vacuum.

Until, before nightfall, it all vanished. Freezing fog and vapour descended like a stage curtain, sealing out the light and dropping visibility to a few dozen metres. Then snow began to flutter again and our speed decreased. The weather had caught up with us.

'Gregor?' I had been watching the snowstorm. 'Come in here.'

Crezia beckoned me through the connecting door. Medea was awake.

The cyberskulls hovered back to give me room as I sat down beside her cot. She looked tired and drawn, faded almost. But her eyes were half open and she managed a thin smile as she saw me.

'Everything's okay. You're in safe hands.'

Her mouth moved, but no sound came out.

'Don't try to speak,' Crezia whispered.

I saw curiosity in Medea's eyes as she focused on Crezia.

'This is Doctor Berschilde. A good friend. She saved your life.'

'...long...'

'What?'

'How long been sleep?'

'The best part of a week. You were wounded in the back.'

'Ribs sore.'

'That will pass,' said Crezia.

'They... they get us?'

'No, they didn't get us,' I said. 'And they're not going to get us either.'

Shrouded by the bitter blizzards and maintaining no more than sixty kilometres an hour, we journeyed on across the roof of the world. I ventured out into the public areas and even to the salon a few times, and found that diverting entertainments had been laid on: buffet meals, music, card schools, a regicide tournament, screenings of popular hololithic extravaganzas. Uniformed Trans-Continental personnel were out in force, keeping everybody happy and volubly disseminating the notion that being caught in an Atenate icestorm was all part of the romance of the famous rail line.

And not a potentially lethal misfortune.

If the locomotive derailed, or the power plant malfunctioned, and the train became stranded in the midst of a blizzard that lasted more than a couple of days, we'd freeze to death and they'd have to wait until spring to dig us out.

Of course, in the nine hundred and ninety years of the Trans-Atenate Express's operation, that had never happened. The train had always got through. It was a remarkably secure form of transport, given the terrain it crossed.

But there is a first time for anything, as people can be forgiven for thinking. Years of experience warned the train staff to start reassuring and distracting the passengers the moment weather closed in, or they'd have a panic on their hands. The idle rich can be such worriers.

* * *

We came to a halt four times before dawn the next day. The first time was at about ten in the evening. The tannoy informed us that we were waiting for wind speeds to ease before crossing the Scarno Gorge Bridge and that there was no cause for concern. Less than five minutes later, we were on our way again.

I was still awake at one when we gently coasted to a stop again. I felt uneasy, and after fifteen minutes, tucked the autopistol into my belt, strapped Barbarisater to my hip and covered them both with Aemos's long green over-robe.

The hallway was dark, the lights dimmed to an auxiliary amber. Little green cue lights glowed on the staff-only monitor display that was set in the panelled wall at the end of the car.

I heard someone coming up the spiral stairs from the car's lower deck and turned to see a steward who regarded me quizzically.

'Is everything all right, sir?' he asked.

'That was my question. I was wondering why we'd stopped.'

'It's just routine, sir. We're just coming over the Scarno Gradient and the Master Engineman has ordered a check of the braking elements in case of excess icing.'

'I see. Just routine.'

'Everything's perfectly safe, sir,' he said with well-rehearsed assurance.

As if to prove him right, the lights flickered and we were moving again. He smiled. 'There we are, sir.'

I went back to my cabin. I barely marked the two further stops we made that night. But I kept my weapons to hand.

The second full day of travel passed without incident. The weather alternated between long, furious blizzards and quick, glorious episodes of sunlit calm. We stopped five more times before supper. Five more routine hesitations. The tannoy whispered that though we were behind schedule, we were likely to make up time once we were clear of the mountains and crossing the Southern Plateau in the latter part of the following day.

I was growing impatient. I found myself pacing the train a lot, end to end. I even took Crezia to the salon for lunch and stayed long enough to play a board or two of regicide with her.

Medea was gaining strength. By the afternoon, she was sitting up and eating for herself. The cyber-skulls disconnected all her drips except the vital monitor. We took turns to sit with her. I let Eleena tell her the details of what had happened since the attack on Spaeton House. Medea listened intently, increasingly dismayed.

When it was my turn to spend an hour at her side, she said, 'You came back for me.'

'Yes.'

'You might have been killed.'

'You would have been.'

'They killed Jekud,' she said after a pause. 'We were running across the paddocks and they cut him down.'

'I know. I felt it.'

'I couldn't help him.'

'I know.'

'I felt terrible. After all he had done to show me my father. And I couldn't save him.'

'It was probably quick. The Vessorine are ruthless killers.'

'I thought I heard him call out, after he had fallen. I was going to turn back for him, but they were everywhere.'

'It's alright.'

She took a beaker from the bedstand and sipped. 'Eleena says they killed everyone.'

'I'm afraid they might have.'

'I mean, not just here. The Distaff. Nayl. Inshabel.'

I nodded. 'Someone was very thorough that night. But here's a thought to cheer you: Nayl's alive, and so's Fischig. We're going to meet up with both of them.'

That made her smile. 'How did Nayl get away?'

'I don't know. He hasn't given me any details. It would seem he got wind of something and left Messina before the attack. I'm looking forward to finding out what he knows.'

'Like who's behind this, you mean?'

I winked. 'That, Medea, I already know.'

Her eyes widened. 'Who?'

'I'll tell you when I've confirmed my suspicions. I don't want you worrying unnecessarily.'

'Now that's just cruel,' she scolded. 'I won't be able to think about anything else now.'

'Then see what you come up with,' I suggested. Medea was privy to most of my operation, and I thought it might be interesting to see if she arrived at any conclusion herself.

The jolt made me strike my head against the side panel of the bed and woke me up in time to feel two more hard judders before the train came to a complete stop.

It was nearly three in the morning and pitch black. I could hear the ice flakes pattering like small arms fire off the window of the cabin.

Every halt we had made so far had been smooth and gentle. Not like this.

Aemos had woken too, and sat up as I turned on the sidelight and strapped on Barbarisater.

'What is it?' he asked.

'Nothing, I hope.' The inter-cabin door opened and Eleena looked in.

'Did you feel that?' she asked sleepily.

'Find your pistol,' I told her.

We woke Crezia and got all three of them into Medea's cabin. Crezia looked befuddled and worried. Eleena was wide awake by then and checking the cell of her weapon.

I pulled on Aemos's over-robe to conceal my own armaments.

'Stay here and be vigilant,' I said and then left the connecting suite via the door to my cabin.

In the gloomy hall, I could hear movement in the other cabins, low voices and the occasional pip of a summoning alarm as worried passengers tried to call the stewards.

I went back down the car to the monitor display the moment I saw the two red lights shining amongst the green ones.

I slid open the display's glass cover and fitted my signet ring to the optical reader. The potent Inquisitorial authority codes loaded into my signet ring rapidly overcame Trans-Continental Line's confidence software and gave me access to the express's master system.

The monitor's little screen woke up, and flickered with user-friendly graphics and bars of data. I requested clarification of the red warning lights.

Alert code 88 decimal 508 – a systematic trigger of active brake units, cars seven through ten, forcing main brake arrest.

Alert code 521 decimal 6911 – irregular breach of door seal, door 34, car eight, lower.

I hurried along the upper deck of the train, heading for the rear. Some cabin doors opened and anxious faces looked out. 'No need for concern!' I called in my best Trans-Continental tone, backing it up with a gentle surge of will that slammed doors after me like a drum roll.

At car six, I had to go down to the lower deck because of the dining salon. Passing into car seven, I saw three train staffers hurrying down the companionway in the direction of car eight.

The lower hallway of car eight was bitterly cold and a gale was blowing down it. I saw six or seven rail employees pulling on foul weather gear and lighting flares as they jumped down out of the open wagon door into the night. Several more were grouped around the monitor display and one, a steward, saw me approach.

'Please go back to your cabin, sir. Everything's fine.'

'What seems to be the problem?'

'Just hurry back, sir. What is your cabin number? I'll bring along complimentary liqueurs in a few minutes.'

'The rear brakes have just thrown and door 34 is open,' I said.

He blinked. 'How did you–'

'What's going on?'

'Sir, I want to guarantee your comfort, so if you'd just like to–'

I didn't have time for a debate. 'What's going on, Inex?' I asked, reading his name off his brass lapel badge and juicing my words with just a touch of will. A name always helped to enhance the mental coercion.

He blinked. 'The brake systems in the rear four wagons have engaged, which triggered an overall braking incident,' he said, quickly and obediently.

'Did someone pull the emergency rope?'

'No, sir. We'd have a source for that, and anyway the train's entire brake system would have fired simultaneously. We believe it's ice in the aft units.'

'That would cause a partial brake lock?'

'Yes, sir.'

'What about the door?'

'It opened just after we stopped. The chief steward thinks it was one of the engineers, opening the door to get out and check the brakes without informing the system he was unlocking the door.'

'It wasn't forced?'

'It was opened from inside. With a key.' The effects of my will were ebbing and his jocular tone returned. 'We've got personnel out lineside now, sir, checking the brakes.'

'Including this engineer who supposedly opened the door in his eagerness to find the fault?'

'I'm sure, sir.'

'Find out,' I said, using the will more forcefully.

He ran back to the monitor panel, and his colleagues stood back, puzzled, as he operated the device.

'Who has access to door keys?'

'Who the hell are you?' one of the others asked.

'A concerned member of the public,' I said, blanketing them all with will power. 'Who has keys?'

'Only engineers of level two and higher, class one stewards and the guards,' said another, stammering in his desperation to tell me.

'How many people is that?'

'Twenty-three.'

'Are they all accounted for?'

'I don't know,' said Inex.

'Stand aside,' I ordered, and used my ring on the monitor. The train had a staff and crew of eighty-four. Each one had a sub-dermal tracker implant so that the train master could account for the location of his people at all times. The display showed a graphic map of the train, but the screen was so small I had to scroll along it, looking at the schematic bit by bit. Master personnel were shown in red, engineers in amber, stewards in green and guards in blue. Ancilliary staff like chefs, waiters, porters and cleaners were pink.

Red and amber dots clustered in the locomotive section, and blue and green ones were speckled throughout the wagons. The upper deck of car nine, the crew quarters, was full of pink lights. I saw a cluster of green and blue cursors that represented the men grouped around me at the back of car eight's lower deck, near door 34. A sub-menu listed the amber and blue lights that had left the train to inspect the running gear.

There was one green light amongst the pink ones in car nine. I called up more information. The green light belonged to Steward Class One Rebert Awins. He was in his quarters.

The express had made an emergency stop and all the staff apart from the ancilliaries were moving to secure the train. Except Awins.

'Awins is class one. He'd have keys.'

'Yes, sir,' said Inex.

'Why isn't he assisting?'

They all looked at each other.

'When did you last see him?'

'He was on the morning shift today,' said one of them.

'I saw him in the rec room at shift change having his lunch,' added another.

'Since then?'

They shook their heads.

'He should have come on again at nine,' said Inex. 'Shall I check on him.'

No, I was going to say. Because he's dead. But there was no point scaring them.

I changed my mind. 'Do that, Inex.' I reached over and took the intercom headset off the man nearest me. He didn't protest. He didn't even notice.

'Go to his room and tell me what you find. Vox channel…'

I studied the headset's small ear piece and adjusted the responder. '...six.'

'Yes sir,' said Inex. As he turned to go, I reached out and touched him briefly on the forehead. He shuddered. My psi-imprint would stay with him for a good thirty minutes now, even once he was out of my vicinity.

Inex ran off.

I looked at the car door. It had been pulled to, but the 'unsecure' light was still blinking. There were thawing cakes of dirty ice on the metal deck inside the door.

'How many people went out?' I asked.

One of them checked the display. 'Twenty, sir.'

'How many have come back inside since you got here?'

'None,' they all said.

They would be looking for me. For us. They knew we were on the train, and they'd got someone aboard at Fonette or Locastre. Someone who had befriended Rebert Awins, killed him and taken his pass keys. Someone with the technical expertise to trigger a partial brake lock, stop the train and then use Awin's keys to open an exterior door and let his associates aboard.

Someone who, by now, surely knew which cabins we were occupying.

I ran back down the train towards car three, using the lower deck hallways. I slid Barbarisater from its nedskin scabbard. It seemed so incongruous to be hurrying down a train's companionway brandishing a sword. But the cabins around me were full of innocent Imperial citizens and I didn't dare use my pistol.

I also didn't dare use the intercom.

I reached out psychically. Eleena was an untouchable blank, so I called to Aemos, Crezia and Medea.

Be ready. Trouble coming.

I passed several train staff in the hall as I made my way past and they jumped back in alarm as they saw the blade.

Forget! I willed at each one as I passed, and they just went on their way.

I reached the front end of car four and prepared to go up. A Trans-Continental steward lay face down on the stairs, his neck snapped.

Just then, the frantic voice of Inex wailed into my earpiece. 'He's dead! Oh God-Emperor! He's dead! Rebert's dead! Sound the alarm!'

The distress klaxon started to warble and recessed light plates in the wall began to blink orange. I saw a third red light had lit up on the car-end monitor panel.

I jammed my signet ring against the reader and cued information.

Alert code 946 decimal 2452 – irregular breach of window seal, window 146, car three, upper.

I clambered over the steward's corpse and made my way up the stairs.

The upper hallway of car three was even colder than the chill of car eight. The end window on the port side, beside the intercarriage articulation, was wide open and freezing air and snow was whirling in. The window had been cut out of its frame with a powerblade or melta torch.

The light was bad. Gloomy, half-dimmed lamps aggravated by the fretful blink of the alarm lights. The klaxons still whooped.

I realised there were three dark shapes halfway down the hall ahead of me, skulking low. They hadn't heard me arrive over the howl of the blizzard and the shrill of the alarms.

I hugged the panelled wall. Barbarisater throbbed, hungry.

Even passively, I could sense the three men were psi-shielded. They made big silhouettes. Combat armour. I saw the ugly shadow of an assault weapon as the point man waved his partners forward.

Forward towards the doors of our compartments.

I edged closer.

The point man, oozing professionalism as he visually checked his rear, saw me.

And all hell broke loose.

FOURTEEN

Barbarisater versus the janissaries
Etrik, blade to blade
Lunchtime drinks in New Gevae

The two killers nearest me turned and opened fire with blunt, large calibre autoguns. I suppose the sword in my hand was a damn give away, but they'd have killed me anyway, even if they had mistaken me for a wayward bystander.

They were professional killers, Vessorine janissaries. They had a job to do, a contract to fulfill, and anyone in their way was a target.

The fact that they were using solid-round weapons confirmed they were Vessorine. The ultimate military pragmatists. They'd tailed the train in a poorly-insulated speeder and deployed through a blizzard. In those conditions, standard las-weapons might have died, their cell-power drained by the cold. But a well-lubricated autogun would fire below freezing. It had only to rely on its percussive hammer action.

Vessorine janissaries. I had faced them before without knowing what they were. Now I knew, and their formidable reputation almost gave me pause. Vessorines, three of them. Plated in combat armour and firing heavyweight man-stopper ammunition. Frankly, I'd rather have squared off with angry Kasrkin.

But Barbarisater was in my hand, alert and alive. I had been using my will openly for some time, and that had quickened its strength. I made a *ghan fasl*, the figure-eight stroke and smashed the first three shots away, impact sparks sheeting from the energised sword blade. Then I struck an *uwe sar*, an *ulsar* and a *ura wyla bei* in rapid series, deflecting squashed rounds into the panelling around me. Wood splintered.

I dived sideways as further shots punched into the hallway carpet and exploded on the inter-wagon doors. People were screaming in the cabins all around.

I rolled and came up on my feet as the first Vessorine rounded the car-end corner and fired half a dozen times. His ejecting shell-cases pattered off his torso in a fog of blue smoke and his gun muzzle lit up like a blowtorch. Point blank.

Except I was behind him.

His gunfire shredded the wagon wall and ruptured the window frame. Barbarisater removed his head.

The second one was charging and firing too. He let out a mask-muffled bellow as he saw his comrade collapse in pieces.

I threw an *ura geh* sequence that diverted the white blurs of his bullets, then followed in with a *uin tahn wyla* that chopped the barrel off his weapon, a reverse *tahn* stroke that severed his forearms, and then the *ewl caer*. The death stroke.

Hot red blood was already spurting from his arm stumps and steaming in the freezing air as Barbarisater plunged through his ceramite chest armour and burst his heart. The gunshot walls were painted with instantly frozen dribbles of bloody ice.

A bullet creased the corner of my jaw with enough force to rip open the flesh of my chin and knock me to the carpet. I tried to rise, but the third Vessorine was right over me. I heard his weapon rack.

He screamed. I smelled a burning in the cold air.

I looked up.

The Vessorine was trying to shield himself, as if from a swarm of stinging insects. Crezia's cyber skulls were flitting around him, stabbing repeatedly with their surgical lasers.

His yelps were cut off by the double crack of a las-weapon. The janissary collapsed like a deadweight at my feet.

I looked down the hall and saw Eleena Koi in the doorway of my room, holding her pistol in a defiant two-handed grip.

'Eleena!' I yelled. 'Get the others out of the compartment! Get them out into the hall and move them this way!'

'But Medea–' she began.

'Do it!'

I ran to the cut-out car window and hauled myself out into the vicious chill. I had to sheath Barbarisater and it didn't like it. Outside, it was bone-achingly cold and the blizzard pummelled me with hail hard as stones. There was precious little in the way of handholds and the exterior of the car was iced up.

I found something to cling to... solid runnels of ice, I think. My fingers went numb.

I hauled myself up onto the roof of car three, the vast snow-peppered blackness of the Atenate night above me.

The blizzard ensured I couldn't see far. I could barely stand up. The convex aluminium roof of the wagon was iced smooth as a skating rink.

A few steps along and my legs went out. I fell smack on my front, dazed and winded. Blood filled my mouth; I had bitten my tongue.

Spitting blood and made angry by the pain, I dragged myself forward through the elemental deluge. I saw shapes ahead of me in the white-on-black maelstrom. Three more armoured figures on the edge of the roof.

They had lowered a directional detonator onto the window of the cabin I had shared with Aemos. As I watched, they triggered it and blasted the window inwards in a hail of glass and fire. The first janissary began to rope down to swing in through the blown window. His comrades were hunched on the rooftop, anchoring his lines.

I leapt up and Barbarisater flew out, crackling in the wet air.

The augmented Carthean warblade came down, splitting the lines in two and cutting deeply into the wagon roof. The descending killer shrieked as he fell away down the side of the two storey carriage.

The other two jerked round like lightning, one going for his sidearm, the other leaping at me with clawing hands. A *tahn wyla* met him and bisected his head like a ripe gummice fruit.

The corpse rolled off the car top into the darkness. I stood ready, Barbarisater twitching in my hands. The remaining Vessorine backed away, aiming a large calibre autopistol at me. The two of us could barely stand, such was the blizzard's windshear.

He fired once. An *ulsar* flicked the round away. He fired again, his feet slipping, and I made an *uin ulsar* that spat the bullet off into the darkness.

'My name is Gregor Eisenhorn. I am the man you have been paid to kill. Identify yourself.'

He hesitated. 'My nomclat be Etrik, badge of Clansire. Clan Szober.'

'Clansire Etrik. I've heard so much about you.' I had to raise my voice over the storm. 'Vammeko Tarl mentioned your name.'

'Tarl? He be–'

'The one who let you aboard?' I finished for him. 'I thought so. I had a feeling he'd been tailing me.'

'Be it he you just slew.'

'Is that so? Tough. Give yourself up.'

'I will not.'

'Uh huh. Tell me this, then... how much is Pontius paying your clan for this work?'

'Who be Pontius?'

'Khanjar, then. Khanjar the Sharp.'

'Enough.'

He fired again and then lunged at me, swinging a power sword up in his left hand. Barbarisater knocked the whizzing slug away and then formed an *uwe sar* to block the downswing of the glittering blade. There was a bark of clashing energies.

I switched to a double-handed grip and ripped Barbarisater in a cross-wise stroke as Etrik tried to use his pistol again. The tip of the blade cut through the gun's body and left him with only a handgrip. But the Clansire's sword, a short yet robust falchion of antique design, darted in and sliced through the meat of my right shoulder. I howled.

I snarled into a *leht suf* that rebounded his thrust and swung reversing *ulsars* that parried two more fast cuts and put me on the front foot. Etrik was a big man, with a considerable reach and alarming strength. That meant even his most nimble and extended strikes were delivered with punishing force. I did not recognise the blade technique he was using, although I was aware that the warriors of Vessor considered sword skill one of the three primary battle arts, devoting as much time to it during their training as to gun lore and open hand. The very fact he was the owner of an heirloom power weapon identified him as an expert.

My skills were a heterodox blend of methods that I had mastered over the years, but at the core of them was the *Ewl Wyla Scryi* or 'the genius of sharpness', the ancient Carthean swordmastery system.

On top of the Trans-Atenate Express, any blade methods had to be semi-improvised. Neither of us were steady on our feet, our boots sliding on the iced metal, and the gale dragged at us hard.

He kept attacking high, aiming for the throat, I imagine, and I was driven into a variety of *tahn feh sar* parries with a tightly vertical blade that defend the head and ear. My own attacks were lower, *fon uls* and *fon uin* strokes that targeted the heart, belly and swordarm.

His defence was excellent, especially a sliding backdrag that fouled every *fon bei* I struck in an attempt to push his blade down laterally and open his guard. His attack strokes were inventively arrhythmic, preventing all but the most last moment anticipations. He was hideously skilful.

I wondered if that was why Pontius Glaw had hired these Vessorines. He was such a connoisseur of martial skills and warrior breeds. He didn't just want killers. He wanted masters of the killing art.

In Clansire Etrik, he'd got his money's worth.

I realised that the mercenary, with a combination of cross parries and driving thrust strokes, was pressing me back towards the gap between carriages three and four. I was cornered with my back to the drop, my combat options restricted. I didn't dare risk a backwards jump without looking, and I couldn't take my eyes off his sword for a moment. I knew he would be building up to a sharp frontal attack that would either catch me with no room to dodge or topple me off the edge.

Carthean sword-craft teaches that when an imminent attack is unavoidable, the only practical response is to limit or force it. The technique, which has many forms, is called the *gej kul asf*, which means 'the bridled steed'. It imagines the adversary is an unbroken mount who is going to charge no matter what you do, and that your blade is a long-reined bridle that will control that charge on your terms. Etrik was going to lunge, so I needed to reduce the lunging options. I went into an *ehn kulsar*, where the sword is raised, two-handed, with the hilt above shoulder height and the blade tipped down in a thirty-five degree angle from the horizontal. Sharp, lateral blade turns robbed him of any sideways or upper body opportunities. His only option was to come in low, parrying up, to get in underneath my guard. I was forcing him to target my lower body, an area his swordplay had shown he didn't favour. It also required him to extend in a low, ill-balanced way.

Etrik made the lunge, shoulder down and sword rising from a hip-height grip. My 'bridle' entirely determined the height and direction of the thrust.

Instead of backing or attempting to knock his rising blade aside with a diagonal stroke, I sidestepped, like a bull-dancer evading a head-down aurox in the karnivale pits of Mankareal. Now he was running his sword into empty space.

He tried to pull in, but he'd committed his weight behind it. His left foot kicked out on the roof ice and his right one went skidding sideways. Etrik grunted out a curse and did the only thing he could. He turned his lunge into a leap.

He just made the roof of the next wagon, his chest and arms slamming into it, his legs wheeling over the drop. His falchion had a pommel spike and he slammed it down into the roof to anchor himself, his boots trying to get a grip on the weatherproof plastic sides of the intercarriage articulation.

I had seconds to turn my temporary advantage into a permanent upper hand.

But my hasty sidestep had left me with no more purchase on the iced roof than Etrik. My legs suddenly flew out from under me and I crashed down on my back. I rolled as fast as I could and fumbled for a handhold, but it cost me Barbarisater. The precious sword squealed as it tumbled over the edge of the roof.

I was holding on, barely. Etrik's pommel spike shrieked across the roof metal as he put his weight onto it and dug in. With a few scrabbling kicks, he hoisted himself up onto the roof of car four and looked back at me. He chuckled an ugly jeer as he saw me worse off than he was.

Still chuckling, he gingerly took one step out onto the top of the intercarriage articulation, and then another, balancing as he crossed back to car three to finish me off.

Another two steps, and he would be within stabbing range.

I decided which of my handholds was most secure and let go with the other, fumbling round behind myself.

Etrik came off the articulation, took the last step, his sword raised to rip at me, and found himself looking down the barrel of my autopistol.

It was contrary to all the noble rules of the *Ewl Wyla Scryi* to start a sword duel and finish it with a gun. The Carthean masters would have been ashamed of me. But I wasn't feeling particularly noble by then.

I fired just once. The shot hit him in the sternum and slammed him backwards. With a cheated look on his face, Etrik disappeared off the far side of the roof.

I was exhausted, and drained from the extreme cold, by the time I got back inside the car. The upper hallway was full of people. Stewards were ushering terrified and distraught passengers into other cars. Master personnel were gazing in perplexed dismay at the fight damage and the trio of Vessorine corpses. Eleena was arguing heatedly with one of the master crewmen.

Everyone looked round and someone screamed as I slithered back in through the window. I must have looked a sight: caked in frost and frozen blood from the wounds to my arm and chin.

Crezia and Aemos pushed through the onlookers and reached my side.

'I'm alright.'

'Let me look at that... Golden Throne!' gasped Crezia, twisting my head to study the gash in my chin.

'Don't fuss.'

'You need–'

'Now's not the time. Is Medea all right?'

'Yes,' said Aemos.

'So you're all unscathed?'

'You're wounded enough for all of us,' Crezia said.

'I've had worse,' I said.

'He has,' agreed Aemos. 'He's had worse.'

Eleena was still shouting at the train master, who was shouting right back at her. He was a tall, distinguished man in an ornate, brocaded version of the Trans-Continental uniform topped with a Navy-style cap. Clearly very old, his eyes, nose and ears had been replaced with augmetic implants: primitive, functional devices finished in boiler-metal black that probably had been handcrafted for him by the locomotive's devoted engineers. Even his teeth, framed by a spectacular white tile beard, were cast iron. His name was Alivander Suko, and I later discovered that he had been master of the Trans-Atenate

Express for three hundred and seventy-eight years. He looked like a bearded locomotive in human form.

I pulled Eleena back and faced him.

'I demand an explanation,' Suko growled, his voice reverberating from a mechanical larynx, 'for this... outrage. Nothing like this has ever happened aboard the Trans-Atenate. This vulgar violence and impropriety–'

'Impropriety?' I echoed.

'Are you responsible for this?' he asked.

'I would not have chosen for this to occur, but... yes.'

'Detain him now!' Suko yelled. A pair of burly train guards who had withdrawn laspistols from the express's emergency locker the moment the alarms had started sounding, stepped forward.

'There are three dead here, three more outside,' I said softly, looking into the train master's electric-shuttered eyes and pointedly ignoring the guards. 'All armoured, all armed... combat warriors. Do you really think it's a good idea to mess with the man who killed them?'

Silence fell on the corridor, colder and harsher than the ice storm still gusting in through the shattered window. All eyes were on us, including, to Suko's discomfort, the last of the gawping passengers still being herded out.

'Shall we continue this in private?' I suggested.

We went into one of the vacated cabins. I opened the hinged wooden cover of the suite's little cogitator, switched it to hololithic mode and pressed my signet ring against the data-reader. The little desk projected a hologram of the Inquisitorial seal, overlaid by credential details, followed by a slowly turning three dimensional scan of my head.

'I am Inquisitor Gregor Eisenhorn of the Ordos Helican.' Suko and his guards were speechless.

'Do you accept that, or would you like me to rotate slowly in front of you until you're convinced?'

The train master looked at me, so taken aback he barely knew what to say. 'I'm sorry, my lord,' he began. 'How can Trans-Continental assist the work of the mighty ordos?'

'Well, sir, you can get this train moving again for a start.'

'But–'

I'd had enough. 'I have been travelling incognito, sir. But not any more. And if I'm going to reveal myself as an inquisitor, I'm damn well going to behave like one. This train is now under my control.'

We remained halted long enough for the engineers to service the brakes and secure the exploded windows. And long enough for the train guards, under my direct supervision, to search the entire vehicle for any other passengers without tickets.

Wrapped in crew-issue foul-weather gear, I went outside and retrieved Barbarisater, which complained fractiously about being left in the blizzard. I sheathed the whining blade and went to check on the three janissaries who lay sprawled and stiffening in the snow.

The express resumed progress at five and there were no more interruptions. We thundered out of the night and into a more temperate dawn where the land was thick with snow but the ice storms had abated.

Suko raced the locomotive right up to the safety margins to make up time. The express cut down through the southern extremities of the Atenate Range, descending through hill country and rocky glacial plains. If I'd been awake, I would have seen hard pasture and scree slowly blooming into forest and deciduous woodland, and then the first little hamlets of the vast Southern Plateau, sunlit in the morning air.

But I was deep asleep, my wounds dressed, Barbarisater slumbering fitfully at my side and Crezia watching over me.

I woke after five, with the express still making excellent time. We were due in at New Gevae at midnight. I'd given Suko strict instructions to send no word ahead of our plight.

It was likely that Pontius would try again at New Gevae. I studied the route map and thought about getting Suko to make an unscheduled stop at one of the satellite stations in the towns north of New Gevae. We could disembark and hire air transport, and the train could run on to the city.

I thought my implacable and attentive enemy might anticipate this move. And I also considered that arriving in plain view at a major city terminal might be the safer plan.

I lay on my cabin's cot, meditating as the lowland scenery of the plateau zipped by outside. Medea was up and around by then, hobbling painfully and using, of all things, my runestaff as a crutch. Only she would have the wit to dare such disrespect.

She limped into my cabin and flopped down on the edge of my cot, nursing her sore back. Crezia was asleep in the opposite berth.

'Never a dull moment, eh?' said Medea.

'Never.'

She nodded over at Crezia. 'She didn't leave your side, Gregor. All day.'

'I know.'

'She's more than just an old friend, isn't she?'

'Yes, Medea.'

'You and your secrets.'

'I know.'

'You never told me.'

'I never told anyone. Crezia Berschilde deserved the privacy.'

She glanced at me. 'Gregor Eisenhorn deserved the privacy too, don't you think? You may be a great and terrible inquisitor and everything, but you're a human being too. You have a life outside this awful work.'

I thought about that. Sadly, I didn't agree.

'But you're together again, then. You and the good doctor.'

'I have renewed a friendship I should never have allowed to lapse.'

'Yeah, right. Renewed.' She made a surprisingly coarse and graphic gesture.

I couldn't help but smile. 'Was there something else, or did you just come in to demonstrate the vulgar extremes of your miming ability?'

'Yeah, there was something else. What do we do when we get there?'

New Gevae was a cluster of monolithic hive pyramids covering the delta of the Sanas river. We could see its twinkling lights in the distance over an hour before we arrived. The Trans-Atenate Express rattled and hissed into the main terminal at two minutes to midnight. I got out ahead of the crowds and strode across the wide concourse under the arched glass roof to the Astropathic Guild's office near the freight cargo pens.

I accessed the Aegis account and read the reply from Nayl. He agreed that it was like the trouble on Eechan, and cursed Sadia's name. He said the *Caucus* was ready to ship out, and that he would be at a bar called Entipaul's Lounge at noon the next day. The bar was in hive four, level sixty.

I looked at the communiqué sadly and then glanced at the waiting adept. 'Two-word reply. "Rosethorn attends". Send it.'

I walked into Entipaul's Lounge the next day at a minute before noon. It was a cage of aluminium tubes and spray-painted flakboard panels artfully wired up so that the ropes of lights pulsed in time to the pound music the place pumped through the caster system. The place wanted to seem tough and underhive and dangerous, but it was all for show. This was a lunchtime and after-work watering hole for mid-hive clerks and Administratum graders, a place for assignations with winsome girls from the logosticator pool, the celebrations that accompanied promotions or retirements, or rowdy birthday drinks. I'd been into real twist bars and heard genuine pound. This place was just sham, theatre.

I was shrouded in Aemos's over-robe, the hood pulled up, wearing a rebreather mask I'd borrowed from the express. I wanted to look like some tech-adept on his lunch break, or a warewright stealing off for a tryst with his girl.

The place was largely empty. A bored-looking steward polished glasses behind the narrow sweep of the bar, and two uniformed waitresses chatted in the rear doorway, holding their glass trays like riot shields. Half a dozen men sat in the booths that radiated off the bar's central hub, and a hooded figure was sitting, drinking alone, with its back to the door.

I sat at one of the hub tables. One of the waitresses approached. She smelled of obscura and her pencilled eyebrows framed wildly dilated eyes.

'Choice?'

'Tunderey clear-grain, double, in a chill-sleeve.'

'Dokey-doke,' she returned as she stalked away.

The music continued to blast. She returned with a single

shot glass on her suspensor tray. The glass was actually a cup of pressure-moulded ice. She tonged it onto my table and caught the coin I flipped at her.

'Keep the change,' I murmured.

'Big spender,' she mocked and paced off, wiggling a backside that had no business being wiggled.

I didn't touch the drink. Gradually, the ice melted and the oily liquid began to seep out over the table top.

The hooded figure got up and wandered over to me.

'Rosethorn?'

I looked up. 'That's me.'

She dropped the hooded cloak away from her shoulders. She had sharp features and long, straight black hair. Her kohl-edged eyes glinted like jade.

Not Harlon Nayl at all. Marla Tarray.

She sat down opposite me and knocked back my drink, licking the ice-water off her long fingers.

'You knew we'd get you sooner or later.'

'I guess so. Who's we?'

The other drinkers in the bar had got up and formed a circle around us, sitting at adjacent tables. Marla Tarray clicked her fingers and they all drew back coats or cloaks to reveal the handguns they carried. She clicked again and the weapons disappeared.

'So this is a trap?'

'Of course.'

'The astrograms weren't from Nayl?'

'Evidently.'

'You've broken Glossia?'

'How clever are we?'

I sat back. 'How did you do that?'

'Wouldn't you like to know, Mr Eisenhorn?'

I shrugged. 'Seeing as you've got me cold, yes. These men are more of your damned Vessorine, aren't they? I'm dead in my seat. I can't see the harm.'

'I imagine you've guessed already.' she said. She smiled. I could feel her powerful mind trying to delve into mine.

'Jekud Vance.'

'That's right, Mr Eisenhorn. Your astropath proved to be very useful. With the right persuasion. And the Janissaries excel at persuasion. Vance sent the communiqués, pretending to be Nayl. He knew Glossia.'

She probed at my mind again.

'You're using shielding techniques,' she said, her face darkening.

'Of course I am. You would be too if the situation was reversed. I have to say though, I'm disappointed. I was hoping that Pontius might be here himself. This is a trap after all. Eisenhorn's last stand. He might have been civil enough to come and watch me die.'

'Pontius is busy elsewhere,' she snapped, and then realised what she'd said.

'Thank you for that confirmation,' I said.

'You bastard!' she snapped. 'You're dead! What good will it do you? This is a trap!'

'Yes, it is. A trap.'

She hesitated. The janissaries had all risen, guns out, aiming at me. The bar staff were fleeing, terrified.

Marla Tarray slowly reached out and took the rebreather mask off my face.

'Etrik?' she stammered, her jade eyes wide.

'Yes,' I said, three kilometres away in a locked lodging house room, sweating and straining as I channeled my will via the runestaff and animated the body of Clansire Etrik.

Tarray leapt back from the table, knocking over her chair. 'Damnation!' she shrieked. 'He's got us! He's got us! How the hell did he know?'

'You could talk like Nayl and use Glossia thanks to Jekud, but Jekud didn't know what Nayl knew. We fought Sadia on Lethe Eleven, not Eechan,' I had Etrik say.

Marla Tarray drew a plasma pistol and shot Etrik through the chest. The Vessorines all around opened fire with their autoguns and las-carbines.

As my puppet was torn apart, I let go of the warp vortex that had been spinning in my mind ever since I had summoned it.

It surged out of Etrik's collapsing body and expanded, annihilating the janissaries, Entipaul's Lounge and the entire level sixty deck of hive four in a radius of fifty metres.

Marla Tarray was atomised. In the last milliseconds of her life, her mental shields collapsed in terror and I got a precious snapshot into her powerful psyker mind. Not everything, but enough.

Enough to know that I had just annihilated Pontius Glaw's daughter.

FIFTEEN

Sanctum, Catharsis and Fischig
Teht uin sah
Promody

Fifteen days later, we were a long, long way from New Gevae, a long way from Gudrun itself. I had, for the time being, evaded the clutches of Khanjar the Sharp.

The morning before my meeting – or my puppet's meeting, I should say – with Marla Tarray in the mid-hive bar, Aemos and I had arranged passage on a packet lighter called the *Spirit of Wysten*, and by the evening, we were leaving the planet. Five and a half days out from Gudrun, in the vicinity of Cyto, we rendezvoused with the *Essene*.

My old friend Tobias Maxilla, eccentric master of the sprint trader *Essene*, had come in response to the Glossia code word 'Sanctum' without hesitation, breaking off from his merchant runs in the Helican spinwards and laying course for Gudrun. He had never been a formal part of my operation, but he was an ally of long standing, and had provided the services of his ship on many occasions.

He always claimed to do this for financial reward – I regularly made sure the ordos remunerated him handsomely – and to keep on the good side of the Imperial Inquisition. Privately, I believe his allegiance to me was the product of an adventurous streak. Getting involved in my business offered more diverting occupation than a trade voyage down the Helican worlds.

There was no ship, and no ship's master, that I trusted more than Tobias Maxilla and the *Essene*. With my life shattered, my back to the wall and an enemy after my blood, he was the one I turned to for rescue and escape.

One could also always rely on Maxilla to lift a company's spirits. In truth, the mood in my little group had been uncomfortable since New Gevae. And that was largely my own fault.

As soon as I had realised that 'Nayl' was just another of Glaw's deceits, a ruse to lure me into a trap, I had set my trap in return. Certain sections of the *Malus Codicium* concerned the creation and remote animation of thralls – human beings psionically controlled as puppets. I had never tried the technique, for it seemed ghoulish. The *Codicium* suggested the process worked best with a freshly killed cadaver. But on the other hand, it was simply an elaborate extension of my use of will, and it suited my purpose.

I didn't go into detail about what I was going to do, but Medea, Eleena, Crezia and Aemos knew something unorthodox was afoot, and they were all concerned when I had Etrik's body covertly taken from the train to a lodging we had rented in hive four. Crezia mumbled something about body snatching, and Medea was dubious. Back aboard the *Pulchritude*, she'd shrugged off as a joke the idea that I was dabbling too far. She seemed to have accepted the whole business with Cherubael.

Now she seemed less confident about esoteric psyker tricks.

Even Aemos seemed reserved. He had not said a word about the *Malus Codicium* since he'd seen me remove it from the safe in my study. And he'd made it clear on several occasions that he trusted my judgement.

But there had still been a feeling in the air.

I kept them out of the room while I performed the rituals, and that may have been a mistake too. Except for Eleena, who was spared the sensations, they all felt the unnerving, creeping backwash of the act.

I had also never used a warp vortex before, but it seemed the only weapon I could equip my thrall with that would trap the trappers. In hindsight, I wonder if the *Malus Codicium* had planted the idea in my head.

The vortex worked. It destroyed the enemies who had tried to snare me. I doubt I will use one again. The feedback left me unconscious, and I was ill and weak for two days afterwards. My friends had to break down the door of the room to get at me, and they must have been shaken by the sight that greeted them. The burnt circle on the floor, the psy-plasmic residue trickling off the walls, the symbols I had painted. I think they felt for the first time that I had attempted something I wasn't quite in control of.

Perhaps they were right.

None of them had wanted to talk about it. Aemos had found the *Malus Codicium* on the floor beside me and slipped it into his pocket before the others could see it. Later, aboard the *Spirit of Wysten*, he'd handed it back to me privately.

'I don't want to touch it again,' he said. 'I don't think I want to see it again.'

I was unhappy at his reaction. His life was devoted to the acquisition of knowledge – it was an actual clinical compulsion in his case – but there he was rejecting a source of secret data, albeit dark, that could be found almost nowhere else in the galaxy. I thought he alone might appreciate its worth.

'It's the *Malus Codicium*, isn't it?'

'Yes.'

'They never found it. On Farness Beta, after Quixos fell, the ordos searched for it and never found it.'

'That's true.'

'Because you took it for yourself and never told them.'

'Yes. It was my decision.'

'I see. And that's how you learned to control daemonhosts too, isn't it?'

'Yes.'

'I'm disappointed in you, Gregor.'

Maxilla was, as ever, the perfect host, and the general spirit did pick up a little once we were in his company. He met us at the *Essene's* fore starboard airgate, dressed in a chequered sedril gown-coat, a blue silk cravat pinned with a golden star pin and a purple suede calotte with a silver tassel. His skin dye was gloss white with black hearts over his eyes, and a fine platinum chain ran between the diamond earring in his left lobe to the sapphire stud in his nose. Behind him, gold-plated servitors waited with salvers of refreshments. He greeted us all, flirting with Medea and making a particular fuss of Crezia and Eleena, two females he had not met before.

'Where to?' was his first question to me.

'Let me use your astropath, and set course for the place we first met.'

I sent word, in Glossia, to Fischig, telling him to alter his route to avoid Gudrun and meet me at a new rendezvous point. 'Thorn wishes Hound, at Hound's cradle, by sext.' Maxilla's cadaverous, nameless Navigator performed his hyper-mathematical feats of divination, and set the *Essene* thundering into warp space as fast as its potent drive could carry it.

As always, I was unable to rest easily while travelling in the hellish netherworld of the warp, so instead I retired with Maxilla to his stateroom. He was a terrible gossip and always relished a few hours catching up whenever we were reunited. Surrounded as he was by a crew that was more servitor than human, he did so crave company.

But I had been looking forward to a private talk. I'd never confided in him particularly before, but now I felt he might be the only man in the Imperium who would give me a fair hearing. And if not fair, then at least one free of harsh judgment. Maxilla was a rogue. He made no excuses about it. His entire life had been devoted to testing the ductile qualities of rules and regulations. I wanted, I suppose, to find out what he thought of me.

His stateroom was a double-storey cabin behind the *Essene's* cathedral-like main bridge. A ten-seat banquet table of polished duralloy that I had dined at many times before occupied a mezzanine area at the far end under a domed section of roof that could peel back shielding at the wave of a control wand to become an observation blister.

Curved stairways, with tefrawood balustrades that Maxilla claimed had been salvaged from a twenty mast sunjammer on Nautilia, ran down from either end of the mezzanine onto the main deck area, a wide hall with a floor of inlaid marble. Works of art – paintings, statues, antiques, hololiths – were displayed all round the room between the crystelephantine wall pillars. Some were protected by softly glowing stasis fields, others hung weightlessly in invisible repulsor beams.

Elegant scroll-armed couches and chairs, some draped with

throws of Sampanese light-cloth, were arranged on a large rectangle of exquisite Olitari rugwork in the centre of the room. The rug alone was worth a small fortune. The room was illuminated by six shimmering chandeliers from the glass-works of Vitria, each one suspended by a small antigrav plate so they floated below the dished ceiling.

I sat down on a couch and accepted the balloon of amasec Maxilla handed to me.

'You look like a man who wishes to unburden himself, Gregor,' he said, taking a seat opposite.

'Am I so transparent?'

'No, I fear it is rather more a case that I am hopeful. It's been a boring few months. I crave excitement. And when the only man I know who makes a habit of getting involved in the most ridiculously perilous ventures anyone ever heard of calls to me for help, I perk up.'

He fitted a lho-stick into a long silver holder, lit it with a tiny flick of his digital ring weapon and sat back, exhaling spiced smoke, rolling the amasec in his glass around with an experienced hand.

'I...' I tried to begin, but I didn't really know where to start.

He put his glass down and made a gesture with his control wand like a theatrical conjuror. The air became close and slightly muffled.

'Speak freely,' he told me. 'I've activated the suite's privacy field.'

'Actually,' I admitted, 'my hesitation was more to do with not knowing what to say.'

'I deal in routes and journeys, Gregor. In my experience, the best place to start is always–'

'The beginning? I know.'

I told him, first in general terms and then with increasing

detail, about the events as they had unfolded. Durer. Thuring. The battles with *Cruor Vult* and Cherubael. His dyed face became tragic, like a clown's, as I told him about Alizebeth. He had always had a soft spot for her.

Though I felt I had taken his advice and started from the beginning, I realised more and more that I had not. I kept going back, filling in details. To explain Cherubael, I had to go back to Farness Beta and the struggle against Quixos, and that in turn required mention of the mission to Cinchare. I told him about the assault on Spaeton House and our desperate flight across Gudrun. I recounted the murders that had taken place across the sub-sector. He'd known Harlon Nayl and Nathun Inshabel, not to mention several other members of my team. My account of Pontius Glaw's revenge was a litany of bad tidings.

Once I had begun, I couldn't stop. I spared nothing. It felt liberating to confess everything at last and unburden myself. I told him about the *Malus Codicium*, and how I might have compromised myself by keeping it. I told him about my dabbling with daemonhosts. And thralls. And warp vortices. I owned up to the deal I had struck with Glaw on Cinchare and how that had empowered him and turned him into the threat that now pursued me.

'Everyone, Tobias, everyone in my operation – my family, if you will – everyone except you, Fischig and the handful I brought aboard here with me, has died because of what I did on Cinchare. Something in the order of... well, I haven't made an exact count. Two hundred servants of the Imperium. Two hundred people who had devoted themselves to my cause in the firm belief that I was doing good work... are dead. I'm not even counting the likes of Poul Rassi, Duclane Haar and that poor bastard Verveuk who perished in what turns out to be the overture to this bloodbath. Or Magos Bure, who must have been killed by Glaw for him to have escaped.'

'Might I correct you, Gregor?' he asked.

'By all means.'

'You called it *your* cause. That they were devoted to your cause. But it isn't, is it?'

'What do you mean?'

'You still, passionately, believe that you are doing the Emperor's work?'

'Damn right I do!'

'Then they died in the service of the Emperor. They died for His cause. No Imperial citizen can ask for anything more.'

'I don't think you were listening, Maxilla–'

He got to his feet. 'No, I don't think you were, inquisitor. Not even to yourself. I'm pressing this point because it's so basic you seem to have overlooked it.'

He walked across the stateroom and stood looking up at a hololithic portrait of an Imperial warrior. It was very old. I didn't want to think where he might have got it from.

'Do you know who this is?'

'No.'

'Warmaster Terfuek. Commanded the Imperial forces in the Pacificus War, almost fifty centuries ago. Ancient history now. Most of us couldn't say what the damn war was about any more. At the Battle of Corossa, Terfeuk committed four million Imperial Guardsman to the field. Four million, Gregor. They don't do battles like that any more, thank the Throne. It was of course the age of High Imperialism, the era of the notable warmaster, the cult of personality. Anyway, Terfeuk got his victory. Not even his advisors thought he could win at Corossa, but he did. And of those four million men, only ninety thousand left the field alive.'

Maxilla turned and looked at me. 'Do you know what he said? Terfeuk? Do you know what he said of that terrible cost?'

I shook my head.

'He said it was the greatest honour of his life to have served the Emperor so well.'

'I'm happy for him.'

'You don't understand, Gregor. Terfeuk was no butcher. No glory hound. By all accounts he was humane, and beloved by his men as fair and generous. But when the time came, he did not regret for a moment the cost of serving the Emperor and preserving the Imperium against all odds.'

Maxilla sat down again. 'I think that's all you're guilty of. Making hard choices to serve the Emperor the best you can, to serve him where maybe others would not be strong enough and fail. Doing your duty and living with the consequences. I'm sure dear Terfeuk had sleepless nights for years after Corossa. But he dealt with that pain. He didn't have any regrets.'

'Committing men to battle is not quite the same as–'

'I beg to differ. Imperial society is your battleground. The people you have lost were your soldiers. And soldiers are only martial resources. They are there to be used. You used your own resources to win your battles. This book you speak of. This daemonhost. He sounds fascinating. I'd love to meet him.'

'You wouldn't, I assure you. And it's an "it" not a "he".'

Maxilla shrugged. 'I fancy you wanted to talk to me about this because you thought you might get a sympathetic ear. Me being an old rogue and everything.' There were times, I swear, I believed Maxilla could read my mind.

'Let me tell you something, Gregor. I love you like a brother, but we're nothing alike. I am a rogue. A gambler. A liar. A reprobate. My vices are many and unmentionable. I never bend the rules; I break them. Snap them. Shatter them. However

312 DAN ABNETT

and wherever I may. In that regard alone, I am a kindred spirit. You are bending the rules of the Imperium, of the Inquisition. You are, undoubtedly, what they call a radical. But that's where the similarity ends. I break the rules for my own gain. To get what I want, to amplify my wealth and status. To make things better for me. Me. Just me. But you're not doing it for yourself. You're doing it for the system you believe in and the God-Emperor you worship and by damn, that means your conscience can be clean.'

I was taken aback by the passion of his speech. I was also taken aback by the suggestion – one that no one had dared make before – that I had become a radical. When had that happened? My actions may have been radical but did that make me a radical to the marrow?

Sitting there, in that opulent room, I realised Maxilla had hit on the truth, a truth I had been denying. I had changed without recognising that change in myself. I would always be grateful to Tobias Maxilla for that bruising realisation. I felt better for it.

'I suppose you can't turn to your superiors for help?'

'No,' I said, still reeling from the fresh viewpoint.

'Because you'd have to tell them things you don't want them to hear?'

'Of course. To get any kind of official help, I'd have to make a full report. And that report would fall apart under the lightest scrutiny if it omitted the *Codicium*, Cherubael. By the Throne, the list goes back! I even hid Pontius Glaw from them. What could I say? Pontius Glaw is exterminating my forces. Where did he come from, my lord grand master? Well, to be honest, I've known of his existence for centuries, but I kept him hidden from you. And he's only up and around now because I decided to give him a body.'

He chuckled. 'I see your point. What will you tell Fischig? Dear Godwyn is as straight up and down as any man I know.'

'I'll deal with Fischig.'

'So what is your next move? You mentioned this daughter of his, the psyker. You saw things when you killed her, didn't you?'

I had indeed. Marla Tarray's entire mental shield had crumbled just before the vortex annihilated her. The picture I had obtained was far from complete, but it was plentiful.

'Marla Tarray was much older than she looked or claimed. She was the bastard offspring of Pontius Glaw and a serving girl from Gudrun that Glaw had taken with him to Quenthus Eight. Marla was born in 020, corrupted from conception by the tainted torc Pontius wore. Several notorious heretics who have evaded the Inquisition in the last three hundred years were actually her under different guises. Many cases could be closed now she is dead.'

'Pontius won't be too pleased.'

'I imagine Pontius Glaw now wants me dead even more than before. But they were after the *Malus Codicium*, you see. I learned that from her undefended mind. Glaw knew Quixos must have it and, once Quixos was dead, realised it must be in my possession. He wants that book so much.'

'Do you know why?'

'I saw images of an arid world just before Marla Tarray died. A dried out husk where primaeval cities lay buried under layers of ash. Glaw's after something there, and he needs the *Codicium* to help him.'

'What?'

'I don't know.'

'Where?'

'I don't know that either. There was a name, a word in her

mind. *Ghül*. But I don't know what it means or what it refers to. Her mind was in collapse. Very little made sense.'

'I'll consult my charts and my navigator. Who knows?' He sat forward and looked at me. 'This book. This *Malus Codicium*. May I see it?'

'Why?'

'Because I appreciate unique and priceless objects.'

I took it from my jacket and passed it to him. He studied it with reverence, a smile on his face.

'Not much to look at, but beautiful for what it is. Thank you for the opportunity to hold it.' He handed it back to me.

'I can't believe I'm going to say this,' he added, 'me of all people. But... I'd destroy it, if I were you.'

'I think you're right. I believe I will.'

I put down my empty glass and walked to the doors. Maxilla evaporated the privacy field.

'Thank you for your time and hospitality, Tobias. I think I'll turn in now.'

'Sleep well.'

'One last thing,' I said, turning back in the doorway. 'You said you break the rules to get what you want. That you serve no one but yourself and everything you do is for your own ends.'

'I did.'

'Then why do you help me so often?'

He smiled. 'Good night, Gregor.'

The *Essene* put in at Hubris four days later. Hubris was an outlying world in the Helican sub-sector and Fischig, Bequin, Maxilla and I had all met there for the first time in 240.

Indirectly, that's where we'd first stumbled across Pontius Glaw too. Everything was turning full circle in the strangest way.

I had rerouted Fischig here as a convenient and out of the way meeting place, but it seemed apt. He'd been a chastener in the local Arbites when he'd first crossed my path. It was his homeworld.

For eleven out of every twenty-nine months, Hubris orbits so far beyond its star that the population are forced to hibernate in massive cryogenic tombs to survive the blackness and the cold. Those winters of eternal night are called Dormant and I had experienced one on that last visit.

But now we arrived at the start of Thaw, the middle season between Dormant and Vital.

The tombs had emptied and the great cities were waking under a pale sun. The population was engaged in a frenzied jubilee of feasting and dancing and general excess that lasted three weeks and was supposed to celebrate the society's rebirth, but which probably had deep rooted origins in the traditional methods of recovery from extended cryogenic suspension such as forced physical activity and high-calorie intake.

I offered to travel to the surface to meet him, partly because I thought Crezia, Eleena and Medea could do with the relaxation of a festival and Maxilla had never been one to turn down a party.

But Fischig answered he would as soon come up to the *Essene*, and he arrived, piloting his own shuttle, a few hours later.

I could tell he was tense from the moment he stepped aboard. He was polite, and seemed pleased to see Medea, Aemos and Maxilla. But with me he was reserved.

I told him it was good to see him, and that I was relieved he had escaped Glaw's purge.

'Glaw, eh?' he said. He had heard all about the fall of the Distaff and our other holdings. 'I had wondered who it was.'

'We need to talk,' I said.

'Yes,' he said. 'But not here.'

Maxilla lent us his stateroom and I turned on the privacy field.

'There's nothing you couldn't say in front of the others, God-wyn,' I said.

'No? Glaw's killed everyone except us few. Because–'

'Because?'

'You should have destroyed that monster years ago, Eisen-horn. That, or handed him over to the ordos. What the hell were you thinking?'

'Same as I'm thinking now. I did what was best.'

'Nayl? Inshabel? Bure? Suskova? The whole damn Distaff? That was best?' His tone was venomous.

'Yes, Fischig. And I never heard you contradict my decisions.'

'Like you'd have listened!'

'To you? Yes. Not once did I hear you say we should turn Glaw over to the ordos.'

'Because you always make it sound so logical! Like you know best!'

I shrugged. 'This is beneath you, Godwyn. It sounds like sour grapes. Things didn't turn out the way I would have wished and you're making out it's all my fault. I took tough decisions that I thought were right. If you'd ever – *ever* – objected, I'd have considered your opinion.'

'Too easy, too damn easy. I was only ever your lackey, your minion. If I'd said we vapourise Glaw, you'd have said yes and then hidden him anyway.'

'Do you really think I'm that underhand? You, of all my counsel, I respect the most!'

'Yeah?' He tossed his gloves onto a couch and helped him-self to a schooner of Maxilla's clawblood. 'Who told Bure to build Glaw a body without telling any of us? Who suddenly knows how to conjure daemons like an expert? You cover your secrets with such an almighty righteous air we all thank the stars and the Emperor Himself you chose us to help you in your work. But you're a liar! A conspirator! And maybe worse!'

'And you're too much a puritan idealist for your own good. And mine,' I hissed. 'I dearly wanted your help, Godwyn. You are one of the few men I really trust and one of the few humans in space with the stalwart spirit to keep me on the level. I needed you now, in my fight to destroy Glaw. I can't believe you're turning against me like this.'

He stared down at the contents of his glass. 'I always did warn you I would if you crossed the line.'

'I've crossed no line. But if you feel that way... go. Get off this ship and leave me to my work. You'll always have my gratitude for the service you put in. But I won't have this bitterness.'

'That's what you think?'

'Yes.'

He hesitated. 'I gave my life to you, Gregor. I admired you. I always believed you were... right.'

'I still am. I serve the Emperor. Just like you. Get rid of your rancor and we can work together again.'

'Let me think about it.'

'Two days, and we're leaving orbit.'

'Two days then.'

Apparently, his ruminations only took him a day.

I had just received, via the *Essene*'s astropath bank, a rather fascinating communiqué, and I went looked for Fischig. I found Crezia playing regicide with Maxilla in a mid-deck suite. He'd taken quite a shine to Doctor Berschilde.

She got up as I entered the room, and excitedly displayed

the stunning funz-silk gown she was wearing. 'Tobias had his
servitors make it for me! Isn't it gorgeous?'

'It is,' I agreed.

'The poor woman had virtually no wardrobe at all, Gregor.
Just a few travel bags. It was the least I could do. You wait
until you see the epinchire dress they're embroidering for her.'

'Have you seen Fischig?' I asked.

Crezia looked at Maxilla sharply and the ship master suddenly became occupied with his study of the game board.

'What?' I asked.

Crezia took me by the arm and walked me over to the cabin
windows. 'He's gone, Gregor.'

'Gone?'

'Early this morning. He left in his shuttle. Dreadful man.'

'He was my friend, Crezia.'

'Not any more, I think.'

'Did he say anything?'

'No. Not to me. Or to Tobias, except a quick goodbye. He
was up late last night though, talking to Medea and Aemos.'

'About what?'

'I don't know. I wasn't included. Tobias took Eleena and me on
a guided tour of his art collection. He has some extraordinary p–'

'They talked and this morning he just left?'

'I like Medea, but I think she may be a little careless. I'd
never have told that Fischig man about the things you did
in New Gevae.'

'And she did?'

'I'm just saying. She might have.'

I had servitors summon Aemos and Medea. They arrived
in my stateroom at about the same moment. Both of them
looked awkward.

'Well?'

'Well what?' snapped Medea.

'What the hell did you say to him?'

She looked away. Aemos toyed with the hem of his cloak.

'I simply tried to make him understand, Gregor. About what you were doing... what you had done. I thought if he knew it all he might see it like I see it.'

'Really? It didn't cross your mind he was a puritanical son of a bitch on a hair trigger? Just like he's always been?'

'I felt honesty was the best policy,' Aemos muttered. Medea said something under her breath.

'Oh, say it so we can all hear!' I snarled.

'Honesty is the best policy,' Medea said. 'I was appreciating the irony.'

'How so?'

'The stuff you never told us. The honesty you withheld.'

'That's rich coming from you, Medea Betancore. In point of fact, I believe I told you everything. Shared everything. Sworn on my secrets.'

'Yeah, well...' she looked away.

'Oh Throne, you told him, didn't you? You told him about Cherubael and the *Codicium* and Glaw and everything!'

She turned on me, tears in her anguished eyes. 'I thought he would understand if everything was out in the open...'

'No wonder he left,' I said, sitting down.

'Medea was only doing the same as me,' Aemos said. 'We were defending you to him, trying to make him understand and see things the way we saw them. We thought–'

'What?'

'We thought he might change his mind and trust you again if he knew it all.'

'I thought you both had more sense,' I said as I strode past them and out of the room.

* * *

There were several craft cradled in the *Essene's* hangar. Two ferry pods, a bulk pinnace, three standard shuttles and a number of small fliers.

I was busy directing the deck servitors to make a two man speeder flight ready when Medea came in, red-eyed and dressed for the surface in a fleece jacket.

'I'll fly you down,' she said.

'Don't bother. You've done enough.'

'It's my job, Gregor! I'm your pilot!'

'Forget about it.'

I clambered into the tight cockpit of the bright red speeder, pulled the canopy shut and fired up the single, in-line thruster.

The launch chute opened and I shot away from the *Essene* at full throttle.

I tracked his flight path to Catharsis, the capital city of Hubris. Festival flares and fireworks were spitting up above the slanted roofs of the vast inland metropolis. The jubilee was in full swing. Once I had parked the sprightly little flier at Catharsis downport, I found myself weaving through a dense river of jumping, whooping people that clogged the winding streets. All of them showed the grey pallor of recent cold-sleep. All of them were drunk.

Bottles were pressed into my hands and young women and men alike planted kisses on my face. I was jostled and shoved and scattered with petals and confetti. The smell of the cryogenic chemicals sweating out of them permeated the entire town.

It took all afternoon to find him. He was alone in an upstairs suite in a crumbling but characterful hotel overlooking the Processional Tombs.

'Get out,' he said as I opened the door.

'Godwyn...'

'Get the hell out!' he yelled, smashing a shot glass against the far wall. He'd been drinking hard, which was unlike him, although everyone else on Hubris except me must have been in the same state.

Fireworks coughed and whizzed in the square under his windows.

Fischig glowered at me for a long time, and then disappeared into the suite's bathroom. He emerged with two more shot glasses and a dish of ice.

I stood in the doorway and watched as he slowly and carefully prepared two drinks. Anise, poured over smashed ice.

He placed one in front of himself and slid the other one towards the chair opposite.

To me, that was an act of diplomacy.

I sat down facing him and lifted the glass.

'To all we've been together,' I said. We knocked back the shots.

I slid the glass back across the table top towards him and he made two more.

He passed the second one back to me and caught my eyes for the first time. I stared into his face, saw the eye-fogging scar that had already marked him by the time we met, saw the faint mauve scar tissues where the side of his face had been rebuilt after our clash with the saruthi on the warped world orbiting KCX-1288.

'I never meant to run out on you,' he said.

'I didn't ever suppose so. When did Godwyn Fischig last run out on a fight?'

He laughed bitterly. We sank the second drink and he fixed a third.

'Whatever Medea told you. Whatever Aemos told you... it's true. But it's not what you think.'

'Yeah?'

'I'm no heretic, Godwyn.'

'No?'

'I think I might have become what you'd call a radical. But I'm no heretic.'

'Isn't that what a heretic would say?'

'Yes. I guess so. If you'd let me into your mind, you'd see...'

'No thanks!' he shuddered, shoving his chair back with a squeak.

'Okay.' I sipped my glass. 'It won't be the same without you.'

'I know. You and me. Bastards! The Eye of Terror itself was shy of us!'

'Yes it was.'

'We could do it again,' he said.

'We could?'

'We could work side by side like old times and hunt out the darkness.'

'Yes, we could. I'd like that.'

'That's why I'm sorry I ran out like that. I should have stayed.'

I nodded. 'Yes.'

'I owe you that much. I should have tried harder. You're not gone. Not all the way. You're just slipping.'

'Slipping?'

'Into the pit. The radical pit. The pit no one comes back from. But I can pull you out.'

'Pull me out?'

'Yes. It's not too late.'

'Too late for what, Godwyn?'

'Salvation,' he said.

The crowds outside were screaming and clapping. Barrages of fireworks were being launched into the early evening air, scattering new stars in their wake like fireflies.

'What does "salvation" mean?' I asked.

'It's why I'm here, why the Emperor put me at your side. To keep you centred. It's destiny.'

'Is it? And what does destiny entail?'

'Renounce it all. All of it. Give over the *Malus Codicium* to me... the daemonhost, your runestaff. Let me take you back to the ordos headquarters on Thracian. You can do penance there. I'll plead for you, plead for leniency. They wouldn't be too hard on you. You'd be active again before too long.'

'You actually believe that you could take me back to the ordos, tell them what I've done, and they'd let me practise again?'

'They'd understand!'

'Fischig, you don't understand!'

He looked at me, disappointed. 'You won't then?'

'I think this is where I say goodbye. I admire your efforts, but I can't be saved, Godwyn.'

'You can!'

'No,' I shook my head. 'You know why? I don't need saving.'

'Then this is where I say goodbye too,' he said, pouring another drink.

'Remember what we did,' I said.

'Yes.'

I shut the door behind me and left.

It took me three hours to get back to the landing field through the solid mob of revellers. I powered the quick-heeled red speeder back up to the *Essene*.

They were all waiting for me in the hangar as I docked. Maxilla. Crezia. Eleena. Aemos. Medea.

I tugged the rumpled copy of the astropathic communiqué I had received earlier out of my pocket and tossed it at Maxilla. 'We're breaking orbit. New destination: Promody.'

'What about Fischig?' asked Eleena.

'He isn't coming.'

There is a move in Carthean blade work called the *teht uin sah*. The phrase literally describes a position of the feet, but the philosophy is deeper. It means the moment in a duel when you gain the advantage and begin to win home. It is the turning point, the little fulcrum on which a life or death fight turns. The moment your fortunes change and you realise victory can be yours if you rally hard enough.

I felt that the astropathic communiqué from Promody was the equivalent of the *teht uin sah*. It had been sent to me, uncoded, by a trusted friend I hadn't seen in a long time.

It read simply 'Khanjar must be stopped.'

It took the *Essene* ten weeks to reach Promody, a jungle world on the trailing hem of the Scarus sector, specifically the Antimar sub-sector.

I went planetside alone, using the little red speeder, in case it turned out to be a trap.

They were waiting for me on a tropical hillside, below a break of pink-lobed punz trees. The evening was warm and fragrant. Insects fidgeted in the gathering dark. The air was humid.

I got out of the steaming speeder.

My old pupil, Gideon Ravenor, sustained by his force chair, rolled forward across the mossy ground to greet me. To his left, he was flanked by Kara Swole. To his right, Harlon Nayl.

SIXTEEN

Surviving Messina
Gideon's omen
Nothing lasts forever

Harlon gave me a great bearhug and Kara timidly kissed my cheek on tiptoe. I gazed at them both, hardly believing it.

'You have a habit of coming back from the dead,' I said to Harlon. 'I'm just glad it's real this time.'

He frowned. 'What do you mean?'

'I'll explain later. I refuse to explain anything more until you tell me how this is possible.'

'Why don't we go inside?' Ravenor suggested. He led us back up the path through the punz trees and across glades where the light was stained gold by the fleshy orange leaves that formed the canopy. Brilliantly feathered lizards flitted from branch to branch and diaphanous insects the size of man's open palm fluttered like seedcases in the humid breeze.

Ravenor's force chair hissed over the ground a few centimetres in the air, surrounded and suspended by a spherical field generated by the slowly revolving and tilting antigravity hoop that encircled it.

Beyond the wooded slope, the ground was flooded. A vast lake of yellow liquid stretched out under the jungle canopy that sprouted up from the water in lurid clumps. Fronds, rushes and fibrously rooted trees formed hammock islets in the lake, along with batteries of puffy mauve or orange zutaes with giant leaves and tangles of saprophitic vines.

Antigrav walkboards bridged out across the resinous water, linking the dryland to Ravenor's camp by way of several of the hammocks.

The camp had been raised on a duralloy raft twenty metres square, held above the water by locked, cycling repulsor lift-pods. Angular, geometric, the structure the raft supported looked like a large tent, but I realised from its gentle shimmer that it was formed from intersecting fields of opaque force energy.

We went in through the one-way field membrane that formed the door and entered a cool, climate-controlled chamber lit by glow-globes. Equipment was stacked up in metal containers and there were several items of collapsible furniture. Further screens denoted adjoining rooms, veiled off. A grey-haired man in a linen robe was working at a small camp table, reviewing data on a portable codifier.

Kara unfolded three more of the stacked camp chairs while Harlon fetched bottles of chilled fruit-water and some shrink-wrapped ration packs. A young woman came in from one of the other rooms and conferred quietly with the man at the codifier.

'You're busy here, I see?' I said.

'Yes,' said Ravenor. 'The view should be good.'

I didn't quite understand what he meant but I let it pass. There were other things on my mind.

Harlon thumb-popped the cap of a bottle and passed it to me before taking his seat.

'Here's to us all, still alive despite the odds.' He clinked his bottle against mine and Kara toasted with hers.

'Well?' I said.

'A bunch of hard-arse merc bastards smoked the Distaff. Took the whole spire out. Killed the lot of them,' Harlon said, matter of factly, but there was still an edge of rage in his voice.

'And you?'

'Madam Bequin saved us,' said Kara.

'What?'

'We got her back to Messina okay, stable,' said Kara. 'The medicae facility at the Distaff hall made her comfortable. They got me back on my feet in about a week. Then Madam Bequin suddenly took a turn for the worse.'

'She stroked out,' growled Harlon. 'A really bad whassit called–'

'Cerebrovascular ischemia,' Ravenor said quietly.

'It was beyond the abilities or resources of the hall's medicae, so we rushed her to Sandus Sedar Municipal General for surgery,' said Kara. 'We knew you wouldn't want us to leave her there alone, so we stayed with her in shifts. I took one watch, and alternated with Nayl. On the night the hall was raided, I had just started my shift.'

'And I was on my way back to spire eleven in an air cab,' finished Harlon.

'So neither of you were there?'

'No.'

'You two... and Alizebeth... all survived?'

'Lucky us, eh?' said Harlon.

'Where is she?' I asked. 'And how is she?'

'Never regained consciousness. She's on vital support in my ship's infirmary,' Ravenor replied. 'My personal physician is tending her.' I knew Doctor Antribus, Gideon's medicae. Bequin couldn't be in more experienced hands.

I looked back at Harlon and Kara. I could tell the Loki-born ex-bounty hunter was enjoying stringing this tale out. He'd probably been rehearsing it for weeks.

'So... go on.'

'We went to ground. Me and Kara. We couldn't move Madam B, so we signed her in under a fake identity so she couldn't be linked to your operation. Then me and Kara went hunting. We caught up with the hit squad at a shanty town lift-port down in the suburbs. Thirty of them. Vessorine janissaries, no less. Never tangled with those brothers before, though I'd heard of them, of course. Now, could they fight like bastards.'

'I've seen them up close.'

'Then you'll appreciate that two against thirty, even with the drop to us, was hard ball. I smoked three of them–'

'Two,' corrected Kara. 'It was two.'

'Okay, two definites and a probable. Kara, may the Emperor bless her, took out six of the pigs. Blam blam blam!'

'We can split a bottle of amasec while you give me a play by play later, Nayl. Stick to the meat.'

'My family motto, chief,' Harlon grinned. 'Well, as it turned out, me and Kara had probably bitten off a sight more than we could chew, and we ended up cornered in a freight yard next to the lift-port. Backs to the wall time. Last stand. A change of underwear moment. And then, just like that,' he clicked his fingers, 'salvation arrived.' He looked over at Inquisitor Ravenor.

'Just glad I was able to help.' Ravenor demurred.

'Help? Him and his kill team kicked arse! Far as I could tell, only eight of the mercs got out alive. Jumped their ship and ran off-world.'

I set my empty bottle down on the duralloy floor and sat forward with my elbows on my knees. 'So, Gideon,' I said, 'how in the name of Terra did you come to be there on Messina at the right time?'

'I wasn't,' he said. 'I was there at the wrong time. If I'd reached Messina a day earlier, I'd have been there at the right time. But my ship was delayed by a warp storm that also shut down my communications.'

'That's the second time since I arrived you've been enigmatic,' I said. 'Is that any way to treat your old master?'

Gideon Ravenor had been my interrogator and pupil back in the late 330s, the most promising Inquisitorial candidate I have ever met. A level delta latent psyker with a P.Q. of 171, he had also possessed a genius intellect rounded out with a fine education, and an athlete's physique. During the Holy Novena on Thracian Primaris, he had been caught up in the infamous Atrocity and his body had been woefully crippled. Since that time, he had lived within the cocoon of his force chair, a brilliant mind sustained within a paralysed, useless frame.

But that had not stopped him from becoming one of the Inquisition's finest agents. I myself had sponsored his promotion to full inquisitor status in 346. Since then he had successfully prosecuted hundreds of cases, the most notable being the Gomek Violation and, of course, the Cervan-Holman Affair on Sarum. He had also penned several works of considerable insight: the celebrated essays *Towards an Imperial Utopia, Reflections on the Hive State* and *Terra Redux: A History of the early Inquisition*, a study of warp craft that was fast becoming a standard primer, and a work called *The Mirror of Smoke* that dealt with man's interaction with the warp-state with such conspicuous perception and poetry that I believed it would survive as much as art as it was instruction.

Ravenor was all but invisible within the dim globe of his chair's field, just a shapeless shadow suspended in the fizzling gloom. His body was utterly redundant and everything he did was performed by psi-force alone. His mind had grown stronger in his infirmity, compensating for the things denied him. I was sure he was now much more than a level delta psionic.

'My work in the last few years has required me to develop an understanding of divination and prophecy,' Gideon said slowly. 'Things have been... revealed to me. Things of great significance.'

I could tell he was being very careful about what he said. It was as if he wished to tell me more but didn't dare. I decided I should respect his caution, and allow him to tell me only what he felt he could.

'One of those revelations – a vision, if you like – forecast that a violent fate would befall the Distaff on Messina. The event was predicted to the precise hour. But I couldn't get there in time to prevent it.'

'The destruction of the Distaff was predicted?' I said.

'With distressing accuracy,' he replied.

I suddenly realised I was hearing his voice, by which I mean the voice Ravenor had used before his terrible injuries, a voice produced by a man whose mouth and larynx had not been melted by burning promethium. I had become so used to the monotone synthetic speech of his chair's psi-activated voxsponder.

'My work has also allowed me perfect stronger psionic abilities,' he said, and one of them was clearly reading my surface thoughts. 'I ditched the voxsponder about a year ago. I have developed enough psionic control to broadcast my speech naturally.'

'I'm hearing you in my head?'

'Yes, Gregor. Hearing the voice you're used to. It doesn't work with untouchables or psychically shielded individuals of course – THAT'S WHY I KEEP THE OLD VOXSPONDER ON STANDBY.'

He uttered the last part of his sentence mechanically via the toneless voice box built into his chair and the grating, emotion-free electronic words made us all laugh with surprise.

'Though I was too late to save the Distaff, I got Kara, Harlon and Alizebeth to safety off-world.'

'For that, you have my gratitude. But why summon me so far off the beaten track to meet with you?'

'Promody has secrets that we need,' he said.

'What manner of secrets?'

'I have been allowed to see the future, Gregor,' Ravenor said. 'And it isn't pretty.'

'Imperial culture has never set much store by divination,' Gideon told me. 'I have come to suspect that is a great weakness.'

It was much later. Night had fallen over the swampy bayou and the air was dancing with bioluminescent flies. Ravenor and I had taken a stroll along the grav walks behind his camp.

'A weakness? Surely it is a greater weakness to take it seriously? If we believed the rantings of every dribbling marketplace seer, of every demented Ecclesiarchy prophet who claimed to have been granted divine revelations–'

'We would be mad, true. Most of it is rubbish, lies, mischief, the delusions of broken minds. Sometimes prophetic insights are genuine, but they are usually made by psykers who have either done it by accident or who are insane. In either case, the visions are untrustworthy or too confused to be interpreted in any practical, useful way. But just because mankind isn't very good at it doesn't mean it can't be done.'

'It is my understanding that other races are reputed to excel at it,' I said.

'That has certainly been my experience,' he replied. 'Serving the Ordo Xenos has been enlightening. The more I have studied alien races in order to discern their weaknesses, the more I have learned their strengths.'

'We are talking about the eldar, aren't we?' I risked the question. He didn't reply immediately. His last words had been close to heresy. The force sphere around him flickered slightly with anxiety.

'They are a strange breed. They are able to read the invisible geography of space-time and unravel probability with great precision. But they are mercurial. Sometimes they use their insight as a lever to change the outcome of events. Sometimes they stand idle and watch as prophecies play out. I believe there is no human alive who could explain why they make the choices they do. We just don't see things the way they do.'

'Their greater lifespan gives them greater perspective...'

'It's partly that. Although orthodox thinking would say that greater perspective is their curse. The Ministorum believes the eldar are too resigned to destiny. That they are indolent and almost cruel, or else brutally manipulative.'

'You don't think so?'

'I'll admit only a selfish fascination, Gregor. They interact with the fundamental structure of the universe. As you might well appreciate, any talent for living or perceiving beyond one's physical body is attractive to me. My work has–'

He broke off.

'Gideon?'

'I wanted to learn something of the way their minds witness

reality independent of their bodies. Their farseers, for example, have a kinaesthetic sensibility that operates regardless of the restraints of time and space–'

We paused at the edge of a walkway and looked out across the misty nocturnal swamp. Glowing insects and airborne spores drifted in the air, their paths occasionally punctuated by the sudden swoops of aerial night hunters. Sinuous things moved through the glistening water below the floating walkways, barely disturbing the oily surface.

'I've said too much,' he murmured.

'You do not need to be guarded with me, Gideon. I will not judge you for seeking knowledge. I'm... not the puritan you once knew.'

'I know. I would tell you if I could. But in order to learn certain things, I have been forced to make promises.'

'To the eldar?'

'I cannot even confirm that. I am not proud of the promises, but I will honour them.'

'Then what can you tell me? You said that things had been revealed to you.'

'One of their kind has foreseen a great darkness ahead of us all. It is so abrupt and acute that it has twisted and altered the skeins of probability that the eldar read. It was revealed to him in a sequence of connected visions. One of those was the destruction of the Distaff. When that came true, I was shaken. It proved the visions were not fanciful.'

'What else has he seen?' I asked.

'A living blade, a man-machine, bestriding a long-dead world and preparing to strike a blow that will spill human and eldar blood alike,' he said. 'After that... nothing.'

I looked down at him. 'Nothing?'

'Nothing. That vision is the most distant thing he is now able to see. It's no more than six months from now. Beyond that, he has been unable to glimpse anything at all.'

'Why?'

'Because there is no future left to see.'

SEVENTEEN

Psychoarchaeology
Ghül
The barque of the daemon

Gideon's message to me proved that he already knew the name Khanjar the Sharp, but as we talked, I discovered he knew very little besides the name.

'Nayl and I tracked the janissaries after they fled Messina in an effort to discover who had hired them. It was well hidden. The Vessorine take great pains to protect the identity of their clients. There were false trails, payments from bogus accounts and via holding companies. But we wormed it out eventually. Khanjar the Sharp.'

'Which meant what to you?'

'Nothing... except that he was the individual who had ordered the systematic destruction of your operation... and that his name featured prominently in a number of the farseer's visions. We believe Khanjar and the man-machine from the climactic revelation are one and the same.'

'Khanjar the Sharp is Pontius Glaw,' I said.

He was astonished and excited. The revelations had said nothing of Glaw. The Khanjar guise had masked his true identity from the eldar.

'Why target you?' he asked.

'Self-preservation. I am one of the few people who knows he still exists. In fact, I'm sorry to say, he exists *because* of me. He was also searching for something that he believes I possess.'

'Like what?'

I had no choice but to tell him everything. My dealings with Glaw, Marla Tarray, the *Malus Codicium*...

'You weren't joking when you said you weren't the puritan I once knew,' he said.

'Are you shocked?'

'No, Gregor, I'm not. I believe radicalism is inevitable. We all become radicals eventually as we appreciate that we must know our enemy in order to defeat him. The real dangers come from extreme puritans. Puritanism is fuelled by ignorance, and ignorance is the greatest peril of all. That's not to suggest the path of the radical is easy. Eventually even the most careful and responsible radical will be overwhelmed by the warp. The real judge of character is what good a man can do for the Imperium before he is drawn too far.'

'There is one other thing. In the mind of his daughter there was an image of a desiccated world that closely matches the one you describe from the eldar revelations. There was a name connected with it: *Ghül.*'

'Let me investigate that further,' he said, and turned his force chair back down the walkway towards the camp.

Ravenor had brought me to that remote jungle world because Promody had featured in another of the eldar visions. Khanjar the Sharp had been there recently, perhaps as little as six weeks before. Ravenor intended to find out why.

Ravenor's field team numbered about ten individuals – several technicians, six astropaths and an archaeologist called Kenzer, the grey-haired man I had seen earlier.

'But there are no ruins on Promody,' I remarked shortly after I had been introduced to him.

'Not any more, sir,' he agreed. 'But there is compelling theory that Promody was once one of several worlds inhabited by an ancient culture.'

'How ancient?'

He glanced at me nervously. 'Pre-Dawn,' he said.

A culture from before the rise of man. That was breathtaking.

'So this compelling theory,' I pressed, 'this comes from the eldar?'

He didn't want to answer but my rank gave him little option.

'Yes, sir. But this culture predates even them. And was quite dead long before even they came to the stars.'

Ravenor's technicians had spent their time since reaching Promody conducting a survey with the assistance of the astropaths. They had studied the surface and atmosphere of the planet for signs of Khanjar's visit, looking for traces of landing sites, the residual pollution of vehicle exhausts, the echoes of human minds. They were certain now that the campsite on the bayou was close to the place where Khanjar made planetfall. Now the astropaths were preparing for an auto-seance on a scale greater than any I had ever attempted.

Gideon called me to the force tent.

'Ghül is the name of a planet,' he said.

'The dead world in the vision?'

'Quite probably.'

'And where is it?'

'We don't know.'

'Who's we? Where did this information come from?'

He sighed. 'Lord seer?' he called.

One of the inner screens drew aside and a slim, very tall figure in a long, hooded robe stepped through from the privacy of the inner rooms. The robe was made of a gleaming blue material that flashed like shot-silk but seemed heavier and more fluid. There was a strange, unpleasantly sweet scent, like burnt sugar. I knew that hood would never be drawn back in my presence. I was not fit to see the face beneath.

'This is Eisenhorn,' the figure said. It wasn't a question. The words flowed melodically with a strange cadence that no human could ever approximate.

'Who am I addressing?' I said.

'The book is in his coat,' the figure said to Ravenor, ignoring me. 'An insult that he carries it so casually.'

'Gregor?'

I took the *Malus Codicium* from my pocket. The figure made a warding gesture with its gloved right hand.

'It's an insult that your friend will have to tolerate, I'm afraid,' I said. 'This isn't leaving my person.'

'It has contaminated him. It smoulders in his blood. It has yoked him to daemons.'

'And more besides, no doubt,' I countered. 'But take one look into my mind and tell me I'm not dedicated to the salvation of all of us.'

I dropped my psi-shield provocatively, but though I could sense the eldar's temptation to look, he did not touch my mind.

'Ravenor vouches for you,' the hooded figure said after a

moment. 'I will content myself with that. But do not come any closer.'

'So what do I call you?'

'You won't have any need to,' the eldar replied bluntly.

'Please,' Gideon cut in. He was clearly very uncomfortable. 'Gregor, you may refer to my guest as "lord seer". My lord, perhaps you could tell Gregor about Ghül?'

'In the First Days, a race came from the maelstrom and raised settlements in this space. Seven worlds they made, and the greatest of these was Ghül. Then they were overturned and left no trace behind.'

'From the maelstrom? From the warp? You mean a daemon race?'

The lord seer said nothing.

'Are you saying daemons once colonised seven worlds in our reality?'

'They fled a war. Their king was dead and they carried his body for burial. On his tomb they raised the first city, and then made six worlds around it to honour his rest forever.'

'Ghül is the tomb of a daemon king?'

There was no response.

'What? Are you just going to answer every other question? Is Ghül the tomb-world? Is that what Glaw is after? The tomb of a daemon?'

'I have not seen the answer,' said the eldar.

'Then take a wild guess!'

'The daemon king is dead. Khanjar cannot hope to raise him.'

'Unless he has the *Malus Codicium*,' I said.

'Not even then.'

'So what, then?' I snapped.

'Traditionally,' Gideon put in, 'in human culture, anyway, a king is buried with great treasures and artefacts beside him.'

'So there's something in this tomb. Something so valuable that the *Malus Codicium* is just a key to get it. Where is Ghül?'

'We don't know,' said Ravenor.

'Does Glaw know?'

'I think that's why he was here.'

The eldar withdrew and I was glad to be out of his presence. I found it hard to know how Ravenor tolerated him.

Outside, the final preparations were being made. All of Ravenor's people except Kenzer and the six astropaths were withdrawing to his ship. Nayl and Kara were going to the *Essene*.

'A message from Maxilla,' Nayl said to me. 'You've had a communiqué from Fischig.'

'Fischig? Really?'

'It seems he's changed his mind. That he regrets his clash with you and wants to come back.'

'I think it's too late for that, Harlon.'

Nayl shrugged. 'Cut him some slack, I say, boss. You know how hardline he is. He's had time to think about things. Get his head around stuff. Let him come back. From what Gideon's been saying, we could probably use him.'

'No. Later maybe. Not now. I don't think I can trust him.'

'He probably thinks the same thing about you,' grinned Nayl. 'Joke!' he added, raising his hands to pacify me. 'Good luck,' he finished, then walked off to the shuttle where Kara Swole was waiting.

It was just dawn. Before their departure, the technicians had extended the antigrav walkways to form a circular path across the bayou fifty metres in diameter. The astropaths spread out around the suspended walkways under the thick, steaming vegetation. I stood with Gideon and Kenzer on one of the central sections. The evenly spaced astropaths began to murmur as they sank into their trances and the air became charged with psypathic energy.

Instead of focusing on a single object, as Jecud Vance and I had done with Midas's jacket, the astropaths were opening the entire area up, conjuring its psychic traces. A cold, blue glow began to spread around us, quite at odds with the light of the rising sun. Things became filmy and misty.

'I see something...' Kenzer said.

So did I. Shapes, like clouds, writhing and forming above the water at the centre of the circle. Nothing distinct.

I felt Ravenor reach out with his mind and fine tune the coherence of the image. Just standing there beside him, I could feel how strong his mind had grown. My old pupil was frighteningly powerful.

Suddenly the image resolved. Three figures, wading through the bayou's knee-deep water. One, a massive ogryn with a blaster cannon, followed in the splashing wake of a sturdy male human dressed in beige combat armour, his face hidden by a rebreather. This human was scanning the area with a hand-held auspex. The third figure was beside him. It was tall, broad, and moved with a strange stiffness, its body partially draped with what looked at first like a cape of feathers.

They weren't feathers. They were blades. Tongues of polished, sharpened metal interlaced into an armoured garment. Beneath it, I could glimpse a body of burnished chrome, duralloy and steel, a mechanical humanoid body of marvellous design.

The work of Magos Geard Bure, I had no doubt. The late Geard Bure.

This was Khanjar the Sharp. The man-machine... the 'living blade' from the eldar vision. Pontius Glaw.

I could see his face. It was the face of a beautiful young man with a mane of curled hair, but the hair didn't move and the expression didn't alter from a curling smirk. It was a mask worked from gold, like the head of a noble gilded statue. I had seen the face before, in old records that showed Pontius Glaw in his prime.

There was no sound, but Glaw said something to his point man. Then he turned and seemed to address someone or something we couldn't see.

There was a long pause as they waited and then the ogryn shuffled back, as if alarmed by something. The point man set his auspex to close focus. Glaw stood still as if awestruck for a moment, then clapped his metal hands in delight.

'I can't see what they're doing...' Kenzer said.

'There's nothing there to see,' Gideon snapped in disappointment. That seemed to be the case. There was a faint visual distortion where the psychic ghost of the location failed to match its real counterpart exactly. But nothing else.

'No,' I said suddenly. 'I think there is. Get your astropaths to widen the field of the seance.'

'What?' Gideon asked.

'Just do it.'

With a little effort, Ravenor's telepaths managed to increase the diameter of the conjured scene. Almost at once, were able to make out shadowy figures lurking around the edge.

'Psykers!' said Gideon.

'Exactly,' I said. 'The reason we can't see what he's up to is because he did what we're doing!'

'An auto-seance.'

'That's right.'

'How did you guess, Gregor?'

'Mr Kenzer here said there were no ancient remains on Promody. Glaw has to be looking for the past by other means.'

'But we can't resolve what it is he's seeing...'

'Go back,' said a voice behind us. Silently, the eldar seer had joined us on the walkway.

'Go back,' he said again.

It took a few minutes for the astropaths to compose themselves and re-establish the image. Now I could feel the eldar's mental strength supporting them.

We watched as the scene replayed. The three figures approached us just as before. Glaw conversed with his point man and then called back to his psykers.

The world changed.

There was no jungle. No water. Great, smooth cliffs of rock blocked out the sky. Stone columns like giant fir trees towered over us. We were seeing what Glaw's psykers had allowed him to see. The surface of Promody as it had been eons before the age of man. A cyclopean city of glassy black rock that had long since vanished so completely only its psychic phantom remained.

'God-Emperor!' Kenzer gasped and collapsed in a faint. It was terrifying. Mesmeric. The scale was so big. We felt like microbes or motes of dust on the streets of an Imperial hive.

I stared, fascinated. Now when the ogryn shuffled back in fear and Glaw stood awestruck, I could see why. Glaw clapped his hands in delight and the point man began scanning a wide section of the ghostly wall with his auspex.

'There's an inscription!' Ravenor cried.

I leapt off the walkway and waded through the oily water until I was beside the images of Glaw and his men. 'We need to get this before it fades!' I shouted. Ravenor flew his chair in over the water to join me. Recording sensors in his chair began to whir and store the images.

They were written in a language I had never seen before. It made me sick to look at it. There was no linear form. It simply spiralled and meandered up across the massive wall face, looping and circling.

I felt dizzy. Glaw was capering and dancing like a lunatic, his machine body lurching and awkward.

The light around us began to wink and flicker.

'We're losing it,' said Ravenor.

'Probably time we did...' I said, stumbling back towards the walkway.

The colossal city melted away. Then Glaw and his companions vanished and blue light ebbed away.

Ravenor's telepaths were slumped on the walkways, exhausted. The eldar stood, head bowed.

'It looked like a chart.'

'It was a chart,' said the eldar. 'A plan of the seven worlds. And on it was the location of Ghül.'

Pontius Glaw knew where he was going. He'd known for some weeks. He might already have arrived.

It took Ravenor and the lord seer about a day to make sense of the findings. Allowing for procession and sidereal shifts as best they could considering the vast passage of time involved, they determined that the world known before the time of man as Ghül was in an uncharted system designated 5213X, three months outside Imperial space and twenty weeks from our current location.

We made preparation to break orbit the following night. Ravenor explained to me that the eldar had requested to be taken to a secret location en route, where he could access something called a warp tunnel. Ravenor was beholden to him.

We agreed to rendezvous at Jeganda, three weeks short of 5213X, prior to the final leg of our chase.

'Do we inform the ordos?' Ravenor asked.

'No. What strength they could lend us would be outweighed by problems they'd cause. I will prepare a full documented account of everything we know to be transmitted back in the event that we...'

'We?'

'Fail,' I finished.

Before we departed, I dared to visit Ravenor's ship, the *Hinterlight*. I took Crezia and Harlon Nayl with me. Medicae Antribus showed us to the low-lit chamber off the starship's infirmary where Alizebeth lay inside a softly glowing stasis field.

Crezia and Harlon hung back by the hatchway.

Alizebeth looked like she was asleep. Her skin was as pale as the snows of the high Atenates.

'Is she alive?' I asked Antribus.

'Yes, sir.'

'I mean... without these vital supports, the stasis field–?'

'If we shut them down, she may remain the way she is. But she might also fade. It is never easy to tell in cases of such significant injury.'

'Will she recover?' I asked.

'No,' he said, caring enough to look me in the eyes. 'Except for some miracle. She will never regain consciousness or mobility.'

'So she's dead to us? Has she any quality of life?'

'Who can say, sir? She's not in any pain. I believe she is dreaming an endless, tranquil dream. If you consider that to be cruel, we can disconnect the machines and let nature take its course.'

He withdrew. Crezia appeared at my side.

'What are you going to do, Gregor?' she asked.

'I won't turn the machines off. Not yet. My mind's too full of that bastard Glaw. I'll make a decision afterwards.' If there is afterwards, I thought. 'I'd like you and Nayl to stay with her. Look after her. Will you do that?'

'Of course,' she said. I realised this was the first time she'd ever set eyes on Alizebeth Bequin.

'Really? It's a big thing to ask of you.'

'I'm a doctor, and your friend, Gregor. It's not a big thing.'

I turned to go.

'She can probably hear you,' she said suddenly.

'Do you think so?'

Crezia shrugged and smiled. 'I don't know. There's every chance she can. And if she can't, does it matter?'

'Does what matter?'

'Tell her, Gregor. Now, before you go. Tell her, for goodness sake. Do the right thing by one of us at least.'

She left me alone and I sat down beside Alizebeth's cot.

And then, though I don't know to this day if she ever heard or understood, I told her all the things I should have told her years before.

I said goodbye to Ravenor and promised to wait for him at Jeganda. I kissed Crezia goodbye and went to the *Hinterlight*'s hangar to cross back to the *Essene*. Nayl came to see me off.

I shook his hand. 'Keep an eye on Gideon,' I said.

He frowned. 'You don't trust him?' he asked.

'With my life. But I don't trust his friends.'

As the *Essene* pulled away from Promody, gathering speed as it headed for the immaterium translation point Maxilla's Navigator had calculated, I went to find Aemos.

He was in his suite of rooms, puzzling his way through a deep stack of books he'd borrowed from Maxilla's library.

'Something else to divert you,' I said, handing him a pile of data-slates and record tiles. Before we had parted company, Ravenor had copied for me everything he had been permitted to copy, including a pict-file of the inscription as his force chair's sensors had recorded it.

'Gideon has marked some key passages in his notes to get you up to speed, but the inscription, which is a chart, is what really interests me. Gideon's... associate... told me what it means, or the part of it that applies to Ghül, anyway. I'd like to know a little more, in literal terms.'

'You want me to decipher an alien text that was long dead before man appeared?'

Put like that it was a tall order. 'There are some other samples of the same script that Ravenor obtained from other sites. I don't know. Do what you can with it. Anything you can turn up will be useful.'

The voyage to Jeganda was not the longest I have ever undertaken, but it felt like it. I was fretful and ill at ease, impatient to arrive. My mind would not stop thinking about Glaw's head start, or how close the farseer's nothingness loomed.

To fill the time, I meditated and exercised, burrowed my way through Maxilla's library in search of anything pertaining to the eldar and their legends. Kara worked to get Medea up to fitness and, after two weeks, the three of us were running through demanding combat training each day. Sometimes Eleena joined us for the lighter sessions to keep in shape. I was glad I had an untouchable with me, given our destination and Glaw's abilities.

Except for Alizebeth, who didn't really count under the

circumstances, Eleena was the last living member of the Distaff. I wondered if I would ever recruit and build it again.

I wondered if I would even get the chance.

During the third week, Aemos called me to his suite to discuss his findings so far. I wondered why he hadn't simply told me over dinner. We all met for a meal each evening anyway.

He told me he was making progress. The ancient culture which had built Ghül appeared indirectly in several old sources. It seems that early Imperial explorers had known myths of a dead, precursor race from some of their first contacts with xenos species, though Aemos was concerned that some of the references could be to other dead cultures, or to species that had migrated or transplanted themselves.

One theme emerged. The race of Ghül were marked as 'others' or 'outsiders' because they had not originated in our galaxy. The name 'Ghül' itself didn't appear anywhere.

'One minor culture, the Doy of Mitas, have a legend concerning the "xol-xonxoy", daemons who ruled once and would return. The word meant "warped ones".

'A good enough description as any. The eldar seemed convinced that the culture was a colony of daemons from the warp. Not even a race in its own right, more a host, an army... a nation. An exiled daemon-king and his followers, perhaps.'

'There are a few more bits and pieces, not much. I'm getting nowhere with the inscription, though it is extraordinary, and Gideon's footage of that seance most perturbatory. I'd like to borrow your book.'

'You what?'

'Your damned book. I use the adjective advisedly.'

'You said you never wanted to see it again,' I reminded him.

'I don't, Gregor. It chills me to know it is even on board. But what chills me more is what we're going out there to find. And you've asked me to do a job. And that's the only tool available to me that I haven't used.'

I took the *Malus Codicium* from my pocket. For a moment I couldn't bring myself to pass it to him.

'Be careful,' I hissed.

'I know the procedures,' he said grumpily. 'You've had me study prohibited texts before.'

'Not like this one.'

I kept an eye on Aemos after that, visiting him regularly and making sure he came to meals. He became tired and short-tempered. I wanted to take the book away from him, but he said he was nearly done.

We were a week from Jeganda when he finished his work.

'It's incomplete,' he warned, 'but the main elements are there.'

He seemed even more fatigued than before and had developed a slight shake on his left side. His suite was a mess of papers and slates, notes and scrawlings, scattered books. In places, where he had apparently run out of paper, he had continued his notes on tabletops or even walls.

Uber Aemos had performed his greatest work of service for me, the hardest task I had ever set him. And it had cost him. It had damaged his health and, I was afraid, his sanity.

'The daemon-king,' he said, spreading out a large sheet of scribbled-on vellum across the litter on his desk, 'who is represented by this glyph here...' he pointed with a palsied finger, '...and by this triple formation of symbols here was called Y-Y-Y–'

'Aemos?'

'Yssarile!' He all but had to spit the word out of his mouth to make the sound. The gilded clock on the table beside his unmade bed chimed twice suddenly for no reason.

'It keeps doing that,' Aemos growled crossly. His finger stabbed another mark on the paper for me to look at and then traced down a curling line of script. His notes, I realised, had taken the form of the chart itself. 'Here, look. There was a war. The daemon-king Y-Y–'

'Just call him the daemon-king.'

'The daemon-king fought a war of staggering enmity with a rival. The rival's name is not given, but from the marking here, I would guess it was one of what we tentatively understand to be the four primary powers of Chaos, although it seems there were only three at that time. I wonder why?'

I couldn't answer that. I wondered if the farseer could.

'The rival is described as a foul sorcerer,' Aemos continued. 'I don't pretend or want to know the hierarchies of the warp, but in simple terms, Y-Y-damnit! Yssarile! was a lieutenant, a warlord, a prince... whatever you want to call it, who tried to usurp the place of this primary power.'

Aemos unrolled another crumpled sheet and wiped pencil shavings off it. 'The war lasted... a billion years. As we would understand it. The daemon-king was destroyed by his rival. Killed outright. His host fled in terror at this crushing defeat, and sought sanctuary in the material universe. Our universe. There they established a capital and six kindred colonies. The capital, Ghül, was built upon the daemon-king's mausoleum, which was itself constructed around his barque.'

'His barque?'

'I suppose they mean his ship. The word is closer to "chariot" or "galley" in literal terms. And I think this may be the key point. The barque was his war machine, the craft that he rode into battle. It is described – here, and also here – as being of such power and might that the warped ones who wrote this were themselves staggered by it.'

He looked at me. 'The barque of the daemon-king. A weapon of inconceivable power that lies entombed in the mausoleum of Ghül. That prize, so I am told, is what Glaw is after.'

'Told?'

He started, shaking his head. 'I'm tired. I meant that's what I've learned. From this. My work.'

'You said "told".'

'I did not.'

'Distinctly.'

'Yes, well I did. Because I used the wrong word. Learned. That's what I have learned.'

I put my hand on his shoulder, reassuringly, but he flinched. 'Aemos, you've done an extraordinary job with this. I've asked a lot of you.'

'Yes, you have.'

'Too much.'

'I serve you, sir. It is never too much.'

'I'll have Maxilla prepare another room for you. You can't sleep in here.'

'I'm used to the clutter,' he said.

'It's not the clutter I'm worried about.'

He shuffled away, muttering.

'I need to take the book back now,' I said.

'It's here somewhere,' he said, off-hand. 'I'll bring it to you later.'

'I'll take it now.'

He glared at me.

'Now, please,' I repeated.

He pulled the *Malus Codicium* from under a pile of notes

352   DAN ABNETT

that fluttered onto the carpet, and held it out. I took hold, but
he would not let go.

'Aemos...'

I managed to yank the book away. The clock mischimed
again.

'I think you should consider your options, Gregor,' he said.

'What do you mean?'

'The powers we face are great. Too great, perhaps. We are
woefully understrength. I think we should be stronger.'

'How do you propose we do that?'

'Summon the daemonhost.'

'What?'

He took off his heavy augmetic eyeglasses and polished the
lenses with the corner of his robe.

His hands were shaking badly now.

'I didn't approve before, on Durer. But I think I grasp things
a little better now. I understand the choices you've made.
The rules you've bent. All for the good, and I apologise for
ever doubting you. With the daemonhost, we might stand a
chance. Summon it here.'

'How?'

He became agitated with me. 'Like you did on Miquol!'

'That was sheer desperation,' I reproved.

'We're desperate now!'

'And we have no host to summon it into...'

'You didn't then!'

'And it nearly killed us with its raw power before I could
trap it.'

'Then use one of Maxilla's astropaths as a host!'

I stared at him levelly. 'I won't kill a man just to provide
a host.'

'You did on Miquol,' he hissed softly.

'What did you just say?'

'You did on Miquol. Verveuk wasn't dead. You sacrificed him for the good of us all. Why would you flinch from doing it again?'

'Why would I do again something I wish had never happened?'

'Are we not playing for the highest stakes? One life, sir. What is that compared to the millions that may die if Glaw succeeds? Summon the daemonhost. Summon Cherubael to help us.'

I walked slowly to the door. 'Get some rest,' I said with forced lightness. 'You'll feel better for it. You'll have changed your mind.'

'Whatever,' he said, turning away dismissively.

He was entirely unprepared for the will I unleashed at him.

'What did it say to you?' I commanded.

Aemos cried out and his legs gave way. He crashed to the deck and half overturned a table in his efforts to stay upright.

His papers avalanched onto the floor.

'It told you, didn't it? It told you! You damn fool, Uber, what did you do?'

'I couldn't crack the code!' he wailed. 'The language was beyond me! But there was so much more in that book! That beautiful book! I realised I could do more!'

'You spoke to the daemonhost.'

'Nooo!'

'Then how else would you know its name, because I sure as hell never told you!'

He shrieked out and staggered back to his feet, his face locked in a grimace of pain and shame and fear.

'It was there in the pages!' he cried. 'Close like a whisper in my ear! So soft! It said it could help! It said it would tell me everything I needed if I could only arrange its release!'

'Oh, God-Emperor! Everything you've told me today you learned from that bastard thing Cherubael!'

'It was true!' he screamed. 'True! Yssarile! Yssarrrrilllle!'

The clock began to chime furiously. A glass pitcher and three tumblers on the bureau shattered. One lens of Aemos's eyeglasses cracked clean across.

He collapsed onto the floor.

I summoned servitors and took him to the sickbay. For safety, we locked him in an isolation bay. His safety, and ours.

The damn clock was still chiming when I went back to his room to burn the papers.

EIGHTEEN

Meeting at Jeganda
Misplaced loyalties
To the last, to the death

Aemos. All that last week of travel, he was my primary concern. I kept a watch on him in the infirmary, but he was generally unresponsive. He woke a few hours after the confrontation, and then said nothing. He refused to eat at first, and remained awake, day and night, staring at the locked door of the isolation chamber.

I dearly wished I hadn't had to lock it.

After a day he took food and drink, but remained silent. We all attempted to get some reaction from him. Both Medea and Maxilla tried for hours at a time.

By the time we reached Jeganda, a day ahead of schedule, our mood was low.

I had never realised before then how central to our team spirit Aemos had been. We all missed him. We all hated what had happened.

I hated myself for allowing it.

Aemos had been careless where I should have been able to trust him, but even so... it was my doing. I hated myself.

And I hated Cherubael, whose baleful influence had been cursing my life for too long. I wondered if I would ever – could ever – be free of it.

I made a resolution. If I lived, if I vanquished Glaw, I would destroy the *Malus Codicium* and then return to Gudrun and destroy Cherubael. I would take my runestaff and annihilate it, just as I had annihilated its kin Prophaniti on Farness Beta.

Jeganda system is dominated by a huge, ringed gas giant. In orbit above it is an semi-automated waystation established and maintained by a consortium of trade guilds and Navigator houses as a stop-over and service facility.

The *Essene* coasted in. There was no sign of any other vessels. Maxilla made contact with the station master and a drone tug led us into one of the wide docking gantries that extended from the rim of the dish-shaped station.

I crossed via the airgate with Maxilla and Medea and we were met by the master, a hirsute, sluggish man called Okeen. He ran the place with a staff of four. It was a twenty-month contract, he explained, and then they stood down in favour of a fresh crew. They didn't get many visitors, he told us. They'd be happy to resupply the *Essene*'s technical needs, for a competitive price, he told us.

He told us plenty. Isolation does terrible things to men's minds.

We couldn't shut him up. I finally left him with Maxilla. Maxilla could talk too.

Medea and I went to the station's central hub to see if the resident astropath had received any messages for us from

Gideon. It was a dismal place of rotting and poorly maintained hallways and dark hangars. There was a background
smell that I decided was spoiled meat and Medea maintained
was stale lactose.

It turned out that, despite Okeen's non-stop chatter, there
was one thing he hadn't told us.

Someone was waiting for us in the recreation lounge.

'Gregor.' Fischig rose to his feet from a threadbare couch. He
was dressed in black with a waist-length shipboard cape of
dark red, wire-shot fully that was secured at his throat with
a small, silver Inquisitorial crest.

I faced him across the room. 'What are you doing here,
Godwyn?'

'Waiting for you, Gregor. Waiting for a chance to make things
right.'

'And how do you propose doing that?'

He shrugged. It was an open, relaxed, almost apologetic gesture. 'I said things I shouldn't have. Judged you too quickly.
I always was a hard-nosed idiot. You'd think my years of service with you might have taught me the error.'

'You'd think,' quipped Medea.

I held up a warning finger to silence her. 'You made your
feelings perfectly clear on Hubris, Fischig. I'm not sure we
can work together any more. There's a mutual lack of trust.'

'Which I want to do away with,' he said. I'd never heard him
so calm or sincere.

'Godwyn, you questioned my purity, branded some of my
actions heretical and then offered to redeem me.'

'I was drunk for that last part,' he said, with a tiny flash of
smile.

'Yes, you were. And what are you now?'

'Here. Willing. Reconciled.'

'Well,' I said. 'Let's start with the "here" part. How the hell did you know I'd be here?'

He paused. I looked round slowly at Medea who was studying the deck.

'You told him where I'd be, didn't you?'

'Uhm...'

'Didn't you?'

She snapped round to face me, every bit as haughty and rebellious as her dear, damned father. 'All right, I did! Okay? We need Fischig–'

'Maybe we don't, girl.'

'Don't "girl" me, you bastard! He's one of us. One of the band. He kept sending to the ship. Sending and sending. You wouldn't listen to him, so I replied.'

'Nayl told me he'd sent one message.'

'Yeah,' she said snidely. 'And Nayl told me what you'd sent back. The big brush-off. To a man who's devoted his life to you. A man who got a bit angry with you and then thought about it and regretted it. Fischig wants to make amends. He wants to be with us again. Haven't you ever regretted anything?'

'More than you can possibly imagine, Medea. But you should have told me.'

'I asked her not to,' Fischig said. 'I imagined how you'd react. I'm grateful Medea thought so highly of me. Could you not find it in you to trust me again? Trust me like she does?'

'Quite possibly. But I wanted to do it on my terms, when I was ready. There's too much going on just now.'

'Oh, come on,' implored Medea.

'How did you get here?' I asked Fischig sharply.

'I got passage on a tramp trader. It dropped me off here a week ago.'

I'd asked the question so I could test his reply and get a

measure of his veracity. As he answered, and I probed delicately out with my mind, I found the last thing I was expecting.

'Why are you psi-shielded?' I asked.

'Just a precaution,' he said.

'Against what?' I demanded.

'Against this moment,' Fischig said. There was true anguish
in his eyes. He drew the compact bolt pistol out from under
his cape.

'Fischig!' Medea howled in horror.

Barbarisater was already in my hands, humming. 'Don't
be a fool,' I said.

He'd only be a fool if he was doing this alone.

The words were not vocal. They were burning wires of psychic venom wrapped around a monstrous cudgel of mental
force that smashed into the back of my skull. I stumbled forward, half-blind. Medea fell over hard, totally unconscious.

I saw figures emerging from the doorways off the lounge
space all around. Five, six, more. Men dressed in the hooded,
burgundy armour of an inquisitor's personal retinue, their
chest plates decorated with gold leaf in the form of the Inquisition's crest. Two of them grabbed me and ripped the force
sword from my slack fingers. The others aimed their weapons at me.

'Don't hurt him! Don't hurt him!' Fischig cried.

The guards dragged me round to face an individual emerging from the lounge's greasy kitchenette area. I saw a tall man
in black armour and robes, with a monstrous face that had
been surgically deformed to inspire fear and loathing. It was
equine, snouted, with a mouth full of blunt teeth and dark
pools for eyes. Fibre-wire and fluid-tubes formed gleaming
ropes across the back of his skull.

He'd once been the pupil and interrogator of my old,

long-dead ally Commodus Voke. Now he was an inquisitor in his own right.

'Eisenhorn. How simply vile to see you again,' said Golesh Constantine Pheppos Heldane.

The guards dragged Medea and me back on board the *Essene*. I was still dazed. I could hear Fischig begging Heldane to order his men to be more careful with us.

Oh, what a mistake Fischig had made.

As we were bundled through the stations docking gantries, I saw the sleek black shape of an Inquisitorial cruiser now occupying the dock station next to the *Essene*. Heldane's ship. It had probably lain concealed in the atmosphere of the gas giant until the trap was sprung.

They took us into the main stateroom. Heldane's men, and I guessed there must have been a full detachment, had secured the *Essene*.

'How many travellers with you?' Heldane snapped at me.

I made no answer.

'How many?' he repeated, following his words with a blade of psi-pain that made me cry out. I needed to concentrate. I needed to rebuild my mental defences.

Feigning injury, I looked around and took stock. Maxilla stood nearby, surrounded by guards, glowering. Eleena was sitting bolt upright and pale on a couch. Medea was sprawled on the floor, just waking up. There was no sign of Aemos or Kara.

'Four!' said Maxilla. 'These four. The rest are my crew, servitors all of them, slaved into my ship.' He was playing the part of the innocent ship-master, outraged at the invasion of his vessel, distancing himself from his troublesome passengers. But I knew he was frightened.

'You're lying. I can tell,' said Heldane, pacing round Maxilla. 'Your defences are good, I'll grant you that, shipmaster. Don't lie to me.'

'I'm not–' Maxilla began and then cried out in pain.

'Don't lie to me!'

'Leave him alone!' Fischig boomed. 'He's just the captain. The shipmaster, like you said. He's not part of this.'

Heldane looked round at Fischig with a withering stare. 'You made this happen, chastener. You came to the ordos and begged us to save your dear, heretical master from damnation. Well, that's what I'm doing. So shut your mouth and let me get on with it. Or would you rather I probed the minds of these delicious young ladies?'

'No.'

'Good. Because the shipmaster is rather interesting. He's not altogether human, is he? Are you, Tobias Maxilla? Your defences are admirable, but only because your brain isn't entirely organic. You're so much a machine, sir, you hardly deserve the title "man", do you?'

'Look who's talking,' Maxilla said bravely.

I felt the psi-surge from across the room and it made me wince. Heldane's inhuman features folded into an angry, animal roar and Maxilla stumbled, cried out and fell to his knees, showers of sparks exploding from burned-out servos in his neck, right shoulder and right wrist.

'Now will you answer, metal man,' Heldane leered at Maxilla, 'or shall I burn out another part of your blasphemous body?'

'There are five,' I said loudly. 'Five of us.'

'Aha... the heretic speaks.' Heldane switched round to face me, his attention drawn from Maxilla, at least for a moment.

'The other member of my party is my savant, Aemos. I'm sure you remember him. He's in the infirmary.'

'How very obliging of you, Gregor,' Heldane said. I prayed that I had outwitted him. Heldane could undoubtedly feel from our minds that someone was missing. If I showed him Aemos, I hoped he would be satisfied and miss Kara entirely.

'I would advise you to leave him there.'

'Why?'

'He... there was an accident,' I said. 'He is damaged.'

'Warp damaged?'

'No. He will recover.'

'But he is infirm because of contact with the warp?'

'No!'

Heldane turned to a couple of his men. 'Go to the infirmary. Locate this man. Kill him and incinerate his remains.'

'God-Emperor, no!' I cried.

I tried to get up, tried to reach out with my mind to wrest Barbarisater from Heldane's hands. I was too weak and he was too strong. Another psychic assault smashed me to the floor.

'Is everything all right?' a new voice asked. 'There was a lot of unseemly shouting just then.'

'Everything's fine, my lord. Welcome aboard,' I heard Heldane say.

I rolled over and saw the newcomer enter the *Essene*'s stateroom. He was resplendent in his brass power-armour, his augmetic jaw as stubbornly set as the last time I had seen him. 'Osma...' I whispered.

'Grand Master Osma of the Ordos Helican, if you don't mind,' he said sourly.

He had been elevated. Orsini was dead and Leonid Osma had finally achieved the rank he had spent his life chasing. So much had happened in the Helican sub-sector since I had become preoccupied with running and staying alive. Osma, my nemesis, the man who had once tried to have me declared extremis diabolus and who had imprisoned me, tortured and hunted me, had now become the master of the Ordos Helican and my supreme overlord.

The guards dragged me up onto the mezzanine area of the *Essene*'s stateroom and sat me in one of the chairs facing the long banquet table. They stood back, and Osma and Heldane approached. Osma was holding Barbarisater and studying the intricate workings of the blade. His own huge power hammer was anchored to his belt.

Heldane sat down facing me.

'There's no love lost between us, Eisenhorn. I won't insult you by pretending there is. Make things easy for all of us. Confess.'

'Confess what?'

'Your heresy,' said Osma.

'I am not a heretic. And this is not a tribunal of my peers. I cannot be judged so.'

I knew damn well I could. Grand master or no grand master, Osma could deal with me however the hell he wanted.

'Confess,' he said again, sitting down in the seat next to Heldane with a whine of armour servos. He really was fascinated by Barbarisater, turning it over in his gauntleted hands.

'Confess what?'

'We have a list of charges,' Heldane said, producing a data-slate from his cloak. 'Your man Fischig was very specific about his concerns. You have consorted with daemons and conjured one of them as a daemonhost on more than one occasion. You have hidden proscribed texts from the Inquisition. You have shielded a known heretic from the Inquisition and allowed him to roam free.'

I fixed Heldane with a hard stare. 'You mean Pontius Glaw? I'll admit nothing, but I'll tell you this much. If you detain me here, you'll pay a much greater price than you can ever imagine. I am sworn to stop Pontius Glaw and you are preventing me from performing my holy duties.'

'Your days of performing holy duties are long gone,' said Osma.

'Where is the *Malus Codicium*?' Heldane asked.

I toughened my mind shield, hoping against hope that the simple surface truth would not get out. In my pocket. In my damn pocket. Your men searched me for weapons but they didn't bother about a battered old book in my coat.

Heldane didn't read it.' 'He's still wonderfully resilient,' he told Osma.

They were assuming the *Codicium* would be in a secure place. A void safe, a strong box, under my damn mattress! They had no idea it would be right there in front of them, covered only by a layer of leather coat. I had to keep that simple, stupid fact from them.

'Millions will die. Tens of millions perhaps. If you don't let me finish my work.'

'That's what they all say,' said Osma. He rose and leaned over at me, his blunt, grizzled face looming close. 'You're going to burn, Eisenhorn. Burn and suffer. I am only grand master today because I have never suffered heretics like you. You are the worst kind of fool.'

'Tell us about the daemonhost,' said Heldane. 'Where is it secured? How can we find it? What are its command words?'

'Command words?' I replied. 'Why would you need those? Do you intend to control the daemonhost yourself?'

Heldane sat back and glanced at Osma.

'Of course they don't!' said Fischig, who had been lurking on the mezzanine steps. 'They're not heretics like you... they wouldn't–'

He looked round at Osma and Heldane.

'You don't want the daemonhost, do you, masters?'

'It must be contained and dealt with,' said Osma. 'Leave this business to your superiors, please. You interrupt too much.'

'But the daemonhost? You talk like you want it for yourselves.'

Osma glanced at the long-snouted inquisitor. 'Heldane? Tell this man to go away. He's served his purpose.'

'Go, Fischig!' Heldane snapped, and my former friend descended the stairs and sat down on one of the couches, gazing at Eleena and Medea, who were trying to make Maxilla comfortable.

'The daemonhost!' Heldane rasped. 'Give it to us!'

'And you call me a heretic...'

Heldane's psychic slap rocked me back in my seat.

A guard approached Osma. 'We have searched the infirmary, lord. There is no one there.'

Thank the Emperor, I thought. Kara has freed Aemos.

'Kara?' said Heldane suddenly. 'Who is Kara?'

No one, I willed.

'There is a sixth person aboard,' Heldane told Osma. 'Probably now working with the savant.'

'Find them!' Osma snapped, and half of his guard unit hurried from the stateroom. 'Bring more squads across from our ship if you have to.'

There was jolt, followed by a terrible raking squeal of metal on metal from somewhere outside.

'What was that?' Heldane demanded.

He got up and hurried down the steps towards the entrance to the main bridge. The *Essene* jolted again.

Osma rose and pointed the tip of Barbarisater at me. 'Move!' he ordered. 'Watch the rest of them,' he told the guard captain.

We followed Heldane onto the bridge. Fischig joined us, along with Maxilla, who was being held upright by a guard.

We were listing badly. On the main screen, we could see a forward view of the waystation.

The *Essene* had disengaged from its moorings, and was slowly tearing backwards away from the dock. Docking gantries were grinding and buckling against the ship's hull.

'What have you done?' Osma said to me.

'This is none of my doing,' I replied.

A series of minor explosions ripped through the control stations on the right hand side of the huge bridge area, showing the marble floor with sparks and machine-part debris.

Another blast rocked the starboard chapel annex that contained the astropathic vault and buckled the hatch. A helm servitor combusted and toppled over, smashing open its sculptural golden casing.

'Sabotage!' said Osma.

Heldane turned on Maxilla. 'Your handiwork!'

'Mine?' said Maxilla. 'Why the hell would I risk damage to my precious ship just to help these criminals? They mean nothing to me!'

'You're lying, you metal freak!' Heldane barked and grabbed Maxilla by the throat, lifting him off the ground. 'Tell us what you've done! Put it right! Get your crew to stabilise the ship!'

'I've done nothing...' Maxilla choked.

Heldane hurled him across the chamber. The inquisitor was strong by any standards, but he supplemented his physical strength with telekinesis. Maxilla hit the wall with a terrible splintering impact, and Heldane held him there with his powers for an awful moment, squashing him against the duralloy with his mind. There were several loud cracks of bone and metal.

Then he let him go and the limp, broken body of Tobias Maxilla fell to the marble deck and lay still.

'Why did you do that?' Fischig cried.

'Shut the hell up, you idiot,' Heldane answered. 'We need to get this vessel locked down.'

Fischig and one of the guards took a few steps forward towards the main bridge consoles. Fischig knew the *Essene*. He probably thought he could access the thrusters and level us out before the dock gantries did any more damage to the hull.

The astropathic vault blew out in a sheet of white flame that atomised two of the helm stations and threw Fischig and the guard off their feet.

Screaming and writhing, incandescent with green tongues of fire that washed across its naked contorting body, a figure levitated out of the burning vault.

But it wasn't screaming. It was laughing.

It was Cherubael.

It was shining so brightly it hurt to behold it, but I could see enough to realise it was wearing the body of one of the *Essene*'s astropaths. Plug sockets still decorated its gleaming flesh, some still trailing wires. All clothing had burned away, but the astropath's extensive bionic augmentation was clear. The body had no legs, just a dangling assembly of cables and machined connectors where the astropath, like most of Maxilla's crew, had plugged directly and permanently into a vault socket.

Heldane and two of the guards ran towards it, the guards shouting prayers against the warp as they opened fire. Heldane drew a force sword from his waist. I felt the backwash as he assaulted the daemonhost with the full force of his psychic powers.

Osma was staring at the daemonhost in astonishment. It

suddenly occurred to me that despite his rank and authority, he probably had very little first hand experience of abominations like Cherubael.

'You wanted the daemonhost, grand master,' I said. 'Looks like you've got him.'

My words snapped him into activity and he looked round, but Barbarisater was already hissing through the air directly into my extended hand.

'Heretic!' he screamed. His power hammer swung up in his plated fists, crackling with energy and he came at me. He had significant advantage. He was psi-shielded and heavily armoured against an adversary with no armour whatsoever.

Our weapons crashed together. We broke and swung again. There was massive strength behind his blows and I was still weak from the psychic mauling Heldane had given me.

'There's no time for this, you fool!' I yelled. 'I didn't unleash the daemonhost, but I'm the only chance you have to stop it!'

Behind us, Cherubael giggled hysterically as it torched the guards firing at it. It skimmed down and locked in combat with the furious Heldane.

Osma was defiant. He would not break off. He deflected my sword stroke with a hammerblow so powerful I was rocked back, my guard open. His follow-through came right at my face and I threw my body back to evade it. It missed. Barely. The hammer's energy scorched my cheek.

But I had lost my footing.

I crashed over onto the marble deck and rolled sideways as the hammer came down and cracked the stone flags. Osma's weapon, the Malleus symbol of his ordo, rushed up again for the deathstroke.

There was a shriek of energy and the air above me was split by a blinding turquoise beam. It struck Osma full in the face and vapourised his head in a splash of light, bone shards and adipose tissue. His body hit the floor with a metallic crash and the fused remains of his heavy augmetic jaw bounced away across the deck.

I rose.

Maxilla, still sprawled and wretchedly twisted where Heldane had dropped him, slowly lowered his hand. The digital ring weapon on his elegantly gloved finger was glowing.

I turned back to the fight. Medea and Eleena had entered the room along with the remaining guards, looking on in horror. Some of the guards fled.

Heldane was being driven back across the bridge by the radiant, cackling daemonhost. He was throwing everything he had at Cherubael, and the daemon was just laughing, teeth backlit into silhouette by the light of the warp streaming out of its gaping maw.

Heldane's robes were beginning to smoulder.

'Eleena!' I shouted and she ran to me. None of the awestruck guards even tried to stop her.

'There's no time to do this cleanly. I need you next to me. You may be able to block some of its power.'

She nodded and grabbed my coat with both hands. She was terrified out of her wits. But she did not falter.

I pulled the *Malus Codicium* from my coat and leafed desperately through the pages. I couldn't find what I was looking for. I damn well couldn't find what I was looking for!

The marble deck of the bridge cracked and parted underneath Heldane like solid ground split by an earth tremor. One of his feet slipped into the crack and he swayed.

Cherubael snorted with glee and clapped its hands. The deck quaked and the crack closed again, like a vice.

Heldane screamed. He screamed the terrible howl of the

damned. He was pinned into the deck by his crushed leg. Cherubael advanced.

Heldane slashed with his sword in terror. The blade melted. The inquisitor's clothes caught fire. Ablaze from head to foot with green flames, he screamed again. On fire, upright, fixed to the spot, he looked just like a heretic burning at the stake.

Cherubael looked away from his prey, bored with it now it was dying. It surged forward and floated towards me. Eleena let out a sobbing whimper.

'Stay close!' I told her.

'Hello, Gregor,' said Cherubael. Its voice was hoarse and impaired. The astropath it inhabited hadn't spoken for many years and the voice organs had partially atrophied.

'Don't we have fun together, Gregor?' it went on, its blank eyes fixed on me. It was smiling, but there was nothing warm in those vacant orbs. Nothing at all, in fact, except evil.

'It's always such a delight to play these games with you. But this game must be a bit of surprise, eh? Didn't expect to see me, did you? It wasn't you that called me this time.'

It came closer. I could feel, not heat, but burning cold emanating from it. I was still ripping through the pages of the book to find what I was looking for.

'Here's another surprise for you,' it added, dropping its voice to a whisper. 'This is the last time we play. I've had enough of the way you make up all the games. You see what I did to that horse-faced idiot? I won't do that to you, old friend. I'll do something that really, really hurts.'

It lunged forward but then backed off slightly, as if stung. It had touched the psychic deadzone around Eleena. Cherubael turned his attention down towards her.

'Hello. Aren't you a sweet little thing? What a pretty face! Shame I'm going to ruin it.'

'Mmmh!' Eleena sobbed.

'You're a clever old stick, Gregor. Always careful enough to have an untouchable at your side when you meet with me. This isn't the regular one, though, is it? What happened to her?'

I wrenched the book open.

'She won't save you, mind,' said Cherubael, reaching out with hands that were sprouting thick, ugly talons.

I thrust the book up and held it in front of his eyes with both hands, clamping the pages open so that the daemonhost could clearly see.

It was diagrams of the four chief runes of banishment. They wouldn't banish Cherubael, because they hadn't been properly invoked. But I was pretty sure just reading them would hurt.

Cherubael squealed and tumbled back. I stepped forward a pace, keeping the book raised and open.

Wracked with agony, the daemonhost soared back across the bridge, crashed through the main screen and shattered the hololithic plates in a shower of crystal and sparks. It bounced twice off the ceiling like a maddened hornet fighting a window pane, the colour of its flame-halo turning yellow and then furnace orange.

Cherubael dropped, hit the floor and burned through it leaving a circular, smouldering hole.

'Oh dear Emperor–' Eleena gasped.

'Come on!' I said. 'It won't be long before it comes back for another try. Move!'

Medea ran forward. The last few guards were busy beating out the flames swathing Heldane with their capes. He was still screaming.

'Get her out of here!' I told Medea, pushing Eleena towards her. 'Hangar deck! Go!'

They hurried towards the exit. Deep, bass detonations from somewhere deep in the *Essene* rocked the floor. Multiple alarms were sounding. Sparks cascaded from the buckled ceiling of the bridge.

I went over to Maxilla. His eyes flickered and he looked up at me. 'I didn't mean it...' he said in a tiny voice.

'Mean what?'

'I told that brute none of you meant anything to me. But I didn't mean it.'

'I know.'

'Thank you,' he said, and died.

I ran from the bridge into one of the main longitudinal corridors. Smoke was boiling along it from untold damage below. On the floor, I saw weapons and cloaks dropped by Osma's guards in their panic to leave.

I'd taken about a dozen steps when a loud voice told me to halt.

Fischig was coming after me, aiming his bolt pistol with a straight, firm arm. He was bloodied and bruised by the explosion that had knocked him down, but there was an utterly determined set to his face. I'd seen that look before, but I'd never been on the receiving end of it.

'Stop where you are,' he said.

'Come on! We have to get clear. The ship is dying.'

'Stop where you are,' he repeated.

'Come with me. I'll explain everything and you'll see why it's vital for us to–'

'Shut up,' he said. 'It's all lies. It's always been lies. You know you nearly fooled me back then. I was almost convinced I'd made a terrible mistake going to Osma. But then you showed your true colours. Brought that daemon back and proved that everything I feared about you was true.'

'This isn't the time or place, Godwyn. I'm leaving now. Come with me if you want.'

I turned my back on him and walked away.

'Gregor, please–'

I kept walking. I was sure he wouldn't shoot. We went back too far. When it came down to it, he wouldn't be able to stop me.

The boltgun roared. The shot exploded my left knee. I cried out and fell, leaning on Barbarisater. There was blood everywhere. I couldn't believe he'd found the will to do it.

With a yelp of pain I hauled myself up on the sword. He fired again and now my right leg went out from under me, also mangled at the knee.

I lay on my back. I could feel the death throes of the *Essene* quaking and thundering through the deck beneath me. Fischig stood over me.

'Stop this...' I gasped. 'Get me to the hangar.'

He drew back the slide of the bolt pistol. He was shaking with distress, wracked by grief and disappointment and duty and belief.

'Please,' he said. 'Renounce it all. Repent your sins and accept the Emperor for the good of your soul. It's not too late.'

'You're still trying to save me.' I managed to get the words out through the pain. 'Glory be, Fischig... you actually shot me so you could try and save my soul?'

'Renounce the warp!' he stammered. 'Please! I can save you! You're my friend and I can still save you from yourself!'

'I don't need saving,' I said.

He aimed the gun at my head. His finger tightened on the trigger. 'May the Emperor protect you, Gregor Eisenhorn,' he said.

He twitched. Once. Twice. He swayed. The bolt pistol wandered in his lolling hand and fired, harmlessly, against the corridor wall. He dropped to his knees and then fell forward onto his face as if he was praying.

I struggled to pull myself up so I could lean my back against the wall. My legs were crippled, bloody and useless.

Medea crouched down next to me. Tears were streaming down her cheeks. She let go of the needle pistol and let it clatter onto the deck.

Kara appeared behind us, a las-carbine in her hands, with Eleena and Aemos at her heels. They all looked in horror at the sight of me and Fischig.

Aemos was deathly pale, and leaning on my runestaff like a penitent pilgrim.

'Help me up,' I said, from between clenched teeth. Kara and Medea hoisted me up between them.

I looked at Aemos. 'You summoned Cherubael? It was you, wasn't it? You summoned him into one of the *Essene's* poor bloody astropaths?'

'They were going to burn us as heretics,' he said softly, 'and then we'd never be able to stop Glaw.'

'But how did you perform the rituals, Uber? You didn't even have the book any more.'

'That book,' he sighed. 'That damn book. It's all in here now.' He tapped his wrinkled forehead with a scrawny finger.

He'd memorised it. During those weeks of study he'd memorised the *Malus Codicium*. Thanks to a meme-virus, he was a data addict. That's what made him such a fine savant. And now his addiction had taken him to overdose.

'You memorised the whole thing?'

'Word,' he swallowed and then finished, 'perfect.'

There was another juddering boom and a rush of hot air gusted down the corridor.

'Are we gonna stand around like ninkers all day or are we gonna get off this ship?' Kara snapped, bracing against me.

'I think that might be wise,' I agreed.

But the way was blocked. Cherubael had come back for me.

Its malicious rampage had crippled the *Essene*. It was still seething with the pain I had inflicted. It wasn't even talking any more.

It surged down the corridor towards us. I couldn't reach the *Malus Codicium* now. I was having enough trouble just standing up.

Eleena cried out in terror. I cursed, helpless, useless.

Aemos hobbled forward and place himself between us and the charging warp-spawn. He braced the runestaff against the floor and lowered the tip towards Cherubael. He knew what to do. May the God-Emperor show him mercy, he knew better than I.

There was a release of power and light so powerful that it was beyond sound. The host body disintegrated, showering us with a hail of burned flesh, charred bone and blackened augmetic debris.

Aemos and the runestaff shuddered and jerked as they both lit up with corposant that crackled and flashed up and down them.

The last few electrical arcs sizzled away into the deck. Aemos remained standing where he was with the staff still upraised. A tiny plume of smoke licked off the headpiece.

'Aemos? Aemos!'

'I've... dispossessed it... for a moment...' Aemos said without turning round. His voice was low and his words were emerging only by huge effort. 'So it's weak... and confused... but that won't... last... we need... a proper host vessel... for it to... occupy...'

He turned to face us. The destruction of the astropath's host body had singed his clothes and knocked his eyeglasses off.

'What did you do with it?' I asked.

He didn't answer. The effort would have been too great. Aemos would only ever say two more words to me.

'Aemos, what did you do with it?' I repeated.

He opened his eyes. They were blank. Completely blank.

It took us ten minutes to make the daemonhost safe, ten minutes we really didn't have. I was encumbered by the fact I couldn't move unaided. Eleena had to hold the *Malus Codicium* for me as I did the work, making the marks and runes and wardings with blood from my own wounds. I recalled the same hasty rituals I had performed on the beach at Miquol.

'Come on!' Kara urged.

'There! It's done! Aemos, can you hear me? It's done!'

His old hands were shaking. He lowered the staff. I could see his mouth trying to form the words, but he couldn't manage it.

But I knew this part. The incantation, the litany, the abduration against evil. The final sealing words.

'*In servitutem abduco*, I bind thee fast forever into this host!'

Medea nearly burned out the lift-jets of Maxilla's bulk pinnace getting us clear of the hangar deck. Everything shook. It didn't have anything like the kick of the old gun-cutter, but she nursed every last ounce of thrust she could out of it.

We managed to get about sixteen kilometres from the *Essene* when the first of the real spasms shook it. The majestic sprint-trader, Isolde-pattern, pride of its master, looked like a black shell to us, lit from within by raging atomic fires, spilling trails of debris behind it as it slowly tumbled into the embrace of the gas giant.

There was a small bright flash and then two more, almost simultaneous, like a flicker. Then a white dot appeared where the *Essene* had been, and grew bigger, and then became a white line that got brighter and longer and closer, until we could see it was the flaming edge of a huge expanding disk of nuclear energy.

The pinnace vibrated frantically like a bead rattle in the hand of an excited child as the shockwave seared past and around us.

Then it was quiet, and still again.

And the *Essene* was gone.

Aemos was crumpled in one of the high-backed acceleration seats in the pinnace's passenger space. His eyes were closed and his breathing was shallow and ragged.

Kara helped me to the seat next to him. She was saying something urgent about improving the tourniquets and field dressings on my legs but I didn't really hear her.

'Uber?'

As if I had disturbed him in his sleep, he opened his eyes. They were his eyes again. Bloodshot, old, blinking to focus without his eyeglasses.

His breath sounds were getting worse.

'You hold on,' I said. 'There's a portable medicae unit in the cargo section, Eleena's trying to get it working.'

He grunted something and swallowed.

'What?' I said.

He surprised me by suddenly taking my blood-stained hand and gripping it tightly. He turned his head slowly and squinted at the daemonhost we had made together. It sat, strapped into its seat, on the other side of the aisle, head bowed and dormant.

'Most...' he whispered. 'Most perturbatory...'

I was going to reply, but his grip had slackened, his breathing had stopped. My oldest friend had gone.

I sat back, gazing at the cabin roof. The sensations that I had been blocking swept in and overwhelmed me.

I felt frail, as if I was made of paper. I knew I had lost a huge quantity of blood.

The pain in my legs was like fire, but it was nothing compared to the pain in my heart.

I heard Kara calling my name. She called it again. I heard Eleena asking me to say something.

But the void had come up like a wall, and they were too far away to hear.

NINETEEN

In the Halls of Yssarile
Leaves of Darkness
In the name of the Holy God-Emperor

Someone, somewhere close by, was using one of those damned shuriken catapults. I could hear the *jhut! jhut! jhut!* of the launcher mechanism and the thin, brittle sounds of the impacts.

There was blood in my mouth, I noticed. I'd worry about it later. Crezia would fuss no doubt. 'You should not be doing this,' she had warned me fiercely in the infirmary of the *Hinterlight.*

Well, that's where she was wrong. This was the Emperor's work. This was my work.

'Moving up,' Nayl said over the intervox. 'Twenty paces.'

'Understood,' I replied. I stepped forward. It was still an effort, and still very much a surprise to feel my body so wretchedly slow. The crude augmetic braces around my legs and torso weighed me down and forced me to plod, like an ogre from the old myths.

Or like a Battle Titan, I considered, ruefully. One heavy foot-step after the next, lumbering to my destiny.

It was the best work Crezia and Antribus had been able to manage given the time and the resources available. Crezia had passionately wanted me confined to vital support until I could be delivered to a top level Imperial facility.

I'd insisted on being mobile.

'If we throw together repairs now,' she had said, 'it'll be worse in the long term. To get you walking we'll have to do things that no amount of later work can repair, no matter how excellent.'

'Just do it,' I'd said. For the opportunity to reach Pontius Glaw, I'd happily sacrifice prosthetic sophistication. All I needed was function.

Barbarisater trembled in my right fist as it sensed a bio-aura, but I relaxed. It was Kara Swole.

She jogged back down the chasm towards me, dressed in a tight, green armoured bodyglove and a thick, quilted flak coat. She had a dust visor on, and a fat-nosed compact hand-cannon slung over her shoulder.

'All right, boss?' she said

'I'm doing fine.'

'You look...'

'What?'

'Pissed off.'

'Thank you, Kara. I'm probably annoyed because you and Nayl are having all the fun taking point.'

'Well, Nayl thinks we should tighten up anyway.'

I voxed back to the second element of our force. In less than two minutes, Eleena and Medea had joined us. Along side them came Lief Gustine and Korl Kraine, two men from Gideon's band who had subbed as reinforcements, as well as Gideon's mercenary archaeologist, Kenzer.

'Moving up,' I told them.

'You managing okay, sir?' Eleena asked.

'I'm fine. Fine. I just wish you'd...' I stopped. 'I'm fine, thank you, Eleena.'

They were all still worried about me. It had only been three and half weeks since the carnage at Jeganda. I'd only been walking for five days. They all quietly agreed with Crezia's advice that I should still be in the infirmary and leaving this to Ravenor.

Well, that was the perk of being the boss. I made the damn decisions. But I shouldn't be angry with them for worrying. But for Kara and Eleena's frantic emergency work on the pinnace, I'd be dead. I'd crashed twice. Eleena, the only one whose blood-type matched mine, had even made last minute donations.

Pulled apart at the seams, my band was pulling together tighter than ever.

'Let's pick up the pace,' I said. 'We don't want Nayl and Ravenor to have all the glory.'

'After you, Ironhoof,' Medea said. Kara sniggered, but pretended she was having trouble with her filter mask.

'I can't imagine why you think you can get away with that nickname,' I said.

We heard the shuriken catapult buzzing again. It was close, the sound rolling back to us around the maze of the gorge.

'Someone's having a party,' said Gustine. Bearded, probably to help disguise the terrible scarring that seemed to cover his entire skin, Gustine was an ex-Guardsman turned ex-pit fighter turned ex-bounty hunter turned Inquisition soldier. He said he came from Raas Bisor in the Segmentum Tempestus, but I didn't know where that was. Apart from that it was in the Segmentum Tempestus. Gustine wore heavyweight grey ablative armour and carried an old, much-repaired standard Imperial Guard lasrifle.

He'd been with Ravenor for a good many years, so I trusted him.

The whizzing sounds echoed again, overlapping with laser discharges.

'Ravenor's friends,' Medea said. None of us were comfortable about the eldar. Six of them had arrived on Gideon's ship as a bodyguard for the farseer. Tall, too tall, inhumanly slender, silent, keeping themselves to the part of the ship assigned them. Aspect warriors, Gideon had called them, whatever that meant. The plumed crests on their great, curved helmets had made them seem even taller once they were in armour.

They'd deployed to the surface with Ravenor, the seer lord and three more of Ravenor's band.

A third strike team of six under Ravenor's senior lieutenant Rav Skynner, was advanced about a kilometre to our west.

Ghül, or 5213X to give it its Carto-Imperialis code, was nothing like I had imagined it. It didn't at all resemble the arid world I had glimpsed in Marla Tarray's mind, the dried-out husk where primaeval cities lay buried under layers of ash. I suppose that was because all I'd seen was her own imagined view of the place. She'd never seen it. She hadn't lived long enough to get the chance.

I wondered if Ghül matched the farseer's vision. Probably. The eldar seemed unnecessarily precise bastards to me.

We'd approached the world in a wide, stealthy orbit. The *Hinterlight* was equipped with disguise fields that Ravenor was reluctant to explain to me but which I felt were partly created by his own, terrifyingly strong will. High band sensors had located a starship in tight orbit, a rogue trader of some considerable size that didn't appear to realise we were there.

Ghül itself was invisible. Or nearly invisible. I have never seen a world that seemed so much to be not there. It was a shadow against the starfield, a faintly discernable echo of matter. Even on the sunward side, it lacked any real form. It appeared to soak up light and give nothing back.

When Cynia Preest, Ravenor's ship-mistress, had brought us the first surface scans to study, we thought she was showing us close up pictures of a child's toy.

'It's a maze,' I remember saying.

'A puzzle... like an interlock,' Ravenor decided.

'No, a carved fruit pit,' Medea had said.

We had all looked at her. 'The works of the Lord on the heart of a stone?' she asked. 'Anybody?'

'Perhaps you'd explain?' I'd said.

So she had. A some length, until we grasped the idea. The hermits of Glavia, so it seems, thought no greater expression of their divine love for the Emperor could be made than to inscribe the entire Imperial Prayer onto the pits of sekerries. A sekerry, we learned, was a soft, sweet summer fruit that tasted of quince and nougat. A bit like a shirnapple, we were reliably informed. The pits were the size of pearls.

Thankfully, no one had made the mistake of asking what a shirnapple was.

'I don't know how they do it,' Medea had gone on. 'They do it by eye, with a needle, They can't even see, I don't think. But they used to show us liths of the carved pits, magnified, in scholam. You could read every word! Every last word! The works of the Lord on the heart of a stone. All laced together, tight and compact, using every corner of the space. We were taught that the prayer pits were one of the Nineteen Wonders of Glavia and that we should be proud.'

'Nineteen Wonders?' Cynia had asked.

'Golden Throne, woman, don't get her started!' I had cried out. But there had indeed been something in Medea's comparison. The surface of Ghül had been engraved, that's what it looked like. A perfect black sphere, engraved across its entire surface with tight, deep, interlocking lines. In reality, each of those lines was a smooth sided gorge, two hundred metres wide and nine hundred metres deep.

I wondered about Medea's description. I remembered the chart we had witnessed during the auto-seance on Promody, and the way dear Aemos's notes had taken on the same scrolling forms of the chart as he struggled to decipher it.

Ghül could very well be engraved, I decided. The warped ones' entire culture, certainly their language, had been built upon expressions of location and place. I imagined that the inscribed wall we had seen during the auto-seance had been part of just such a maze of lines, from a time when Promody had looked like Ghül, the capital world.

Cynia Preest's sensors had located heat and motion traces on the surface. We'd assembled the teams, and prepared for planetfall. The *Hinterlight*'s ship-mistress had been told to line up on the enemy's ship and stand ready to take it out.

Our three vessels, my pinnace and two shuttles from Ravenor's stable, had sunk low into the thin atmosphere and skimmed across the perfect, geometric surface, their shadows flitting across the flat black sections and the deep chasms.

We'd put down in adjacent gorges near the target zone.

The first surprise had been that the air was breathable. We'd all brought vacuum suits and rebreathers.

'How is that possible?' Eleena had asked.

'I don't know.'

'But it's so unlikely... I mean it's unfeasible,' she had stammered.

'Yes, it is.'

* * *

The second surprise had been the discovery that Medea was right.

Kenzer had knelt down with his auspex at the side of the gorge, studying microscopically the relationship between chasm floor and chasm wall.

I didn't need him to tell me they were perfect. Smooth. Exact. Machined. Engraved.

'The angle between floor and wall is ninety degrees to a margin of accuracy that... well, it is so precise, it goes off my auspex's scale. Who... who could do a thing like this?' Kenzer had gasped.

'The hermits of Glavia?' Medea had cracked.

'If they had fusion beams, starships, a spare planet and unlimited power supplies,' I had said. 'Besides, tell me this: who polished the planet smooth before they started?'

We moved down the gorge. It curved gently to the west, like an old river, deep cut in its banks. Long before on KCX-1288, facing the saruthi, I had been disconcerted by the lack of angular geometry. Now I was disturbed by the reverse. Everything was so damned precise, squared off, unmarked and unblemished. Only a faint sooty deposit in the wide floor of the trench suggested any antiquity at all.

We caught up with Nayl.

'They know we're here,' he said, referring to the sounds of battle in the nearby gorge.

'Any idea of numbers?' I asked.

'Not a thing, but Skynner's mob has found trouble too. Vessorines, so he reckon, wrapped up in carapace suits and loaded for bear.'

'We'd best be careful then.'

I tried Ravenor, using my mind instead of my intervox.

Status?

THE ASPECTS HAVE–

Whoa, whoa, whoa... quieter, Gideon.

Sorry. I forget sometimes you–

I what?

You're hurt, I meant to say. The aspect warriors have engaged. It's quite busy here.

I could feel the sub-surface twinges of power as he channelled his mind into his force chair's psi-cannons.

Opposition? I sent.

Vessorine janissaries and some other heterodox mercs. We–

He broke off. There was a grinding wash of distortion for a moment.

Sorry, he sent. *Some sort of fusion weapon. They certainly don't want us in here.*

In where?

He broadcast a sequence of map co-ordinates and I took the map-slate out of Nayl's hands and punched them in.

A structure, Ravenor sent. *Ahead of us, south-west of you. It's built into the end pier of one of the gorge junctions. Although I can't see how. There are no doors. The Vessorine are coming out of somewhere, though. There must be a hidden entrance.*

More distortion. Then he floated back to me.

The Vessorine are fighting like maniacs. My lord seer says they have already earned the respect of the aspects.

Your lord seer?

Send again. I didn't make that out.

Nothing, Gideon. We're going to try and come round on your flank, around the north-east intersection of the gorge.

Understood.

Come on! I urged. The others all jumped, all except Eleena, and I realised I was still using my psyche. Sloppy. I was tired and in pain. Still no excuse.

'My apologies,' I said, vocal again. 'We're moving forward. This chasm turns south-west and intersects with two others. Target site's at the junction, so Gideon reckons.'

We hurried forward, moving through the steep shadow of the gorge.

'Glory be!' exclaimed Kenzer suddenly. He was looking up.

Bright flashes lit up the starry sky framed by the sides of the chasm. They washed back and forth like spills of milk in ink. Alerted to our presence, Glaw's starship had presented for combat and the *Hinterlight* was answering. Vast blinks of light lit up the sky like a strobe.

'I wouldn't wanna be up there,' said Korl Kraine. Kraine was a hiver who'd never served in any formal militia. His allegiance was to Ravenor first and to the underclan of Tanhive Nine, Tansetch, second and last. He was a short, pale man wearing patched and cut-off flak-canvas. His skin was dyed with clan colours and his eyes were cheap augments. He wore a string of human teeth around his neck, which was ironic as his own teeth were all made of ceramite.

Kraine raised his night-sighted Tronsvasse autorifle to his shoulder and scurried forward. He'd lived in a lightless warren of city all his life until Ravenor recruited him. This gloom suited him.

The sound of catapults grew louder. There were several of them at work now, buzzing out a duet with heavyweight lasguns. I heard the gritty thump of a grenade.

Kenzer, the archaeologist, was lagging. He wasn't part of Ravenor's official troop, merely an expert paid to help out on Promody. I didn't like him much. He had no fibre and no real commitment.

I didn't need to read his mind to see that he was only here for the potential fortune a few exclusive academic papers about the Ghül discovery could make him.

'Hurry up!' I yelled at him. My back was getting tired and the blood in my mouth was back again.

Kenzer was hunched down at the base of the chasm side, fidgeting with his hand-scanner.

I called a halt and stomped back to him, my heavy boots, reinforced with the brace's metal frame, kicking up soot. Iron-hoof, indeed!

I believed my greatest annoyance wasn't the brace-frame or its weight or the lumpen gait I was forced to adopt, not even the non-specific haemorrhage that was seeping into my mouth.

No, the worst thing was my cold scalp.

I really couldn't get used to it. Crezia had been obliged to shave my head in order to implant the cluster of neural and synaptic cables that would drive the augmetic frame around my legs. She had been upset all through the implant procedure. It really was terribly crude, even by basic Imperial standards. But out in the middle of nowhere at all, it had been the best she and Antribus could cobble together.

Needs must, as they say.

I was bald, and the back of my skull was raw, sore and clotted with the multiple implant jacks of the sub-spine feeds my faithful medicaes had installed to make my leg frame work. The steel-jacketed cables sprouted from my scalp and ran down my back into the lumbar servo of the walking brace. The bunched cables were flesh-stapled to my back, like a neat, augmetic ponytail.

I would get used to it, in time. If there was time. If there wasn't, what the hell did it matter?

I stopped beside Kenzer, throwing a hard shadow over him. 'What are you doing?'

'Making a recording, sir,' he gabbled. 'There's a marking here. The carved walls we've seen so far have been blank.'

I peered down. It was difficult to bend.

'Where?'

He pulled a puffer-brush out of his kit-pack and blew the soot away.

'There!'

A small spiral. Cut into the smooth face of the rock.

It looked like a tiny version of the chart we'd seen on Promody, or a really tiny version of the mazed surface of this planet.

'Record it quickly and move on,' I told him. I turned away. 'Let's go,' I called over my shoulder curtly.

Kenzer screamed. There was a flurry of las-fire.

I wheeled back immediately. Kenzer was sprawled on the floor of the gorge, ripped apart by laser shots. He was only partially articulated, such had been the point-blank ferocity of the shots. The wide puddle of blood seeping from his carcass was soaking into the soot.

There was no sign of any attacker.

'What the hell?' Barbarisater was in my hand and had been purring, but now it was dull.

Nayl dropped close to me, his matt-black hellgun sweeping the area of the corpse.

'How in the name of Terra did that happen?' he asked. 'Lief? Korl? Upside?'

I looked back. Gustine and Kraine were walking backwards slowly, scoping up at the cliff tops of the gorge.

'Nothing. No shooters above,' Gustine reported.

I slapped my palm against the cold stone face of the gorge above the marking Kenzer had found. It was unyielding.

We moved forward, following the sweep of the chasm. Kraine was covering our backs. After we'd gone about fifty metres, he suddenly cried out.

I turned in time to see him in a face-to-face gunfight with two Vessorine janissaries in full carapace-wear. Kraine staggered backwards as he was hit repeatedly in the torso, but managed to keep firing. He put a burst of rounds through the face plate of one of the Vessorines before the other one made the kill shot and dropped him into the soot.

Nayl and Medea were already firing. The remaining Vessorine swung his aim and squeezed off another salvo, winging both Eleena and Nayl.

Then he walloped over onto his back as Kara's cannon ripped him apart.

'See to them!' I ordered, pointing Medea at Nayl and Eleena. Nayl had been skinned across the left arm and Eleena had a flesh wound on her left shin. Both kept insisting they were fine. Medea opened his kitbag for field dressings.

I looked at the corpses, Kraine and the Vessorines. Gustine appeared beside me. 'Where the jesh did they come from?' he asked.

I didn't answer. I drew my runestaff over my head out of its leather boot, and gripped it tightly as I focused my force at the gorge wall. Soot and the debris of eons puffed out, and I saw another spiral mark in the wall like the one Kenzer had found.

'Charts,' I said.

'What, sir?' asked Lief.

I bent down, spitting on my fingers then rubbing my hand across the spiral marks. I tried to ignore the fact that there was a smear of blood in the spittle.

'No wonder Ravenor couldn't find a door. We're not seeing this in the right dimension.'

'Pardon me, but what the craphole are you talking about?' asked Lief. I liked him. Always honest.

'The warped ones understood location and moment in way

we can't imagine. They were, after all, warped. We see this as a geometric network of mathematically precise chasms, a maze. But it's not. It's four dimensional...'

'Four?' Gustine began, uncertainly

'Oh, four, six, eight... who knows? Think of it this way, like a... a woven garment!

'A woven garment, sir?'

'Yes, all those thick, intertwined threads, such a complex pattern.'

'All right...'

'Now imagine the knitting needles that made it. Just the needles. Big and hard and simple.'

'Okay...' said Medea, joining us.

'This planet is simply the knitting needles. Hard, rigid, simple. The reality of Ghül is the garment woven from it, something we can't see, something complex and soft, interlaced round the needles.'

'I'm sorry, sir, you've lost me,' Lief Gustine said.

'Lost,' I said. 'That's damn right. These marks on the wall. They're like mini charts, explaining how the overall reality can be accessed and exited.'

Ghustine nodded as if he understood. 'Right... so, going back, where the jesh did the janissaries come from?' he asked.

I slapped the hard wall.

'There. Right there.'

'But it's solid rock!'

'Only to us,' I said.

As we moved on again, down the gorge, we formed a pack that covered all sides, like phalanx of spearmen from the old ages of warfare. The sounds of Ravenor's battle had become frenetic. Nayl reported grimly that he couldn't raise Skynner or any of his force any more.

We all hunted the walls for further carvings

'Here, sir! Here!' Kara sang out.

I ran over to the spiral cut she had found. 'Wait,' I ordered.

Like an eye blinking, the smooth rock opened. Suddenly it just wasn't there. A Vessorine janissary in combat carapace pushed out, weapon raised.

Nayl had him cold, felling him with a single shot. But there were more behind the first.

Medea started shooting. Two more mercs had blinked out of the gorge wall on the far side of us.

There was no cover. No damn cover at all.

In a moment, we were fired on from a third angle.

I had already drawn the big Hecuter autopistol I had borrowed from the *Hinterlight*'s arsenal. Gustine's old las was cracking away beside me and Eleena was emptying her pistol's extended clip on semi-automatic.

They'd just been poaching us up until now. This was a full scale ambush. I counted at least fifteen janissaries, as well as an ogryn with a heavy weapon. Nayl went down, hit in the thigh, but he kept blasting. A las round sparked bluntly against the heavy brace on my left leg.

Time to reset the odds.

'Cherubael!' I commanded.

It had been drifting high above the gorge, trailing us like a kite, but now it descended, gathering speed, beginning to shine.

I had been much more careful in my design of this daemon-host. Elaborating on the basic and hasty ritual construction Aemos and I had wrought in those last few minutes aboard the Essene, I had supplemented the wards and rune markings on its flesh to reinforce its obedience. This daemonhost would not be permitted to have any of the capricious guile of the previous versions. It would not rebel. It would not be a maverick that had to be watched at all times. It was bound and locked with triple wards, totally subservient. I liked to think I could learn from my mistakes, at least sometimes.

Of course, there was a price to pay for such security. This Cherubael could manifest much less power, a direct consequence of its reinforced bindings. But it had enough. More than enough.

It swept down the gorge, warp-flame trailing from its upright body, and demolished one group of attackers in a blurry storm of aether. To their credit, the Vessorines didn't scream. But they broke and started to fall back.

The ogryn fired his heavy weapon at the incoming host. The impact fluttered off Cherubael like petals. It punched its talons into the squealing abhuman's chest and lifted the big brute off the ground.

And then threw him. The ogryn went up. Just simply went up and kept going.

Cherubael changed direction and skimmed across the gorge towards the retreating mercs. Our guns had whittled their numbers down by then and we were in pursuit, though Eleena had stayed with the sprawled, cursing Nayl.

I noticed something else about this new Cherubael. It didn't laugh any more. Ever. Its face was set in an implacable frown. It showed no signs of taking any pleasure in its slaughter.

I was pleased about that. The laughter really did used to get on my nerves.

It was going to take a while to get used to Cherubael's new face, though. Once installed within the flesh host, the daemon had made its usual alterations – the sprouting nub horns, the talons, the smooth, glossy skin, the blank eyes.

But it had not entirely erased the features of Godwyn Fischig.

* * *

It killed the last of the ambushers, all save one who reached the gorge wall and accessed the dimension trap they had emerged from.

'Hold it!' I ordered. 'Hold it open!'

Cherubael obeyed. It atomised the last merc as the trap blinked open and then braced its arms wide, preventing the trap from closing. Even for Cherubael, this was an effort.

'Hurry. Up,' it said, as if annoyed with me.

I reached the trap.

There wasn't time to get us all through. Gustine hurled himself in, headlong, and I followed, shouting to the others to stay back and stay together.

The last thing I heard was a loud, liquid impact that must have been the ogryn finally obeying the law of gravity.

The trap blinked shut.

I felt a sickening twist of translation. I landed on top of the sprawled Gustine in a dim, boxy space that smelled musty.

'Ow!' he complained.

I got to my feet. That in itself was ridiculously hard. I was sweating freely by the time I was vertical.

'You okay?' Gustine asked.

'Yes,' I snapped. I wasn't really. My head was throbbing, and the pain in my legs was beginning to overcome the power of the drugs that were self-administering from a dispenser Crezia had fitted to my hip.

'You had better not expect me to carry you,' Cherubael whispered behind me.

'Don't worry. Your dignity isn't in danger.'

I drew Barbarisater, holding it in my right hand, and gripped my runestaff in my left.

I stomped forward. Darkness. A wall. I turned. Another wall.

'Gustine?'

He'd switched on a lamp pack, but it was showing him nothing but black walls. There was no sign of a ceiling.

'How far can you see?' I asked Cherubael.

'Forever,' it said, floating alongside me.

'Fine. In practical terms, how far can you see?'

'Not far in here. I can see that the wall ends there. There is a gap beyond it.'

'Very well,' I plodded ahead. My back really hurt now where the implants went in and my nose was bleeding. Gustine clipped the lamp pack to the bayonet lug of his las.

He tried to reach Nayl on the vox. Dead and silent.

I made an effort to reach Ravenor with my mind. Nothing.

Heavy footed, I moved through the darkness with my odd companions. The runestaff was trembling, sniffing some focus of power.

'You feel that?' I asked the daemon.

It nodded.

I decided we would follow it.

'Have you noticed we can breathe in here too?' Gustine remarked a few minutes later.

'Gosh, I wouldn't have picked up on that.'

He frowned at me, put-upon. 'I mean, the air's right, inside and out.'

'It's so the enemy can breathe,' Cherubael said.

'What's that supposed to mean?'

'They got here first. They got inside. Ghül made the atmosphere appropriate for them as soon as Ghül sensed they were there.'

'You're talking like Ghül is alive.'

'Ghül has never been alive,' it said.

'It's never been dead, either,' it added a moment later.

I was about to ask it to expand a little on that alarming notion, but Cherubael suddenly surged forward in the blackness ahead of us. I saw the flash of its light, a laser discharge.

It came back, blood steaming off its talons.

'They're hunting for us,' it said.

I have seen wonders in my life. Horrors too. I have witnessed vistas and spectacles that have cowed my mind and dwarfed my imagination.

None of them compared to the mausoleum under Ghül.

I cannot say anything about its size except to use inadequate words like vast, huge...

There was nothing to give any scale. We came out of the black tunnels into a black abyss that was to all intents much the same except that the blackness that had been walls was now immaterial. Tiny, scattered specks of light, dozens of them, illuminated small parts of the face of some impossible structure, as dark and cyclopean as the eternal wall ancient philosophers used to believe surrounded creation. The edge of the universe. The side of the casket an ancient god had wrought to keep reality in.

Which god, I wouldn't like to say.

It was warm and still. Not even the air moved. The dots of light showed small parts of a vast design etched onto the face of the mausoleum. Hints of spirals, lines and swirling runes.

This was where the warped ones had laid their dead king to rest.

This was the tomb of Yssarile, over which Ghül had been raised in the strange eons before man.

The sight even stunned Cherubael to silence. I hoped its lack of comment was down to awe. I had a nasty feeling it had more to do with reverence.

Or dread.

Gustine lost it for a while. His mind refused to deal with what his eyes were seeing. He began to weep inconsolably, and fell to his knees. It was a dismal sight to see such a robust, fearless man reduced in such a way.

I let him be as long as I dared, but the sounds of his weeping carried in the dark and seemed alarmingly loud. Some of the tiny lights on the face of the mausoleum began to move, as if descending.

I took hold of the sobbing fighter and tried to use my will to calm him.

It didn't work. No persuasion could anchor the edges of his sanity where it had come adrift.

I had to be harsher. I numbed his mind with a deep psychic probe, blocking his terror out and freezing his thoughts but for the most basic instincts and biological functions.

We approached the mausoleum across a plain of lightless stone. The further we got, the further away I realised the structure actually was. It was evidently even bigger than I had first realised.

I had Gustine switch off his lamp pack. We simply followed the dots of light up ahead. I suggested that Cherubael might like to warn us if the darkness around us became anything other than a flat table of stone. A chasm, for example.

The only advantage in the mindless scale of the place as I could see it was that the enemy would have a hard job finding us. There was so much space to search.

After what seemed like an hour, we were still a very long way from the tomb. I checked my chronometer to determine precisely how long it had been since we accessed the interior of Ghül, but it had stopped. Stopped isn't right exactly. It was still running and beating seconds, but the time was not recording in any way.

I recalled the clock in Aemos's suite, chiming to mark out times that had no meaning.

As we closed on our destination, I was able to make more sense of the lights. Tiny dots, they had seemed, casting little fields of light.

They were massive lamps, high power, of the sort used to light landing fields or military camps. Mounted on suspensor platforms, they floated at various points in front of the face of the mausoleum, lighting up surface details in patches of glare the size of amphitheatres. There were forty-three of the platforms, each with its own lamp. I counted them.

There were men on the platforms, human figures. Glaw's men, I was sure, some of them mercenary guards, most of them adepts of arcane lore enlisted to his cause.

As we watched, some of the platforms drifted slowly or adjusted the sweep of their light.

They were reading the wall.

By whatever catalogue of means, Glaw had learned of this place, found it and made his way inside to plunder its vile treasures. But its innermost secrets clearly still eluded him.

That was why he had wanted the *Malus Codicium* so badly.

To turn the final lock, to get him through the final barrier.

One of the platforms began to climb vertically, its lamplight flickering across the passing relief of the tomb face. It climbed and then halted far up above at what seemed to be the top of the wall. Its beam picked out an open square, an entrance, perhaps, though who would put an entrance at the top of a wall without steps?

I scolded myself for asking. The warped ones.

'Glaw is up there,' Cherubael said.

It was right. I could smell the monster's mind.

* * *

We hurried the last distance to the foot of the mausoleum wall. Several cargo fliers and two bulk speeders were parked down here, alongside metal crates of equipment and spares for the lamp platforms. Their base camp.

We waited. I considered our options.

Almost at the same time, two of the platforms descended the wall to ground level, dimming their huge lamps. There were about six men on each one.

One settled in and two men jumped down, hurrying towards one of the cargo fliers. I could hear them, exchanging words with the crew on the platform. A moment later the other came down softly beside it.

I could see the men. They were dressed in light fatigues or environment robes. Some carried data-slates.

The men who had gone to the flier returned, carrying an equipment crate between them. They loaded it onto the platform and it immediately began to climb back up the wall, its lamp powering back to full beam to resume its work.

'Come on,' I said quietly.

More men were loading more crates onto the other platform. There were six in all – four in robes and two armoured mercs operating the platform controls.

Barbarisater took the three loaders out with two quick strokes. Gustine dragged a man backwards over the platform rail and snapped his neck. Cherubael embraced the two mercs from behind and they turned to ash and sifted away.

We got on board.

'Get ready with the lamp,' I told Gustine. I studied the platform control panel quickly, and then activated the lift. The attitude controls were a simple brass lever.

We rose. The tomb face whispered by. As we lifted past the lowermost of the working platforms, Gustine powered up the lamp and angled it towards the wall.

I couldn't remember quite how far up the platform had been before it had descended for spares. How long before we passed our designated spot and were noticed by the others?

I hoped they were all too engrossed in their work.

We were about two-thirds of the way up when we heard shots from another platform and a lamp swung our way. Almost immediately, so did several others, tracking our ascent. Las-fire pinged across at us. Gustine dropped down by the rail and returned fire. I kept us rising.

'Do you want me to…?' Cherubael asked.

'No, stay put.'

Gustine's next salvo took out the lamp of a platform rising after us. A huge shower of sparks erupted out and drizzled down the tomb face. I felt multiple jolts as shots impacted against the underside of our rig.

Almost there.

We rose up next to the entrance. It was square, maybe forty metres across. A platform was already floating outside it and, clumsy with the controls, I slammed us against it. The men aboard began firing. There were others inside the dim mouth of the entrance. Gustine blasted back. I saw one topple back onto the deck of the other platform, and then another pitch clean off and drop like a stone.

Las-fire and solid rounds raked our vehicle, tearing strips and nuggets out of the deck plating and the rail. Shot through, the lamp died.

I hauled on the control stick and slammed us sideways into the other platform, deliberately this time. We ground against them and drove them into the tomb face. The edge of their hull shrieked out sparks as it tore against the stone. I did it again. They were screaming and firing.

'Let's move!' Gustine yelled.

He heaved a grenade into the mouth of the entrance to clear us a path.

There was a dull bang and a flash, and two figures came flailing out into the air.

Gustine tossed a second onto the other platform and then leapt over the rail into the tomb entrance, blasting into the wafting smoke haze with his lasrifle.

I followed him, Cherubael drifting at my heels. It was damn hard to step wide enough and span the gap between the platform and the entrance's stone lip.

Gustine's second grenade ripped a hole through the deck of the other platform. It sagged and then dropped, like a descending elevator, trailing flames.

Far below us, it tore through two other platforms and spilled men and debris into the air.

The jolt of the blast had come at the wrong moment for me. Our platform shuddered and yawed out like a boat at a dock, and I was still halfway across, forcing my stiff, heavy limbs to carry me.

I was going to fall. The brace around my body felt as heavy as an anchor, pulling me down.

Cherubael grabbed me under the arms and hoisted me neatly into the entrance.

I was grateful, but I couldn't find it in me to thank it. Thank Cherubael? The idea was toxic. Then again, just as unlikely was the notion of Cherubael voluntarily saving my life...

Gustine was fighting his way forward down the entrance, which we saw now was a long tunnel that matched the dimensions of the opening. Crates of equipment were piled up in the mouth, and floating glow-globes had been set at intervals along the wall. They looked like they went on for a long way.

Four or five mercs and servants of our adversary were dead

on the tunnel floor and half a dozen more were backed down the throat of it, firing to drive us out.

Cherubael swept forward and obliterated them. We came after him. I so dearly wished I could run.

The tunnel opened on the other side of the tomb face. We set eyes on the interior. By now, I had become numb to the inhuman scale of things. The tomb was a vault in which one might comfortably store a continent. The inner walls and the high, stone-beamed roof were lavishly decorated with swirls of script and emblems that I swore I would never allow to be seen by other eyes. This was the crypt where Yssarile lay in death, and the walls screamed his praise and worship.

I could make out little of the dark gulf below, but there was something there. Something the size of a great Imperial hive city. I discerned a black, geometric shape that was fashioned from neither stone nor metal nor even bone, but, it seemed, all of those things at once. It was repellent. Dead, but alive. Dormant, but filled with the slumbering power of a million stars.

The barque of the daemon-king. Yssarile's chariot of unholy battle, his instrument of apocalypse, with which he had scoured the warped fortresses and habitations of his own reality in wars too dreadful to imagine.

Glaw's prize.

From the globe-lit tunnel, we could make our way out onto a massive plinth of dark onyx that extended from the edge of the inner wall. There was a block raised there, a polished tooth of dark green mineral forty metres tall, set deep into the plinth. It was wound with carved spirals.

Glow-globes floated around it and tools and instruments lay at its foot. Pontius Glaw had been studying this discovery himself. But the noise of our violent entry had alerted him. He was waiting for us.

He emerged from behind the standing block, calm, almost indifferent. His tall, gleaming machine body was as I had remembered it from the auto-seance. The cloak of blades clinked as he moved. The ever-smirking golden mask smirked.

'Gregor Eisenhorn,' he said softly. 'The galaxy's most persistent bastard. Only you could scrabble and slash and claw and crawl your way to me. Which, of course, is why I admire you so.'

I stomped forward.

'Careful!' Gustine hissed, but I had long passed the point where being careful was a high priority.

I faced Glaw. He was broader than me and a good deal taller. His blade-cloak jangled as he stroked a perfectly articulated duralloy hand across the surface of the green block. Then he raised the same hand and held it up for inspection.

'Magos Bure did a fine job, didn't he? Such a craftsman. I can never thank you enough for arranging his services. This is the hand I killed him with.'

'There's more than his blood on your hands, Glaw. Do you answer to that name now, or do you prefer to hide behind the title Khanjar?'

'Either will do.'

'Your daughter didn't take either of your names.'

He was silent. If I could get him angry, I could perhaps force an error.

'Marla,' he said, 'so headstrong. Another reason to kill you, apart from the obvious.'

He was about to say something else, but I had waited long enough. I blasted my will through the runestaff, and lunged forward, swinging my blade.

The psychic blast knocked him back, and he half-turned, his cloak whirling out and turning Barbarisater aside with its multiple edges. His turn became a full spin and I lurched back to avoid the lethal hem of his blade-cloak.

Gustine moved in, firing bolts of light that simply reflected off Glaw's gleaming form.

Cherubael came in from the other side. Its searing attack scorched Glaw's metal, and I heard him curse. He slashed at Cherubael with his open hand, extending hook blades from slots in the fingertips.

The hooks ripped into Cherubael's flesh but it made no cry. It grappled with Pontius Glaw, psychic power boiling the space between them and flaring out in spasming tendrils of light. The very air crisped and ionised. Glaw's dancing metal feet chipped flakes of onyx off the plinth beneath him. I tried to get in, to land a blow in support of the daemonhost, but it was like approaching a furnace.

Gustine simply looked on, open-mouthed. He was so far out of his league it wasn't funny.

Glaw tore out a savage blow that spun Cherubael away for a second and followed it up with a lance of mental fury that actually made the daemonhost tumble out of the air. Cherubael got up slowly, like a thrown rider, and rose up off the ground again.

In that short break, I rejoined the struggle, driving at Glaw with alternate blows of staff and sword, keeping the most powerful mind wall I could erect between us.

Glaw smashed the wall into invisible pieces, struck me hard and tore the staff out of my hand. His blades lacerated my arm and ripped my cloak.

I exerted all the force I had and rallied with Barbarisater, cutting in with rotating *ulsars* and heavy *sae hehts* that chimed against his rippling cloak armour. The runestaff had fallen out of reach.

I ducked to avoid a high sweep of his razor-hem, but I had forced myself too hard. I felt cranial plugs pop and servos tear out of my back. Pain knifed up my spine. I barely got clear of his next strike. My sword work became a frantic series of *tahn feh sar* parries, as I tried to back away and fend off his hooks and cloak-blades.

Cherubael charged back at Glaw, but something intercepted it in mid-air. Out of the corner of my eye, I saw Cherubael locked in aerial combat with an incandescent figure. They tumbled away, off the plinth, out over the gulf of the tomb.

'You don't think you're the only one to have a pet, do you?' Glaw jeered. 'And my daemonhost is not restricted in its power like yours. Poor Cherubael. You've treated him so badly.'

'It's an "it", not a "him",' I snarled and placed a high stroke that actually notched his golden mask.

'Bastard!' he squealed and swept his cloak around under my guard. The thick metal of my body-brace deflected the worst of it, but I felt blood welling from cuts to my ribs.

I staggered back. The agony in my spine was the worst thing, and I was certain my already limited motion was now badly impaired. My left leg felt dead and heavy.

Ironhoof. Ironhoof.

He thrust at me with his talons and nearly shredded my face. I blocked his hand at the last second, setting Barbari-sater between his splayed fingers and locking out his strike.

He threw me back. I was off-step, out-balanced by my slow, heavy mechanical legs.

Laser shots danced across Glaw's face and chest as Gustine tried vainly to help out. Glaw pirouetted – a move that seemed impossibly nimble for such a giant – and his cloak whirred out almost horizontally with the centrifugal force.

Hundreds of fast moving, razor-sharp blades whistled through Gustine, so fast, so completely, that he didn't realise what had happened to him.

A mist of blood puffed in the air. Ghustine collapsed. Literally.

Glaw turned on me again. I'd lost sight of Cherubael. I was on my own.

And only now did I admit to myself that I was out-matched.

Glaw was almost impervious to damage. Fast, armoured, deadly. Even on a good day, he would have been hard to defeat in single combat.

And this wasn't a good day.

He was going to kill me.

He knew it too. As he pressed his assault, he started to laugh.

That cut me deeper than any of his blades. I thought of Fischig, Aemos and Bequin. I thought of all the allies and friends who had perished because of him. I thought of what his spite had done to me and what it had cost me to get this far.

I thought of Cherubael. The laughter reminded me of Cherubael.

I came back at him so hard and so furiously that Barbarisater's blade became notched and chipped. I struck blows that snapped blade-scales off his clinking cape. I struck at him until he wasn't laughing any more.

His answer was a psychic blast that smashed me backwards ten paces. Blood spurted from my nose and filled my mouth. I didn't fall. I would not give him that pleasure. But Barbarisater flew, screaming, from my dislodged grip.

I was hunched over. My hands on my thighs, panting like a dog. My head was swimming. I could hear him crunching over the onyx towards me.

'You'd have won by now if you'd had the book,' I said, coughing the blood from my mouth.

'What?'

'The book. The damned book. The *Malus Codicium*. That's
what you were really after when you sent your hired mur-
derers against me. That's why you tore my operation apart
and killed everyone you could reach. You wanted the book.'

'Of course I did,' he snarled.

I looked up at him. 'It would have unlocked the prize
already. Done away with this endless, fruitless study. You'd
simply have opened the tomb and taken the daemon's chariot. Long before we could ever get here.'

'Savour that little triumph, Gregor,' he said. 'Your little pyrr-
hic victory. By keeping that book from me you have added
extra months... years, to my work. Yssarile's weapon will be
mine, but you've made its acquisition so much harder.'

'Good,' I said.

He chuckled. 'You're a brave man, Gregor Eisenhorn. Come
on, now – I'll make it quick.'

His blades clinked.

'I suppose, then,' I added, 'I'd have been mad to bring it
with me.'

He froze.

With a shaking, bloody hand, I reached into my coat and
took out the *Malus Codicium*. I think he gasped. I held it out,
half open, so he could see, and riffled the pages through with
my fingers.

'You foolish, foolish man,' he said, smiling.

'That's what I thought,' I said. With one brutal jerk, I ripped
the pages out of the cover.

'No!' he cried.

I wasn't listening. I fixed my mind on the loose bundle of

sheets in my hands and subjected them to the most ferocious mental blast I could manage. The pages caught fire.

I threw them up into the air.

Glaw screamed with despair and rage. A blizzard of burning pages fluttered around us. He tried to grab at them. He moved like an idiot, like a child, snatching what he could out of the air, trying to preserve anything, anything at all.

The pages burned. Leaves of darkness, billowing across the plinth, consumed by fire.

He snatched a handful, tried for more, stamping out those half-burned sheets that landed on the ground.

He wasn't paying any attention to me at all.

Barbarisater tore into him so hard it almost severed his head. Electricity crackled from the rent metal. He rasped and staggered. The Carthean blade sang in my hands as I ripped it across his chest and shattered part of his cloak.

He fell backwards, right at the edge of the plinth, his finger hooks shrieking as they fought to get a purchase on the smooth onyx. I swung again, an upswing that ripped off his golden mask and sent it spinning out over the gulf. The interior of his head was revealed. The circuits, the crackling, fusing cables, the crystal that contained his consciousness and being, set in its cradle of links and wires.

'In the name of the Holy God-Emperor of Terra,' I said quietly, 'I call thee diabolus and here deliver thy sentence.'

My own blood was dripping off Barbarisater's hilt between my doubled handed grip. I raised the blade.

And made the *ewl caer*.

The blade split his head and shattered the crystal into flecks of glass.

Pontius Glaw's metal body convulsed, jerked back and fell off the edge of the plinth, down into the gulf, into the blackness of the daemon-king's tomb, its cloak-blades chiming.

I was sitting on the plinth, with my back against the tomb wall, blood slowly pooling around me, when a flight flashed out in the darkness of the vault.

It came closer.

At last, Cherubael floated down and hovered over me. Its face, limbs and body were hideously marked with weals, burns and gashes.

I looked up at it. It was hard to move, hard to concentrate. There was blood in my mouth, in my eyes.

'Glaw's daemonhost?'

'Gone.'

'He claimed it was more powerful than you.'

'You don't know how nasty I can be,' it said.

I thought about that. The last of the diabolic book's pages were mere tufts of black ash, scattered across the plinth.

'Are we finished here?' it asked.

'Yes,' I said.

It frowned.

'I'm going to have to carry you after all, aren't I?' it sighed.

words. He fell down on his back. Saur just stood there, watching him bleed out, the bloodied *cutro* low at his side.

Blood formed a huge, dark red mirror on the canvas around the stranger. The mirror crept out. Blood soaked his coat and robes, covered his hands, and flecked his face. He stared at the ceiling, his mouth fluttering open and shut, his legs twitching.

I bent over him. Perhaps he didn't have to die, I thought. We could hold him, bind his injury, call for the city watch. I tried to apply pressure to his ghastly wound, but it was open, and as big as a dog's mouth. My hands were no better at stemming the flow of blood than his had been.

He suddenly, finally, saw me instead of the ceiling and the lights. He blinked, refocused. Tiny beads of blood had lodged in his eyelashes.

'What is this? Who are you?' I asked.

He said a word. It came out of him like a gasp, more breath than sound. It was a word I had not heard before.

He said, 'Cognitae.'

There was a bang, right in my ear, and it made me jump because it was sudden and close and painfully loud. A bark of pressure clouted me along with the noise. I flinched as bloody backspatter hit my face, throat and chest. I had his blood in my eyes.

An extract from

by Dan Abnett

'Who are you?' I demanded.

He rammed me aside with both hands. I staggered and fell, knocking down a rack of wooden exercise staves. I got up, gripping one stave and kicking the others out of my way. The stranger was backing away from me, his hands up. I think he intended to cut his losses and flee.

He doubled up as Saur's *cutro* tore into him from behind. The short sword went through his coat, through his robes, through his under-jack and mesh, and sliced into his waist.

Saur ripped the blade free, and blood squirted out across the canvas. The stranger stumbled away, his head wobbling like a drunkard's, his feet unsure, his eyes confused. He had both hands clamped to his waist, but even tight together, they could not plug the hole in him. Blood poured out, like red wine from a jug. His hands and sleeves were soaked with it.

His mouth opened and closed, without managing to form

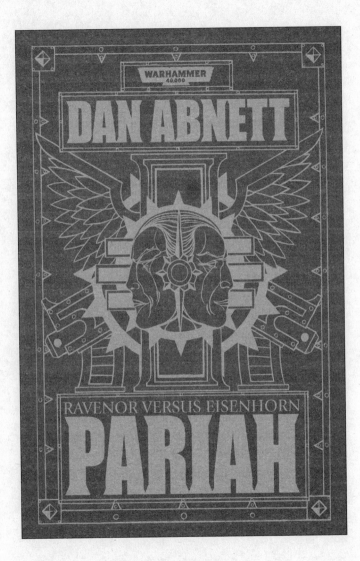

WARHAMMER
40,000

DAN ABNETT

RAVENOR VERSUS EISENHORN

PARIAH

ABOUT THE AUTHOR

Dan Abnett is the author of the Horus Heresy novels *The Unremembered Empire*, *Know No Fear* and *Prospero Burns*, the last two of which were both *New York Times* bestsellers. He has written almost fifty novels, including the acclaimed Gaunt's Ghosts series, and the Eisenhorn and Ravenor trilogies. He scripted *Macragge's Honour*, the first Horus Heresy graphic novel, as well as numerous audio dramas and short stories set in the Warhammer 40,000 and Warhammer universes. He lives and works in Maidstone, Kent.

his reputation. He was killed, following injury, on Menazoid Epsilon in 765.M41.

Harlon Nayl continued in the service of the Inquisition for many years and, along with Kara Swole and Eleena Koi, joined the staff of Inquisitor Ravenor. Their individual fates are not recorded in the Imperial archive, though it is believed that Nayl died circa 450.M41.

Crezia Berschilde returned to Gudrun, where she served as Chief Medicae (anatomica) at the Universitariate of New Gevae until her retirement due to failing health in 602.M41. Several of her treatises on augmetic surgery have become standard authority texts.

Medea Betancore returned to Glavia and became the director of her family shipwright business, a post she held for seventy years. She disappeared en route to Sarum in 479.M41, although several later reports suggest she survived that date.

Lord Inquisitor Phlebas Alessandro Rorken recovered from his ill-health and became Grand Master of the Ordos Helican after the disappearance of Leonid Osma. He held the post for three hundred and fifteen years.

Inquisitor Gregor Eisenhorn is believed to have continued in the service of the Ordos after the events on 5213X, though recorded details of his life and work after that date are conjectural at best. His eventual fate is not recorded in the Imperial archives.

There is no archived mention of the being known as 'Cherubael.'

Dossier addendum
Notes concerning the key individuals in this account

*Inquisitor Gideon Ravenor supervised the annulment of 5213X,
also known in some records as Ghül. Despite long debates amongst
the Sector ordos, no attempt to recover an artefact and material
from 5213X was ever permitted. Under orders from Battlefleet
Scarus, under the command of Lord Admiral Olm Madorthene,
annihilated the planet in 392.M41. Ravenor continued to serve
the Inquisition for several centuries, performing many notable
acts, including the destruction of the Heretic Thonius Slyte, but
his posthumous fame results more from the quality of his writings,
especially the peerless work* The Spheres of Longing.

Inquisitor Golesh Heldane survived the destruction of the Essene *at Jeganda. His bodyguards were forced to sever his leg
to free him and carried him to his ship. He spent many years
recovering from his horrific injuries, which required still more
severe augmetic reconstruction than he had already undergone.
He returned to active service, but his career was blighted by*